"Are you the one who wants to look around?" a deep voice asked from behind me.

"Yes, I . . ." I was speechless. In front of me stood the most beautiful man I'd ever seen. Taller than Jack, he had dark brown, messy, sexy hair and the most unusual ice blue eyes. Built like Adonis . . . he was perfect. Even his voice was hot. I could feel my heart pounding in my ears and I thought I might pass out. Was he a movie star? Was he gay? His jeans, black T-shirt, and tennis shoes were nothing special, but on him they looked like foreplay. First I would peel his shirt off with my teeth and then I would . . .

"Are you okay?" he asked, watching me with concern. "Maybe you should sit down." He took my arm to help me to a chair and I could swear a shot of electricity blasted up my arm and straight to my panties. It was like those vampire romances . . . Maybe he was a vampire. Or maybe I was insane.

ALSO BY ROBYN PETERMAN

How Hard Can It Be?

Size Matters

ROBYN
PETERMAN

eKENSINGTON
Kensington Publishing Corp.
www.kensingtonbooks.com

eKENSINGTON BOOKS are published by

Kensington Publishing Corp.
119 West 40th Street
New York, NY 10018

All Kensington titles, imprints, and distributed lines are available at special quantity discounts for bulk purchases for sales promotions, premiums, fund-raising, educational, or institutional use.

Special book excerpts or customized printings can also be created to fit specific needs. For details, write or phone the office of the Kensington special sales manager: Kensington Publishing Corp., 119 West 40th Street, New York, NY 10018, attn: Special Sales Department; phone 1-800-221-2647.

eKENSINGTON and the k logo are Reg. U.S. Pat. & TM Off.

First Electronic Edition: December 2013

ISBN-13: 978-1-60183-063-0
ISBN-10: 1-60183-063-7

First Print Edition: December 2013

ISBN-13: 978-1-60183-219-1
ISBN-10: 1-60183-219-2

This one is for, Steve.

*You are hotter than any hero I could ever write
and you make my life complete.
I love you.*

ACKNOWLEDGMENTS

A book doesn't come to life with only the author's imagination. There are many people involved, and without them I would simply have a story without the polish. I am grateful and blessed to have so many wonderful people in my life.

First and foremost, my editor, Alicia Condon, who continues to delight me with her expertise as I continue to make her wet her pants! I am a better writer because of you.

My Pimpettes. You ladies are nuts and I adore you. Thank you for continuing to spread the word!

My beta readers. I love you more than you will ever know: Jennifer, Kris, Kim, Jim, Jowanna, and Candace. You spur me to write faster and keep me afloat when I've jumped off the deep end. It wouldn't be half as much fun to write if you guys weren't reading!

My critique partner, J. M. Madden. You are a brilliant writer and have a way with words that can make my biggest and most horrific mistakes seem like simple fixes. I am honored to call you my friend.

And last but not least, my family. Hot Hubby, I wouldn't trade you for all the lottery tickets in the world. You and our kids are the best things that ever happened to me. Thanks for eating peanut butter and having no clean underpants when I'm on a deadline. You guys make it all worth it.

Chapter 1

"You're kidding me," I said, shaking my head in shock.

"I'm absofuckinglutely not." My best friend and roommate grinned, gently stroking her six-foot-tall cardboard cutout of Brett Favre. "Did you think I would take a bet where I might lose my cardboard quarterback boyfriend?"

"B-but you have a real boyfriend," I stammered, realizing the magnitude of my stupidity. I knew there was no way out. I couldn't plead brain damage or lack of sex. Actually I could plead lack of sex, but I didn't really want Rena to know that little tidbit right at the moment. Having a kind-of boyfriend who traveled more than he was in town had put a crimp in any activity south of my belly button.

"I do have a real boyfriend," Rena agreed, "but no one can replace my life-size cardboard cutout of Brett Favre."

"Does it have to be Bigfoot?" I whispered, praying to Lutheran Jesus for a reprieve. "What if I do your laundry for a month? Or babysit the little people that live in your aunt Phyllis's TV?"

"Tempting." My best friend, who I hated at the moment, grinned evilly. "But, no."

"How does this always happen to me?" I moaned, running my hands through the bane of my existence. The wild blond curls all over my head and halfway down my back were the envy of every woman I met, but drove me to drink occasionally. "I'm cutting the hair off," I muttered, trying to extract my hand.

"No, you're not. I will personally kill you if you do," Rena informed me. "I want your hair worse than I want Angelina Jolie's lips. And to answer your question, you said, David Hasselhoff is a big star in France and I said, no, he's not. Then you said, Do you want to bet? and I said yes. I then proved, via some scary Internet footage, that he's a rock star in Germany and they don't give a shit about him in France. The end result is that I'm keeping Cardboard Brett Favre and you're going to accompany my aunt Phyllis to her Bigfoot meetings for the next two months."

"Oh my God," I said. The reality of what I'd done was almost too much to bear.

"What if I pretend I'm you and go for your Pap smear?" I was desperate.

That stopped her cold. Rena had an unnatural phobia of Bryant Gumbel and gynecologists. "How many years?" she asked, eyeing me narrowly.

"Um . . . two?"

"If you had said twelve, I might have considered it," she informed me as she lovingly dusted Cardboard Brett Favre's abs.

"Twelve?" I shouted. "How does twelve years of double Pap smears equate to two months of Bigfoot meetings?"

"Just wait and see, Kristy." She grinned and handed me the Sasquatch get-together schedule.

"You suck."

"You suck more," she laughed.

My eyes darted around Rena's office as I tried to come up with a reasonable way out of this, or at least an alternate exit. I had an office down the hall, where I did fund-raising work for the women's shelter I'd started. The rest of the space was filled with *New York Times* best-selling authors. Long story.

"Oh, I almost forgot, Louise called from the shelter. She's a little concerned," Rena said.

"Why?" I racked my brain trying to remember if there was anything complicated scheduled at the women's shelter today. I had turned the day-to-day running of the shelter over to Louise, one of the most levelheaded and calm people I'd ever met. Hell, it had to be something bad for her to be rattled.

"Apparently Edith and Mrs. C showed up to give knitting lessons."

"Oh, hell no," I screeched as I ran from Rena's office and continued to run all twelve city blocks to the shelter.

"Are they here?" I huffed, trying desperately to catch my breath. My lungs were burning and sweat dripped from my face. I hadn't sprinted like that in . . . ever. I'd never sprinted in my twenty-eight years on earth, but the thought of Edith and Mrs. C alone with women who were trying to get their lives together was comparable to hosting an AA meeting at George's Liquor Emporium.

"They just waddled out," a pale-faced Louise informed me. "It was bad, but most of the women here today don't speak much English."

"Thank Jesus," I gasped, plopping down on the couch in Louise's office. "Did they use the phrase 'Bless your heart'?"

"Yep"—she shook her head ruefully—"right before or after they said something emotionally crippling about someone's hair, shoes, face, clothes, or accent."

Edith and Mrs. C were seventy-year-old evil twins and they scared the hell out of me. I had inherited them from my recently deceased not-evil grandmother along with said grandmother's knitting shop, A Stitch in Time, where the two devil incarnates worked.

"What did they want?" I asked as I covered my eyes and tried to block out the disaster that was my life.

"You," Louise deadpanned. "As I recall, it went something like this . . . Tell that no-good lazy large-bottomed cow she better show her huge ass up at the store or we'll burn it down, bless her heart."

"Oh my God, my ass isn't big," I hissed.

"No," Louise laughed, "actually, it belongs on the cover of *Sports Illustrated*. So, hot ass, great boobs, and amazing hair aside, I think they were serious about burning the store down."

"Motherhumpin' cowballs," I muttered. "I don't want the knitting store and I certainly don't want the two hags that come with it. I already have a job that I love. God, I don't have time for this."

"You're going to have to make time," she informed me in her no-nonsense way. "Mariah Carey almost beat the living daylights out of them."

"What is Mariah Carey doing in this building? I banned her from coming here for three weeks until she completes an anger management course."

"Apparently she did it online in two days and is cured." Louise grinned.

Mariah Carey (no relation) was a 97-pound ball of fury with the voice of a 275-pound Minnesota Vikings linebacker. I had helped her get her GED and six jobs, all of which she'd been promptly fired from. The reasons varied, but a similar theme kept popping up. Someone looked at her funny, so she broke his nose . . . someone tried to return something without a receipt, so she broke his nose . . . someone said their fries were cold, so she broke his nose. Always men, never women. Her past was rough, but she'd never have a future if she kept getting arrested for aggravated assault.

"Mariah Carey," I shouted, "get in here."

All five foot nothing of the unfortunately named pain in my ass entered the office with a sheepish grin on her face. "Sorry, dude," she muttered in a voice that had me wondering for the umpteenth time if she were actually a tiny man with boobs.

"Sorry's not going to cut it, little missy. Why'd you try to smack down on the old ladies?" I asked.

"Well, um." She pulled on her stringy hair, which was dyed blue this week. Possibly to match her fingernails. "They said nasty things to Consuela and Rosita and they called me a man."

Hmm, interesting. "So what happened?"

"Nothing, dude," Mariah Carey mumbled. "I just got up in their faces and threatened them."

"For God's sake, Mariah, last week you put a metal chair through the TV set and the week before that you set the rug in my office on fire and the week before that you painted swear words all over the lobby . . . why in the hell didn't you deck the old bitches?" I yelled.

"Kristy," Louise gasped with disapproval, "you did not just tell her she should have taken out the old ladies."

"I would never tell her to take out old ladies, but they're not ladies . . . they're mean old hags who are making my life a living hell and said I had a big butt. If Mariah had taken them down, maybe they would have . . ."

"Died?" Louise spat.

"Oh crap," I moaned, and dropped my head into my hands. "What is wrong with me?"

"I'll tell you what's wrong," Louise said, sitting down next to me and gently rubbing my back. Mariah Carey wedged herself in on my other side and played with my hair. A little odd, but strangely comforting. "You started this shelter all by yourself three years ago and have worked 24/7 until you hired me six months ago. You have raised enough money, in a shitty economy, through grants and donations so we can keep our doors open the rest of the year. Your grandma died a month ago and your boyfriend seems like a douche. A very attractive douche, but a douche. You now own a store run by Satan's twin spawns and you need a break. But you can't tell Mariah she can bust down on old ladies, no matter how vile they are."

"I'm so sorry," I told Mariah and Louise between the splayed fingers that covered my face. "I think I need a little vacation."

"When's the next major fund-raiser?" Louise asked, pulling my face out of my hands.

"October," I muttered, yanking on a curl and putting it in my mouth.

"That's four months away," she said matter-of-factly. "Do you have savings?" I nodded mutely. "You are going to take the summer off. I have it under control at the shelter and you need to figure out what you're going to do with the knitting shop."

I shuddered inwardly at the thought of facing the Beelzebub twins, but I knew I had no choice. I'd deal with them and take the rest of the summer off. For the first time in a while I felt lighter.

"Thank you," I whispered, giving Louise a hug.

"Can I make a suggestion?" Mariah Carey offered.

"Does it involve killing old women with blunt objects or folding chairs?" I asked, giving her the disapproving eyebrow.

"Um, no," she chuckled, "but that sounds like a good time."

"So what's your advice, Mariah?" I grinned, waiting for something appalling or illegal to come out of her mouth.

She yanked on her hair and punched me in the arm. "You need to get laid."

"Don't I know it," I laughed, flopping back on the couch. "Don't I know it."

Chapter 2

T he shop smelled like my grandma. I realized I hadn't been here since she'd died a month ago. It smelled of freesia and lilies with a hint of brown sugar. Like Grandma. It smelled so familiar, I wanted to cry. I kept expecting her to pop out from behind a tower of purple yarn and plant her wet noisy kisses on my face . . . but that was impossible. She was gone and I was here. I had no choice. Grandma had left me the store and I was supposed to run it.

"God, Grandma, I miss you," I whispered as I ran my hand over a display of quilts she had made.

I now owned the store, the stock, and the lovely old building that the store was housed in. It was in Uptown, a great little trendy nook of Minneapolis. There were two other storefronts in the building that rented from Grandma . . . I mean me. Curl Up and Dye, a hair salon that catered to the young hip crowd, although the older-lady following was quite large too. It was run by a supercute gay couple, Steve and Steve. Tall, skinny Steve and short, fat Steve. The Steves, as they were known, were covered in multiple piercings and tattoos. I love them and my grandma did too. They had coveted my hair for years and had their own wigs made to match my curls. The Steves also happened to be fabulous drag queens. I adore a good drag show.

The other storefront was home to the accounting firm that Rena used to be a slave to before she started her own company. I had temped there for a number of years while I got the shelter up and running. It was lovely to know that the pencil-pushing weenies were now at my mercy instead of Rena and me being at theirs. If I had a nickel for every time one of those nerds had touched my butt, I'd be able to retire. I suppose both Rena and I could have sued for sexual harassment, but that would have been too easy.

It was much more fun to screw with them.

Like the time they hosted accountants from the entire state of Minnesota and we sent them off with pot-laced brownies (compliments of the Steves). Apparently they ate all the brownies, laughed like hyenas throughout all the meetings, and were banned from accountant get-togethers for five years. That, by the way, is a huge slap in the nuts to geeks in the numbers world. They moped for a year about that one. The best though, was when we mailed them explicit secret-admirer notes from each other. It was fabulous to watch them blush and stammer and avoid each other in the small confines of the office. It took eighteen months for them to be able to make eye contact with each other. Good times.

The Steves were great, the accountants were asses, but the old ladies . . . they were scary. Grandma had tolerated them and they'd loved her, but everyone loved my grandma. Nobody except my grandma even remotely liked the old buzzards.

They wore their sweatpants high on the waist, right below their torpedo tits. Sweater sets were their normal uniform, lighter colors in the summer and darker in the winter. Today it was cotton candy pink. Occasionally they wore Disney Princess T-shirts. There is something inherently wrong with combining braless seventy-year-olds and Cinderella. Of course, the crowning jewel of their ensembles was the footwear . . . black rubber rain boots. That offended me beyond words.

Both biddies sported steel gray hair, bushy unibrows and beady little eyes. I never knew what color they were because they were always in slits of disgust when I was around.

This afternoon, nothing had changed.

"Hello, ladies," I yelled at the top of my lungs, feigning joy at seeing them.

"We're old, not deaf, you moron," Edith let me know.

"Yes, yes, of course," I shouted, pointing to my ears. "Double ear infection."

Edith slapped one of her mean little claws down on the counter and pointed at me with the other one. "I thought you had the flu and pinkeye, you dirty liar!"

What the fu . . . ? She'd busted me. I couldn't for the life of me remember what excuse I'd given them to explain my absence. Crap. The self-satisfied smirk on her face was clear evidence of her win. It was going to take everything I had not to kill them. Where was Mariah Carey when you needed her?

"The flu developed into a double ear infection," I screamed, just to piss them off.

They backed away. I realized volume was my friend. They started talking quietly, assuming I couldn't hear them due to the ear infection. I smiled, stared off into space, and let them have at it.

"Bless her heart," Mrs. C said, "what in the Lord's name is wrong with her face? She looks like a shiny albino or a deranged clown."

Ouch, that hurt. I hadn't had any time to sunbathe and I'd sprinted a mile about an hour ago . . . what in the hell did they expect?

"She always looked deranged to me," Edith sniffed.

"I heard her mother, bless her heart, that slut, dropped her on her head repeatedly as a child."

Holy hell, my mother was a lot of things, but slut was definitely not one of them. Plus, if anyone was going to call my mother unflattering names, it was going to be me, not the old bags.

"Look at her," Edith told Mrs. C, barely moving her mouth. To screw with any lipreading skills I might have, I suppose. "She's getting too old to find a husband, so she's going to attract some old geezer with those disgusting knockers. I'm sure this slutty idiot right here got a boob job."

"I think you're right," Mrs. C agreed. "Bless her heart, new boobies won't get her a man. She's as dumb as a box of hair."

"Some men don't care about brains," Edith piped in. "A good set of hooters can go a long way."

"Ladies," I shrieked, making them jump. Shoot, I was hoping to give one or both of them a heart attack. Dumb as a box of hair, my ass. "Apparently"—I kept the volume high because it was so enjoyable to watch them wince—"we've had some complaints. Several customers have left the shop in tears. Many people are swearing never to come back because you two are such horrid bitches."

Mouths agape, they stared at me in shock.

"What did she say?" Mrs. C whispered to Edith.

"She called you a bitch," Edith whispered back.

"No," Mrs. C hissed, "she called *you* a bitch."

"No," I shouted, "I called both of you bitches, because that's what you are. For the sake of clarity," I continued to bellow, "I believe I called you horrid bitches . . . not just plain old, disgusting, putrid bitches."

"She doesn't have a double ear infection, does she?" Mrs. C asked Edith. Edith shrugged her bony shoulders.

"No, I don't," I answered her, grinning from ear to ear.

"That was a dirty underhanded trick, you awful girl," Mrs. C wasped at me.

"I thought it was pretty good. By the way, the boobs are real. Quite honestly, ladies, your obsession with knockers alarms me. It makes me ponder your relationship."

They paled considerably and began to fidget. No. Way. I was just trying to mess with them. I didn't really think they were lesbians. Sweet Lutheran God, the visual was enough to give me nightmares for the rest of my natural life.

"You can't speak to your elders like that, little hussy," Edith snapped, trying to swat me with her claw. It seemed she thought she could scare me or beat me into forgetting they were gay. If it were only that easy.

"You're right, I can't," I said to the pair of self-satisfied smirking old biddies. They looked so superior sitting there, looking down their mean old lesbian noses at me. Bushy unibrows a-twitching. Had they never heard of tweezers? They truly believed they had the upper hand and I would cave to whatever their demands were, enabling them to continue to terrorize the knitters and quilters of Minneapolis . . . while I paid them.

There was one thing they hadn't counted on . . . I was at the end of my rope. I was exhausted, overworked, and undersexed. And I was getting more pissed off with every moment I had to spend with these evil women who gave lesbians a bad name. Life lesson: Never mess with an overly tired, cranky, horny girl.

"You're right, I can't talk to you like that. Come to think of it, I don't want to talk to you ever again." Was I brave enough? My stomach clenched in excitement and my hands shook. "You're fired," I shouted at them.

"You can't fire us, you little potlicker," Mrs. C yelled.

What in the hell was a potlicker? Whatever. I narrowed my eyes at the abominations sitting behind the counter in my beloved grandma's shop and I smiled sweetly.

"I believe I just did." A huge weight began to lift from my shoulders.

They didn't move a muscle . . . just sat there like they owned the place. "You just wait," Edith threatened, "this whole town is gonna hear about that boob job."

"That's okay," I countered gleefully, "I can't wait to tell everyone you guys are muff divers."

Their shrieks of rage were music to my ears, but they still didn't budge from their perch behind the counter.

"I think it's time for you gals to leave," I told them as I walked toward the front door.

"I think it's time for you to read the stipulations in your grandma's will," Edith said smugly.

The blood in my veins turned to ice. "What are you talking about?"

"You can't fire us. We come with the store," Edith cackled.

Who did I screw over in a past life? I simply didn't deserve this crap. "Fine," I snapped, "I'll sell the damn place."

"Can't do that either," Mrs. C chimed in. "At least, not for five years. You might want to pay your grandma's lawyer a visit, girlie."

I gave them a hostile glare and tried to come up with a brilliant parting shot, but I was in shock. If what they said was true, I was screwed. Nothing but the word *assclown* came to mind, and I don't really know what that means . . . so I stayed silent, turned my back on the old cow patties, and left. The lightness I had felt only moments earlier had disappeared. The weight of the world was squarely back on my shoulders. Crap.

Chapter 3

"Gotcha!" Jack jumped out from nowhere and trapped me in a suffocating bear hug while showering me with noogies.

Jack had an apartment downstairs, but since he and Rena were in luurve, he spent all his free time in our apartment . . . hogging the couch and the remote.

"Get off me, you dork," I laughed, pushing the six-foot-two Greek god away.

"Leave her alone," Rena chimed in, smacking him on the butt. "She's had a day from hell."

I moaned in agreement, threw my purse on the kitchen table, and flopped down on the couch. The tension in my neck began to loosen as I grabbed my Minnesota Vikings fleece blanket and curled into a tight ball. I was home. My day from hell was over and I had the entire evening ahead of me to watch bad reality TV . . . Heaven. I closed my eyes, but didn't miss the wild-eyed look of concern that passed between the lovebirds. I really, really hoped they were going out. I so didn't want to rehash my day and have them try to make me feel better.

Rena was the sister I'd never had and by default, Jack had become my overprotective obnoxious older brother. Their love was true and slightly nauseating. As happy as I was that my best friend in the world had found the real deal . . . I was a little jealous. I wanted what they had too. I just couldn't seem to stop dating losers . . . like the douche, oops, I mean Ethan, my absent boyfriend. Why I even labeled him *boyfriend* was becoming a mystery to me. We had only gone out on six dates. He was hot and exceedingly polite. He'd made several bizarrely considerate comments about my rear end. He badly needed to work on his flirting, but his looks made up for his strangely well-mannered lack of finesse . . . I think. Originally from somewhere in

Texas, he'd relocated to Minneapolis three months ago. Oh, and he was Jack's boss. For a cop he sure traveled a lot.

"Are you guys going out tonight?" I asked, snuggling deeper into my purple and gold blanket.

"Um . . . no," Rena replied quickly. "I thought we'd hang out here, eat ice cream, and watch *Housewives of Whatever-the-Fuck*."

I sat up swiftly and narrowed my eyes at a very guilty-looking duo. "All right, who died?"

"Why would you ask something like that?" Rena laughed, not quite meeting my eyes.

"Because you hate the *Housewives* and we only eat ice cream for dinner when really bad stuff is going down," I informed her calmly as my insides danced wildly. I glanced at Jack, who seemed to find the ceiling fascinating. "Spit it out. I've had a crap day and I can't take any more bad news."

"Did Edith and Mrs. C do anything awful at the shelter?" she asked, scooping ice cream into bowls as if her life depended on it.

"No, Mariah Carey threatened them and they left before they could do much damage."

Jack decided the ceiling was just fine and chose to rejoin us. "Did she break their noses?" he asked, trying unsuccessfully not to laugh.

"How do you know about Mariah Carey and her nose-rearranging issues?" I giggled, forgetting for a moment they were the enemy.

"Kristy," he explained, still grinning, "every cop in Minneapolis and the surrounding area knows Mariah Carey. She's at the station almost as much as I am."

"Damn," I muttered. "I keep trying to help her get a handle on her fists, but she clearly has a few anger management problems."

"Jail time might help," Rena offered, shoving a bowl of ice cream into Jack's hands and placing one on the coffee table in front of me.

"Maybe," Jack agreed, "but the irony of it all is every guy that she mangles is the kind of guy we'd all like to mangle if we weren't law-abiding citizens."

"Maybe so," I said through a clump of black raspberry chip ice cream, "but it's kind of hard to hold down a job if you assault the customers, no matter how well deserved."

"She does have a certain charm," Jack admitted, "but that voice . . ."

"What about her voice?" Rena asked, pulling out our last box of Thin Mints. The Girl Scout cookies proved definitively that the pair were hiding something, but I didn't know if I had the strength or the brain cells left to pry it out of them.

"She sounds like a defensive end for the Vikings." Jack, spoon in hand, slapped his hand over his mouth, spraying ice cream all over the wall behind him.

"Oh my God," I shouted. "Did Brett Favre die?"

"No," Rena interjected, grabbing the Thin Mints and shoving them at me. "Brett Favre is just fine."

"Guys"—I closed my eyes, feeling utterly miserable—"stop plying me with sweets and tell me what's going on."

Rena sat on one side of me and Jack sat on the other. Oh shit, this was going to be bad. Jack rarely sat down . . . ever. I drew in a deep breath and blew it out. What could they want to tell me that merited this buildup?

"Oh sweet baby Jesus," I shrieked. "You guys are breaking up." I felt my eyes well up with tears. This could not be happening. They were perfect together . . . of course I would back Rena, but I'd grown to love Jack too. It had taken Rena so long to find the man who could deal with and love her brand of crazy. God, I felt sick . . .

"Hell no, we're not breaking up," Jack said. "If Rena tried anything like that, I'd cuff her to the bed till she changed her mind."

"Oh please," Rena giggled, "if Jack tried to leave me I'd cut his substantial man-bits off with a dull butter knife. We are not breaking up."

"Ookay," I said, trying to escape the visuals they'd just planted. "If Brett Favre is alive and you guys are still together, then what is going on here?"

"Honey." Rena took my hand. "How much do you like Nathan?"

"Who is Nathan?" I demanded.

They exchanged a bewildered look. Jack grabbed the cookies and put four in his mouth. He clearly found my lack of recognition disturbing.

"Again," I said, grabbing the cookies from Jack, "who in the hell is Nathan?"

"Jack's boss . . . the guy you've been dating," Rena supplied, seizing the cookies from my hand and cramming a few into her mouth.

"His name is Nathan?" Even I could hear the faint thread of hysteria in my voice.

"Um . . . yep," Jack said.

"You have got to be kidding me," I yelled, fighting to control emotions I couldn't name. "I've been calling him Ethan for three months. Are you positive it's Nathan?"

"It's definitely Nathan," Jack said, moving away from me. I didn't blame him. I wasn't sure if I was going to laugh, cry, or split in two like Rumpelstiltskin.

"Oh. My. God. I can't believe he didn't tell me I was calling him by the wrong name. What kind of douche bag does that?" I said, dipping my Thin Mint into my ice cream and inhaling it.

"I think there's a lot he didn't tell you," Rena said quietly. "What exactly do you know about him?"

I stood and paced the room. Sitting still was not working. I took the cookies with me. "I know he's from somewhere in Texas. He's polite, almost to the point of creepy. He travels a lot and he's really hot."

"Kristy, he's from Dallas. Born and bred in Dallas, Texas," Rena said, watching me closely.

I felt like the wind had been sucked from my lungs. My knees gave out and I sank to the floor. "No," I gasped.

"Yes," Rena said, kneeling down on the floor with me. She put her arms around me and rocked me back and forth.

"I can't believe this. I just can't believe it," I said, accepting her condolences.

"I know, sweetie, I couldn't believe it either when I heard."

"I am so humiliated that I made out with a Dallas Cowboys fan. I feel . . . dirty," I moaned and shoved the remaining Thin Mints into my mouth.

"Tell her the rest," Jack said, backing away like we were contagious.

"I'm getting there," Rena hissed.

I wasn't worried. There couldn't be anything worse than a Cowboys fan. Nothing in the world could top the fact that he worshipped Tony Romo. Nothing.

"He's also married."

I was wrong.

Dizziness and nausea overwhelmed me. I never should have eaten so many cookies, but more than feeling sick, I was pissed. Really pissed. That freaking jerk had touched my butt and stuck his tongue in my mouth . . . while he was married and rooting for the Cowboys.

He needed to die. Now. Mariah Carey's need to break noses suddenly made sense.

With the renewed strength and purpose of a predator out to kill, I jumped up and lunged for my purse on the kitchen table.

"What are you doing?" Jack asked, alarmed.

"I'm going to call that fucktard and rip him a new one."

"Oh my God"—Rena tried to suppress her glee—"I thought you quit swearing."

"Let me tell you something," I ground out through clenched teeth, rooting through my purse for my phone, "today is not the day for me to release the word *fucktard* from my vocabulary. Maybe tomorrow. Where is my cell phone?"

"You don't need it," Jack, ever the diplomat, said.

"Yes, I do," I yelled, dumping the contents of my purse on the floor and locating my phone. "I'm going to dump the douche."

"Actually, I already broke up with him for you."

I froze mid-dial.

I couldn't decide if that was weird or nice. I elected to go with both nice and weird, if slightly invasive.

"What did he say?" I asked, kind of relieved that the deed was already done.

"He was extremely polite, wanting me to offer you his most sincere apologies. He also wanted to know if he ever got divorced, could he call you?"

"And you said?" I was a ticking time bomb, about to go off.

"Nothing," Jack replied with pride. "I punched him and knocked him out cold."

"Holy shit, Jack," I gasped. "You could lose your job."

"Nope." He shook his head and raised an eyebrow. "Turns out he was also dating the mayor's wife. He's been transferred."

"Effective immediately," Rena added. "And the mayor gave Jack a big bonus."

Stunned didn't cover it. How could I have been dating a married Dallas Cowboys fan who was two-timing me? I'd sunk to a new low.

"Please tell me you didn't play hide the salami with him."

"I think I need to leave," Jack muttered, heading for the door.

"Don't move," Rena hissed.

He rolled his eyes and obeyed.

"Kristy, please tell me you never saw that Tony-Romo-loving douche's pork sword," she pleaded.

"I'm delighted to inform you, Jack, Lutheran Jesus, and all the angels and saints that I. Did. Not." A strange wave of calm washed over me. I suppose if my entire day hadn't been from hell, this latest blow might have bothered me more. Oddly enough, I just felt relief.

"Thank you, Lutheran Jesus," Rena said. "And we do have some good news."

"Short of you telling me I don't have to go to the Bigfoot meetings with your aunt Phyllis, nothing you could tell me would be good news."

"There's this guy and . . ."

"Nope." I cut her off.

"Seriously." She laughed. "He's Jack's best friend and . . ."

"Nope," I yelled. Volume had worked with the gay she-devils. I was hoping for a repeat performance.

"He's hot and he's not married. He's a Vike's fan and he's a cop," she said, speaking faster than an auctioneer.

"What part of 'nope' don't you understand?" I asked as I settled myself back on the couch.

"Oh come on, Kristy, you should see him. His ass could melt butter." She waggled her eyebrows.

"Hey now," Jack protested, turning around to display his fine backside.

"Yours is better, honey," Rena laughed. "Kristy, just meet him."

"You must be brain damaged to think I'm even going to look twice at a cop. No offense, Jack."

"None taken," he said, sitting down beside me.

"I am not going to date anyone. Ever again. Never. Not until the second coming of Lutheran Jesus," I informed them in my serious voice.

"Not even Cardboard Brett Favre?" Rena teased.

"Nope, not even him," I said, grabbing the remote.

"Okay, fine," she huffed, "but once you lay eyes on Mitch, it will be a different story."

"You wanna bet?" I challenged.

She stared at me for a long moment, grinning from ear to ear. "Yes, I do, David Hasselhoff."

"Fine." I grinned back, knowing I was finally going to own Cardboard Brett Favre. "If I win, the Cardboard God is mine."

"And if I win, you have to eat dinner with Edith and Mrs. C every night for two weeks."

That gave me pause. She had chosen well. I'd rather yank my own toenails out with pliers than break bread with Lucifer's Lesbians. There was no way in hell I would ever date a cop, but . . . No, I had the upper hand here. She was going down.

"Deal," I said. "Enjoy Cardboard Brett while you still have him."

"Oh, I will," she said smugly.

"How about I take both you lovely ladies out to dinner?" Jack suggested.

"How about we stay here and watch *Housewives of Whatever-the-Fuck* and we eat more ice cream? I'm a little fragile right now," I said innocently, knowing it would kill both of them to sit through a half hour of the *Wives*.

"Okay." Rena blew out a defeated breath and sat down beside me. "Can we order in Thai?"

"Sure, I'll grab the menu," Jack said, heading for our menu drawer.

"The food should be here right about the time the show is over," Rena said, trying to hide her relief.

"This is fantastic," I squealed, turning the volume up. "There's a *Housewives of Whatever-the-Fuck* marathon tonight!"

"Holy shit," Jack muttered under his breath, grabbing the counter for support.

"Um, okay. That sounds, um great." Rena's forced enthusiasm made me bite my lip to stifle my giggles.

"I just want you two to know how much I love you. You are my best friends, and after the *Housewives* marathon I thought we could watch the *Kardashians* marathon." I was greeted with appalled silence as I hopped up to retrieve my purse.

"What are you doing?" Rena choked out, attempting to hide her horror at the evening ahead.

"Getting my purse so we can go out to dinner. I hate the *Kardashians* and I've already seen all the *Housewives*, but it was too much fun to watch you guys suffer."

"You are such a bitch," Rena shouted as she ran for the front door before I could change my mind. Jack was close on her heels.

I giggled as I watched them trip over each other to escape. "Yeah, but you love me," I yelled as they disappeared down the stairs. And I knew they did. As bad as my day had been—and it was bad— at least I had fucking amazing friends. Tomorrow. I'd quit swearing tomorrow.

Chapter 4

M y grandma's lawyer's office space hadn't been updated since the eighties. It was U-G-L-Y, ugly, but it was clean and smelled of Old Spice aftershave and peppermints. Mr. Lundberg and his wife had been dear friends with my grandma for many years. They were lovely people. But I was less than delighted to see Tandy Lundberg McOath, their granddaughter, sitting behind the reception-ist's desk.

"If you don't have an appointment, Kristy," she snapped, staring at my boobs, "my grandfather won't be able to see you."

She was clearly trying to figure out if my chest had been enhanced. Damn, those old lesbos worked fast.

"Would that be because his office is so full of clients?" I politely inquired, indicating the empty lobby. She huffed and went back to her computer, ignoring me.

Me and Tandy Lundberg McOath. We had history.

High school. Junior Miss Pageant. Talent competition.

Right before the talent portion of the pageant, Tandy Lundberg stole my black jazz shoes. Of course at the time I didn't know it was her, but I had my suspicions. All I knew was that I had a three-minute interpretive-style jazz dance to the theme from *Star Wars* coming up and no jazz shoes. How in the hell was I supposed to become Darth Vader, Yoda, Princess Leia, and Luke Skywalker without jazz shoes?

In a fit of desperation, I ripped the feet out of my tights and danced barefoot. I did stick to the floor a couple of times during the Jedi Fight Sequence, but I only wiped out once. The beauty of it all . . . I still kicked Tandy Lundberg's ass.

Even hitting the deck and giving myself a mild concussion, I reigned victorious over her display of self-made garments accompanied by a bizarre and disgusting monologue. Her monologue droned on and on while she frantically changed from one butt-ugly homemade outfit to another. She changed behind a screen completely decoupaged with photos of herself sewing. She then ran out, delivered more monologue, and sprinted behind it again. Sixteen times. I don't want to gloss over the importance of the monologue: a diatribe about having stabbed herself with a sewing needle and how she bled like a stuck pig, culminating in how the needle broke off in her hand and would be with her the rest of her life.

After the show, the pageant directors did a search and rescue for my jazz shoes. They busted Tandy when they found them at the bottom of her sewing basket. She was disqualified and still living it down to this day. Suffice it to say, there was no love lost between us.

I leaned over her desk, giving her a fantastic cleavage shot. "Your grandfather knows I'm coming," I told her cheerfully. "If you don't let him know I'm here, I'll tell everyone that you didn't even make those butt-ugly clothes for the pageant. Your aunt Tudie did."

"Who told you that, you silicone piece of trash?" she screeched, growing pale and visibly uncomfortable.

No. Freakin'. Way. I was right? I had pulled that one out of my butt, just like the lesbian thing . . . Maybe I was psychic. "Your mom told me," I cooed.

"You're a boob-job liar," she yelled, turning a mottled red.

God, it would be so easy to call her a fucktard, but I was letting that word into the universe and out of my vocabulary. I would have to settle for giving her more crap.

"First of all," I announced slowly and clearly, "my boobies are real." I laughed, lifted my shirt, and flashed my tatas. "One hundred percent real."

She gasped and covered her eyes. "You are so uncouth," she hissed.

"Correct. And you"—I grinned—"have sticky fingers." I hummed the theme from *Star Wars*.

She screamed like a fishwife and climbed over the desk to choke me. This had gotten slightly out of hand. I backed away and ran smack into Mr. Lundberg. Both Tandy and I froze.

"Well now," he said kindly, stepping between us. "Tandy, it looks like you could use a break and a higher dosage of your medication. Why don't you take the rest of the day off, dear."

Tandy muttered something about humongous plastic hooters and left in a huff. Mr. Lundberg gave me the eyeball and a hot flash of shame settled in the pit of my stomach.

"I'm sorry," I mumbled.

"You girls need to put the past behind you. I think it would be a fine idea if you two went to lunch sometime and worked out your differences."

"I'll get right on that, sir." I smiled, attempted to convey sincerity, but failed. I think I almost threw up in my mouth.

"I don't believe you girls will ever be friends, but it would make me happy if you could get along."

"Yes, sir," I said, caving. He was right. The pageant was forever ago, plus I knew my grandma would agree with Mr. Lundberg. "I'll try."

"Good, good. Now what can I help you with?" he asked, shuffling slowly back to his office.

"Well, when we went over Grandma's will, I was still really upset and I think I may have overlooked a few important details."

"Of course, my dear. Mrs. Lundberg and I miss your grandma terribly. She was a wonderful old gal," he said fondly, seating himself behind a big mahogany desk.

"I miss her too," I replied quietly.

We sat in comfortable silence for a bit. When his head nodded over to the right, I was concerned he might have died or fallen asleep, but thankfully I was mistaken. "Now about your questions," he said, pulling out a file.

"Yes, um, I was wondering about Edith and Mrs. C. I think they're under the false impression that they come with the shop." I laughed a little shrilly, praying to the Virgin Mary they were mistaken.

"You know that your grandma found the good in everyone," he said, flipping through the file.

"Yes, she did." I didn't like the direction this was going. Damn it, I knew praying to the Virgin Mary had been a bad call. I was Lutheran . . . what in the hell had I been thinking?

"Most people find the old sisters, um, rather difficult."

"I believe that might be an understatement, Mr. Lundberg," I said as sweat began collecting on my upper lip. I wondered if it was too late to make a deal with God . . . the Lutheran one.

"Yes, well, your grandma knew it would be difficult for the old gals to find jobs, since they've offended most of the town, so she guaranteed them employment after her death for five years."

"Shit, I mean shoot," I said, slapping my hand over my mouth. "Is there any way around this?"

"If you want to contest the will . . ."

"No, I would never do that. I'm sure Grandma had good reasons for, um . . . making my life a living hell," I told him, trying to figure out what Grandma had seen in the old lesbos.

"Maybe she found something in them that we're missing," he said, gently.

"Possibly." I shook my head and wondered how much it would cost me to pay Mariah to kill them . . . or maybe just maim them.

"I think your grandma would want you to show compassion."

I felt the heat creep up my neck and land squarely in my face. My guilt over the planning of their demise weighed a lot. I would try . . . and if all else failed, I was armed with some good lesbianic blackmail.

As I left Mr. Lundberg's office, I got a call from Mariah Carey that made my gut twist. The shelter had been broken into and the intruders were still there. She was there alone, painting over all the swear words she'd decorated the lobby with recently.

"Mariah," I yelled, "get out of there."

"I can take them," she whispered into the phone.

"You listen to me right now. Get your skinny ass out of there. If something happens to you, I will kill you," I hissed.

"You like me, you really like me," she whispered, giggling.

"I am serious. I want you out of there. Did you call the police?"

"They're on the way," she murmured. "I'm not letting these dick-wits get away."

"Yes, you are," I insisted, frantically. "They might be armed. You could end up dead. For real dead."

"Nah, it's not my day to die." She laughed like a psycho and hung up on me.

Son. Of. A. Bitch.

I got in my car and drove like a bat out of hell to the shelter.

Thankfully the police had arrived before I did. I raced into the shelter and found Mariah Carey on the floor, giving a statement to Jack while nursing a black eye and a bloody lip.

"Oh my God," I gasped, dropping to the floor by Mariah, "are you okay?" My heart seemed to be beating throughout my entire body and I was shaking with relief. "Why didn't you leave?" I demanded. "I told you to get out."

"This is my safe place." Her voice broke and her eyes welled with tears. "They can't come to my safe place."

"Oh, baby." I cradled Mariah, tough little Mariah Carey, in my arms and rocked her. "It will be okay," I promised. "This will still be your safe place."

Jack took me by the arm and led me away when the paramedics came in to check out Mariah.

"She'll be okay," he said. "The intruders suffered far more damage than she did."

"What do you mean?" I asked, looking back at Mariah. She looked so tiny and young.

"There were two of them. She broke both their noses and crushed one of their hands. Not to mention she kicked their man jewels up into their chest cavities." He laughed. "She is a walking menace to society."

"How do you know all this?"

"We apprehended them crying and limping down the street."

"Were they armed?" I asked. We'd never had any problems in this area. It scared and infuriated me that someone would steal from a shelter.

"Nope. They were kids. Fifteen years old—looking for some money for booze or drugs." Jack ran his hands through his hair and sighed. "I have to finish talking to Mariah before they take her to the hospital. I want you to look around and see if anything is missing."

"Is it safe?" I asked, scanning the mess.

"It should be, but I'm sending an officer with you," he said, giving me a funny look. "Wait here."

"Fine," I said, wondering if the cops would let us open our doors tomorrow. The mess wasn't bad at all considering the injuries sustained by the intruders and Mariah. It looked like the main room was the only one that had suffered any damage. The computer was smashed and a couple of chairs seemed to be broken.

"Are you the one who wants to look around?" a deep voice asked from behind me.

"Yes, I . . ." I was speechless. In front of me stood the most beautiful man I'd ever seen. Taller than Jack, he had dark brown, messy, sexy hair and the most unusual ice blue eyes. Built like Adonis . . . he was perfect. Even his voice was hot. I could feel my heart pounding in my ears and I thought I might pass out. Was he a movie star? Was he gay? His jeans, black T-shirt, and tennis shoes were nothing special, but on him they looked like foreplay. First I would peel his shirt off with my teeth and then I would . . .

"Are you okay?" he asked, watching me with concern. "Maybe you should sit down." He took my arm to help me to a chair and I could swear a shot of electricity blasted up my arm and straight to my panties. It was like those vampire romances . . . Maybe he was a vampire. Or maybe I was insane.

"What's your name?" he asked as he squatted in front of my chair. He smelled like heaven—Irish Spring soap, fresh laundry, and man. He was talking to me . . . God, if he was gay, I'd have a sex change for him . . . He asked me a question, but he was so pretty . . . Wait, what the hell did he ask?

"I'm sorry," I said in a porn-star voice I seemed to have no control over. "I didn't understand the question. Could you repeat it?"

"I asked you what your name was." He chuckled. Was he staring at my mouth? He reached out and pulled on one of my curls and my brain stopped functioning.

"My name," I stammered. What in the hell was my name? I knew it earlier, I swear I did. Balls, he's going to think I'm mentally challenged or just really stupid. Oh my God, his eyes . . . Why can't I remember my freakin' name? How hard can it be? I think it starts with a C or maybe a K.

"Her name is Kristy," Jack interjected, grinning at me like an idiot. "And this is Mitch, my best friend and new partner." He waggled his eyebrows and kept tilting his head toward Mitch.

Kill me now.

Why oh why did the man who sent electrical shockwaves to my undies have to be the cop who could make me lose Cardboard Brett Favre and have to dine with Edith and Mrs. C for two weeks? And why in the hell was he looking at me like he wanted to eat me? If I could just rip my eyes away from his perfect mouth, I'm sure my grasp on the English language would return.

"Hi, Kristy." Mitch grinned. "Why don't we take a walk around the shelter?"

"Um, no . . . that's okay," I stammered, jumping to my feet and putting some distance between us. I had a very real fear of grabbing his ass. "It's all good. You must be really busy with all that hair and those eyes." Motherhumpin' assclowns, what in the hell was I saying? "I'm just going to look around and then call all my husbands to help me clean up this mess." I smiled and started backing into my office.

"Ookay," Jack said, enjoying himself immensely. "There are a couple of problems with that."

"Really?" I hissed at Jack through clenched teeth.

"Yep." He grinned. "First of all, I didn't realize your office was in the men's bathroom and unless you did it this morning, I'm pretty sure you're not married or Mormon."

"Did I say *husbands*?" I laughed heartily at my mistake. "I meant my band . . . my folk-rock, um . . . thrash, you know . . ." I was dying here. "Punk band."

They both stared at me in bemused silence. I gave Jack a death stare, daring him to dispute the crap that had just flown out of my mouth. He didn't.

"So, it was nice meeting you, Mitch. I'm absolutely sure I will never see you again. So have a nice butt, shit, I mean life."

I literally ran to my office, trying to escape before anything more appalling could pass my lips . . .

"Hey, Kristy," Jack said as I sprinted across the lobby, "maybe I can bring Mitch to one of your gigs."

I had quite the hate-on for Jack right now. He was going to suffer for this. "Oh, well, we're not playing right now because, um . . . twelve of my band members died in a bizarre gardening . . . accident with weed whackers and . . ." I started out strong but ended in a whisper. Even if I was free to pursue Mitch, the hottest guy I'd ever laid eyes on, I'd blown it. No one in their right mind wants to marry, date, or travel south of the belly button with a certifiable nutbag.

Thankfully, before I shut and locked the office door I spied Louise, her husband (not her band), and her four teenage sons arriving. They would start the cleanup, and as soon as the police left, I would come out of my hidey-hole and help.

As I sank down to the floor, I wondered how much more karmic poop was going to land on my head before I was permanently buried? God knows it wouldn't take much.

Chapter 5

"I'd like you to call me Aunt Moon-Unit from now on," Aunt Phyllis said, offering me some Crock-Pot Reuben dip.

After hiding in my office from Jack and Mitch for one hour and thirty-seven minutes, I'd helped Louise and her family clean up the shelter. Then, thanking them profusely, I went home, showered off my day, and drove over to Aunt Phyllis's house to pick her up for the dreaded Bigfoot meeting.

"Are you a Frank Zappa fan?" I asked, trying to figure out why her Crock-Pot creation smelled so weird.

"Who's that, dear?" she asked as she heaped a large lump of the odd-smelling goo onto a plate for me. "Is he a friend of yours?"

"Um, no, he's a singer who named his daughter Moon Unit," I muttered, examining the bright orange pile on my plate. "I thought maybe that's where you got the name."

"Oh, sweet baby Jesus, no," she giggled. "It came to me in a vision from the aliens."

Rena's aunt Phyllis, I mean, aunt Moon-Unit, is one of the kookiest people I know. She's also one of the most generous and loving, but she was best in small doses.

"Is everything all right at the shelter? I was listening to my police scanner and heard all about the break-in," Aunt Moon-Unit said, handing me a pile of Ritz Crackers to scoop up the dip.

"Yep," I said, not a bit surprised that she owned a scanner. "It was some kids looking for drug money. One of my gals beat the hell out of them. Um, Aunt Phyl-Moon-Unit, is this dip supposed to be orange?"

"Oh yes," she informed me, filling four more plates with the offending dip. Was she expecting company? "I added orange rinds to zest up the Thousand Island dressing, Miracle Whip, and sweet pickle relish, but the color wasn't quite to the trolls' liking, so I added orange food coloring. Can you see them?" she asked.

I examined the orange vomit and tried to find some rinds. "I don't know."

"Oh, they're not in there," she told me solemnly. "They're on the couch next to you."

"The orange rinds?" I asked, bewildered.

"No, dear, the trolls. Can you see them?"

I glanced to my left and right. After the day I'd had, I half expected to see trolls. "Um, no. Sorry." This was going to be a long evening.

"That's all right, dear, sometimes I have to wear 3-D glasses to make them out. They're very sneaky bastards. Quite violent too, kind of like our little friend Mariah Carey."

"You know Mariah Carey?"

"Of course I do. She's one of the most passionate Bigfoot followers I've ever met. I knew immediately that was her handiwork when I listened to the police scanner earlier."

"Really?" I asked, beginning to piece together the horror of the evening that lay ahead . . . locked in a room with Aunt Moon-Unit, Mariah Carey, and God knows who else, discussing Sasquatch.

"Oh yes," Aunt Moon-Unit said gleefully. "When I heard broken noses and damaged testicles, I knew Mariah had been involved."

I had absolutely nothing to add to that, so I stayed silent. I wanted to know who the other plates were for, but I knew the answer might be too alarming for me to handle.

"Well, dear, we should get going, but I want to ask you a question first. I need you to concentrate and become one with the earth. Let all of the static that the government has planted in your brain flow gently out of your ears."

"Okay," I said, feeling slightly nauseous. Rena was going to owe me so big time. I couldn't decide who I disliked more . . . Rena or David Hasselhoff.

"Can you feel it?" she asked.

"Feel what?" I whispered, getting a bit freaked out.

"The chi. The chi in my house is off. Listen," she demanded.

I listened . . . and heard nothing.

"There it is," she hissed, scaring the hell out of me. "Do you hear it?"

"Um, no. What exactly does it sound like?" I needed to be shot for encouraging this, but I couldn't stop myself.

"It sounds like feral cats fornicating during an ice storm," she whispered.

Before I could ask her what that sounded like, she grabbed my arm and yanked me to the floor. Holy Lutheran Jesus, she was strong for an old lady.

"Don't move. The bad chi wants to embed itself within our neurons."

I eyed the front door. I could be out of here in six seconds . . . but what if she was right? I simply could not afford bad chi embedding itself in my neurons, whatever the fuck that meant. I knew I'd taken a trip to Crazytown when I stayed huddled on the ground with someone who'd renamed herself Aunt Moon-Unit. My life was deteriorating quickly.

"It's gone," she said, hopping up as if nothing weird and disturbing had just happened.

"Are you sure?" I asked, slowly standing up, looking around for some kind of evil green mist.

"Absolutely," she chirped, clapping her hands together and doing what appeared to be a hip-hop step. "It will be back, but I'll be ready. I need to find the source and kill it."

"Ookay then." I wanted out really bad. Bigfoot was starting to sound like the better end of the bargain. "Should we clean up the plates of orange shi-dip before we go?"

"Oh no," she laughed, grabbing her purse and a stuffed Bigfoot doll. "That's for the trolls. The plates will be licked clean by the time I get home."

"Of course they will," I muttered as I speedwalked out of her chi-infested house. From now on, I would sit in my car in the driveway and beep till she came out.

Apparently the Sasquatch Society used to meet at the community center until they got kicked out for scaring the living daylights out of small children, neighborhood dogs, and senior citizens. Roaring and wearing full-face and body camouflage in public was against the rules. Who knew? So now they met at the public library. I followed

Aunt Moon-Unit through the stacks to the meeting room with my head down. God forbid I ran into someone I knew . . .

"Aunt Moon-Unit, can we sit in the back?" I asked, wanting to have a quick and unencumbered escape route.

"Oh no, silly girl," she said, dragging me toward the front row. "We'll miss too much back there. Besides, the homosexual twins like the back row and I'm not real fond of them."

I froze. A gnarly tension gripped my insides and my head started pounding. "What did you just say?"

"Oh my," she giggled. "I don't want to sound homophobic, because I'm not. Most Martians and hobbits are gay and lesbian and I love them, but those old rug-munching sisters are just mean. They give all nice respectable muff divers a bad reputation."

I turned around to flee, but the crowd of overexcited Bigfoot believers made it impossible. Trying to make myself tiny (which is difficult for someone who's five foot ten with tons of wild blond hair), I followed Aunt Moon-Unit to the front. I sat down on the hard metal folding chair and slid as low as I could go. I will never make a bet with Rena again. Ever . . . but wait, I already had and it sucked large cowballs. My mind drifted to Mitch. Why in the hell did I make that bet? I'd take Mitch and his perfect ass over Cardboard Brett Favre any day of the week. Maybe I could see him secretly . . . no. I am never going to date a cop again. Ever. Why would he want to see me anyway? I'd told him I had multiple husbands and was in a punk rock–folk-thrash band. Plus, eating with Mrs. C and Edith for two weeks would kill me dead. No guy was worth that, no matter how bitable his lips were.

I glanced around and tried to spot the old hags . . . nothing. Thank you, Jesus. Could there possibly be two sets of mean twin sister lesbians? I racked my brain for ways to escape without hurting Aunt Moon-Unit's feelings or defaulting on the terms of the bet. My mind was blank . . . and then the meeting started. I had gone to hell.

An eerie hush fell over the room as a fully camouflaged woman, roughly the size of a Sub-Zero fridge, shimmied toward the front of the room on her stomach. She was trailed by a short, skinny little dude, who if I'm not mistaken, was beatboxing with his mouth, alternating with humming the theme from *American Idol*. He walked in a low squat behind the crawling woman, reminiscent of a chimp . . . or a tiny caveman.

"That's Kim and Hugh Jensen Johnson," Aunt Moon-Unit whispered excitedly. "They're our leaders."

Oh. My. God.

Kim Jensen Johnson reached the front of the room and leapt to her feet. An impressive move for a gal that size. Hugh Jensen Johnson jumped up on the table behind her and channeled Mick Jagger . . . in a bad scary way. The crowd went nuts . . . Wait a minute, the crowd *was* nuts.

"My people," Kim yelled above the roar of Yeti fanatics. She then bent at the knees, lifted her hands like they were claws, and growled at the audience. All around me people lifted their own hand-claws and growled back, except for Hugh. He was balancing on his hands and grunting out a barely recognizable version of Queen's "Bohemian Rhapsody."

"There have been sightings," Kim shouted, "and one of our members has a new theory that gives me chills and makes me want to break-dance."

Which she did. Hugh, clearly not one to miss an opportunity, sang a warped version of the lyrics "I like big butts" while his wife sweated and grunted on the ground, performing moves that should never be seen in public. The crowd went ballistic.

"This is so exciting," Aunt Moon-Unit shrieked above the noise, as she growled and rocked out to Hugh's attempt at music.

Kim Jensen Johnson, sweating like a pig, stood and raised her hands above her head . . . The room got quiet; even Hugh put a cork in it. "I have news," she said, looking to the heavens. "We are being considered to head up a team for the reality TV show *Searching for Sasquatch*."

"Never heard of it," a grossly familiar voice yelled from the rear of the room.

"Sounds like a pile of shit," its evil twin chimed in.

"It's a new show, you mean old biddies. It's not a pile of shit, and don't you dare back-sass my honey pie," Hugh yelled back, taking a short break from providing background music. Sensing his lapse in song, he immediately morphed from speech back into the theme from *The Dukes of Hazzard*.

"Bless his heart," Mrs. C said loudly. "He clearly donated his brain to science before he was done with it."

Edith, not to be outdone by her sister, shouted, "Hugh, guess you forgot to pay your brain bill this month, bless your heart."

"Nope," Hugh told them, grinning from ear to ear. "I have a direct withdrawal from my bank account. Unlike you gals, and I use that term loosely, who are a few bearded ladies short of a freak show."

Hugh had just gone up in my estimation from weird boom box guy to superhero. The crowd of fictional-hairy-myth enthusiasts whooped their approval of Hugh's comeback. The old ladies shouted insults at everyone. This might be a fun evening after all . . .

"Now, now," Kim bellowed, quieting the crowd. "Mrs. C and Edith, if you don't have anything nice to say, then don't say anything at all. Do you understand me?" She eyeballed them in a way that had me trembling. She was a tough mambajamba.

"Yes," they muttered, pissed.

"Yeti believers." Kim Jensen Johnson rocked back and forth like a preacher. "Our sister Boo would like to share some amazing evidence she has uncovered. Boo Carey," Kim boomed, "come and testify!"

No one stood and no one spoke. Was Boo here? Was she even a real person?

A shuffle and some swearing erupted on the left side of the room and from out of the crowd came a bruised and bandaged Mariah Carey dragging a girl who looked alarmingly like her minus the blue hair. People smiled and patted both Mariah and Boo (I assumed) on the head as they passed.

"She's coming," Mariah grunted in her manly-man voice. "She's being a little shy."

Right on cue, Hugh had his out-of-tune way with the death march song. Kim rolled her eyes and whacked Hugh in the back of the head. He immediately changed his song to Queen's "We Are the Champions."

"Come on up here, sweetie," Kim said, reaching out for the very timid Boo. "And bring your sister with you. Everyone here is your friend. Right, my Bigfoot disciples?" The rabid followers clapped their approval and yelled bizarre yet encouraging comments to Boo. She quietly stood in front and pulled a worn and tattered novel from her purse. Mariah stayed close and gave her sister a quick hug.

"I believe," Boo whispered, not sounding even remotely like a linebacker, "that Bigfoot has lived in relative peace with humans all these centuries because he is a shapeshifter."

The crowd gasped and began muttering excitedly.

"Do you have proof?" someone asked from the middle of the hubbub.

"Yes, I do. This book I'm holding in my hand has a secret code written into it, proving without a doubt that Bigfoot is an immortal shapeshifter living among us."

"Makes sense," said a partially bald woman sitting next to Aunt Moon-Unit.

"Of course it does," Aunt Moon-Unit agreed. "I myself was leaning toward the cyborg theory, but this one is so simple it's brilliant."

I looked around and felt like the sane orderly in the loony bin. Were all these people buying this shapeshifter crap?

Yes, they were.

I swallowed hard, realizing I was going to be with these people for the next two months because of that fucktard David Hasselhoff. Giving up swearing was going to be a losing battle. Thank Jesus I hadn't made a bet concerning that. Little snippets of conversations about naked shapeshifters, the diets of dragons, and the merits of mind-reading Pygmy trolls rolled over me. I felt like I was high on something. Mariah Carey waved frantically until she caught my attention. She gave me a thumbs-up and I gave her the finger. She thought that was hilarious and proceeded to call me a string of swear words even I wouldn't use.

Making my escape was easier than I expected. Aunt Moon-Unit was going to Taco Bell with Hugh and Kim Jensen Johnson. After they promised to get her home safely, I ran. Fast. I didn't pass Go or collect my two hundred dollars. I ran for my life.

Chapter 6

Running for your life while looking over your shoulder for mean gay women and Sasquatch enthusiasts is a bad idea. A very bad idea. Thankfully I turned my head before I took out a stack of encyclopedias and a cute old guy with a walker. After apologizing and promising to slow my pace to a walk, I spotted the best man-butt I'd ever seen in my life. What was a man-butt like that doing in the public library on a Thursday at this time of night? And why couldn't I have a man-butt like that for myself? I would take such good care of it . . . I would grab it and love it and talk to it and show it off. I wondered if the face matched the butt and the rest of the ridiculously gorgeous body that belonged to the butt. Damn, if he would just turn around . . . yessss. Oh shit, no, no, no, no. I know that man-butt—

It was Mitch. The hot cop who made my girlie parts sing and could cause me to have to break bread with hateful rug-bumpers for two weeks. Damn it to hell, how did he look better than he had this afternoon? It wasn't fair. Sexy man-butt or not, it didn't erase the fact that jumping him in a public venue could make me lose Cardboard Brett Favre and have to dine with mean old hags. Besides, he was a cop and cops were untrustworthy, married Dallas Cowboys fans.

Maybe he wouldn't see me if I stood really still. That was stupid . . . Please, Lutheran God, let him walk by and not notice that I'm trapped between the two tables he's headed toward. Please, please, please . . . damn.

He stopped dead in his tracks about three feet from me. His eyes started at my hot pink toenails and girlie-sandaled feet, then slid slowly up my bare (thankfully shaved) legs. They paused at my strapless sundress-clad breasts for I'd say twelve seconds too long. From there his gaze traveled lazily to my neck, my lips, my eyes . . . I saw delight and something I couldn't define flash in his beautiful icy blue eyes as recognition hit. A slow sexy grin spread over his face and I had to remind myself to breathe.

"Hi, Goldilocks, I've been thinking about you," he said, walking toward me.

"That's not my name," I said, backing up into the table. "And you shouldn't be thinking about me . . . because I have, um, some unresolved issues about some, uh, stuff and I have to go, you know, to work right now." I slapped my hand over my mouth before I could dig a deeper stupid-hole.

"Do I fluster you, Goldilocks?"

"Of course not," I laughed, beginning to like the Goldilocks thing. "Why would you ask that?"

"Because it's nine thirty on a Thursday night," he chuckled, pinning me with those damn eyes.

"Oh, right." I felt the heat crawl up my neck. "What are you doing here?" A change of subject was in order. *And what in the hell was he doing here?*

"Checking out a book." He stepped closer and held up some odd-looking purple police manual and a Stephen King novel.

"You can read?" I asked, trying to be conversational . . . and failing.

He threw his head back and laughed. My knees buckled . . . he was even hotter when he laughed. I just wished I had made a joke instead of a joke of myself.

"I'm sorry, I didn't mean that. I'm sure you can read. I would imagine you had to know how to read to become a cop and um . . . Okay, fine," I huffed. "You fluster me."

"Feeling's mutual, Goldilocks," he said, moving closer. "What are you doing here?"

"Bigfoot meeting," I mumbled, glancing wildly around for an escape. I was forty-two seconds away from tackling him to the ground and shoving my tongue down his throat.

"Oh," he laughed, "you're one of those."

"No, I'm not. I lost a bet."

"I see," he said. Clearly not seeing at all.

"I said that David Hasselhoff was a big star in France and he's not, he's a big star in Germa . . . oh my God, please forget I said that. Suffice it to say, I'm here against my will. I am not a Sasquatch devotee or a David Hasselhoff fan."

I tried to back away, but the damn table was bolted to the floor. Out of the corner of my eye I spotted danger . . . more danger than what stood in front of me invading my personal space. Crap. Mrs. C and Edith were headed my way.

"Hide me," I squeaked, pulling Mitch flush to my body. All I needed was for them to tell Mitch my boobies were impostors. The fact that it was untrue was irrelevant; having to explain would be mortifying.

They passed without seeing me. Thank you, Jesus.

"Oh my God," I gasped, realizing I was smashed up against what felt like a brick wall. I tried to pull away and almost went down. The fact that my knees had turned to jelly might have had something to do with it . . . As I struggled for balance, I grabbed on to a perfectly muscled arm. "I am so sorry," I stammered, which may have come out slightly muffled because the arm gently pulled me back to the chest. The best-smelling, most beautiful chest ever. I was so tempted to bite it . . . or lick it. What the fu . . . ? What was wrong with me? Was I so horny that I would jump a forbidden cop in the public library because he smelled good and had an awesome man-butt? Yes, unfortunately the answer was yes.

"Kristy?" Mitch asked, putting a warm, slightly calloused finger under my chin and lifting my face to his. "Can I ask you something?"

"That's a bad idea," I muttered, trying unsuccessfully to move out of his arms.

"Why's that?" he asked in a voice that made me weak.

"Because I have no idea what's going to come out of my mouth," I told him truthfully. He was in grave danger of my grabby hands. I balled them into fists, willing them not to touch his insanely kissable lips or slap his man-butt.

"How about I talk and you just nod your head?"

I nodded my head in agreement and giggled.

"Good," he grinned. "I want to take you out for ice cream and I . . ."

I started to shake my head to tell him no, but he cut me off.

"No nodding or shaking till I finish," he informed me, tucking my hair behind my ear. "I promise to do all the talking until you feel less flustered. Although, it would be fascinating to hear about your band," he chuckled.

I rolled my eyes and tried to shove him away, but he was going nowhere fast. I was amazed I didn't feel trapped or freaked out. This big, beautiful man who reduced me to a blubbering idiot actually made me feel safe . . .

"Mitch, I can't," I whispered, so close to his mouth I could almost touch it with my own.

"Why?"

"Um, because of lesbians and Brett Favre," I mumbled, sure he'd drop me and run like hell.

"I'm not going to touch that one," he said.

"That's a good idea," I said, trying to pry myself away.

"So you won't come out with me for ice cream." He gave me a pouty lip with a twinkle in his eyes.

Damn it, I wanted to suck on that lip . . . "No, I can't."

"Well then, I do believe the price for denial is a kiss," he said in a husky voice, staring at my mouth.

Oh. My. God.

Was he serious or joking? If the expression on his face was anything to go by, he was very serious. The butterflies in my tummy were break-dancing with more gusto than Kim Jensen Johnson had exuded twenty minutes ago. My mouth felt dry and I knew if he let me go I'd be in a puddle at his feet. Would kissing him mean I'd lose the bet? No . . . I wasn't going out with him or having sex with him . . . although I certainly wouldn't mind that. Hells bells, he was a cop. I would not date or sleep with or dry hump a cop. Ever. No matter how freakin' outstanding his man-butt was, not to mention his impressive package, which was kind of hard to miss—being smacked up against it.

Who was ever going to know if I kissed him?

"You can't tell Jack," I said, eyeing him narrowly.

"Do I look like a guy who kisses and tells?" he asked, pulling on my curls. "God, I want to sink my hands into your hair."

"Really?" I whispered.

"Really, really. So, pretty girl, what will it be? Do we spend the night locked together in the library or do you give me a kiss?"

"One kiss," I blurted. "No tongue."

I closed my eyes and waited . . . and waited. What the hell was he doing? Where was my kiss? I opened my eyes to find the object of my desire and possibly the instrument of my having to eat with unpleasant lesbians and lose Cardboard Brett Favre a mere breath away from my lips. His eyes bored into mine and his sexy smile made the blood roar in my ears. Damn, he hadn't even kissed me yet and I was ready to have a Richter scale–shattering orgasm.

"Keep your eyes open, Kristy," he said as he erased the distance between us.

As he leaned in, my fingers tangled in his hair and I pulled his lips to mine. All coherent thought left me when he teased my lips with the tip of his tongue. I vaguely remembered telling him no tongue, but that was stupid. I loved his tongue. I'm fairly sure I loved his tongue as much as I loved his man-butt. He slanted his mouth across mine and gave me the most toe-curling kiss I'd ever had . . . without tongue. Dang it, that just wouldn't do . . .

I parted his very willing lips with my tongue and laid one on him that almost made me pass out. The sounds he made sent heat coursing through my body and straight to my panties. If kissing him was this good, sex with him would probably kill me.

"Oh my God," he said against my mouth. His hands were in my hair and he ran his lips along my jawline and down to my neck. "I have to stop," he groaned, "or I won't be able to."

"Excuse me," a pissed-off bespectacled librarian hissed, throwing a metaphorical bucket of icy cold water over us. "The library is closing. I would suggest that you two get a room . . . at a hotel."

She pivoted on her heel and stomped off, muttering something about teenagers in heat. She got the age wrong, but the rest was fairly accurate.

"I'm sorry," I said, backing away from the hottest lip smack I'd ever participated in.

"I'm not." He grinned, watching me like he was going to pounce.

"Well, um, it was lovely seeing you again," I said, trying not to giggle. "Have a nice life and enjoy your books."

I walked away. I knew he was watching my butt. I could feel it . . . and I liked it. Wait a minute . . . I turned back to him and much to my delight, caught him staring.

"Mitch, did you know I'd be here tonight?" I asked, wondering if it was coincidence or providence.

"Possibly." He grinned and shrugged his broad shoulders.

I stared at him for a moment and decided I liked his answer. I knew I would avoid him at all costs from now on, but it was flattering to find out he was stalking me. I turned and left, knowing full well his eyes were back on my butt. Why not let him enjoy the view? God knows, I'd certainly enjoyed his.

"So how was the Bigfoot meeting?" Rena asked gleefully.

"It was informative," I groaned, flopping down on her bed. "Your aunt is now going by the handle Moon-Unit and apparently Sasquatch is an immortal shapeshifter living among us."

"Holy shit," she laughed. "I knew about the name change thing. Mom is fit to be tied. She refuses to address Phyllis as Moon-Unit, so Phyllis won't answer her when she speaks."

"Sunday family brunch must be awesome," I deadpanned, grabbing her pillow and trying to wipe Mitch from my brain.

"Hell yes . . . So, little missy, I heard you met Jack's supersexy partner earlier," she teased, raising her eyebrows.

Crap, had she been hiding at the library? Did she know I'd kissed him? "What are you talking about?" I croaked, fully ready to take my punishment.

"Well," Rena gushed, "I hear sparks flew and then you informed him you had eight husbands and played in a classical-country-techno-pop band."

"I never said how many husbands and it was a folk-rock-thrash-punk band. Jack clearly has a memory problem or brain damage." I breathed a huge sigh of relief when I realized she knew nothing about the library.

"Did you think Mitch was hot?" she asked, gathering up the dirty laundry that covered her floor.

"He's okay," I said, tossing her a bra and sweats that I found under her pillow.

"Hmm, he certainly had a higher opinion of you than you do of him." She gave me the look . . . and waited.

"What?" I yelled.

Rena cackled and continued to clean her room. "He said you were hot, crazy hot."

"*Crazy* being the operative word," I moaned, putting her pillow over my head.

"Nah," she assured me. "He told Jack he couldn't say much because everything about you took his breath away."

"He didn't say that," I gasped, sitting up on her bed and throwing the pillow at her.

"Did."

"Not."

"I swear he did." She lobbed her pillow back at me. "Jack said so."

"Yeah, Jack also said I had eight husbands and a country-techno band." I rolled my eyes and flopped back on her bed. My tummy was tingling and it was all I could do to keep my voice normal. There was no way I could let on how I felt. If I did, Rena might drop the bet so I could be happy. And the bet was the main thing holding me back. My fear and disdain of dating cops seemed to disappear every time I laid eyes on Mitch. Sad thing was, Nathan/Ethan wasn't my first law enforcement romance failure . . . There was David, the beat cop who was more into his own reflection than me, and Tommy, the dispatcher, who was such a momma's boy all our dates were threesomes (and not the kind you read about in erotic romance novels). How many times did I have to date a cop before I learned my lesson? The bet was still on and it was going to stay that way.

"Jack didn't say eight husbands or country whatever-the-fuck band," she grinned. "I did, just to screw with you. The Mitch stuff is true."

"Doesn't matter," I quipped casually. "I'm not interested. I don't date cops anymore. I don't want to dine with Mrs. C and Edith. Ever. And I'm looking forward to owning cardboard Brett Favre."

Rena considered me for a long moment. "Okay," she said cryptically. "Have it your way."

"I will," I shot back.

She scooped up the laundry basket and started out of her bedroom.

"You know, Kristy, it's really going to be fun hearing about all the wonderful meals you'll be sharing with Edith and Mrs. C."

She was out of the room before I could nail her with anything. I lay on the bed and stared at the ceiling. Motherhumpin' assclowns, the psycho part of me hoped she was right.

Chapter 7

"It's going to be fine, and the damage wasn't too bad," Louise said, emerging from under a pile of donated clothes. "Hell, Mariah causes more destruction than this on her own—even without teenage hooligans ransacking the place."

"I know," I agreed. "I'm just glad she's okay, and I'm glad there were no weapons."

"Her knee and her fists seem to be fairly lethal," Louise chuckled.

"I wasn't talking about Mariah."

"I know," she sighed. "This just stinks. We lost the lobby computer, a couple of tables and chairs. Oh, and Mariah destroyed the TV two weeks ago."

I blew out a long breath and looked around. "I'd have her come in and work the TV off if I didn't think she'd demolish the entire shelter in the process."

Louise laughed and began sorting clothes. Sitting down next to her, I started making lists. Lists made me feel sane, not that I followed them. But in the tsunami that was my life, I was grasping at anything.

"I suppose I could call around and see if anyone would donate a computer and television," I said wearily. "I'll bring my old laptop over and set it up so we can still help these gals learn to use the Internet. I got it last year, so of course, it's almost obsolete." I rolled my eyes.

"You're supposed to be on vacation," Louise chided. "You should be going out on romantic dates with Ethan."

"Nathan."

"I'm sorry, what?"

"Ethan's name is Nathan," I said, leveling her with a look.

"Back up," she groaned, "that jack-off gave you the wrong name?"

"Nope. Apparently he was too polite to correct my faux pas."

"Creepy." She shuddered and stopped folding. "Are you still . . ."

"Nope." I cut her off. "Turns out Ethan/Nathan was married, also dating the mayor's wife, and a devoted Dallas Cowboys fan. Jack knocked his lights out and dumped him for me."

Louise was speechless.

"Oh, and I never poked him," I added before she asked.

"Well, thank baby Moses in a basket for that," she said, shaking her head in shock. "I think you need to pick another profession for your dating pool."

Mitch flitted through my mind and I firmly grabbed his shapely man-butt and shoved him to the very, very back. "I couldn't agree with you more."

"Anyway," she continued, "I never liked that guy. He was so damn polite and well . . . creepy."

"Why didn't you say anything when I was dating him?" I demanded.

Louise burst out laughing and shook her head. "*Creepy* is a kill-the-messenger word. I don't get into your private business, young lady."

"Well, next time I would greatly appreciate it if you would," I huffed, trying not to grin. "If I show up with someone creepy, psychotic, or, god forbid, polite, I want you to smack some sense into me. Deal?"

"Deal. Just don't show up here with another cop. Now get your bad self out of here. I have about ten volunteers coming in to get this place all spick-and-span. You are officially on vacation . . . starting now. Go."

"I'm gone," I said, ducking to avoid the wad of clothes she tossed at me. "Hey, Louise . . ."

"Yes?"

"Thank you."

"You're welcome, sweetie."

Today was the day of "I don't want to do it, but I have to." As I pulled up to A Stitch in Time, I thought about what Louise had said. She was right. No. More. Cops. Mitch was trouble. He was another in a long line of stupidly hot cops who were going to either break my heart or destroy every bit of self-confidence I owned . . . and I needed my confidence. I had to deal with the vicious sisters.

I laid my head on the steering wheel and blew out a frustrated breath. Suck it up, baby. Grandma had left me a beautiful building with three thriving businesses inside. The responsibility was overwhelming, but clearly Grandma thought I could do it . . . and I could. I would deal with Mrs. C and Edith. I would make sure the icky accountants and the wonderful Steves were happy renting from me. My God, I didn't have any real problems. I had a great life, great friends, a business that made a difference . . . and shitty taste in men. That, too, I could change—and I would. I pasted a smile on my face, got out of my car, and was greeted with hysterical squawking. Crapitty-crapcrap . . .

"Thank the gay Lord above," Short Fat Steve yelled, running out of the salon and straight at me. "It's just awful," he shrieked. "My Steve is going to get his pepper spray and blind them. If he does that, he'll go to jail and we're going to the Bahamas tomorrow. I've never been to the Bahamas! Do you hear me, Kristy? Never. Been. To. The. Bahamas. I will not let those swamp-ass lesbians send my man to jail. I'm all pasty and I need to get some Caribbean sun. I mean, my God, they're crying."

He dropped to the ground in front of me and buried his face in my stomach. I was so confused, I was dizzy. "Mrs. C. and Edith are crying?" I tried to peel Short Fat Steve off me, but he was clamped on tight. Although, I must admit, an evil joy flitted through my mind as I pictured Big Tall Steve shooting pepper spray into the old hags' eyes. I definitely had a suite in hell waiting for me when I died.

"No, they're not crying," he said into my tummy, tickling me. "They made the big burly construction guys cry."

"What big burly . . ." I turned my head and saw them . . . three huge men, standing in front of A Stitch in Time, sobbing. Holding each other and sobbing. WTF? "What did they do?"

"It was just awful, like Taylor Swift singing live. Awful," he whimpered, detaching himself from my body and pacing the sidewalk in front of me. I sucked my lower lip into my mouth to keep from giggling. When Short Fat Steve got going, he looked like a tattooed, pierced Weeble. "The poor guy had a wandering eye and they just kept screaming 'look at me' . . . over and over."

"Wait . . . what? They were hitting on Mrs. C and Edith?" I had entered an alternate universe and I wanted out. Why in the hell would big hunky construction guys hit on those two?

"Oh God, no," he gasped, wringing his hands. "The poor guy's eyeball doesn't shoot straight, and instead of ignoring it, like any polite human being would do, those rug munchers made him cry."

"Holy hell," I muttered, grabbing Short Steve by the shoulders so he would quit moving. His flair for the dramatic was killing me. "Why were construction workers in a knitting shop?"

"Kristy," Steve hissed, "that's sexist. There is no reason big boys can't knit."

"Or cry," I mumbled because I couldn't help myself.

"This is not the time for random pop-culture references to obscure songs."

"I'm sorry, you're right," I said, glancing over at the blubbering men. "So they're . . . um, customers?"

"No, they're not customers," he shouted. "They're construction guys."

"Now who's being sexist?" I asked, raising my eyebrow.

"I am not sexist," he informed me. "I'm gay. Homosexual people cannot be sexist. Sexy? Yes. Sexist? No."

"I'm not going to touch that, but I'd like to point out that you got the word *sex* into that sentence five times."

"Well, color me impressed with myself," he giggled.

"Oookay, they're not customers. They didn't hit on the lesbians, yet they're sobbing on the sidewalk in front of my store . . . What gives?"

"They start work tomorrow and they were checking out the premises," he said, smoothing out my shirt, which he had wrinkled when he was buried in it.

"Work on what?"

"Ohh, snookie bottom, you probably don't know what I'm talking about," he said as his own eyes filled with tears. I knew this had something to do with my grandma. Every time either Steve brought her up, they cried.

"Steve, I've had a really long and horrific week, so could you get to the point of all this? Quickly?"

"Yes, yes, of course," he said, wiping his eyes on my shirt, the shirt he'd just de-wrinkled. "Before your grandma died, Lutheran God bless her soul, she scheduled work on the building. New roof, new electric, some plumbing issues . . . So we all knew the building would be closed for two weeks and that's why Steve and I are going to the

Bahamas. And now those nasty bitches made the guys cry and the boys said they wouldn't go back in there until the dykes left."

"Did they actually say *dykes*?" I asked.

"Um, no," Steve admitted. "I just added that because I thought it sounded good."

"I'll take care of it," I sighed and pulled on my hair. "Could I ask you a question you might not know the answer to?"

"Absolutely. And if I don't know the answer, I'll make one up."

"Okay, um . . . great. Are Mrs. C and Edith, um, girlfriends?"

"Oh, sweet Jesus in heaven up above, I think you've made me permanently lose *my* appetite," he groaned. "And I like to eat." He demonstrated his love of food by lifting his shirt and gracing me with a view of his ample, hairy tummy. I was fairly sure he'd made me lose my appetite . . . at least till I was able to block out the visual he'd just gifted me.

"Well, are they?"

"Hell no, those old geezers have different gal pals every other week," he said, shaking his head in disbelief.

"Did you make that up?" I asked, feeling nauseous.

"Shockingly enough, no. I couldn't make something like that up. Even thinking about it makes my manhood shrivel." He shuddered.

"You did not just use the word *manhood* in place of *penis*," I groaned.

"I most certainly did. Steve and I are having a contest to see who can use more penis slang in public and get away with it," he said, grinning like a twelve-year-old.

"Have you tried pork sword, divine rod, man-tool, or skin flute?" I asked, leaving my short rotund buddy almost speechless.

"Kristy, those are fabulous," he squealed, hopping up and down like a Mexican jumping bean. "Where did you learn such dirty lingo?"

"Rena."

"Of course." He slapped his head and laughed. "She has a mouth like a sailor after my own heart. I have to run inside and write those down so I don't forget them. Can you handle this clusterfuck?"

I nodded mutely and he laid a big wet one on my cheek. As he skipped back into the salon, he gushed, "I'm gonna kick Steve's ass in the penis game."

"Glad I could help," I muttered as I made my way over to the weeping husky guys. "Hi, um . . . I'm Kristy, the owner. I understand that there was a . . ." Holy shit on a stick. Wandering eyeball, my butt. That eyeball didn't just wander, it raced around in the socket like a pinball. It was all I could do to look at the stationary eye. I bit down hard on the inside of my cheek to keep from shouting "look at me." Stopping myself was difficult, but I was better at it than the two nasty women peeking out the window at us had been.

"How can eye help you?" I bit down hard on my lip, praying they hadn't noticed my homonym.

"Well, ma'am, these working conditions are unacceptable and unless those women are removed from the area . . . we won't be able to honor our contract."

I barely heard a word. Something about unacceptable, removed . . . contract. Focus, damn it. He couldn't help it that the Indianapolis 500 was taking place in his ocular cavity.

"Eye will take care of that," I whispered, racking my brain for a replacement word for first-person singular. Slowly, I backed away. I prayed to Brett Favre and all the quarterbacks in the NFL for strength. I would not make a grown man cry. I am a good person and God knows there's plenty in my own life to poke fun at . . . it just wasn't as obvious to the naked eye. Son of a bitch, even my inner thoughts were trying to bring me down.

I'm pretty sure I heard them say "thank you" as I turned and ran into the shop. I slammed the door behind me and slid to the floor. Sweating . . . profusely.

"You wanted to yell 'look at me,' didn't you?" Edith barked, scaring the hell out of me.

"No, I did not," I lied, getting to my feet and putting my back against the wall so neither one of them could sneak up on me. Holy hell, Mrs. C and Edith were dressed up. They'd traded their sweatpants for tight polyester leggings paired with house slippers and sequined stretch tops. It was hard to look away, kind of like a train wreck. The house slippers were hurting me bad. I closed my eyes to block out the horror, but alas, their new look had embedded itself on my brain. Shitcrapballs. Flushed with anger that I would never be able to forget these outfits, I decided to let them have it. "That was hateful and mean, what you did to those men."

"God bless him," Mrs. C chimed in, "but I wouldn't let some wild-peepered freak work on my electric or my roof or my plumbing."

"Or my hooha," Edith added.

I ignored her and threw up in my mouth a little bit. I refused to have a conversation with them about vaginas. I grabbed a bottle of water from my purse and took a huge swig.

"Here's the deal," I said, wiping my mouth on the sleeve of my shirt. It was already wrinkled and had Steve's tears all over it, so what the hell. "The building will be closed for two weeks and you two can't be here—at all."

"I call bullshit," Edith snapped. "We can be here whenever we want and you can't tell us what to do," she smirked.

"That's right, you little hussy," Mrs. C cackled. "I'm guessing all the silicone in your hooters ate your brain. We run this place and you answer to us."

"First of all"—I smiled sweetly—"my hooters are real, and if I didn't think it would excite you so much, I'd show you."

They gasped and tried to speak. "Quiet," I bellowed. The volume thing was a great tool with these gals. I decided shouting the rest of my conversation would be fun. "It's true I may not be able to fire you, but I can absofuckinglutely tell you what to do. I can cut your hours, make you clean toilets, or have you work from ten p.m. till five a.m. . . . counting buttons."

"I dare you," Mrs. C hissed and narrowed her eyes beneath her gnarly unibrow.

"Actually," I continued as if she hadn't spoken, "I think what we need in here is some new blood. Bless your nonexistent hearts, you two are getting up there in years and I don't want you to strain your-selves. I'm going to hire several homophobic, right-wing, militant, religious zealot, superpreppy, bored housewives."

"You wouldn't dare," a very pale Edith spat.

"Try me," I shot back, refusing to break eye contact.

They glanced at each other uncertainly as I smiled benignly at them. While they exchanged some kind of weird silent lesbian-sister telepa-thy, I realized this was another omen in my quest to ban cops from my bedroom—I mean life. Losing the bet and eating with Mrs. C and Edith would be a fate worse than death. Between my talk with Louise and my time spent with Satan's gay spawns, I knew my decision to avoid Mitch for the rest of my life was a sound one. Depressing, but sound.

"Fine," Edith said tersely. "We'll take two weeks off."

"Give me your keys," I said with my hand out.

Very reluctantly and cursing the entire time, they handed over their keys. Lutheran God was watching over me. I wasn't going to lay eyes on these abominations for two whole weeks! I grinned as they waddled out of the store. The construction guys screamed and ran for cover when the old gals walked out. I found them still hiding in their truck a half an hour later. I handed them the master key to the entire building and left. My vacation started . . . now.

Chapter 8

As I entered my apartment building, ahead of me was one smokin'-hot man-butt. Who in the hell was he and why was he in the lobby of my apartment building? I wondered if his man-face matched his man-butt . . . the hell with Mitch, this man-butt was way better than his and this one potentially lived in my building. Things were looking up. I pretended to get my mail so I could check him out. His hoodie sweat jacket hid his face and hair color from me, but as he retrieved his mail, I saw his left hand, and it was ringless. Awesome.

"Did you say something?" Hottie McMan-butt asked with his back still to me.

Oh my God, did I say any of that out loud? That was a total asshat move. I mean, he had a great behind, but I didn't want him to think I regarded him as a piece of meat. That would be sexist, not to mention rude. Although if he were a piece of meat, I suppose he'd be a filet mignon . . . maybe. I hadn't seen the face yet, but a butt that great had to have a good face. Right? Wait, what was wrong with me? He was not a piece of meat. He was probably a very nice guy who was going to think I was a crazy dingbat with loose morals and a man-butt obsession. Balls.

My gut clenched and I wondered if I could make it to the stairs without the new hot neighbor guy seeing me. The odds were slim, but I had to try. I shut my mailbox and ran.

"Goldilocks?"

I jerked to a halt on the third stair. No, no, no, no . . . Could this day get any worse?

"Mitch?" I choked out.

"How are you?" he asked, grinning at me.

I grabbed the stair railing because my knees were about to give out. Damn it, what the hell was it about this guy that turned me into a noodle?

"I'm good. What are you doing here?"

"I live here," he said, pointing to Jack's apartment.

"You can't," I gasped, willing my spaghetti legs to work.

"Why not?" His silky voice held a challenge. He stepped closer, and because my lower body was useless, all I could do was sit down to get a little farther away.

"I live here," I stammered. "And since I'm avoiding you until I die, you can't live here. It would make my life difficult and I'd be tempted to break my vows."

"Are you going into a nunnery?" he asked as he sat down next to me and made my brain short-circuit.

"Of course not," I giggled. "I'm Lutheran." I tried to move away, but instead, conked my head on the railing. "Shit," I muttered.

"Come here." Mitch leaned in and felt around in my hair for a lump. For such a big strong guy, his hands were incredibly gentle. I wondered how they'd feel on my . . . Stop. Don't go there.

"I'm okay," I whispered, aching to kiss him. I stood up shakily and put a little distance between us. "I have to go."

"Wait—" Mitch grabbed my hand. "Why won't you go out with me? It feels like you're liking me and God knows, I'm liking you."

"Mitch, you seem like you're very, um . . . nice, but I don't date cops." I tried to pull my hand away, but his grip tightened.

"Well, you're in luck. I'm not a cop. I'm a DEA agent, so that argument won't stand." He grinned lazily and my heart skipped two beats.

"That's the same thing," I told him, trying not to smile.

"Nope, it's not. You'll have to come up with a better excuse for not going out with me than that."

"Okay, fine." I pulled my hand from his and crossed my arms over my chest so I wouldn't bury them in his hair. "I can't go out with you because if I do, I'll have to eat lots of dinners with hostile lesbians and I'll lose Brett Favre forever." If that didn't scare him away, then I didn't know what would.

He laughed and I almost jumped him in a very sexual way. "I'm a little confused," he said. "Let's break this one down . . . I'm very sure Brett Favre is married. Am I wrong about that?"

"It's not real Brett Favre. It's Cardboard Brett Favre," I explained rationally, halfway hoping my crazy would make him give up and move to Alaska. Of course the other half of me wanted him to grab me by the hair and shove his tongue in my mouth.

"You mean like the one in Rena's office?" he asked.

"Yes," I answered slowly. I was beginning to wonder what he already knew. Was he in on this? Had Rena convinced him to hit on me so I would lose the bet?

"And the hostile lesbians?" he asked, pulling on one of my curls.

"I'm sure you know exactly what I'm talking about," I said with a sarcastic edge to my voice. I was sooo not falling for this. He was as bad as all the rest of the loser cops I'd dated . . . maybe worse.

He stared at me for a long moment and I almost forgot how much I didn't like him. Those damn blue eyes. "No, I have no idea what you're talking about. If I did, I wouldn't ask."

"Right," I snapped. "I really have to go, Mitch. Good luck with the new apartment. I'll be moving out next week." I turned and ran as quickly as my stupid pasta legs would carry me . . . which was not very fast.

"Kristy. Stop." The sexy command in his voice made my throat go tight and everything inside my body tingle in anticipation. God, this jack-off knew how to push every one of my hoochie mama buttons. "Look at me," he instructed.

I turned and waited.

"Your reasons aren't good enough. I'm not quite understanding the Brett Favre and hostile lesbian thing, but it's very clear you have dated some asshole cops. I'm not one of them. I'm the guy who can't get you out of my head ever since I saw you the other day. That kiss in the library is burned into my brain and I keep replaying it."

"Me too," I whispered, then purposely banged my head against the wall. Admitting I wanted to trade spit with him was not going to help my case. His sexy answering smirk lit my panties on fire.

"Give me a chance," he said, sending some kind of magic hoodoo straight to my brain and other unmentionable parts of me. "Get to know me . . . Let me take you out."

I was pretty sure I wouldn't have been able to say no even if the fate of mankind was resting on my answer.

"Okay," I said in a voice that belonged in a porno. I quickly cleared my throat and tried again. "Okay, but here's the deal . . . You can't tell anybody. Not Jack, not Rena . . . no one."

He put his hands on his hips, stretching his T-shirt across his insanely hot chest, and tilted his head to the side. My mouth went dry . . . "Are you ashamed of me?" he asked with mock severity.

"No," I gasped. "It has something to do with the, um . . . lesbian–Brett Favre thing."

"I'm going to take your word on that," he chuckled. "Hell, short of doing something illegal, I'd do anything to go out with you. So if you want to keep it a secret . . . it's a secret."

"Thank you," I blurted, grinning like an idiot.

"Tomorrow night?"

I thought for a moment. Rena and Jack were going to a concert . . . perfect. "Yes, tomorrow night."

"Seven o'clock," he said. "Do you want to meet me somewhere?"

"Um, no. Rena and Jack won't be here; you can pick me up at my apartment . . . if you want to." Crap, did that sound like an invitation for nookie?

"I'll be there." His voice was so damn hot I found myself leaning toward him. Thankfully I caught myself before I tumbled down the stairs and landed in a broken mess at his feet.

I righted myself, turned, and walked up the stairs with a little extra swing . . . I knew full well he was watching my butt. I might have to break bread with the hostile lesbos, but I had a weird feeling it would be worth it.

"Aunt Moon-Unit has called six times for you," Rena informed me as I scrounged through the fridge looking for something that didn't have a past-due date or wasn't growing fur. Damn, nothing but salad dressing and hot dog buns.

"What did she want?" I pulled out a hot dog bun, checked it for mold, and ate it.

"No clue, I didn't answer," Rena said, grabbing another bun and joining me. "Holy fucking hell, we need to go grocery shopping."

"Agreed," I replied with a mouth full of dough. "Did she leave a message?"

"Not really. She just kept yelling your name louder and louder— like you would answer if she broke your eardrums."

"Why didn't you pick up?" I asked, searching for something that might taste a little better than an old stale hot dog bun.

"Because I spent an hour on the phone with her this morning dis- cussing ways to murder bad chi with spatulas and fly swatters when I should have been crunching numbers for my clients."

"'Nuff said. I'll call her back in a minute."

"How was your day?" she asked, unearthing some vanilla pudding from the salad crisper.

"Sucked. What's the date on that stuff?" I asked, digging my own pudding cup out of the drawer.

"I can't make it out."

"I didn't buy this crap. Do you remember buying it?" I asked, searching the little container frantically. I realized I was starving. In the midst of my hellacious day, I'd forgotten to eat.

"I never buy shit like this."

"Well, we don't have a pudding fairy as far as I know," I snapped, still searching for an expiration date.

"Relax your crack," Rena laughed. "Jack loves this stuff and the only time he ever grocery shopped for us was a week ago, so knock yourself out."

I did and it was amazing. "God, we should buy this all the time," I said grabbing another pudding out of the veggie drawer.

"You know what?" Rena said, stopping mid-pudding-shovel. "I think that wanker hid these. He thought if he put dessert in the veggie bin, we'd never find it."

"What else do you think that rat bastard hid?" I asked, giving the crisper another search.

"I don't know, but I'm going to find out."

Ten minutes later we were settled on the couch with chips and salsa we'd found in the laundry room, cheese puffs we'd found under the bathroom sink, and beer we'd found on the top shelf of Rena's closet.

"Jack's a dick," I said, enjoying the fruits of our hunt.

"Totally," Rena agreed. "I think I'll withhold sex for a week."

I almost choked on a puff ball I laughed so hard.

"What?" she yelled. "You don't think I'm capable of keeping my legs closed?"

"Nope." I took a swig of warm beer to wash down the cheese ball that almost ended my life.

"You're right, I'm not. Not where Jack's concerned." She rolled her eyes and laughed. "Speaking of not keeping your legs closed . . . Mitch is staying in Jack's apartment."

"First of all, that made no sense and second, why do you even call it Jack's apartment when he's completely taken over this one?"

"He has, hasn't he?" she giggled, looking like a lovesick teenager. "All I'm saying is that Mitch thinks you're a total babe and you need to have sex . . . like yesterday."

"That's just lovely," I huffed. "I don't know how to make it any more clear . . . I am done with cops. I will not poke the po-po or pork the pig. Ever."

"Okay, that's just disgusting and I'm the queen of inappropriate and gross."

"You're right," I muttered. "Sorry."

"Kristy, if you really like the guy, I'll drop the bet."

"You will?" I was shocked. Rena never backs off of anything. Especially something that would cause me massive embarrassment and involve Bigfoot or lesbians. To be fair, I'd do the same thing to her, only never on such a grand scale.

"No fucking way," she yelled, laughing. "Although I would be really happy for you if you got laid by the fine specimen living downstairs."

"Not to mention the inordinate amount of time I'd be spending with Edith and Mrs. C."

"That's just an added bonus," she said gleefully.

Before I could call her a fucktard and fail yet again at having a curse-word-free existence, the phone rang and saved me from myself. "I'll get it."

I sat in shocked silence for six minutes and forty seconds while I listened to Aunt Moon-Unit's dilemma. Pale, pissed, and confused, I told her I'd be there in a half an hour.

"What in the hell was that about?"

"Apparently an emergency Bigfoot meeting has been called for tonight and the trolls and fairies have told Aunt Moon-Unit if she doesn't go, either the world will end or *Jeopardy!* will be cancelled.

I'm not sure. I kind of zoned out after she said she knew something was wrong when she caught the cyborgs trying to copulate with your dead uncle Carlton."

"Oh my God," Rena groaned. "I'm worried if other people hear her talk, she'll get institutionalized. Look, this is above and beyond the terms of the bet. I'll take her."

"No," I sighed. "She said she'd rather I take her. The trolls said I was the one to solve the riddle of injustice, whatever the hell that means, and Moon-Unit said all you do is laugh and make fun of everybody."

"Oh shit, I didn't think she noticed that the last time I went with her."

"Apparently everyone did."

I went quickly to my room and changed into a cute sundress and sparkly flip-flops. Could this day be any longer? I was so looking forward to cheese balls and *Toddlers & Tiaras* . . . and all because of that jack-off *Baywatch* star, I was going to hang out with Yeti lovers.

"I just have one thing to say," I told Rena as she finished off her beer, looking contrite about my evening. "David Hasselhoff is a fucktard."

Chapter 9

"Where is everybody?" I asked Aunt Moon-Unit as we made our way to the front of the practically empty room. Being back at the library reminded me of kissing Mitch. I firmly put him out of my mind and glanced around. There were literally six people there, including us. Something was off.

"I have no idea. It was last minute . . . maybe everyone is busy or under the influence of government voodoo," she said.

Staying silent was the best response I had to most of the things Aunt Moon-Unit said, so I did. Kim and Hugh were in the corner of the room deep in discussion with two very short men who were definitely not from Minnesota. Overly tan and slick, they wore skinny jeans and silky shirts. They seemed bored with the mounds of information that Kim was throwing at them and slightly disturbed at the garbled sound track coming from an overexcited Hugh.

"Aunt Moon-Unit," I whispered. "Who are Kim and Hugh talking to?"

"Oooo, those must be the L.A. producers," she said. "This is big, Kristy. Mark my words. This. Is. Big."

A strange surge of panic washed through me. I actually breathed a sigh of relief when I saw Mariah Carey and her odd, shapeshifter-loving sister Boo walk in the room. They were followed by a huge guy that I didn't remember from the last meeting . . . and I would have remembered him. Bless his heart, he was shaped like a pear, his teeth were something to behold, and the curly black hair on his head resembled pubes. He was dressed in a light blue muumuu type of shirt and sweatpants. Looking at him from where I stood, I wondered if he might be mentally challenged.

I took a seat next to Moon-Unit and prayed this would go quickly.

Lost in my own world, fantasizing about a DEA agent that I should have nothing to do with, I was startled when the big, unfortunate-looking guy sat down next to me. Hell, practically every seat in the room was available . . . did he really have to sit right next to me? I glanced over and realized he also had man-boobs. Everything about him was so wrong, I knew I had to be nice.

"Hi, I'm Kristy," I said, offering him my hand. This poor guy had been smacked hard with the ugly stick. On top of all his challenges, he had one green eye and one brown. I imagined growing up had been difficult.

"Rich," he said in an accent I couldn't quite identify. British? That would explain the teeth . . .

"So, you, ah, believe in Bigfoot?" I said, trying to make conversation.

"Oh yes. Don't you?" he asked in an accent I now thought might be Australian . . . or possibly Scottish.

"Well," I hedged, "I'm not against the possibility."

Crap, I didn't want to pull a "Rena" and make fun of these people, but pretending to worship Sasquatch was not gonna happen. Again, I cursed David Hasselhoff. I wanted to get this show on the road. Small talk with man-boob Rich was not very appealing and Mariah and Boo were all the way on the other side of the room. I turned to Aunt Moon-Unit to avoid my new large buddy, but she was in some bizarre meditative state, mumbling about cyborgs.

"You have lovely hair, Kristy," the unidentifiably accented Rich said.

"Thank you. You, um, smell good," I said, fumbling for something nice to say. God, please don't let this guy and his bad teeth be hitting on me. Although he actually did smell good. He smelled a little like Mitch. Maybe they used the same laundry detergent.

"That's such a kind thing to say," he said, smiling and running his hands over his muumuu and mussing his hair. "This is my first meeting. I'm trying to get out into the world and make some friends with similar interests."

Oh hell, did he not have any friends? I am such a sucker for the underdog. If he would get a haircut and some braces and go on a diet . . . Darn it, I needed to stop judging. Here was a huge, looks-and-fashion-impaired guy trying to fit in somewhere. The least I could do was be kind.

"So, Rich, what do you do for a living?" I asked, giving him my full attention.

"I'm unemployed at the moment," he said, lowering his eyes. "But I'm a magician by trade."

"Oh. Wow," I stammered, trying not to laugh. "That's fantastic. You know, I run a women's shelter and we have a lot of children come through . . . maybe, you could do a, um, magic show sometime."

"That would be wonderful," he said. "I'm a very good magic man."

"I'm sure you are. Of course, we'd have to do a background check." I hated saying that, but it was the way it was.

"No problem." He smiled. "My male hooking days are long past me now."

"Oh my God, what?" I gasped and choked on my own spit.

"I'm joking," he laughed. "If I was a male hooker, I would starve to death. And as you can see"—he slapped his big belly—"I'm not food deprived."

"You're fine the way you are," I said, giggling. I meant it. His looks might be unusual . . . and somewhat alarming, but he was nice and had a sense of humor.

"I understand the group will be going on a Bigfoot search," he said. "Are you going?"

"Absolutely not," I told him. "The only reason I'm here is because I drive my friend." I leaned back so I could introduce Rich, but Aunt Moon-Unit was deep in conversation with something invisible on her lap.

"Is she okay?"

"She's fine," I assured him. I didn't want him to think she was insane. "She's um, psychic and communes with the . . . dead." Shit-balls, so much for distracting him from Aunt Moon-Unit's crazy. Not to mention, letting on that I wasn't quite right either.

"That's too bad; it sounds like an interesting trip," he said.

"Talking to dead people?" I asked.

"No, no, no," he said, laughing and shaking his head. "Searching for Sasquatch. I understand there have been some sightings up north."

"I don't know anything about that," I told him, "but the others here will know. Over there"—I pointed to Mariah and her sister Boo—"Mariah and Boo are way into Sasquatch, just don't get in nose range of Mariah's fists."

"Okay," he said, looking at me strangely.

"Trust me on that one." I pointed to the corner. "Kim and Hugh are the leaders. They're, um . . . lovely people and Hugh is quite a singer."

"Good to know," he said. "And who are those ladies?"

"What ladies?"

"The ones in the back wearing sequins and giving everyone dirty looks."

"Oh shit, no," I moaned and tried to duck down. Too late. According to my plan I wasn't supposed to lay eyes on those lesbians for two weeks. Maybe I had picked up some bad chi at Aunt Moon-Unit's the other day.

"Bless your heart. How are those titanium hooters?" Edith yelled across the room to me.

"With dinglebobbers like that, I'd be surprised if you could see your toes," Mrs. C bellowed joyously.

That was it. I was so done with those hags. "For the last time, you hateful old rug munchers, my boobs are one hundred percent real. If you'd like to join me in the ladies' room, I'll show you," I shouted back.

The entire room went silent and gaped at me. I have never in my life wanted the floor to open up and swallow me more than I did in that hideous moment. Even Aunt Moon-Unit had come out of her trance to stare at me in shock.

"Sorry about that," I muttered, sliding as low as I could possibly go in my chair.

"I can tell they're real," Rich said kindly.

"You can?" I whispered, still wanting to die.

"Absolutely." He nodded solemnly.

"Thank you," I said gratefully. He was a really nice guy. Really unattractive, but really nice. I would definitely sit next to him for the next two months of meetings.

"Allrightyroo," Kim Jensen Johnson sang as she took the spotlight off me and started the meeting . . . with all seven of us. "I have the most exciting news!"

She bounced up and down like I do when I have to pee really bad. Hugh, standing next to her, was doing the Michael Jackson crotch grab and humming "Billie Jean." It was beyond disturbing, but thankfully it took everyone's attention away from me and my funbags.

"The producers from *Searching for Sasquatch* have chosen our group to go to Duluth for two weeks to look for Bigfoot. We're going to be on TV," she shrieked, knocking Hugh to the floor with her out-of-control enthusiasm.

Hugh, not one to miss an opportunity, slid into the splits and played his chest like a drum. I snuck a quick look at Rich to see his reaction. He seemed a bit puzzled, but happy. God, everyone here was nuts . . . or maybe they were all sane and I was losing it.

"We are blessed to have the producers from *Searching for Sasquatch* here with us tonight. Stu Greenberg and Stan Angelusi, all the way from Los Angeles, California. Home to my favorite movie hunks, Steven Seagal and John Stamos! They're going to tell us all about our adventure!"

Everyone began applauding wildly. Since the group was so small, I felt I had to go with it. I clapped and hooted and felt like a dork. Stan or Stu, I didn't know which—they were kind of interchangeable—stepped in front of Kim and started talking.

"Thank you for your interest. We are pleased that you've accepted our offer and will all be going on the trip," he said.

I froze. What in the hell was that shiny little guy saying? I wasn't going on a Bigfoot hunt with the bonkers group sitting in this room. I needed to stay in town and possibly, yet secretly, boink Mitch. Wait, no . . . I wasn't going to boink Mitch. That would mean I'd have to eat with Satan's gay handmaidens . . . Nope, not gonna boink Mitch. My deal with Rena was meetings . . . not overnight field trips to Duluth. I. Hate. David. Hasselhoff. Should I speak up now? Should I pretend to go to the bathroom and never come back? No, how would Aunt Moon-Unit get home if I left—I suppose Kim and Hugh might take her home, but she would be worried. Maybe I could pass out and they'd have to call the paramedics and I could go to the hospital in an ambulance . . . No, that was stupid. The ambulance guys would probably know I was faking it, and God forbid that Kim or Hugh . . . or the lesbos . . . tried to give me CPR. No, I'd just . . . Motherhumpin' assbuckets. Why was everyone staring at me?

"So will you do it?" Stu or Stan asked me.

"Do what?" My voice drifted into a hushed whisper.

"Host *Searching for Sasquatch*," he said as if he were offering me a million dollars.

"Host?" I choked out.

"Yes," the short shiny man said. "We need some good-looking T and A eye candy for the ratings." He looked around the room disdainfully. "And you're it."

A panic like I'd never known welled in my throat and I was speechless.

"They're going to donate fifty thousand to the charity of our choice," Mariah gushed all aflutter. "And we voted for the shelter!"

"What?" I stared at Mariah, baffled. "When did all this happen?"

"It's all right, dear," Aunt Moon-Unit said, gently rubbing my back. "While you were busy having your inner monologue with yourself, the tiny man in the girlie shirt gave us all the details."

I remained absolutely motionless for a moment while my brain tried to catch up. They wanted me, my boobs, and my butt to host a bunch of misfit freaks running around Duluth looking for Bigfoot. That was bad enough, but it was going to be televised . . . on TV—for the world to see. No. Fucking. Way.

"I can't," I said. Thank you, Lutheran Jesus, my mind and my lips were finally working together. "I have a shelter to run."

"No, you don't," Mariah said.

"Yes," I hissed through clenched teeth, "I do."

"Clearly you're having a brain fart," Mariah reminded me. "You took the summer off. Louise is running the shelter so you can get laid and get your life back in order."

"Right," I said, scrambling. Why did I have to be such a crappy liar? And why in the hell did she have to announce to the room I needed to get laid? "You're right. I forgot about that little detail, but I also have a sewing shop that I have to manage. So, I'm sorry. I'll have to pass."

"I call bullshit," Edith yelled, waddling toward me. I jumped out of my seat and hid behind Rich's overly ample body. "The store is closed for two weeks, you little hussy . . . unless you were lying."

"No," I gasped in terror, imagining the sisters going down to check the store and sending the acrobatic-eyeballed construction worker into sobbing hysterics. The whole crew would quit, and finding last-minute construction workers, plumbers, and electricians would be impossible. Crap, the old biddies had me cornered. "I wasn't lying. The shop is closed."

"Well, aren't you just a few fries short of a Happy Meal," Mrs. C chimed in, enjoying my pain way too much.

"That solves it then," Kim cried out with great pleasure. "Kristy will host and we will find our hero Yeti!"

"No," I insisted. "I can't. I'm not even part of this group. I'm just Moon-Unit's driver. It should be hosted by someone who has the passion. I really, really don't have the passion."

"I know why you don't want to do it," Edith said slyly. "You don't want the world to know your love puppies are filled with rubber."

Love puppies? Was she kidding? I stepped out from behind Rich and got right up in Edith's face. "You are a shining example of why people should avoid inbreeding. For the last time, my badoinkies are real. Go ahead, touch them," I shouted.

"Girls, girls, there will be no more fighting and no touching private parts," Aunt Moon-Unit said, separating me and Edith. I cringed, inwardly noticing Edith's disappointment at not getting to poke my puppies. "Kristy, I do believe you should consider this opportunity. You could have fifty thousand dollars in your budget at the shelter in two weeks. That's a lot of money. You're fancy-free and clear of work commitments at the moment and I'm fairly sure the short shiny men don't want to do the show without you."

Stu and Stan nodded in unison.

I glanced around the room; ten sets of hopeful eyes peered back. Poor unfortunate-looking Rich winked at me with his green eye. The money was a huge incentive. We could do so much at the shelter with that money . . . and the trip would also keep me from getting involved with Mitch.

"Okay," I said slowly, somehow knowing I would regret my decision for the rest of my life or at least the immediate future. "I'll do it."

The cheers were loud and frightening. So terrifying that the shiny little L.A. guys quickly made their escape, promising to be in touch. Hugh lost his mind and did a medley of Disney songs in a rap style. Kim danced furiously while Boo cried. I assumed and hoped they were tears of joy, but who knew? Mariah punched the air with her skinny little arms and Aunt Moon-Unit smiled and spoke animatedly with the invisible things flying around her head. What had I gotten myself into? I got passed around and hugged so hard I could barely breathe. Even the scary sisters embraced me. I ended up squished by Rich's man-boobs, which while sweet, was also a little gross. I extricated myself and watched the joyful misfits around me and questioned my sanity. Maybe this would be a win-win for all of us. Of course I didn't for a minute believe we would find Sasquatch, but then again . . . who in the hell knew?

"I bet we'll go to Hollywood for the premiere," Boo shrieked, startling me. Her voice was the exact opposite of Mariah's . . . high and squeaky.

"Oh my God." Kim paled and began to shake. Sweet baby Jesus, was she having a heart attack? "If we go to Hollywood," she said, shushing Hugh's Disney extravaganza, "there's a good chance I could see Steven Seagal or John Stamos. Or at least drive by their houses repeatedly."

"Or Cher's house!" Hugh shouted triumphantly, breaking into a dizzying version of "Gypsys, Tramps & Thieves."

"What is wrong with you idiots?" Edith barked. "There's only one man in Hollywood worth shit."

"Yeah," Mrs. C said. "He's the one man we'd go straight for."

Eww, the thought of them getting it on with anything made the vanilla pudding in my stomach curdle.

"George Clooney?" Mariah guessed.

"Nope, not hot enough," Edith said. "Guess again."

"Sylvester Stallone?" Boo volunteered.

"God, no. I can't understand a word he says," Mrs. C said, clearly enjoying the game.

"Jay Leno," Kim yelled.

"He is hot," Edith admitted, "but not as hot as my man."

"All right then, who is it?" Aunt Moon-Unit asked, taking a break from her trolls or fairies or whatever.

"It's David Hasselhoff, you imbeciles! He's the hottest piece of man-meat to put his pecker in a Speedo," Edith shouted, waving her claw at everyone.

"And he sings like a wet dream," Mrs. C added.

"Oh shit, that's disgusting," Mariah moaned. She was joined by a chorus of groans from the rest of the group.

"What in the hell is wrong with you nose pickers? David Hasselhoff is a god," Edith screamed over the boos and hisses.

As a loud argument ensued over the quality of David Hasselhoff's package, I lost it. I was laughing so hard I was crying. I sat down on the floor and rocked back and forth, hoping I wouldn't pee myself.

"Care to share?" Rich asked as he settled his big old self on the floor next to me.

"Oh my God," I sputtered, "David Hasselhoff is why I'm here."

"You know him?" he asked, impressed.

"No, actually I think he's a fucktard." I collapsed in another fit of laughter. "Sorry," I wheezed. "I made a bet with my roommate Rena about David Hasselhoff and I lost, so I had to bring Aunt Moon-Unit to these meetings for two months."

"So you're really not a Sasquatch believer?"

"No, I'm sorry . . . I'm not," I said, hoping he'd still be my friend. Even with his bizarre accent and regrettable looks, he was the most normal person there.

"Do you make bets often?" he asked, smiling.

"Unfortunately yes," I told him. "And I usually lose. My latest is a real doozy."

"Tell me."

"You don't really want to hear this," I said, trying to keep my eyes on his face instead of his pubic head.

"I really do."

"Okay, you asked for it." I grinned.

I explained to him my hideous record with dating cops down to the married, two-timing, Dallas Cowboys bastard and the bet Rena had made about me not sleeping with this really sexy cop named Mitch. How I had taken the bet knowing full well I would win, until I laid eyes on Mitch. He was every fantasy I had ever had rolled into one package, but so much was at stake . . . Cardboard Brett Favre and dining with the dykes. Problem was, I really wanted to tackle this Mitch guy to the ground and do all sorts of nasty things to him . . . plus I'd already made a secret date with him. I even confessed how I was cheating on the terms of my bet.

Rich sat silently for a moment, looking shell-shocked. Shit, I'd probably scared the hell out of him.

"TMI?" I asked in a worried tone.

"No, no," he said. "I'm just trying to get all of this straight in my head. So, if you sleep with this hot cop guy, you'll have to eat with Mrs. C and Edith for two weeks?"

"Right." I nodded. "And I'll lose Cardboard Brett Favre."

"Do you like this guy?" he asked.

"Yes, but with my luck, he's probably a serial killer or has a harem stashed in Iowa."

Rich laughed and his man-boobs jiggled. I jerked my eyes back up to his face. Pubic head was far easier on the eye than man-boob. "Well, Kristy, you are already paying for the bet, whether you sleep with the womanizing serial killer or not."

"How do you figure?" I asked, confused.

"You will be eating all your meals with the lesbians for the next two weeks on our little sojourn into the wilds of Duluth looking for Bigfoot. So, Brett Favre aside, you can sleep with your hot cop because you're already paying the price of losing."

"Motherhumpin' cowballs," I gasped. "You're right. What should I do?"

"I can't tell you what to do," he said. "You should do whatever your heart tells you to."

"Or my lady bits," I muttered.

"Those too," he chuckled.

"Rich, you are a great guy and I'm sure we're going to be good friends. Thanks for listening to all my crap and not laughing at me," I said, giving him a hug and getting squished by the man-boobs again. Amazingly, this time I didn't care. He can't help what he looks like on the outside. He was quickly proving he was quite good-looking on the inside.

"Good luck, Kristy."

"Thanks, Rich."

I grabbed Aunt Moon-Unit as the Hasselhoff discussion turned into a brawl. Hugh, in regular form, was screeching the theme to *Baywatch*. Kim was trying to hold Mariah and her fists back from Edith and Mrs. C, and Boo just stood there crying. The next two weeks were going to be fucking fantastic. Watching the mayhem around me, I decided to give up swearing in the fall . . . possibly.

Chapter 10

"Get out of town!" Rena laughed, examining me like I'd had a lobotomy.

Maybe I had. Sitting on the couch retelling the events of last night sounded ridiculous even to my own ears. I pulled my knees to my chest and grabbed my Minnesota Vikings fleece blanket. I needed comfort.

"Son of a bitch," Rena moaned, ransacking the cabinets. "We don't have any breakfast food. Do you want pudding and a beer?"

"Too early for a beer, but I'll take a pudding," I said. "Did you tell Jack we found his stash?"

"Nope." She giggled. "I'm going to let him discover it for himself. He'll be horrified."

"You're awful," I laughed.

"Yep," she agreed.

She handed me a pudding cup and a spoon and plopped down next to me on the couch. We ate our healthy breakfast in companionable silence. I vowed to grocery shop that day. There was no way I was going to drink salad dressing for lunch.

"So let me get this straight . . . You're going to Duluth to hunt down Bigfoot for a reality TV show."

"Um, yes." I bit my lip and wondered how much more I should tell her. In the light of a new day it was mortifying.

"And you're going to find the elusive Yeti with Aunt Moon-Unit, Kim, and Hugh."

"Yep," I muttered, deciding I'd only answer questions . . . not offer up any excess humiliating information.

Rena already knew Kim and Hugh from her own tenure of taking Aunt Moon-Unit to her meetings. She'd also met with them for research on her on her appalling book, *Pirate Dave and His Randy Adventures*. She'd invented an oversize, hairy, Bigfoot-ish character named Sam in the piece of crap novel that had brought Evangeline O'Hara's romance writing career to a grinding halt. Sam was an immortal time-traveling pirate shifter with a huge package. So huge, he'd been unable to fornicate for centuries.

"There seems to be a lot missing from this story," Rena said, stealing some of my blanket.

"Yep."

"Spill."

"Fine," I sighed and pushed my hair out of my face. "I'm whoring myself out for fifty thousand dollars for the shelter. I'm going to host the show with my tits and my ass, leading a band of freaks through the wilds of Duluth, looking for something that doesn't exist."

"Sounds reasonable," Rena said, licking her spoon. "Is Hugh doing the sound track?"

"Yes," I giggled. "Yes, he is."

"Then it's sure to be a big hit. I hope he does a few originals about the unknown mating habits of Sasquatch."

"Oh my God," I groaned, trying not to laugh. "Stop joking. This is my life we're talking about."

"Okay." Rena grinned and swiped the rest of my blanket. "Honestly, I'd do the same thing if I were you."

"You would?"

"Kristy, I tried to become the new Sunshine Weather Girl by showing up at the news station every day for a month, which clearly didn't end well. You think I wouldn't make a gaping ass of myself by hosting an imaginary monster show for fifty thousand dollars?"

"Point taken."

"Exactly," she said, getting excited. "You have the summer off and you'll make a shitload of needed money for the shelter. The way I see it, it's a win-win."

I knew I should be wary of anything Rena thought was a good idea. My mind was swirling with paranoia and doubt. My best friend's good ideas have often landed her in the slammer. I might not end up in the pokey, but there was a fine chance I'd land on YouTube . . . forever. Crap, what had I done?

"There's more," I whispered.

"It gets better?" Rena's eyes grew wide.

"There are other Yeti believers coming with us."

"Oh my God." She hopped up and grabbed two beers. Handing me an open bottle, she made herself comfortable again. "I know it's early, but I have a feeling we might need this."

I took a swig and then a deep breath. Maybe if I said everything out loud, it wouldn't be so awful . . . or maybe I'd wake up and realize it was all a dream. I pinched my leg to test my theory. Ouch . . . balls, not a dream.

"Mariah Carey is going on the trip."

"Holy shit, the singer? Damn, her career is in the toilet if she's doing crap like that. I read this thing where she only washes her hair in champagne . . . no, wait, maybe it's orange juice or buttermilk and . . ."

"No," I cut her off. "Not the singer. The nose breaker from the shelter."

"No way," she cackled.

"Yes way, and it gets better." I took three deep calming breaths. I realized if I said the next part out loud it would be true. "Edith and Mrs. C are going."

That shut her up. Rena turned white and grabbed my hands, spilling beer all over the couch. "You'll die," she gasped. "Or end up serving a life sentence for murder."

I hadn't thought about that. Was I really capable of killing the old girls? I'd been so focused on the amazing fact that I could jump, I mean date, Mitch, I hadn't really thought about being with the twins 24/7.

"I can't do this," I muttered frantically, grabbing the runner off the coffee table to mop up the spilled beer. Rena was right, I might off them. The temptation to permanently get rid of the lesbians could be too much to handle. It would probably be self-defense, but since I'd considered the kill, it would be ruled premeditated murder. Fuck-monkeys, I had to get out of this.

"Wait," Rena said, sensing my hysteria. She soaked up the remaining beer with my beloved Vikings blanket. If I hadn't been in such a panic, I would have wept that she'd desecrated my blanky. She grabbed me by the shoulders and pushed me down on the still-damp couch. "Is anyone normal going on this clusterfuck of a trip?"

I pressed my hand to my forehead and tried to refocus. "Well, *normal* being a relative word, there's one guy who seems nice," I said, still feeling ill.

"How relative is normal?"

"He's shaped like a pear, his hair would look better on a crotch, his teeth are very British, and he has man-boobs, but he's funny and kind."

"Well, there's something." She rolled her eyes and sat down next to me. "I feel really guilty."

"Why?"

"Because I'm the reason you had to go to these stupid meetings."

"Nope," I told her. "I took the bet. It's my own fault."

Rena jumped up off the couch and started pacing the room like a caged tiger. She grabbed two new beers and handed me one. "Kristy, there may be a silver lining here."

"And that would be?" I asked skeptically.

"You can boink Mitch now," she shouted. "This is great! You're such a freaking rule follower, you never would have let yourself cheat and be happy. Since you're eating with the skanks for two weeks anyway . . . you're free and clear to boink away. Of course, you would lose Cardboard Brett Favre."

"I don't want Cardboard Brett Favre."

Rena was speechless.

"Okay look, I have to tell you something . . . I was already going to cheat. I'm going on a date with Mitch tonight."

She grinned from ear to ear. "So it's a self-fulfilling prophecy," she said.

I waited for her to continue . . . I knew she would.

"You were destined to sup with the muff divers, just as much as you were meant to do the nasty with Mitch. The bet was just a fore-telling of the future."

"That is totally fucked-up and discombobulated," I told her. "It doesn't even make sense."

"It makes perfect sense," Rena argued. "But you do realize Mitch is a cop."

"He's not a cop, he's a DEA agent."

"Same thing."

"Nope," I informed her, not wanting to admit I'd had the same con-versation. "It's different."

"Ooo, you really like this guy," she laughed.

"Well, I definitely lust him and I think I like him too."

"You're more than in lust with a guy when you're willing to forgo Cardboard Brett for him," she said smugly. "You'll be bumping uglies tonight."

"I will not be bumping anything tonight," I insisted forcefully. "I'm going to get to know him first." I got up off the beer-soaked couch to make my point. If I could make her believe me . . . maybe I would too.

Rena just smiled the kind of smile that made me want to slap her.

"Rena, I can't, won't, will not sleep with him tonight," I yelled. "I'll be screwed if I do it . . . No pun intended."

"Okay fine," she said in her "I've got a great plan" voice. "Go out with him tonight. Tell him you're going away on business for two weeks and then have nightly phone sex while you're on the mission to capture Sasquatch. Get to know him while having great orgasms in the privacy of your own tent or whatever-the-fuck and then come back and screw him till his eyes cross."

I thought about it for a moment. "I think that sounds good."

"You see?" she chirped gleefully. "You need me."

She tackled me on our couch, which now smelled like it belonged in a bar, and hugged me so hard I had to tickle her to get her off me.

"What should I wear tonight?" I wheezed and tried to get my breath back.

"Do you have any clean good-butt jeans?" She balled herself up on the couch, covering all her tickle spots. "Sweet baby Jesus, the couch reeks." She jumped up and ran to our cleaning supply closet.

"Yes, it reeks and yes, I have clean good-butt jeans," I laughed, removing my wet rear end from the couch.

"Okay, wear those, but put on some granny panties and don't shave your legs," she said as she began spraying the offending couch with air freshener.

"Stop," I coughed and took the aerosol can of floral stink away from her. "You're making it worse. Why in the hell would I go out with gross panties and hairy legs?"

"If you really don't want to sleep with him, do as I say. Nasty panties and stubbly legs will be an extra incentive to keep your pants on."

"Oh my God, you're brilliant," I gasped. That had never occurred to me before.

"I know." She grinned. "I'm taking the day off from work because all my clients are away on book tours. So I say we are going for manicures, pedicures, and therapy shopping. You need a sexy new top for tonight and some rugged yet revealing pieces for your stint as the host of the Bigfoot bonanza."

"Don't remind me," I said, and snatched my purse off the table. "I'm ready. Are you?"

"Kristy, Kristy, Kristy," Rena chuckled. "I was born ready."

I rolled my eyes and giggled. I had the greatest best friend in the whole fucking world.

Chapter 11

In the dimly lit back room of the most charming Chinese restaurant in Minneapolis, I sat across from the most beautiful man in the world. Of course, Asian Wind, the name of the restaurant, brought to mind unpleasant gastric explosions, but the food was delicious. It was owned by the Wang family, who swore they were first-generation Americans. Their insanely heavy Minnesota accents belied their claim, but no one in their right mind would call them on it. Mr. Wang was a very sensitive culinary genius and Mrs. Wang was a ball-buster. Mr. Wang was the chef and Mrs. Wang, the hostess. Frighteningly, Mrs. Wang fancied herself a chef too. Her Peking duck slathered in cream of mushroom soup and Ritz Crackers was a hit only amongst the most hard-core casserole-loving Minnesotans.

"You look beautiful," Mitch said across the table.

My insides tightened at his compliment. I did feel pretty. Rena had insisted I buy a flirty, sexy, off-the-shoulder top that was way out of my price range and now I was glad I did. With my good-butt jeans, sexy top, and shocking pink toenails, Rena declared me hot to trot. My strapless push-up bra gave my not-fake tatas that extra oomph. Mitch was having a difficult time peeling his eyes away from my oomph. Hell, since he had picked me up forty-eight minutes ago, it was everything I could do to keep my hands to myself. He had on his own good-butt jeans and a lightweight, long-sleeved blue shirt that hugged his muscles and made my mouth water.

"Thank you," I said, feeling the heat crawl up my neck. "You do too. I mean, you look handsome, not pretty . . . or, um, beautiful." God, this was probably going to end up being a first and last date. When in doubt, ask a man about himself . . . and I was in doubt.

"So, have you ever been married?" Appalled at the first thing that flew out, I shoved a spring roll into my mouth before I could ask him if I could touch his butt, if he had commitment issues, or if he wanted to marry me.

"Married?" He grinned. "Nope. You?"

He observed me closely, probably hoping I wouldn't choke on the huge wad of spring roll I'd consumed. "No," I said with my hand over my very full mouth.

"Kristy," he said in a low voice that twisted my panties into a wad.

"Yes?" I said as I force swallowed the spring roll.

"You need to relax. I wanted to be with you in public because it's too hard to keep my hands off you in private."

Oh. My. God. I nodded in agreement, unable to speak.

"This might sound crazy, but I haven't been this attracted to anyone in a long time."

A green frisson of jealousy ripped through me as I wondered how long ago and who he'd been attracted to. I quickly snatched another spring roll off my plate to cork my mouth before I said something mortifying.

"So"—he grinned and I felt my nipples tighten—"have I scared you to death?"

I looked at the intense and sexy man sitting across from me. My body was on fire and my mind was a jumbled mess. Did he scare me? Hell yes. He scared me in the best way possible. My brain was screaming Danger!, but my body wanted to crawl across the table through the lo mein and tackle him.

"Kind of," I murmured. "I thought I might have scared you too, or possibly scared you off."

"You terrify me." He gave me a lopsided grin and my tummy flipped. "So how about this: you tell me everything I need to know about you and I'll do the same. It'll be like we've been dating for three months, and then we can go out to my car and make out like horny teenagers."

My heart and my girlie parts sang with delight. "I think I like that idea."

"You first," he said, taking my hand. A little zing flew up my arm in response to his touch.

"Okay," I said, running my free hand through my hair and taking a deep breath. My heart was pounding so hard in my chest, I was sure he could hear it. "I'm an only child. My mom is retired and lives in

Arizona. My grandma, who I worshipped, died a month ago and left me her sewing shop. I can't stand abuse of any kind, which is why I opened the women's shelter. Graduated from the U with a degree in social work and did my grad work in psychology. I live and die by the Vikings, winning season or no. I'd sell my soul to protect the people I love and for black raspberry chip ice cream. I think women deserve the same pay as men and I'm a very loyal friend. I'm trying to quit swearing, but my favorite word is still *fucktard*. Also, I think you have the most amazing butt I've ever seen." I slapped my hand over my mouth. "Sorry," I muttered. "That last part probably should have gone in a different conversation."

He couldn't control his burst of laughter. Damnity damn, he was hot when he laughed. Gorgeous blue eyes that matched the shirt he'd chosen sparkled. Instead of feeling silly, I was bizarrely happy that I made him laugh. What was that about?

"My turn?" he asked.

"Your turn," I said, gripping the table so I wouldn't lunge across it. My body had detached itself from my brain and was being ruled by my inner horny-monster.

"I was born in Appleton, Minnesota. My parents still live there. Went to Marquette and majored in computer science and Spanish. It's also where I met Jack. My blood is purple and gold, no matter where I live. Favorite colors are your eyes and your hair. I'll never say no to pizza and my shameful secret is that I TiVo *American Idol*. I'm tone deaf and I love to sing. I've been all over the country and trained at the FBI Academy in Quantico, Virginia." He paused for a moment; his eyes lost their glow and hardened. "I have four sisters, but one died when I was in tenth grade."

"God, I'm so sorry," I said, reaching for his hand.

"It was a long time ago." He shrugged and gave me a smile that didn't reach his eyes. "Some asshole was dealing drugs to high school kids and my sister got hooked." He blew out a long breath and ran his thumb over my knuckles. "I'm sorry. That was probably a little much for a first date."

I smiled and squeezed his hand. "I'd say we're at least two months in. Maybe even two and a half since I mentioned *fucktard*."

He chuckled and I felt better. I'd always wanted to absorb everyone else's pain; it's what put me in therapy . . . But his? I wanted to erase it. I was in big trouble here. In a matter of days, I'd gone from wanting to avoid him till hell froze over, to wanting to grab his ass and choke him with my tongue, to wanting to take care of him forever . . . Crapmonkeys.

"That's why I became a DEA agent," he said quietly, watching me with those beautiful icy blue eyes.

"If we're going really deep," I said hesitantly . . . Was I really going to tell him this? Yes, I was . . . "I wasn't completely straight with you about why I opened the shelter . . . My real reason for opening the shelter was because of my mom. I didn't mention my dad, because as far as I'm concerned . . . I don't have one. He wasn't a nice man. If it wasn't for my grandma taking us in, my mom and I would have needed a place like my shelter."

"I think you're amazing," he said.

"Back at ya, big guy," I giggled. "That kind of wore me out. Should we drive the car back onto the road so we have something to make out in later?"

"Yes, we should," he said with a sexy evil glint in his eye. "I would hate to crash and burn before we even got started."

We went back to our meal. Mrs. Wang surprised us with a complimentary cheesy mushroom sweet and sour pork. My gag reflex kicked in over the aroma alone, but Mitch bravely took several bites while Mrs. Wang looked on in delight. He gave her a kiss on the cheek and pronounced the vomitous dish life changing. Mrs. Wang waddled off on cloud nine and I fell just a little bit more for the guy sitting across from me.

"Holy God Almighty," Mitch gasped. "I can't even explain that. It tasted like . . ." He searched for the right word.

"Butt?" I asked, feeling his pain.

"I can't say I've ever had butt before," he laughed, "but, no pun intended, I would guess *butt* might adequately describe that."

"I don't think I can eat any more with the butt still on the table," I said, holding my breath.

Mitch raised his hand for the check. Mrs. Wang came back over with the check and a large to-go box. She put our dinners and the butt all in the same gigantic box. Our eyes grew as huge when we realized we had to leave the premises carrying the butt.

"I'm not touching that." I shuddered.

"You have to," Mitch moaned. "I actually took a bite."

"Shit," I muttered and grabbed the odiferous box of lo mein and butt. "There better be a trash can outside."

Turns out there was, but it also turned out that Mrs. Wang walked us to our car. She was so excited that someone liked her cooking, she just didn't want to let us go. We got in the car with the butt between us and listened for fifteen minutes to how that son of a bitch Mr. Wang didn't want her in his kitchen. We nodded and made the appropriate ohs and ahs. I understood Mr. Wang perfectly . . . and sympathized. I just wanted to go. Get the butt out of the car and jump on top of the sexiest, sweetest, hottest man I'd ever met.

"Thanks again, Mrs. Wang," Mitch said, starting the car and slowly pulling away. She looked a little crushed at our departure, but promised to make another special dish next time we were in.

"I feel kind of sad," I said, pinching my nose closed.

"Sad? Why are you sad? We're on our way to the make-out session of the century."

I giggled, which sounded kind of funny with my nose plugged. "I'm sad because I can never go to Asian Wind again. I now live in fear of what special cheesy creamy dish Mrs. Wang will bring us."

Mitch pulled over and stopped the car. "Is that really the name of the restaurant?" he asked, shocked.

"Yeah, Rena and I call it Chinese Farts."

He threw back his head and let out a huge laugh. "God, you make me happy."

Mitch jumped out of the car and disposed of the stinky bag, but the damage was done.

"Um, I don't think I can suck face in your car," I said apologetically, leaning toward my open window.

"It still smells like butt, doesn't it?" He shook his head in disgust. "Yeah, it does."

"Fine." He grinned and my stomach flipped over. "I have a better idea."

Chapter 12

We split up in the lobby of our building. Mitch insisted on brushing the butt off his teeth and said he needed to get a few things from his apartment. I took the stairs two at a time to my own apartment. My stomach was in knots and I felt as if I was in high school. My heart was bouncing around in my chest like a Ping-Pong ball and my hands were shaky. I quickly freshened up and waited . . .

He was a cop. Kind of . . . But he wasn't like the others. He was smart and funny and kind and so very hot. He was a Vikings fan and I was quite sure he wasn't married. I'd never wanted to tackle any of the other guys I dated. I'd never lost the power of speech or felt like my entire body was a live wire either. Hell, I'd never slept with a guy, cop or no, this fast in my life. Crap . . . Was I going to know him in the biblical sense tonight? I really shouldn't, but we did cover a lot of territory at Chinese Farts. The bonding over the butt alone, not to mention I told him stuff only Rena and my therapist know, put us well into a relationship . . . Who was I kidding? I was in heat. I wanted to knock boots with him more than I wanted to breathe. Did that make me a ho-bag? Would he think I was easy? Monkeyballs, maybe we should just swap spit and roll around on the floor with our clothes on.

That was what we'd do. We'd talk some more and kiss a little bit . . . but I'd make him leave before it got too out of control and then I'd spend an hour or so with Vinnie the Vibrator. I wouldn't be a hooker. He'd respect me and I could screw his brains out tomorrow . . . I was a modern woman. That's how a modern woman should handle it. Right? Of course that's right. If I peeled his clothes off with my teeth and rode him like a cowboy, he might think I was loose.

I'd ask him out on a second date. That way it would be like we'd been dating three and a half to four months . . . I could totally poke a guy after dating that long. Fucktard, I was leaving tomorrow to ferret out Bigfoot from the boonies of Duluth. I forgot to tell him about that. If we didn't bump uglies tonight, I'd have to wait two weeks . . . But that wasn't necessarily a bad thing. We could have phone sex and then when I got back . . .

I was jerked out of my shaboinkie plans by a harsh clipped banging on the door. WTF? I was sure we'd paid our rent this month. If it was the weirdo from down the hall selling vacuums again, I'd rip him a new one. I know everybody has to make a living, but not at nine thirty at night when I need to suck face with my new boyfriend.

"Who's there?" I asked as I peeked through the peephole.

"It's Officer Sanderson, ma'am. I need you to open the door. Now."

Oh. My. God.

I grabbed the doorknob to keep me from falling into a mush pile on the floor. Mitch, in full-on cop mode, was standing on the other side. My breathing was erratic and my live wire hooker body was ready to pass out.

"Mitch?" I choked out.

"It's Officer Sanderson, ma'am. You need to open the door now or I'll have to use force."

Every bell in my hooha and elsewhere went off. The alpha man standing outside my door was turning my crank like it'd never been turned. With trembling hands I unlocked the door and let in the man who didn't realize he was my future husband.

"I'm sorry, ma'am, but I'm going to have to ask you to step over to the counter and turn around," he informed me in a no-nonsense tone. He locked the door behind him and watched me with hooded eyes.

God, he looked hot. He'd changed into a fitted black T-shirt, fatigues, and black boots. He was every fantasy I'd ever had all rolled into one . . . and then some.

"I'm sorry, what?" I giggled.

"This is not a laughing matter, ma'am. You're in a lot of trouble. I don't think you want to go down to the station. Do you?"

"Um, no." I bit my lip and tried to suppress the huge grin that was threatening to split my face. "Like this?" I asked as I slowly turned around and walked to the kitchen counter. I let my hips sway just a little more than normal and was rewarded with his quick intake of breath. I took my sweet time bending forward and placing my hands on the counter. Thank the Lutheran God above I hadn't listened to Rena about the granny panties and hairy legs. I was wearing a hot pink thong and matching push-up strapless bra under my jeans and overpriced shirt, and my legs were as smooth as a baby's bottom.

He came up behind me. The heat of his body made me glad I had the counter to hold me up. Something clicked and I gasped as the cool metal of his handcuffs made goose bumps erupt on my arms. I shivered as he snapped them shut over my wrists and attached me to the silverware drawer.

"Is this normal police procedure?" I whispered as excitement took the express shuttle through my body.

"Yes, it is," he replied silkily. "Especially in cases as egregious as this one."

"Can I ask what the charges are, Officer?"

"Yes, you can," he answered in a clipped tone.

"Well?" I laughed.

"Well what?"

"I asked you what the charges are."

"No, ma'am, you didn't. You asked me if you could ask me, and I said yes."

"Oh my God," I groaned. "You are such a dork."

"I'm not sure I like the tone of your voice or your choice of words," he whispered in my ear. His hot breath on my neck and his hard body pressed against mine sent everything south of my belly button into a tizzy.

"I'm sorry, Officer," I said as contritely as I could manage, considering his voice alone was making my knees buckle.

"Not good enough. Someone with your attitude is likely carrying concealed weapons. I'm afraid I'm going to have to do a strip search."

"Really?" I squealed. This was the best night of my life. Ever. This was exactly what I'd wanted even if I'd tried to convince myself it was better to wait. Of course, I didn't envision it happening in my kitchen with me handcuffed to the silverware drawer . . . but what the hell.

His large beautiful hands slowly slid under my shirt, feeling around for weapons. There was definitely something hard in my bra, but it wasn't metal. My nipples were aching to be touched.

"Are you all right, ma'am? You seem to be shaking. Am I hurting you?" His voice was gruff and his breathing belied his calm demeanor.

"I'm good," I gasped, biting down on my lip so I wouldn't cry out as his fingers lightly brushed my nipples. "Did you find anything?"

"I think I did," he said as he pushed up my shirt and ran his tongue along my spine.

My brain skitzed out and I would have dropped to the floor if his arm hadn't been wrapped around me. With deft fingers, he unhooked my bra and cupped my breasts in his hands.

"God, you are so fucking hot," he hissed as he pinched my nipples and sent shock waves through my body and straight to my panties. I moaned when he slid his hands to my hips and ground the most frighteningly impressive package I'd ever felt into me. "Do you have any other weapons on you, ma'am?"

"Um, I think I might have accidentally tucked something into my jeans," I giggled, shocked with my boldness.

"I'm sorry, but I'm going to have to remove your pants," he said tightly. "Will that upset you, ma'am?"

"*Upset*'s not really the word that comes to mind," I gasped as his fingers undid the button to my jeans. He unzipped me with excruciating slowness and eased my jeans down with sure hands.

"Your ass is perfect," he said as he ran his hands possessively over me.

After a quick sharp slap on my bottom, which practically threw me into a massive orgasm, he went to work. I was completely helpless; he could do whatever he wanted to do to me . . . the feeling of being controlled by him was a turn-on like I'd never known. Breathing became something I had to concentrate on. Passing out wasn't an option. I refused to miss a minute of the most intense, hot, and scary sex in the world.

He put one hand in front of me and one behind. Brain cells floated out of my body. He pressed down on my clit with the heel of one hand and inserted two thick fingers of the other inside me. Everything inside my head went fuzzy and someone was making all sorts of noise . . . Who in the hell? Wait, oh my God . . . that was me.

"Your entire body is a weapon," he whispered as he buried his face in my neck.

"Mitch," I whimpered as I bucked against his hand, bringing me closer to Lutheran God than I'd ever been. I felt faint, and colors exploded behind my eyes as the most mind-blowing orgasm known to man ripped through me. I screamed and collapsed limply on the counter. The blood was still roaring in my ears, but I vaguely heard him kick off his shoes and unzip his pants.

"Please tell me you have a condom," I said, trying to keep my noodly legs from giving out.

"The police always come prepared, Kristy," he told me in a voice that was pure sex.

I glanced back over my shoulder at the mention of my name and my libido shot through the roof. All the air whooshed out of my lungs . . . behind me stood a naked freakin' Greek god with a package that made a Fourth of July display zing through my girlie parts.

"Is this what you want?" he ground out, lightly running his hand up and down his beautiful cock.

"God yes." I pressed my legs together, afraid I was going to come again before he was inside me.

A key jangling in the front door yanked us both out of our sexual frenzy. Violently.

"What the fuck?" Mitch muttered, pulling my jeans back up and diving for the handcuff keys.

"Oh my God," I hissed. "It's Jack and Rena."

"Shit. Am I still a secret?"

"No," I said in a panic, "but this doesn't look good."

"Right."

The handcuff dropped off my left hand. Mitch scooped up his clothes and ran around the room buck-ass naked, looking for a place to hide. If I hadn't been so freaked out, I'd've been convulsed in laughter.

"The closet," I said, pointing to our cleaning supply closet. "She'll never look in there."

"Got it." He sprinted for the closet and shut the door behind him just as Rena entered the apartment. Mitch was hidden. I was dressed . . . braless, but dressed. Everything was great . . . except my right hand was still cuffed to the silverware drawer. Fuckmonkeys. I quickly arranged myself with the cuffed hand behind me and leaned back on the counter. I plastered a big fake smile on my face and racked my brain for a legit way to get her out of here.

"Hey," I said.

"Holy shit," Rena screeched. "You scared the hell out of me." She eyed me curiously for a moment. "You're supposed to be out with Mitch."

"I am, I mean, was. You're supposed to be at a concert with Jack."

"Concert sucked." She plopped down on the couch and made herself comfortable. "We bailed."

"Where's Jack?"

"I sent him out to buy more pudding and beer." She grinned evilly and I laughed. "Kristy, Jack's going to be back in a few and I need to talk to you." She patted the couch beside her. "Come sit by me."

"No," I said casually. "I'm good here."

"You're not going to like what I have to tell you. Jack told me to stay out of it, but I can't."

A bad juju feeling swept over me. If I hadn't been cuffed to the drawer, I would have run from the room.

"How much do you like Mitch?" she asked carefully.

"Oh my God, not this conversation again," I yelled. "What? You're going to tell me his name is Stitch or Rich or Pitch or Bitch? His name is Mitch Sanderson. He's not married. He loves the Vikings. He's hotter than hell, he likes my butt, and he thinks I'm funny. He had a sister who died and he knows my sorry excuse of a dad beat on my mom. I'm halfway in love with him and had the best orgasm of my life tonight. So what do you want to tell me that I don't already know?" I was so close to breaking. All I wanted to do was cry.

"Shit, Kristy." Rena's tone was hushed. "Please come sit with me."

"I really can't," I told her truthfully. I had no intention of letting her know I was attached to the drawer.

"There's something else. There's a reason you shouldn't get too involved."

"Rena." My voice was icy. "Did I ever try to fuck with you and Jack?"

She shook her head *no*.

"Then why are you doing this to me?"

Rena froze and looked around the apartment. "Did you hear something?"

"No," I said, hearing exactly what she'd heard. It was Mitch trying to get dressed in the supply closet. Hell, I'd forgotten he was still here.

"It sounds like mice." She grimaced. "No, bigger than mice . . . rats. It sounds like fucking rats. I'm going to kill our landlord."

"I don't hear anything, so finish what you have to say. Now."

"He's a DEA agent."

"So?"

"He's here on some big secret case. He didn't join Jack's department. He's not here to stay," she said.

I opened my mouth to speak, but nothing came out. My eyes had no such problem . . . tears spilled down my cheeks. That was a fairly large fucking omission in our speed-dating session at Chinese Farts. I was just an easy lay for him. *Easy* being the operative word . . . a quick fuck. How could I have been so stupid? My heart felt like it was shattering, but my pain was massively overshadowed by my anger. At myself . . . and at Mitch.

"Are you dressed?" I ground out through clenched teeth.

"Um, yes. I'm dressed," Rena said, bewildered.

"Not you. Him."

"Yes," came a muffled voice from the closet.

"We don't have rats, do we?" Rena asked with wide eyes.

"Actually, we do," I told her, wiping my tears away. "I think you should come out here."

"I think that's a good idea," Mitch agreed.

He stepped out from the cramped closet looking disheveled and more beautiful than an opportunist asshole had a right to.

"Rena," he said firmly. "Would you mind going down to Jack's apartment? I need to talk to Kristy."

Rena gave him a death stare and then turned to me. "Is that what you want, Kristy?"

"No, but I think it's best."

"Okay, fine." She hesitated. "I'll be downstairs if you need me."

With one final skin-flaying glare at Mitch, she left.

"Kristy, I can explain," he said quietly.

"I seriously doubt it, but go ahead and try."

Chapter 13

We stood silently and eyed each other. My body was calm and still on the outside, but my heart was shattering. What in the hell was wrong with me? It's not like we'd dated for four years and were breaking up . . . We hadn't done anything tonight that I didn't want as much as he did. I refused to look away first. I may have been used, but I wasn't a victim.

"I would greatly appreciate it if you could uncuff me from the silverware drawer," I said coldly. Boy, there's a sentence I'd never thought I'd say and most likely never would again.

"I can't do that yet."

"Because?"

"Because," he said logically, "I don't want you to run away before I can convince you I'm not an asshole."

"That could take a while and I have to pee. So unless you'd like me to humiliate myself more than I already have tonight, I'd suggest you let me go."

He approached me warily. Who could blame him? I was attached to the silverware drawer, full of forks and knives . . . He quickly and efficiently detached me from the drawer and just as quickly reattached me to him.

"What the hell?" I hissed, trying to yank myself free. Oww, metal biting into skin hurts. "I have to pee and I don't recall asking you to join me."

"I'll stand outside the door and I'll hum," he said, gently pulling me to where he assumed the bathroom might be.

"But, we're attached," I stammered, my stupid traitorous heart tap-dancing with excitement in my chest. "I get pee fright. It could take hours."

"Then I'll wait," he said.

I really did have to pee, damn it. I blew out a frustrated breath when I realized he wasn't going to budge. Fine, if the assmonkey wanted to hear me pee . . . so be it.

After shutting the bathroom door as far as it would go with his arm wedged in it, I did a bizarre one-armed maneuver and got my jeans down. I idly wondered how in the hell I was going to get them back up, but I really had to go. And then pee fright set in.

"I can't do this," I muttered, furious at him and myself.

"Turn on the water," he suggested.

Of all the stupid things . . . Wait, maybe he was right. The water might disguise the sound and I'd be able to go. I pretzeled myself over to the sink and turned the faucet on full blast and then to up my odds, I turned on the shower too . . . and I still couldn't do it.

"Not working," I yelled over the cascading water.

"Just relax," he chuckled, giving my arm a squeeze.

Shitclowns, his touch still made electricity shoot up my arm. Was I so pathetic that I was wildly attracted to someone who wanted a one-night stand and treated me like a floozy? Yep, I was. In a last-ditch effort to block out all sound, I turned on the blow-dryer. It was far away enough from all the running water to eliminate the possibility of electrocution, but he didn't know that. When he tried to open the door in a panic, I slammed it back down on his arm. His yelp of pain was delightful. After ten more seconds of waiting, I finally peed. Thank you, Jesus. Although, just to screw with him, I sat in the bathroom for another thirty-two minutes.

After a struggle that would have won the ten-thousand-dollar prize on *America's Funniest Home Videos*, I got my pants back up. Not buttoned, but up. I flicked off the blow-dryer and turned all the water off after doing an awkward one-handed wash. This was ridiculous.

"You're a dick," I said, whipping open the bathroom door and startling him.

"Noted."

"And a jackass," I added, trying to block out how good he smelled.

"Agreed," he said, carefully leading me back to the living room.

Seated entirely too close to him on the couch, which still smelled like beer, I was torn between leaning into him and lifting my foot to kick his balls up into his throat. Thankfully I was able to stifle both instincts.

"I want to apologize."

"Don't." I cut him off. "Tonight was mutual. I wanted you and you wanted me. We're adults. You're leaving. We're done. Uncuff me and go away."

"Will you please hear me out?" he asked, piercing me with those damn blue eyes.

"You haven't given me much of a choice," I replied, holding up our linked wrists.

"I was afraid you'd run."

"Why would I run?" I asked, exasperated. "This is my home and I didn't lie about anything."

"True." He ran his free hand through his dark hair and looked up at the ceiling. "I didn't actually lie . . . I omitted."

"And that makes it better . . . how?"

"I suppose it doesn't," he sighed. "I'm treading in uncharted territory here."

"Well, that's just fantastic for you," I snapped. "Unfortunately, I'm not. I'm the idiot that should know better than to date cops or DEA agents or any loser that has something to do with law enforcement. You're all the same . . . and I'm the idiot."

"You're not an idiot." His voice was low and intense. He scared me a little bit, but most of all he turned me on. I was having a hell of a time blocking out the feeling of his hands and lips all over my body. To kill this train of thought I did what any rational, sane person would do . . . I imagined David Hasselhoff doing the polka naked and lashed out at the former possible love of my life.

"The getting-to-know-you speech at Chinese Farts should have included the part about you not living here. Call me crazy, but I thought you . . ." I stopped. I was digging a hole that would put me in mourning for years. I kept my eyes trained on the floor. All of a sudden I was so tired. I just wanted to be alone to lick my wounded pride in private.

"You thought I liked you? I did, I do. I am completely confused right now. I'm not a feelings guy. It's been stripped out of me from training, but you make me feel . . . Shit, I'm not doing this right."

I continued my love affair with the floor. I would not give him the opportunity to suck me back in with those eyes. I wanted to make waaay more out of what he was telling me, but that had been my problem in the past and today was the day I started being a big girl.

"Look, Mitch," I said quietly, "you don't live here. I can't get involved with you any more than I already have. I don't separate well. I can't just have, you know . . . um, sex, or almost sex and then walk away. I know that might sound old-fashioned, but I think tonight should prove that I'm not that old-fashioned . . . Actually, tonight proves that I'm a slutbag," I groaned, pressing my free hand over my eyes.

"No," he disagreed, removing my hand from my face and forcing me to look at him. "You are amazing and beautiful and I think I'm falling . . ." He stopped and regrouped. "Which makes no sense because I hardly know you."

"Mitch, stop," I pleaded. "You're saying all the things I want someone who's going to be around to say, but you're not staying."

"Kristy, my job is unusual. I don't really live anywhere, but this hasn't ever happened to me."

"Well," I said with a lump the size of a golf ball in my throat, "that's not my problem. It's yours."

"If I could promise to stay, would you want to be with me?" he asked, holding my chin so I couldn't look away.

"I would probably drag your ass to the courthouse and marry you," I laughed, knowing the impossibility of such a thing happening.

"Then what's the difference if I have to travel?" he asked confidently, thinking his logic was sound.

"One, because you failed to mention something huge, which leads me to believe there are other huge things you've left out. Two, I don't want to have a relationship where I see someone every so often. I've done long distance. It doesn't work . . . I want . . . it doesn't matter what I want. I can't have it."

"If what you want is me, you can have it," he said, running his fingers along my lips.

Why in God's name did his hands on me have to feel so right? Was he correct? Could I have him? Could we actually make this work?

"Okay," I said slowly. Hope was doing a cautious jig in my tummy. "Why are you here in Minneapolis?"

He took a long pause. "I can't tell you."

"I see." The jig had turned into a death march. "How long are you in town?"

The pain and anxiety he was feeling were coming across loud and clear. I almost felt sorry for him. Almost. "I'm unsure," he admitted, realizing how fast this conversation was going south. "I know this sounds hopeless." He spoke quickly so I couldn't butt in. "It's not hopeless. I'm not like the other guys. Yes, I have secrets, but they're about work, not my personal life. If I could tell you everything, I would, but that might put your life and others in danger, plus I'd get fired in a big way. I am one hundred percent single and I'm crazy about you. It'll be complicated, but it can work. I swear."

By the time he'd finished speaking, he had hold of both of my hands. The handcuffs made it a little uncomfortable, but I didn't care. He held me like I would disappear if he let go. I wanted to believe him . . . I really, really did.

"After you're done with whatever big secret mission you have, when will I see you again?" I asked, realizing I was drinking the Kool-Aid. The part about my life being in danger was a bit unsettling, but the massive orgasm he had given me earlier made death seem like an even trade.

"Um, I don't know," he said, gripping my hands tighter. "As soon as I can."

My heart dropped to my toes. As much as I wanted to say yes, I knew I couldn't. This was possibly worse than being cheated on by a married Dallas Cowboys fan. Worse because I cared. He was asking too much. I would resent him and we'd end up hating each other. I wished I'd never met him.

"Unlock the cuffs, please," I said.

He did.

I got up and paced the room. I knew after tonight I'd never see him again and if I did, it would be in polite passing. The words that should come out of my mouth didn't want to, so I forced them.

"Mitch, I am wildly attracted to you. I like you and I think a tiny part of me started to fall in love with you, but I can't do this."

"Kristy." He got up and moved toward me.

"Stop. This is hard," I said, pulling on my curls and trying not to cry. Part of me wished he wouldn't listen to me. I wanted him to cuff me again and refuse to let me go until I promised to be his, but that was a fairy tale. A fucked-up fairy tale, but in my life those seemed to be the only ones available. "I need you to leave. Please."

It felt like an eternity before he spoke. "I understand," he said in that voice that made my knees weak and made me wonder if I was

making the wrong decision. "And I'm sorry . . . to you and for me."
He took several steps closer. "Can I kiss you good-bye?"

"I think that's probably a bad idea," I said as I did nothing to stop
his lips from meeting mine. I also did nothing to stop my arms from
wrapping themselves around his broad shoulders.

Tears filled my eyes as his tongue, so forceful earlier, gently parted
my lips and explored my mouth with such focused care, I almost
passed out. The kiss, which started out soft and sweet, turned into
something that was changing me from the inside out. I knew I was
more than halfway in love with him; even his dedication to the stupid
job that was tearing us apart was admirable. Everything about him
was stand-up and honorable; he just wasn't supposed to be mine.

I wanted a partner and kids and date nights. I couldn't live worrying
I would never see him again. I grew up without a father . . . I wasn't
going to raise my kids the same way. But I could still get lost for a
few more moments . . . and I did.

I felt raw and broken. I curled up on the stinky beer couch with
my Minnesota Vikings fleece blanket and I gave in to the tears that
had been threatening me for the last hour. Why did this hurt so bad?
Watching him walk out the door was gut-wrenching. I couldn't possibly have fallen for someone I'd known for only a few days . . .
could I? Hell, that only happens in romance novels and Rena's life.
I'm more grounded than that. It had to have been the sex. I was in
lust with him and I could get over him just as quickly as I'd fallen
in love with him, I mean lust . . . lust with him. Fucktards. Going
on a trip with crazy Bigfoot freaks sounded like a vacation to me.
Sitting home alone with my thoughts of what might have been
sounded like hell. I snuggled down into the hops-scented cushions,
turned my brain off, and let her rip. Maybe my tears would detoxify
the couch . . .

"Hey, are you okay?" Rena asked from the doorway of our apartment.

"No, not really," I sniffed pathetically.

"Do you need more cry time?" she asked, hovering in the doorway.

"No, I'm good."

She came into the apartment bearing gifts . . . beer, pudding cups,
black raspberry chip ice cream, and two spoons. I loved her so much
the waterworks started to flow again.

"Come on now. Ice cream will make you feel better." She spooned a big clump into my mouth. Although she almost choked me, she was right. I did feel a little better. I nodded and gave her a weak smile.

"See?" She grinned and wrapped me in a bear hug. "Motherfucker, this couch reeks! Get off that thing," she demanded, hopping up and staring at our couch. "I think it's a goner."

"I don't know," I said, opening a pudding and then a beer. "Maybe we could get it dry-cleaned."

"That would probably cost more than the couch is worth." She eyed the offensive couch as if it was stinking up the room on purpose. "The only reason I'd miss it is sentimental. I've screwed Jack's brains out more times than I can count on that piece of furniture."

"Oh my God," I gasped in disgust, jumping up off the couch like it had bitten me. I groaned, remembering all the times I'd spent lounging on Rena and Jack's plaid instrument of fornication. "I really wish I didn't know that."

"Oh shit, I'm sorry. That was totally insensitive of me," she said sheepishly.

She pulled me to the kitchen table and gently pushed me down on the chair. She quickly retrieved the beer and snacks from the coffee table and plopped them down in front of me. She opened four beers, placing two in front of me and two in front of her. After a moment of intense contemplation, she shoved one of her beers across the table toward me.

"So, do I need to have him killed?" she asked in total seriousness.

"No. Absolutely not. No," I said. Rena actually had friends with Mafia connections, or so they claimed. Vito and Angelo, two of the sweetest, hairiest, and horniest little sixty-year-old Italian guys I'd ever met. They owned a small coffee shop in the WMNS building, where Rena had hung out for a month trying to become the Sunshine Weather Girl a while back. They made mean white chocolate apricot scones, were obsessed with women's private parts, and had the reputation of offing people. I was unsure if it was real or just big talk, but I was taking no chances.

"Fine," she huffed. "Jack wouldn't let me do it anyway. He likes that douche hole."

"I like that douche hole too," I sighed and stuck my finger in the pudding. "I just can't do the long distance, the 'I can't tell you what I do,' and the 'I don't know when I'll be back' thing." I smeared the pudding around the open rim of the beer bottle and took a sip. Holy Jesus, that was disgusting. Hopping up and running to the sink, I had to spit and rinse several times before I could sit back down.

"I could have told you that would be gross," she informed me.

"Then how come when you eat pudding and beer together, but separately, it tastes good?"

We pondered the question in silence. "I don't know," she muttered, "but you make an interesting point."

"Thanks."

"So, are you okay?" she asked carefully.

"Not at the moment, no, but I will be. I'm always okay," I said, pushing the puddinged beer bottle to the far side of the table and swigging off a fresh one.

"Yeah, that's always worried me about you," Rena said thoughtfully.

"Look, I liked him and he liked me. It won't work. Period. I'm a little raw right now, but I'll live. There are people with much bigger problems than mine."

"I know," Rena chimed in, "but everything is relative."

"Relative is for assmonkeys," I said, making a very weak joke. "I leave tomorrow anyway. It might even be easier to forget him while trying to fend off the advances of Mrs. C and Edith."

"Kristy, you really don't have to go on that trip."

"Actually, I really do. I'm glad I'm leaving. It was just a meaningless little fling. Maybe he'll be gone by the time I get back." All the words I spoke were correct. I suppose if I kept saying them . . . eventually I would believe them.

"Maybe he will," Rena agreed. "Do you want me to help you pack?" she asked, thankfully not challenging me on any of the lies I'd just told.

"Yes, I do."

She took my hand in hers and led me back to my bedroom. The sister of my heart proceeded to pack two suitcases for me, tuck me into bed, and kiss me good night . . .

Chapter 14

Morning came and I was still breathing. I hadn't died of a broken heart. A man, no matter how hot, could not break me. Although traveling with Mrs. C and Edith . . . might. I had worried that two suitcases might seem excessive. That was nothing compared to the six oversize behemoths that the old ladies arrived with. Nine o'clock in the morning was just too early to deal with the twins.

"Bless your heart," Edith yelled at Rich. "Could you bring your fat ass over here and get my cases to the van?"

"For God's sake, Edith," Mrs. C hissed, "they all have fat asses. You have to be more specific."

"Fine," Edith spat. "Hey, you, with the big man-boobs, bless your heart, come get my goddamn cases."

"See?" Mrs. C nodded approvingly. "How hard was that?"

Rich started across the parking lot to assist the nasty lesbos. I grabbed his beefy arm and stopped him.

"You"—I pointed at the ladies—"will not speak to people like that. Rich has a name and he's a person," I said, staring daggers at the pair.

"With man-boobs," Edith muttered, snickering.

"Enough," I snapped. "Everyone has, um . . . issues, including you two," I said, defending Rich and his unusual body. "If you are going to point out things people can't help, you'd better be prepared to have some 'bless your heart' thrown right back at you."

"Can I break their noses?" Mariah whispered to me.

"Not right now . . . maybe later," I whispered back. Mariah grinned and gave me a high five. Asscracks, I can't give Mariah permission to smackdown on the old biddies.

"Bless your heart," Mrs. C said, waving her claw at me. "My guess is your plastic buppies have addled your tiny brain. You might boss us at the store, but you can't boss us here."

Buppies? Where in the hell did she even get that word? I was so going to give Mariah permission. "We will leave my buppies and your unibrows out of this." They gasped and pulled their matching visors down low. Ahhh, I might have found a chink in the armor . . . "You will apologize to Rich and then you will bring your own cases over."

"Sorry," they mumbled insincerely as they dragged their monster bags across the parking lot. What in the hell had they brought?

"Kristy, I don't mind helping them," Rich said in an accent that sounded kind of South African today. I really wanted to ask him where he was from, but I had a feeling the accent was fake and he'd been embarrassed enough for one morning. Did he think it made him mysterious? Or, God forbid, sexy?

"No," I said firmly. "Until they can be civil, they're on their own."

I glanced around the empty asphalt parking lot of the Lutheran church where we'd decided to meet before our big adventure. Where in the hell was everyone? It was ten after nine . . . Kim had said we were leaving at nine on the dot. No Kim or Hugh or Aunt Moon-Unit. No slick shiny little producer guys, just me, Boo, Mariah, Rich, and the devil's spawns.

"Where is everybody?" I asked. "I thought Kim said we were leaving at nine."

"She did," Mariah confirmed.

"So?"

"She lied. We leave at ten. She didn't want anyone to be late."

"You mean I got up at seven, got ready, and got here when I could have slept another hour?" I asked, shaking my head.

"Yep." Mariah grinned. Holy Lutheran God, she'd dyed her hair green. Maybe she thought she'd blend in with the trees better. How did I not notice that immediately? Was weird my new normal?

"This bodes well for a great trip," I muttered as I rolled my suitcases over to the trailer hitched onto the back of the passenger van. "Dang it, it's locked."

"Let me see," Rich said, fiddling with the lock.

"Want me to pick it?" Mariah inquired as if there was nothing unusual or illegal about breaking into things. Her skill set was alarming . . . breaking noses, relocating testicles to chest cavities, popping locks, graffitiing walls with swear words . . . no wonder I couldn't find her a job. I wasn't sending her out for the right things. I'd have to research organized crime families when I got back.

"Um, no, but thank you. We'll just wait till the shiny guys get here." I sat down on my suitcase and questioned my sanity. I told myself this trip was a good thing. Well, not good in the sense it was good. Good in the sense that it would give me something to do so I could forget about Mitch. Like that was going to happen anytime soon . . .

"Are you okay?" my buddy with the seriously bad teeth asked. I was going to carve out some time on this trip to talk to him about the wonders of orthodontics. He was batting such a big zero. Between the crotch hair on his head, his body, and his teeth, he was a hot mess.

"No," I sighed and gave him a smile, "but in time I will be."

"Man trouble?" he asked, sitting down on my other suitcase. Crap-monkeys, he was huge. I wondered if that was the suitcase with my blow-dryer and vibrator in it. I needed both of those things on this trip. I stared at him for a moment and realized there was no graceful way to tell him to remove his gargantuan ass from my luggage. Whatever. There were stores in Duluth. Blow-dryers and vibrators were replaceable . . .

"Yep," I told him. "My own fault."

"Do you want to talk about it? I'm a great listener. I bet I could make you feel better," he said.

I felt my eyes well up with tears. This poor, sweet, ugly guy wanted to help. I would knock those old lesbians' heads together if they were mean to him anymore. "No, I'm a little too close to it to talk about it yet, but thanks." I gave his hand a squeeze.

"Well—" He smiled. I quickly jerked my gaze from his frighteningly toothy smile to his bizarrely mismatched eyes. "Whenever you want one, I'll be your ear."

With a sweet pat on my shoulder, he walked away. I watched Mrs. C and Edith grunt and groan and curse at each other as they made their way over. I had a difficult time imagining them being attractive to anyone. They wore identical outfits. Stonewashed blue jean gauchos that should have been burned in the seventies, paired with tight black tank tops that hugged their torpedo tits in a very bad way. Their bravery was astonishing. The most revolting was the footwear . . . white socks and black sandals. I looked down at my own cute little white miniskirt, blue tank, and sparkly flip-flops and thanked the Lutheran Lord Jesus above for good genes and fashion sense.

"Would you like a bible?" Boo asked, startling me.

"A bible?" I eyed the gaily wrapped and bejeweled package she held in her hands.

"Not the religious one," she giggled. She was adorable, with big soft gray eyes and wavy auburn hair. She was as tiny as her sister Mariah, but without the hard edges or green locks. "The Bigfoot bible," she added solemnly.

"Um, that's okay," I told her, sucking my bottom lip into my mouth to keep from laughing. "You should give it to someone else who would get more, you know . . . more enjoyment out of it."

"You're a nonbeliever." Her eyes clouded with sadness.

Balls, now I just felt bad. She seemed so fragile, but I couldn't lie to her. Could I? "I wouldn't say nonbeliever per se. I just think I need a little more um, proof."

"Do you believe in God, Kristy?" she asked, piercing me with those gray eyes.

"Yes," I answered, alarmed at the bizarre direction this conversation was taking. What direction? I had no clue.

"Have you ever seen Him?"

"Well, not exactly," I hedged.

"But you still believe."

"Yes, but . . ."

She silently held the wrapped Bigfoot bible out to me, cutting off any further religious debate. "You need this more than any of us."

Never in my twenty-eight years on earth had I equated Bigfoot's existence with God's, but clearly she had. For the umpteenth time, I questioned my sanity, but fifty thousand dollars for the shelter was a gift I couldn't refuse . . . no matter how scary the task to claim the money. I gingerly took the package from Boo and slid it into the side zipper pocket of my suitcase.

"Thanks," I muttered, hoping our God-Bigfoot conversation was over.

"No," Boo said, gripping my hands with the strength of a man three times her size. Damn, the Carey family was strong. "Thank you. You are a beautiful person, Kristy. I can see your pain . . . so much hurt. You need love in your life," she murmured, closing her eyes and squeezing my hands even tighter. "It's all in front of you," she whispered. A shiver skittered up my spine and I felt cold despite the eighty-two-degree heat. WTF? "It's all right here . . . right now. You just have to see through the haze of disbelief. You are worthy." Boo released her iron-man grip and wandered off in a daze.

She was coo-coo crazy loco and I was never going to hold hands with her again. What the hell was that about? She was kind of spot-on . . . but her assessment could apply to plenty of people. Everyone has pain and wants love. What was that "all in front of you" crap? It was all in front of me last night and I made it leave . . . Oh my God, if Boo kept spouting shit like that the entire trip, I would tear my own head off. Between the lesbians and the tiny wannabe psychic, this was going to be a long two weeks.

At nine forty-five a beat-up aqua minivan roared into the parking lot, followed by a nondescript black sedan. Before the van had stopped, Hugh jumped out, sporting night-vision goggles and red bike shorts. Nothing else. He did cartwheels all the way from where he landed on the pavement to where we were standing. No one reacted. Was this normal behavior? Did they all cartwheel through life in bike shorts? Holy hell, the thought of Rich or the muff divers in bike shorts was enough to make me want to throw up in my mouth. I pushed the image away and waited for instructions from our mentally challenged leader, Hugh.

"Allrightyroo!" Kim yelled, making a much less splashy entrance than her husband. She ambled over wearing a T-shirt that said *Bigfoot or Bust.* Her hair was in a ponytail sprouting out of the top of her head and she had a grin on her face that was contagious. The shiny L.A. guys parked next to the van, got out, and immediately began making calls on their cell phones. I couldn't for the life of me remember which one was which. I decided to call them Frick and Frack. Kim, barely able to contain her excitement, continued. "We, the talent, will ride in the van, and our producer–film crew will ride in the sedan."

"Where do we put our goddamn luggage?" Edith yelled.

"The trailer is padlocked," Mariah added.

Frick quickly ended his call and addressed our concerns. He gave us a big, overly white smile and placed his little hands on his little hips. "The luggage will go with you in the van. There's a baggage compartment underneath." He eyed the massive pile of suitcases and his smile disappeared. He pinched the bridge of his nose in annoyance. "And whatever doesn't fit will ride inside the van with you."

"Where's the rest of the crew?" Boo asked.

"You're looking at it, baby!" Frick said, giving us the thumbs-up. Frack, finally off the phone, joined his cohort. Frack slapped Frick on the ass and shot us the finger-gun. Were we really going on a trip organized by these morons?

"Fags?" Mrs. C inquired.

"Bags," Kim yelled before the old gal could add anything more offensive. "That's right, Mrs. C," Kim ground out through tight lips. "The bags go in the van." If looks could kill, Mrs. C would be so dead right now.

Hugh, ever helpful, decided this would be a fine moment to warble a medley of Village People tunes. The irony escaped no one, except for Hugh. I'd bet my savings he thought he was showing solidarity with the gay world. I choked back my laughter by chomping down hard on my lip. Most of our group stared at the pavement. Fortunately, Frick and Frack seemed confused.

"You're the entire crew?" Rich asked, surprised. He put his hand on Hugh's shoulder and thankfully Hugh stopped singing. God, Rich had to be burning up in his muumuu and sweatpants. I wondered if he ever wore shorts. The thought made me gag. Literally.

"You okay?" Mariah asked, pounding me on the back.

"Yep, I'm good," I lied. "Excuse me," I said, giving the shiny goobs a big smile. "I don't think all the luggage will fit in the compartment and the van with all of us in it. Is there any way we could put some of it in the trailer?"

"Absolutely not." Frick gave me an oily grin. Frack examined me for a moment and then went back to his cell phone. "The trailer has very expensive camera equipment and lights in it. Insurance company won't allow it. Of course, you could always ride in the sedan with us, Kristy."

Okay, eww freakin' gross. His pathetic attempt at hitting on me left me feeling dirty. I bet Mitch would have kicked his ass . . . but Mitch wasn't here. He was busy saving the world from bad guys.

"She rides with us," Mariah barked. "She happens to be a homo and my girlfriend. If you so much as look at her again, I'll shove your foot up your ass and pull it out of your mouth."

"She's joking," Kim shrieked. "We have a group of jokesters! It's going to be a great show. Big ratings," she bellowed. I guess she figured if she was loud enough, she could distract the little Napoleons from how crazy we all were. I'd used the loud method several times myself and found great success. From the looks of bewilderment on Frick's and Frack's faces, it was working for Kim too.

"No problemo," Frick said, giving us all a big L.A. smile. "Just pile in and follow us."

"Thanks," I whispered to Mariah as we got in the van.

"No problemo." She rolled her eyes, mimicking the douche bags. "This is going to be an interesting two weeks."

I laughed and returned the eye roll. "My sentiments exactly."

We piled into the van. Edith and Mrs. C in the back row, Rich and me in the middle, Boo and Mariah in the front row, and an assload of luggage that didn't fit in the compartment under our feet. Kim drove and Hugh was the radio. We were off. I wasn't sure if the lead ball in the pit of my stomach was about Mitch or the fact that I was about to hunt down a mythical creature with a bunch of insane people headed up by two smarmy little shiny guys.

Leaning back in my seat I closed my eyes. Maybe if I fell asleep I could pretend this wasn't happening. Why did I feel like I was forgetting some . . .

"Shitballs," I shouted, causing Kim to slam on the brakes. Everyone flew forward, including poor Hugh, who almost went through the windshield. "Aunt Moon-Unit! Was I supposed to pick her up? We have to go back. We forgot Moon-Unit!"

Kim turned around and gave me the stare. I shrank down like a beaten dog. "Sorry," I whispered, "but we forgot Aunt Moon-Unit."

"Kristy, you cannot yell like that when I'm driving. We did not forget Moon-Unit. She has opted to be our liaison from her computer. She's on her police scanner as we speak. She will let us know the traffic and weather reports."

"That doesn't make any sense. She was so excited about this trip," I said, getting worried. "Are you sure something isn't wrong?"

Kim and Hugh exchanged a look. Kim heaved a big sigh. "All right, this is top secret info, but Moon-Unit would be okay with the team knowing."

Oh my God, was she ill? Rena hadn't said anything about Moon-Unit being sick. Did she have cancer . . . had she been institutionalized? I felt dizzy and panicked. I was on the verge of tears. I adored Aunt

Moon-Unit and all her crazy. If something bad was happening, maybe I should stay in Minneapolis . . .

"The chi in Moon-Unit's house has gotten worse. If she leaves, she fears the chi will take over and the aliens won't land at their expected time. She's hosting a small gathering of E.T.'s and has to eradicate the chi before next Thursday," Kim told everyone while Hugh grunted out the theme from *Close Encounters of the Third Kind*.

"Has she tried spreading saltpeter around the house?" Edith inquired.

"I don't believe she has," Kim said. "What does the saltpeter do?"

"Chi can be horny little bastards and multiply like rabbits. Saltpeter will make those chi dongers useless. The less chi fornicating . . . the less chi," Edith explained.

"Sounds reasonable." Hugh nodded. "I'll text her the info immediately."

Was everyone in the van a fucktard except me? I glanced over at Rich. He seemed a little shell-shocked and confused by the information. Boo was buying it hook, line, and sinker. Mariah looked like she was trying not to laugh. I refused to turn around and look at the old bags. It was their idea, after all.

I realized my mouth was hanging open. Were they for real? "Um, guys, chi is not an animate object. It can't have intercourse and it can't procreate. Chi does not have, um . . . private parts. Therefore, saltpeter won't help all that much."

"Do you know this for a fact, Dingleboobers?" Edith demanded from behind me. She wedged her head in between me and Rich, making me scream in fear. Holy Jesus, she smelled like my grandfather. She was wearing Old Spice aftershave.

"Yes, it's a fact," I said, gingerly pushing her head back to her section of the vehicle.

"Have you ever seen chi?" she questioned.

"No, and neither have you," I said, wondering if this would degenerate into a fistfight.

"Have."

"Not," I shot back.

"I most certainly have and they have wangs and cooters," she shouted. "They also have badoinkies bigger than yours," Edith informed all in the van, with the authority of an asylum inmate who'd forgotten her meds.

"Oh my God." I expelled a huge breath and realized entering a debate about chi wangs and cooters was a losing proposition. "I'm going to take a nap so I don't have to listen to you tell us that auras give blow jobs."

"How did you know that?" she asked, impressed with me for the first time ever.

"I quit," I muttered, closing my eyes and ending the conversation. I mentally beat the hell out of myself for willingly entering into a situation that was going to add years of therapy to my life. I contemplated getting out of the van and walking back to my car, but I stayed . . . At least the talk of randy chi had made me forget about Mitch for a few minutes. I suppose if I didn't give in to my secret fantasy to kill the lesbians, they'd provide some much-needed distraction. Small doses, I reminded myself as I drifted off to sleep. Just take them in small doses. Teeny, tiny, small doses . . .

Chapter 15

"*He slid through space and time like a pirate on a ship of bloody eels. His huge feet and oversize member often froze solid when he traversed more than a hundred years through the warped black suck-holes of time. Ginormous appendages were a hindrance to him and made his life miserable.*

"*He felt most at home in the Pacific Northwest and the rural South, although he did enjoy cooler climates. Being such a hairy bastard made living near the equator a clusterfuck, so he didn't. Many a time he had tried to remove his hair-coat and hair-pants, but to no avail. With every wax, shave, and depilatory product he used, the hair came back thicker and coarser. His entire body resembled a six-foot-ten-inch walking and talking pubic region.*"

What an effed-up dream. I snuggled deeper into my squishy and slightly lumpy pillow and tried to go back to sleep. I couldn't for the life of me remember what I had to do today . . .

"I think the 'cooler climates' part is referring directly to Minnesota," Hugh said and started into a New Age concert.

"My Hubie has a good point," Kim said. "So many sightings in Minnesota!"

WTF? That wasn't a dream and my lumpy pillow was not a lumpy pillow . . . it was Rich's man-boobs. I jerked to an upright position and nailed my head on the passenger window. "Ouch," I moaned, rubbing my head.

"Are you okay?" Mariah asked, holding her own head in sympathy.

"I'm fine. I thought I was dreaming, but . . ." I faded out. My grandma always said, If you don't have something nice to say, then shut your cake-hole. "What were you um, reading?" I asked Boo, realizing hers was the voice from my nightmare.

She held up the tattered, coverless bible reverently. "What did you think of it, Kristy?"

Motherhumper, why didn't I just stay asleep? The silence in the van was deafening. I could taste the metallic flavor of blood in my mouth. I had bitten down so hard on the inside of my cheek to keep from informing everyone in the van they were unbalanced, I'd mutilated myself. Surely they didn't believe that stuff . . .

"I thought it was . . . interesting but slightly repugnant," I said as calmly as if I were discussing the weather.

"I think it's tragic that he's ashamed of his body hair," Kim said.

"I believe the size of his man-tool, God bless him, is the reason why people search for him," Mrs. C said.

Not to be outdone by her sister, Edith chimed in too. "I would guess his testicles are the size of cantaloupes."

I stared down at my balled-up hands in my lap. I had several choices here . . . Go with it and pretend they're making sense . . . tell them they're all mental . . . or keep my mouth shut. Shut. I would keep my mouth shut.

"While I find the time-travel part to be kind of bullshit, I'm totally into the shapeshifting thing. Read that part," Mariah told Boo as she opened up a can of Red Bull.

She so didn't need any stimulants.

"Okay," Boo said, flipping through the Bigfoot bible. "I just need to find the section."

"Wait a minute." I burst out laughing, unable to hold back any longer. "Do you guys really, really believe that?"

Hugh stopped his concert mid-mouth-guitar solo and gaped at me. "It's all true."

"Come on." I rolled my eyes. "A time-traveling guy with hair-pants and a huge thingie? Please, I've seen Bigfoot specials and I've never heard of Sasquatch being described that way."

"That's because people don't know yet," Boo insisted, refusing to back off her ludicrous claims.

"Just because you haven't seen it doesn't mean it's not real," Edith snapped, defending Boo. "There are plenty of things you can see with your own eyes that are fake, bless your heart, like your overinflated funbags for example."

"Oh my God." I let my head fall back on the seat. "My funbags are real and you're certifiable." I knew I sounded like a sarcastic buzz-kill, but this was too much. Maybe the reason I was here was to keep these people from going off the deep end. I think I was probably too late . . .

"Kristy, you have lovely funbags. Edith and Mrs. C are just jealous," Kim laughed, and the old ladies huffed with indignation. "I have a question for you, dear."

I held my breath and waited for a boob question or a Sasquatch interrogation or possibly a lecture on how sad my lack of faith was . . .

"Do you take the Bible stories literally?" she asked.

"Well, um . . ." Holy hell, I worried we were veering dangerously close to the God-Bigfoot debate again. "I think that the Bible is a book of stories to teach us to be good."

"Do you think the stories are true?" she pressed.

I started to sweat. Which answer would end the conversation? "Um, sure?"

"So you believe Noah's ark happened, but you can't believe in the possibility of Bigfoot."

Assclowns, I was stunned to silence . . . a rare and unsettling occurrence. Anything I said could and would be held against me. Damn, for being crazy, these people were smart.

"I think that little pervert Noah was into bestiality," Edith said, very pleased with herself. "He took all those animals onto that boat and then he . . ."

"Oh, for shit's sake," Mariah bellowed. "You are the most fucked-up old lady lesbo I've ever known . . . and I know fucked-up."

"Girls, girls," Kim admonished. "This conversation is not about fornicating with animals or lesbians. It's about helping Kristy."

Everyone in the van was looking at me, including Kim, which was alarming because we were still moving. "Kim, would you mind watching the road?" I asked politely. Even though death might be the preferable option to spending two weeks with my team, it just didn't feel like a good day to die.

"So talk to me about Noah's ark," Kim pressed.

I was silent. Any answer I gave would backfire.

"I think the animals represent people of different cultures. I don't think they were animals at all," Rich said, trying to save me from answering. Damn, he was sweet. "If you put all those animals together, they would have eaten Noah and his family first and then each other. Although I don't believe it happened at all."

"That's an interesting theory, Rich," Kim said with enthusiasm, "but it wasn't your turn. It was Kristy's."

"I actually really like Rich's theory," I said, giving his hand a squeeze, "but if you want to know my take, I think it's a story to teach us that if we believe, we will be taken care of."

"Believe without seeing?" Hugh, the human boom box, asked me with the shit-eating grin of victory.

"Yes," I groaned. "You guys win. I suppose Bigfoot could exist. I think equating him with God would put most churchgoing Christians into a coma, but I'll give you that he could exist."

"Amen," Boo shouted.

"But, that crap you were reading was utter bull," I told her.

"Kristy, it's like the Bible," Boo giggled. "It's got lots of fiction wrapped around the truth. The ridiculousness of it is to confuse non-believers."

"And you know this how?"

"I just do," she said simply and with such great conviction, I almost believed her for a second.

"If we're done with Sunday school, I've got a few goddamn questions," Mrs. C snapped.

"Go ahead, dear. Oh, son of a bucket," Kim gasped. "We've lost Stu and Stan."

And we had. The black sedan was nowhere in sight. Kim started to hyperventilate and Hugh stopped singing. My stomach felt queasy. I realized I had no idea, other than Duluth, where we were going . . . not the hotel, not the phone number . . . nothing. My stomach gave a sickening lurch and I wondered if anyone knew.

"You must have an itinerary," Rich said calmly.

"Kind of," Kim muttered almost inaudibly.

"What did you say?" Edith yelled from the back.

"Do you have their numbers?" I asked, ignoring Edith and beginning to take on some of Kim's panic. She didn't answer.

"Hotel name?" Boo asked in her sweet, high-pitched voice.

"I think he said Paul Bunyan Lodge and Getaway Resort," Kim whispered, close to tears.

"This is a clusterfuck," Mrs. C bellowed. "I'm stuck in a van an hour from home with a bunch of freaks who have no clue where we're going?"

"Well, if that's not the pot calling the kettle black," a man shouted back.

I whipped my head around, looking for an extra man . . . Wait, it was Mariah. Would I ever get used to her voice?

"Maybe we should turn around," I suggested. Unfortunately my comment spurred full-on outbursts from everyone. For the next six minutes, suggestions, accusations, and swearwords flew.

"Calm down," Rich said with the force of someone in charge. The van went silent. Never in my wildest dreams did I think I'd willingly look to a ginormous man with boobs, bad teeth, unidentifiable accent, and a crotch on his head for sane leadership . . . but I was. "There is a Paul Bunyan Lodge and Getaway Resort on the northwest side of Duluth."

"And how do you know that?" Edith demanded.

"I know that," Rich said slowly and clearly, "because while you were shouting things that should get your mouth washed out with soap, I looked it up on my phone. I also e-mailed them to see if we had a reservation, and we do."

"Thank you, Jesus," Kim said, back to her old self. "Rich, you are the man!"

"Rich for president," Hugh shouted and then broke into "Hail to the Chief."

I giggled, so happy for Rich. The wonderfully odd man, who was striking out into the world to try to find friends, was on his way. After a high five with Mariah and a hug from Boo, he handed Hugh his phone and instructed him to put the address into the navigation system. I quickly called Rena to give her my information, but her voice mail was full. No big surprise there; she was totally technically challenged except for number crunching. I ended up leaving a message on Jack's cell with instructions to give my whereabouts to both Rena and Louise down at the shelter. I threatened him with a slow and painful death involving the *Kardashians* and the *Housewives* if he forgot.

"This sure is some rinky-dink operation," Edith huffed. It was the first time I ever thought she was right . . . about anything.

"I'm a little surprised that Stu and Stan are both the producers and the entire crew," Rich agreed.

"It is only the pilot." Kim defended the smarmy little men. "My guess is they're going to shoot it like *Blair Witch Project*. Very rough, very real."

"Gritty," Hugh grunted.

"Or shitty," Mrs. C added.

I bit back a laugh. I couldn't have agreed with her more, but I was not defecting to their side. I'd rather chew glass and swallow it. The nasty old gals pulled out their knitting needles and went to work. Kim drove and bounced happily to Hugh's bizarre and off-key rendition of "King Tut." Mariah and Boo, the sisters who couldn't have been more different, played travel Yahtzee, and Rich had a mean game of Angry Birds going on his phone. I called Aunt Moon-Unit to update her and check in. I found out the roads were clear and the weather was good. She felt she was close to destroying the bad chi and was positive her long-dead cheating husband, affectionately known as "that bastard Uncle Fucker," was somehow responsible for the evil life force invading her home.

I made her promise not to do anything dangerous and she swore the trolls and imps would keep her safe. She then suggested doing an Internet check on Frick and Frack. She knew the company they worked for was legit, but she wanted to find out what else they had produced and if it sucked. Why none of this was done before we left, I didn't know. She had to go because the chi was thickening. I wished her luck and sanity and hung up.

The rhythmic clicking of the knitting needles paired with the Yahtzee dice bouncing around in the plastic cup, made me sleepy again. Even Hugh's "Walk Like an Egyptian" and Kim's alarming backup singing calmed my jangled nerves and broken heart.

I curled myself into a little ball on the seat and leaned toward the window. As my eyes were getting heavy, Rich gently poked me.

"You can lean on me," he whispered. "I'm pretty fat and squishy, kind of like a pillow with a heartbeat."

"You're like a giant teddy bear," I murmured as I moved to take him up on his sweet offer. Never thought I would willingly cuddle up to man-boobs, but I never thought I would go on a search for Sasquatch either. At least Rich was safe; he could never hurt me like Mitch did. But then again, I wasn't in love with Rich. Damn it to hell, I decided to close my eyes and try to sleep off my depression. I didn't really expect it to work, but what other choice did I have?

Chapter 16

Paul Bunyan Lodge and Getaway Resort was everything I expected it to be . . . and less. At one time it was probably a lovely place . . . like in 1983, but now, not so much.

A long sprawling one-story building flanked by beautiful dense forest sat on an unpaved pothole-ridden parking lot. The door of each connected cabin (and I use that word loosely) was painted a dull mustard yellow. The rest of the building was painted (again loosely) to resemble logs. It did look clean and well maintained. Either the owners had horrid taste or no funds to update the resort.

The best and most awe-inspiring part was Fiberglass Paul Bunyan himself. He stood about twelve feet high in the middle of the parking lot, surrounded by purple morning glories that had crept up his large legs and covered most of his bright red pants. His axe was chipped and broken, but more alarming than the axe and flower legs was that half of his head was missing. The left side. He held a large sign in his axe-free hand: WELCOME! SEARCHING FOR SASQUATCH and VACANCIES. Yet again, I questioned the wisdom of coming on this trip, but fifty thousand bucks for the shelter was fifty thousand bucks.

"Here are the keys to your rooms," Kim trilled, handing us keys that resembled tiny axes. We stood like a band of lost souls under the watchful eye, *because he had only one*, of Paul Bunyan.

"Where in the hell are the shiny fags?" Mrs. C grumbled.

"Mrs. C!" Kim admonished.

"Sorry," she said. "I meant, where in the hell are the shiny fags, bless their hearts."

"Mrs. C, you have got to curb your mouth. This is a huge opportunity for us and I won't have you ruin it with your homophobic slurs," Kim told her firmly.

"You know," Mariah Carey said, sounding every inch the tiny linebacker that she was, "it surprises me that you'd have a problem with the girlie boys since you're a rug muncher."

"Listen, you little green-haired man with teeny tiny boobies," Edith shouted, turning an unbecoming shade of red, "we don't like that term, we prefer *lesbos* or *queers*. If you insist on using that name, I will cut your hair off while you sleep, knit it into a merkin, and super-glue it to your forehead."

Everyone froze for a moment in shock and then started to laugh. Hard. Even the old lesbos were laughing. I laughed too, although I had no idea why.

"Oh my God, what's a merkin?" I gasped, gathering myself. They all stared at me like I had three heads. "What?" I said. "I don't know what it is."

"I'll explain later," Rich whispered, still chuckling. He patted my back and I felt like an idiot. Maybe I should have pretended I knew what it was . . .

"Um, okay," I said, not quite ready to give up. "Is it always made out of green hair? Is it gross?"

My question set everyone off into hysterics again. Thankfully Frick and Frack pulled up, and all the joy over my lack of merkin knowledge disappeared.

"They're here," Kim squealed. Hugh started dancing around the parking lot like his feet were on fire. I truly hoped they weren't going to film this.

"It's really going to happen," Boo whispered, teary eyed. She clutched her Bigfoot bible to her chest and grabbed her sister's hand.

"Are you ready to find Bigfoot?" Frick yelled, giving us the Sasquatch pose. Knees bent, arms raised in the air, and claws out.

"Yes!" my crazy group shrieked back, assuming the pose. I stood there wondering when I had entered the twilight zone. Rich gave me a gentle prod and I took up the mortifying position too. Thankfully no camera was in sight.

"All right, the *Duluth Daily Gazette* will be here soon to get photos," Frick said. "Let's move the van and trailer in front of Paul Bunyan. It'll be a great shot." He glanced up at the half-headed Paul and winced. "Jesus Christ," he muttered. "Pull the van up on the right side. Don't want to scare off the fans with a lobotomized lumberjack."

Hugh jumped in the van and parked on Paul's good side. The excitement was contagious. Kim was practically vibrating and Boo couldn't stop crying. An SUV with DAILY GAZETTE printed on it pulled in minutes later. Hugh dove out of our van and started an Irish jig that was disturbing to everyone.

"Hugh." Rich put his hand on Hugh's shoulder. "Take it down a notch, buddy."

"Right," Hugh gasped, breathing hard from his shocking performance. "I guess I'm a little gobsmacked," he said with a grin.

"We all are," Rich agreed, "but let's play it cool."

"Cool. I got it," Hugh said, sticking his chest out and shoving his hands into the waistband of his biking shorts. I was grateful that he'd put on a T-shirt during the drive. I couldn't imagine what the *Gazette* would have made of his bare chest.

A curvy-in-all-the-right-places gal wearing tight clothes and too much makeup below her blond helmet-head hair greeted us with a Minnesota accent so heavy, I could barely understand her. She was accompanied by two generic bald guys carrying cameras and lights.

"Hi, I'm Heidi Kugelschmooson," she said enthusiastically, taking in our motley crew. She blanched as she noticed Mariah's green hair, but she almost passed out when she got a glimpse of Rich. "Boy, oh boy, oh boy," she mumbled. "Don't get paid enough to deal with this . . ."

"Heidi." Stu sidled over and handed her his card, touching her hand for about fourteen seconds too long. Not that she seemed to mind. She giggled and tried to toss her hair over her shoulder. It didn't move. It was so hard, it probably could have been used as a weapon. "How wonderful they sent someone so beautiful to welcome us to Duluth."

"Ooo, you're a charmer," she cooed at our shiny smarmy little producer.

"Can't seem to help myself around a piece of . . . woman like you."

"Well," she said, batting her overmascaraed eyelashes at him, "I'm not just a reporter. I'm the local weather girl too!"

Holy God Almighty, Rena would crap her pants. She should have come to Duluth to try her hand at broadcasting. Surely she would have beaten out Heidi Kugelschmooson with her unmovable blond hair and overmade-up face, meteorology school or not . . .

"The weather in Duluth is blessed," Stu said to her abundant cleavage.

"Ohhh, Mr. Greenberg," she giggled, running her hands up and down his hairy, skinny arm.

"Call me Stuey," he said, trying to reach around for a quick grab-ass.

Heidi Kugelschmooson did a move that most pro football players would have admired to avoid Stu's slimy little hands. I was impressed and completely grossed out at the same time. Did she find Frick, I mean Stu, attractive? I glanced around at my people. They were mute and confused. Even Hugh had no backup sound track for this disaster. It was kind of like watching the mating ritual of things that shouldn't breed . . . you knew you should turn your head away, but you couldn't.

"So Stuey," Heidi said breathlessly, à la Marilyn Monroe, "I'd like to follow the team and do a daily article on the search . . . if that's okay with you, sweet cheeks."

Frack's, I mean Stan's, head shot up from his cell phone and he gave Stu a measured look. Stuey, as he shall be known henceforth, turned away from his partner's silent whatever and put all of his focus on the hot mess also called Heidi.

"On one condition, you feisty little thing . . . you come out to dinner with me tonight." He grinned and stood up to his full height. About five foot two.

After the briefest moment of indecision or possibly revulsion, Heidi agreed. Maybe it wasn't indecision . . . maybe she was playing hard to get. Oh my God, why in the hell was I dissecting the thoughts of someone who used more hairspray in a day than I used in an entire year?

"Well, if you two are done making your revolting, God bless you, pre-fornication plans, let's take the goddamn picture. I'm hungry," Edith huffed.

Heidi blushed thoroughly, Stuey, with great pride, did a Michael Jackson crotch grab, and I pretty much threw up in my mouth. Now on top of everything else, I was going to have the pleasure of watching Stuey Greenberg try to bag Heidi Kugelschmooson. Could life get any better than this?

"Line up in front of the van for the picture," one of the bald newspaper guys barked.

We did. Chattering the whole time, we made our way to the van. Only Rich was unusually quiet. Edith and Mrs. C pushed their way to the front, only to be repositioned by the bald guy to the back. After they blessed his heart, I'm fairly certain they called him a hairless asscrack. Unfortunately I was put right smack in the center. Boo was next to me and everyone else was lined up behind. Heidi examined all of us with a critical eye. Her gaze rested on Rich a bit too long for my liking. If she said one derogatory thing about my friend, I would yank her blond helmet wig . . . ? WTF? She was wearing a wig? A wisp of dark brown hair fluttered around her temple. That brown hair must be pretty awful if she chose to cover it with the blond monstrosity she was wearing.

"Stuey, would you and your partner like to be in the picture?" Heidi inquired in a sultry tone. "It won't be the same if you're not in it."

"Nope," Stan said, holding Stuey back. "We are the producers, not the talent."

"Ooooo, come on, you handsome devils," she purred.

Stuey was practically salivating, but Stan stood firm. He swatted Stuey across the back of the head and let Heidi know in no uncertain terms that he and Stuey would not be in the picture.

"Okay," she pouted. "On three, everybody smile. One, two, three . . ."

It took about an hour to take pictures. Mostly because the old ladies kept flipping the photographer off. Once we realized what was causing the delay, Rich and Hugh stood behind the nasty old gals and held their arms down. We took pictures in front of the van and in front of the trailer and two with Hugh and Mariah on top of the trailer. That, bizarrely enough, was at Stan's request.

Heidi Kugelschmooson and her bald buddies left after she and Stuey made their evening plans. We then brought our luggage to our rooms and planned to meet back up in the parking lot in an hour. I was pissed to see Rich and Hugh helping the old ladies despite the way they'd treated them, but Hugh and Rich were just good guys. Weird, but good.

My room was . . . well, it was clean and that's about all I could say for it. The mustard-colored door theme was carried out everywhere. Clearly the owners had gotten a really good deal on the pukey brownish yellow paint. After staring at it for about twenty minutes I was sure they must have gotten it for free. No one would have used this particular color everywhere and paid for it. I changed into some jeans, tennis shoes, and a pink henley. I glanced in the mirror at my hair. My curls had taken on a life of their own. I spent thirty-seven seconds trying to tame them and gave up. Crapmonkeys, how was I supposed to control my life when I couldn't even control my hair? Whatever. I took a deep cleansing breath and decided to just go with it. At the appointed time, I grabbed a jacket and headed back out to the parking lot. Even though it was July, Minnesota was chilly at night, especially this far north.

Mariah and Boo stood next to the van. They were both wearing beautifully made, but garishly colored knee-length sweater coats. We'd gotten a donation of them at the shelter. Most of the women who came through didn't want them due to the lime green and Day-Glo orange color palate, but Mariah had no such issue. She had several and had asked if she could have one for her sister. Louise and I had obliged happily. Since we couldn't get rid of them, I even took one. I wore it only around the apartment. The knitwork was exceptional and the yarn was soft and cozy. Rena was jealous . . . I'm pretty sure another box of sweaters had been delivered to the shelter with less offensive colors. The boxes always came in the middle of the night with no note. I needed to remember to look when we got back. That would be a good bargaining tool for future bets with Rena. Although I was done betting with her. The last two bets had landed me in Duluth to find Bigfoot and in love with someone I could never be with . . .

"Bless your heart," Mrs. C said, eyeing Mariah. "Your sweater matches your hair, which would make you a yarn-head." Mrs. C and Edith laughed heartily at the joke that made no sense.

"Yep." Mariah grinned, completely unoffended. "And your face matches your butt, which makes you an ass-head."

I laughed at Mariah's joke, which not only made sense, but was accurate.

"I wouldn't laugh, titanium badoinkies," Edith snapped at me.

"You're right, merkin brains. I should be kinder to people who are hateful to everyone," I shot back, throwing that *merkin* word in again.

I still didn't know what it meant, but I knew it was bad. I'd clearly hit my mark. The ladies were speechless and Mariah and Boo laughed so hard they were crying. What in the hell was a merkin?

Before I could pry an answer out of anyone, Kim burst out of her room in a panic, dragging Hugh behind her. "Where's Rich?" she asked frantically. "I have news."

The way she said *news* made my tummy tingle . . . in a bad way.

"Here I am," Rich said, ambling over. He had changed muumuus and had on a fresh pair of sweats.

"Moon-Unit called. The good news is she's got the evil chi narrowed down to the two back guest rooms in her house."

"And the bad news?" Boo asked, wrapping her blinding sweater coat tightly around herself.

"The bad news is that when she researched the TIT network, there was no mention of *Searching for Sasquatch* anywhere," Kim said, wringing her hands.

"You mean TNT network," Boo corrected her. Jeez, I was out of the loop. I thought this show was for Animal Planet or something like that.

"No," Kim said. "I mean TIT. Totally Inspirational Television."

"You mean to tell me I've come all the way out here to find Bigfoot for Jesus with boobs?" Edith shouted. "I've never even heard of that channel! I thought it was TNT and I had a chance to meet Ted Turner, goddamn it."

I was having an out-of-body experience. This was wrong on every level. I was out in the middle of nowhere at a lodge where Paul Bunyan had only half a head, with psychotic people, possibly working for a network that had a name synonymous with breasts. I would have been better off wallowing with my broken heart in my bed at home.

"Okay," I said sharply, cutting off Edith's rant before the talk of boobs reminded her that she believed mine to be fake. "If TI . . . um, the network knows nothing about the show, then it doesn't exist. We need to repack and get the hell out of here. Now."

"What about Stuey and Stan?" Hugh asked, confused and songless.

"Those little shiny homos are up to no good," Mrs. C bellowed.

"They're not homos, you jackass," Mariah yelled at Mrs. C. "The really short one hit on the weather girl earlier. Besides, you shouldn't call them homos, even if they are."

"What in the hell am I supposed to call them?" Mrs. C shot back.

"Homosexuals or gay men," Boo answered for her sister, who was dangerously close to rearranging Mrs. C's nose.

"Ohhhh, so it's just fine and dandy for you to call me a rug muncher, but I can't call the little shiny guys, fags? Bless their hearts."

"Oh. My. God," Mariah shrieked. "I'm not calling you that anymore. I'm only going to call you lesbo and queer."

That shut Mrs. C up . . . for a second. "Well, in that case, I'll use the term *homosexual*."

"There has to be a reasonable explanation," Rich said as Kim nodded like a bobblehead.

"There is," came a voice from behind us.

"Shit," Hugh squealed, startled. He jumped into his wife's arms and buried his head.

"There's a very good explanation." Stan approached our group with Stuey close behind. I think that was the most words I'd heard Stan speak so far.

"It better be good," Edith said, getting up in his face, "you little homo . . . uh, sexual." She quickly glanced at Mariah for approval. Mariah gave her a curt nod. Pleased with herself, she continued. "I have never heard of your badoinkie network. So speak up or I'll let the little green-haired menace have at your man-jewels."

Stan pulled Stuey in front of him. Clearly, he didn't want to risk his testicles. "Tell them, Stuey," he hissed.

"Okay," Stuey began, looking at the ground in embarrassment. "It's not on the network website because they cancelled it." There was a collective gasp from my group. "They took away most of our funding."

"That doesn't make sense," Boo said gently, sensing Stuey's discomfort. "If they cancelled it, why didn't they take *all* your funding?"

"We had already rented the cameras and the van and had the lodge reservations before they pulled the plug." He was shaking and his voice was clogged with tears. I started to feel kind of bad for him. "Stan and I failed at our last two projects," he whispered, "so we put up the money ourselves so we could shoot the pilot. We have to prove to TIT that we can do it."

"When did they cancel the show?" Kim asked, putting Hugh down.

"The day before we came to your meeting," he muttered morosely, "but when we saw how enthusiastic you were and how hot Kristy was, we knew we could have a hit on our hands."

"Were you going to tell us this?" I asked, mortified that my hotness had anything to do with our being in this mess.

"We were kind of hoping it never came up."

"So lay out your plan," Rich said. "Tell us what we're doing here and why we should stay."

"Right. Of course," Stuey said, all business. "We have one camera. We'll go out to designated spots each morning and shoot as much footage as we can. We have been given secret locations by our Yeti scientists of potential dens and hangouts of Sasquatch."

"There are Yeti scientists?" Hugh was amazed.

"Absolutely." Stuey nodded solemnly. "Men and women, well, mostly men, who have dedicated their lives to scientific research of the habitat, rituals, and existence of Bigfoot."

"I knew it," Hugh shouted gleefully, giving Kim a high five.

"So you want us to spend two weeks here searching for Bigfoot to save your shiny little asses." Mariah summed it up in the way only Mariah could.

"Basically, um, yes." Stuey nodded.

"Sounds reasonable to me," Hugh said.

"What about the fifty thousand dollars for the women's shelter?" Rich questioned. "Is that gone too?"

"No," Stuey interjected quickly. "Brooks Spewter, the CEO of TIT, was caught with hookers at a major Jesus conference a month ago. TIT took a big hit, being a religious network and all, so they're looking for some good press. The publicity department jumped at the chance to give to a women's shelter. They're playing it like it was Spewter's idea."

"Oookay," I said. "That's a lovely story." At least the shelter would still get the money. How did I forget to ask that? I reached over to Rich and squeezed his hand gratefully. He winked his green eye at me.

"So are you guys in?" Stuey asked timidly while Stan stood mutely behind him.

"What if we can't find Bigfoot?" Boo asked. "Will the show be a failure?"

"No," Stan finally spoke. "We just need to get close. He's been spotted here repeatedly."

"As long as we can find some evidence or a print or some hair, we could make it work," Stuey added.

We all looked at each other. I was good to stay. We were already here and I felt sorry for Stuey. Not Stan so much, he seemed kind of like a dick, but Stuey was sweet . . . in an oily, smarmy way.

It alarmed me that I was understanding the silent group telepathy. Boo, Kim, and Hugh were all for staying. Mariah would do whatever made her sister happy. The old ladies were a bit torn, but leaning toward a yes. Rich was the only one I couldn't read. He watched Stuey and Stan with an odd expression on his face. I'm not sure he bought the whole story. I'm not sure I did either, but I didn't think they were out to get us. They'd probably been fired from TIT for incompetence or sexual harassment. Rich glanced over at me and I raised an eyebrow in question; he just smiled and gave a thumbs-up. God, I wish he'd get his teeth fixed.

Kim made eye contact with each of us and received a brief nod in return. "We'll stay," she told the little shiny guys.

Stan and Stuey blew out huge sighs of relief and my group went wild. I even got into it a little too . . . I was becoming as crazy as they were. Shit.

Chapter 17

Rose and Popo's was an all-you-can-eat buffet and karaoke bar. Hugh was so excited I thought he was going to spontaneously combust. Kim lovingly had to yank him back down in his seat repeatedly during dinner. At one point I thought she was going to spank him. As much as I feared his post-dinner performance, I couldn't help but be tickled. His song list was huge and I had a bad feeling this would be a long evening.

We were crammed into an oblong table for eight right next to the buffet line. Mrs. C referred to our area of the restaurant as the clusterfuck section. I marveled at her use of the English language. Apparently all-you-can-eats were popular in Duluth. The place was packed and the atmosphere was happy. I found myself relaxing and having fun. My heart was still hurting, but I was moving forward with my crew of crazies.

"Did you try the chipped beef Stroganoff?" Edith inquired with a mouthful of what looked like something a cat would cough up.

"Um, no." I quickly turned away from her open-mouthed query before my gag reflex kicked in.

"I think it's Spam Stroganoff, not chipped beef," Kim said, examining her huge mound of food.

"No, it's fish," Mrs. C corrected, taking a swig of her beer. "Tastes like ass."

"How do you know what ass tastes like?" Mariah asked, biting back her smirk. Boo giggled and everyone else waited, scared to death of Mrs. C's reply.

"Smell it," she said logically and shrugged. "If it smells like ass . . . probably tastes like ass."

"Good point." Hugh leaned in and sniffed his food. "What if it smells like feet?"

"Tastes like feet," Mrs. C replied.

Now everyone was smelling their food . . . including me. WTF? Everything smelled kind of like butt-feet. Crapmonkeys, my appetite was gone.

"Would you guys like to hear another chapter or verse?" Boo asked, pulling out her bible.

"You betcha." Kim beamed. "I have a good feeling about this trip. I know it's a little screwy with the show being cancelled and all, but if we find him . . ."

"Or her," Boo cut in.

"Or her." She nodded at Boo. "We can help the guys with the show and fulfill our destinies."

"I don't really want to be on a station called TIT," Edith grumbled. "But, bless your heart, Kristy, that seems like a good channel for you."

"I'd love it." I grinned. "And I heard they're creating a show specifically for you and Mrs. C. It's called *Badoinkie Envy*."

The old bags flipped me the bird, which I happily returned, much to the shock of the family at the next table.

Boo leaned in and began to read. The restaurant was so loud and her voice was so soft, it was difficult to hear her.

"Fornication for the hairy bastard was next to impossible. With a schlong the width of a two-liter soda bottle and the length of a laptop computer, women, men, and sheep wanted no part of him. He had developed carpal tunnel syndrome from masturbating, so he took to humping trees and large furniture."

I could not have possibly heard that correctly. Everyone at the table looked kind of dazed and freaked out. Thank Jesus. No one could be dumb enough to buy that crap.

"How exactly would you interpret that?" Kim asked carefully.

"Well—" Boo pondered the question. "I believe that means he is overendowed and hasn't been able to mate. I believe he has a healthy sexual appetite and no partner, human or animal. It's really tragic if you think about it. This must be why there are so few Bigfoots."

"She's right," Hugh agreed. He sniffed Kim's food and must have decided it didn't reek of butt-feet because he started to eat. How the hell anyone could eat after that story was beyond me.

"She has a good point," Kim said thoughtfully. "The actual text is disturbing, but when correctly interpreted, it's undeniable."

"Oh, for shit's sake," Mrs. C griped. "We're trying to find Bigfoot, not fuck him."

"Knowing the size of his tallywhacker is not going to help us find the hairy bastard," Edith huffed.

"Actually, it might," Mariah said, earning a grateful glance from her sister. "If he's been humping trees, that would be a good place to find hair. I would assume his weenie is as hairy as the rest of him?" She looked to Boo for confirmation.

"Yes, of course." Boo nodded. "It might have slightly less hair from the friction of the constant masturbation, but it would still be quite furry."

Kill me now.

"So, when we go out tomorrow, we should examine the trees carefully," Mariah concluded.

"And any large furniture we find in the woods," Hugh reminded us.

"Riiiight," Mariah said. I knew she wanted to bust him for being an idiot, but she held back. It was impossible to be mean to Hugh. He was just too damn sweet . . . bizarre, but sweet.

"All they need to make the show successful is some kind of proof," Kim added.

"I want to find the hairy bastard," Edith said. "I want to have my picture made with him and I want to go on Jay Leno and Dr. Phil and become a star."

"I get the Leno thing," I said to Edith. "But why Dr. Phil?"

"He's hot."

"What do you think, Rich?" Kim asked.

"About Dr. Phil being hot?" he asked, confused.

"No, no, dear," Kim laughed. "We all know that Dr. Phil is hot. What do you think about our ideas to find Yeti?"

He smiled and gave everyone the thumbs-up. "I think it's a plan."

Ooookay then, I was the only sane person here. I was appalled and somewhat nauseous about going out and searching for Bigfoot's pubic hair. I peered around the table. The old ladies were excited and ready for their close-ups with Jay and Dr. Phil. I hadn't noticed till this moment that they were wearing gold lamé tops. *How in the hell had*

I missed that? Boo was calm and focused in regard to her quest and Mariah seemed happy when Boo was happy. Kim and Hugh were in heaven, this was their raison d'être, plus Hugh planned on singing himself mute tonight. Rich looked a bit dumbstruck even though he was on board with the strategy. I think his idea of Bigfoot was more in line with what the general public knew. I think all the talk of Sasquatch's genitalia had thrown him. It had certainly thrown me. Rena would have laughed herself silly and Jack would have stared at the ceiling and run when he had the chance. Mitch . . . What would Mitch have done if he was sitting here right now? I knew exactly what he would have done. He would have been kind to everyone and made them feel good about their whack-job ideas. I mean, he ate the freakin' cheesy mushroom sweet and sour pork at Chinese Farts so he wouldn't hurt Mrs. Wang's feelings.

My eyes filled with tears as I thought about him. Asshats, I have to let it go. Now.

"Are you guys ready for some Bon Jovi?" Hugh yelled to everyone in the restaurant within hearing distance. Well, that certainly yanked me out of my pity party and made me wince.

"I want some Justin Bieber!" Kim insisted.

"Eminem," Boo and Kim said at the same time.

"David Hasselhoff," Mrs. C shouted. Edith pulled out a lighter, fired it up, and held it over her head. I was in hell.

"Kristy and Rich, what do you guys want?" Hugh asked, ready to charge the makeshift stage on the other side of the room.

"I'm good with anything, buddy," Rich said in that peculiar and unidentifiable accent.

"Me too," I added quickly. I didn't want to be personally responsible for Hugh butchering any artist I really liked.

"All right then," Hugh squealed. "I'm gonna do it!"

He screamed as he ran across the restaurant, scaring every man, woman, and child in his wake. The stage cleared immediately when they saw the insane little guy in shiny red bike shorts barreling toward them. I wondered for a moment if he knew what he was doing. He had put the fear of God, Jesus, Moses, and Beelzebub into everyone. No one would go near the stage now . . .

"I'm not sure I can do this," Rich whispered.

I noticed he was sweating. He was so overweight, I wondered if he was having a heart attack. "Are you okay? Do you need a doctor?" I asked, feeling his damp forehead.

"No, no, nothing like that. There are so many people in here and I've been listening to Hugh sing for eight hours straight. It's just . . ."

"Too much?" I grinned. I realized Rich probably hadn't been around this many people in a long time, if ever. He was striking out into the world with the wrong group . . . or possibly not. How many people would accept him and not make fun of him? My team might be nuts, but they were kind. Well, not the old lesbos, but even they had thawed a bit.

"Yeah." He looked down. "I feel kind of bad, but I think I need some air."

"Come on," I said, taking his hand. "I do too."

No one from our group even noticed our exit. They had all run to the edge of the stage like crazed groupies. Edith and Mrs. C held lighters over their heads and kept chanting "David Hasselhoff, David Hasselhoff." Leaving was an excellent idea.

There was a lovely park next to Rose and Popo's. Rich and I wandered over and sat on the swings. I unsuccessfully tried not to flinch when he shoved his ginormous derriere into an apparatus that was made for someone an eighth of his size. Thankfully he didn't notice, or pretended not to.

"Do you feel better now?" I asked, wondering if the swing would hold him. Maybe I should suggest the bench . . .

"Much." He smiled. In the dark his teeth weren't as bad and I couldn't see that his eyes were different colors, but his hair . . . it reminded me that we would be searching for Sasquatch's pubes in the morning. "How are you doing?" he asked.

"I've been better. It's been a rough couple of days," I said, pushing off and letting the swing glide.

"I'm sorry."

"Me too." I looked up at the stars. They were huge. Aside from the lights illuminating Rose and Popo's, it was very dark out. The sky was breathtaking in this part of the country. "Have you ever seen the northern lights?" I asked.

"Yes, a long time ago."

"It's so beautiful. It makes you know there's a God."

"And a Bigfoot?" he teased.

"And possibly a Bigfoot," I giggled. We swung in companionable silence for a bit. I wondered if Rich might be gay or asexual . . . I really needed a friend to dump on. It would be so much easier if he liked guys too.

"Um, Rich, have you ever been in love?" I asked. As soon as the words left my mouth, I regretted them. He was so unfortunate-looking, he probably hadn't ever been in a relationship.

"Yes. Once," he answered, quietly.

I felt shame and was so glad he couldn't read my mind. There was someone out there for everyone. Rich might not be pretty on the outside, but he was lovely on the inside.

"Did this person love you back?"

"I believe she did." He smiled. Was I getting used to his teeth or was it too dark to notice how British they were?

"What happened?" I asked.

"Oh, you know," he said vaguely. "This and that."

I bet the bitch broke his heart. I felt sick. I needed to steer this conversation away from the horrible woman who'd broken his heart. I would tell him about the rat bastard who broke mine . . .

"I was in love once too," I told him. "I mean, I think I was. It happened so fast. I mean, it was just last week and I only knew him for a couple of days . . . maybe I was just in lust. God, I don't know, but I feel shredded inside and I think I might have made a mistake."

"By falling in love?"

"Lust," I corrected him. "No, I guess it was love . . . or is love. Hell, I don't know, but I told him it wouldn't work. I made him leave."

"Why?" he asked. God, he was such a good listener.

"Because he lied, well, not exactly lied. He omitted some rather large things about his life."

"Was he married?" Rich asked, trying to resituate his ass in the swing.

"Nope, not married." I stood up and moved to the bench. Rich gratefully followed.

"Alcoholic? Drug addict?"

"No and no," I told him. "He has a job where he travels a lot."

"Is that all?" he asked, raising his eyebrows above his mismatched eyes.

"Yeah, I guess that makes me sound kind of stupid, but my dad . . . well he, um, you know . . . he wasn't around much and . . ."

"Kristy, you don't have to tell me anything you're uncomfortable with," he said gently.

"I know," I whispered. I looked at Rich. I wondered why someone so sweet had gotten smacked with such a huge ugly stick. I was going to help him. If we walked every day maybe he would lose a few pounds. I could get the Steves to do something with his crotch head when we got back, and Rena's dad was a dentist . . . If Rich didn't have insurance, maybe I could help pay for some braces. Rich would be my new project. I knew in my gut I could trust him. "Rich, my dad used to beat my mom and me. My mom stayed for a long time and then one day he threw me into a wall and knocked my two front teeth out and broke my collarbone. That was the last time I ever saw him."

"Did this man you lust for hit you?" he asked, appalled.

"No, God no. He would never hurt me that way," I said quickly. "I'm not being clear. In fact, I'm not even sure why I told you that." I paused. "I suppose what I was trying unsuccessfully to say is I want to love someone who will be around."

"And he can't do that?"

"No, he can't. His job dictates his life. He can't tell me where he will be or when he'll come back, if at all."

"If you don't mind me asking, what in the hell does this guy do?"

"Some kind of supersecret agent thing." I laughed at how silly that sounded. "Even after what my dad did to my mom and me, I used to dream of him coming back to us . . . and being sorry . . . and wanting to be a real family. I want a real family, I want to know that someone is coming home. This man can't do that."

"I'm sorry, Kristy," he said.

"Me too." I smiled. Talking to Rich felt good. If I was going to get over this overwhelming feeling of sadness, I needed to talk about it. "Rich, thank you for letting me dump on you."

"The pleasure was all mine, Kristy. Any time you want to talk, I'll be here."

I was so going to help this guy . . . I was going to make him over. The next time he ran into that assclown who broke his heart, she was going to regret her decision.

Chapter 18

We all met in the parking lot at seven a.m. I had on good-butt jeans, a cute bright blue long-sleeved fitted T-shirt, hiking boots, and a full can of bug spray. I looked around at my tired and hungover group and worried I was underdressed. Mariah wore a bright green sundress with fishnet stockings and matching green combat boots. Her green hair finished off the outfit in an unexplainable way. Boo wore an ensemble that was very safari-ish, complete with an Indiana Jones hat. Kim and Hugh were in camouflage from head to toe . . . including their faces and hands. They had to have been up for hours to have created that look. The old ladies wore sweatpants and sequined flowing tops with rain boots. They rolled one of their huge suitcases behind them. Rich was the only one who appeared semi-normal, if you could call sweatpants and a size XXXXXL muumuu normal . . .

"Hey there! Hi there! Ho there!" Stuey yelled, running over to our group. His volume and enthusiasm made my head hurt. It practically put the rest of the hungover group on the ground. "You guys ready to search for Sasquatch?"

"Listen, you shiny little bastard," Edith hissed, grabbing him by his overstarched Hawaiian shirt, "if you don't dial it back, I'm going to remove your spleen."

Stuey blanched and continued his greetings in a whisper. "Okay, we're going to take the van and trailer and go out to our safe house in the woods. We'll use it as a base camp and a bathroom."

"What about food?" Kim asked.

"I picked up a bunch of subs this morning from Rose and Popo's," Stuey said.

"Do. Not. Mention. Rose and Popo's. Ever. Again," Mrs. C said between clenched teeth.

Apparently, while Rich and I talked last night, our team got a little rowdy. Well, Edith and Mrs. C got rowdy . . . and of course Mariah, being Mariah, got in on the action. Shots of vodka and lighters are not a good combination. After Edith tried to set a family of four on fire when they asked if Mariah was a man, and Mrs. C punched the owner because he said David Hasselhoff couldn't sing, everything went south. Mariah took offense at the tone of voice used on the old lesbos, so she drop-kicked the bouncer and kneed his man-jewels up into his chest cavity. Of course, that went over well, but the crowning moment was when Hugh sang the unsanitized medley of Eminem . . . in a family restaurant.

The police and the fire department showed up. Miraculously, no arrests were made. Boo explained why we were in town, and the locals were so impressed, our crew left with just a slap on the wrist . . . and a firm warning never to step foot in Rose and Popo's again. Ever.

"Where's Stan?" Rich asked, scanning the parking lot.

"He's pulling the sedan around," Stuey said. "You won't need your suitcase," he told the old gals dismissively, and handed Kim directions to the base camp.

Edith and Mrs. C ignored him and shoved their monster bag into the luggage compartment under the van. I had no idea why they needed it or what was in it, but I refused to ask. I valued my spleen.

"You won't be riding in the van with us?" Boo asked.

"No, sweet cheeks," Stuey said, winking suggestively at Boo. Mariah growled and Stuey backed off. "We could only afford insurance on one driver for the van and that's Kim, so Stan and I will take the car. We might need an extra vehicle if we capture Sasquatch. Plus I get carsick in vans."

"That's a waste of gas," Hugh croaked, sounding like a baby dinosaur. Clearly his concert last night had left him practically mute. Sweet baby Jesus, I hoped it would mean he would be on vocal rest today.

"Don't worry about it." Stuey grinned. "The network forgot to get their credit card back." He flashed a gold card at us and gave us the double thumbs-up.

He was such a douche, it was difficult to believe anyone would entrust him with anything. The network didn't have to physically have the card to cancel the account, but he was so pumped about getting one over on the company, I didn't have the heart to tell him how stupid he was. I wondered how his date with Heidi Kugelschmooson had gone last night. If her not being here was any indication . . . I'd guess, pretty bad.

"So here's the deal. We go out and I take a camera and follow you guys through the woods and we find us a goddamn Sasquatch!"

"We're searching for Bigfoot's pubic hair today," Boo said in a matter-of-fact tone.

"I'm sorry, what?" Stuey asked, appalled.

"We'll be looking for hair and footprints and evidence today," I added quickly, before Boo described Sasquatch's genitalia and our plan of action.

"Right, right," he said and then turned his eyes to me. "So you got some kind of intro set up?"

"What do you mean?" My gut clenched. Was I supposed to have memorized something? "I didn't get a script," I said, starting to sweat. Assmonkeys, this just kept getting worse. I'd forgotten I was supposed to be the host.

"No script," he said, looking me up and down. "Just stand there, look hot, and say some shit about Bigfoot. Then we'll run all over the woods for a couple of hours, eat, and come home."

"Is this one of the areas where Bigfoot has been sighted?" Kim asked.

Stuey answered her, but I didn't hear a word he said. My ears were ringing and I wanted to run away. Far away. What in the hell was I going to say? I didn't even really believe Bigfoot existed. Any true believer would be able to see right through me. Maybe I should try to find a tame part of the Bigfoot bible and read from it. Holy hell, who was I kidding? From what I'd heard so far, that was probably a very bad and profane idea. Maybe I could talk about the bar fight last night . . . the producers of most of these reality shows loved some violence. Wait, no . . . that's Jerry Springer. Shitballs, I can't do this. I'm not an actress, I'm a social worker . . .

"How far away is this base camp?" Mariah asked.

"What did you say?" Stuey asked Rich.

"*He* didn't say anything," Mariah said, menacingly. "I did. I asked how far to the base camp, and just because someone has a low voice doesn't mean they're a man." Her volume increased as her anger skyrocketed. Rich grabbed Mariah as her little hands clenched into fists and she narrowed her gaze, zoning in on Stuey's nose. Rich held her firmly against his big belly and whispered in her ear. She immediately calmed and sagged against him. What in the hell had he said to her? I needed to know. He had some kind of weird magic with people. After all, he was a magician, if I remembered correctly . . . I was simply grateful we weren't going to start the day with Stuey lying on the pavement in a pool of his own blood.

"Half hour," he said, answering Mariah's question, blissfully unaware that his nose had been in grave danger only moments ago. "Let's do it!"

Stan pulled up. Stuey jumped into the sedan and they took off.

"Does anyone find it odd that they leave us in the dust all the time?" I asked as we piled into the van.

"At least they gave us directions this time," Kim muttered, putting her seat belt on and checking to make sure Hugh had fastened his correctly.

Hugh turned around and faced us all with tears in his eyes. "I'm sorry," he croaked. "I won't be able to sing for you today. I blew my wad last night. I should be okay by tomorrow."

"That's okay, Hugh," Boo said sweetly. "You were amazing last night."

"That's my Hubie." Kim grinned and patted him on the head like a dog. He leaned over and kissed her cheek. Theirs was an odd love . . . but, hey, whatever works.

"Kristy, I feel your tension and fear," Boo said in her creepy psychic way. "Would you like me to read from the bible to give you some ideas for your intro?"

"Um, no," I said quickly. "I'll think of something."

"Talk about your boob job," Edith said, completely serious.

"For the last time, my boobs have not been jobbed," I snapped.

"Yeah, right," she muttered under her breath. I rolled my eyes and gave up.

"Why don't you talk about why you came on the trip?" Mariah suggested.

"I think telling the world that I was bribed by a fifty-thousand-dollar donation to the shelter might get us off on the wrong foot," I said.

"Point," Mariah agreed.

"How about why you've dedicated your life to Sasquatch?" Kim offered. "Oh, wait," she remembered. "You haven't actually dedicated your life yet, have you?"

"Ahh, no. Sorry," I muttered.

"That's okay, dear." She smiled. "You will."

Dear Lutheran God in heaven, I had no response to that whatsoever. I wouldn't hurt her feelings for the world, but she was on crack if she thought I would dedicate my life to a fictional creature with a man-tool the size of a two-liter soda bottle. I stayed silent and racked my poor brain for a way to not insult the intelligence of the rabid Bigfoot believers. I did not want to screw this up.

"Maybe you should introduce yourself and explain that we're on a serious quest to find a creature that many believe to be a myth," Rich said, saving me from frying my brain.

"I think that's perfect," Boo said approvingly. "But I'm going to read a passage just in case."

I smiled gratefully at Rich and held my breath in anticipation of the frightening words that I knew were about to come from Boo's lips. She read with passion and conviction in her sweet little voice.

"Time travel made him weary. He longed for stability and a woman with a cooter large enough to accommodate his bulbous pecker. He wandered aimlessly, depressed and lonely. There had been one, with a deformed vagina, but she had been evil to the core. She had tried to kill his fearless leader and his leader's concubines.

"Her punishment had been death. Her skin had been flayed from her body and her toenails yanked from her feet with pliers. She had enhanced her bazooms to epic and disgusting proportions. While he found that to be revolting, it was slightly arousing. He often pondered the probability of large hooters equating to large hoohas, but because of his stench, he'd never gotten close enough to a stripper or a porn star to test his theory. Instead he'd taken to masturbating in the dark corners of bedrooms belonging to large-breasted women."

You could hear a pin drop. Even the old queers had been stunned to alarmed silence . . . for a moment.

"What in the fuck is that supposed to mean?" Edith shouted from the back of the van. "Bless your heart, Boo, but that's a crock of bull-honkey and makes me want to puke up my breakfast."

My sentiments exactly.

"Don't you talk to my sister that way, or I'll come back there and make you eat your own vomit," Mariah threatened, unbuckling her seat belt.

I quickly opened the window to try to tamp down my gag reflex. This was such a bad idea on so many levels. Just when I felt close to my crew, I realized they weren't playing with a full deck. Some of them were playing with no deck at all.

"Now, now, girls, no fighting or force-feeding stomach bile," Kim admonished. "Yes, that passage was a bit disconcerting, but it's the interpretation, not the text, we need to pay attention to. If this was easy, everyone would know how to find Bigfoot."

I was losing it. Kim was making sense to me in a bizarre way. By the time these two weeks were over, I would need to be institutionalized.

"Boo, can you decipher that one for us?" Kim inquired. I noticed she was driving way over the speed limit. Maybe we would crash and die before we got there. It was beginning to sound like a good alternative.

"I believe that Bigfoot is sad and lonely. He longs for love and sexual satisfaction. I think the time travel may be a metaphor for something, but I'm not sure. The actual manipulation of space and time seems highly unlikely, but then again . . . stranger things have happened. If he can time travel or shape-shift, it would explain why he's so difficult to track."

"What about the evil woman with tremendous watermelons? What does that mean?" Hugh questioned in a gravelly voice.

"I think that implies he's made bad choices in his mating search. Something that appears appealing on the outside may be all wrong on the inside. With his looks and his stench, he may have experienced great abuse in his youth. He simply wants to be loved and cared for . . . like we all do," Boo added quietly.

Was I in an out-of-body therapy session? Take out the looks and stinky part and Boo could have been talking about me. Fucktard. Heat crawled up my neck and I felt clammy. I stuck my head out the window . . . maybe a tree or phone pole would knock it off. Wait a minute, with Kim's erratic driving, that was a distinct possibility. I pulled my head back in the car and made myself sit with my own thoughts.

I had been searching for love and I thought I might have found it. No, that was stupid. You couldn't fall in love with someone in a matter of minutes . . . or could you? I didn't really know Mitch, but somewhere deep inside, I did. Damn, damn, damn, why should his job matter so much? I didn't have a traditional growing up . . . I'd had a horrific childhood, so I'd thought the only way to be happy was to find the perfect model of what I'd never had. I was drawn to police officers because they were supposed to be above reproach. That had blown up in my face time after time. Why was Mitch different? *Was* he different? Did it even matter? He would probably be gone by the time I got back . . .

"Are you okay?" Rich asked, giving my hand a light squeeze.

"No," I told him truthfully. "I think I might have really screwed up."

"The guy or this trip?"

"Both," I laughed without much humor.

"Look," he said logically, "the trip insures funding for your shelter and the guy will always be there. He'd be crazy not to."

I gave Rich a bright smile. "You're right," I said. I believed the money part, but the guy? Not so much. Whatever. I took a deep breath. I would be okay. I was always okay. These nut jobs in the van needed me and I was beginning to wonder if I needed them too . . .

Chapter 19

"And in conclusion," I stuttered, feeling a sweat droplet roll from my eyebrow down the bridge of my nose, "Bigfoot is a tragic and misunderstood creature . . . looking for love and friends."

"And sex," hissed Mrs. C from off-camera.

"And sex," I repeated before I really heard what she had said. "Shit, I mean . . . oh sorry, I didn't mean to say shit. God, I did it again." My entire body heated in embarrassed panic. I scanned my surroundings and wondered if it would be odd if I took off running into the woods. I decided that might be more humiliating than having said *shit* on national television. Somehow, despite the fact that I pride myself on my common sense, I had agreed to this. Because I'm a gal of my word, I would see it through . . . Assbuckets. I took a huge breath and tried to smile at the camera. I'm fairly sure it came out as a pained grimace. "Pardon my French. Bigfoot may or may not be real, but if this many people dedicate their lives to finding him, there must be something to the story. That's why we're here . . . We're *Searching for Sasquatch*."

"And cut," Stuey said, lowering the camera.

"Was that okay?" I asked, biting my lower lip with worry. "Sorry about the shit thing."

"Oh yeah, no problemo. We can cut that stuff in editing. The most important thing is that your tits look great. You are one hot broad," he said, leering. "All that sexy hair, the long legs, the tight ass, the . . ."

Edith grabbed him by the scruff of his neck. "Scrotum," she spat into his ear, spraying old-lady spit all over his face. "If you'd like to keep your scrotum, you need to shut your shiny cake-hole. Now."

"Got it," he muttered, moving away from Edith.

Stan was still in the sedan talking on his cell phone. He'd been there the entire hour we'd spent on my disastrous intro. That guy had some serious lack of social graces. He barely spoke and when he did, it was clipped and short. Stuey said he was the silent brains of the operation. Help us, Jesus. I guess the brains decided a small deserted hunting cabin in the middle of nowhere was a good spot to hunt Sasquatch. Maybe it was, but this place was gross and clearly a hangout for someone. Cigarette butts and beer cans littered the area. The cabin itself was large for a hunting shack. It didn't look lived-in, but it seemed well visited. If I believed in Bigfoot, which I didn't, I'd have a difficult time seeing him hanging out here.

Stuey backed up and stood about ten feet away from all of us. He kept the camera lowered in front of his privates. He seemed unsure whether Edith had been serious about removing his scrotum. He was taking no chances. "Allrightyroo," he shouted. "Let's go into the woods and find that big hairy bastard!"

We stood frozen in a clump, unsure what to do.

"Do we just take off into the woods?" Mariah asked. "Do we stay together or split up or what?"

Stuey ran his hand through his hair in confusion, pinched the bridge of his nose, and started a staring contest with a nearby tree. Clearly he hadn't thought out his shot list very well . . . aside from my boobs. Stan, sensing a problem, got out of the sedan and approached his doofus partner. "What's the problem?" he asked Stuey.

"No problemo, my friend," he said. "I just need to figure out the . . . you know, um . . ."

"We don't understand what exactly you want us to do," Rich told Stan.

Stan gave Rich a measured look. "Find Bigfoot."

"Yes, we know that. But do we search together, since there's only one camera? Do we split up?" Rich was trying to be polite, but his undertone of frustration was obvious.

Stan and Stuey eyed each other silently. Holy hell, this was ridiculous. My guess was when TIT cancelled the show, they cancelled the crew and the director and God knows what else. I wondered if Stan and Stuey had any idea what they were doing. From the silent conversation going on, my deduction was: no.

Their wordless conversation lasted three minutes too long. "You will stay in a group. Walk north for about twenty minutes before you start your search. Stuey will film all of you. You can take turns, or whatever. I don't care, just find some proof," Stan said as he walked back to the sedan.

"Oookay then," Kim bellowed joyously, completely oblivious to Stan's rude behavior. "You heard the man. Let's go!"

Hugh did a cartwheel and an impressive toe touch. Boo, with her bible in hand, skipped ahead of the group. Her excitement, Hugh's toe touch, and Kim's glee made the awkwardness of the situation disappear. Their delight was contagious. Mariah followed after her sister, grinning like an idiot. I prayed to Lutheran Jesus that Boo wouldn't read from the bible on camera. That could be bad, way worse than my intro gaffe. Rich ambled along with Kim, Hugh, and Stuey, and the old lesbos and I brought up the rear.

"Um, thanks for sticking up for me with Stuey," I mumbled to Edith. Saying thank you to one of the women who had made my life a living hell was akin to chewing glass and swallowing it, but it was the right thing to do. Surprisingly, it felt pretty good.

"Well, it's your own fault," Edith sniffed. "Bless your heart, if you hadn't had those disgusting dingleboobers put in, I never would have had to threaten his ball sac."

Maybe it didn't feel *that* good. I rolled my eyes and tried to think of a comeback, but decided against it. Mrs. C and Edith's boobie envy knew no bounds. There was no winning this fight.

"So are we walking for twenty minutes because there's been a sighting out this way?" Kim asked Stuey.

"Yeah, yeah," Stuey replied, distracted and sweating like a pig.

"Where's Stan?" Hugh asked. Unfortunately his voice was coming back. I suspected we'd be hit with some background music soon.

"He's staying close to the cabin. Don't tell him I said this, but he's got a tiny bladder and has to stay near a toilet."

That didn't make a whole lot of sense. As far as I knew, a guy could whip it out and pee anywhere . . . but then again, these little shiny dudes were weird.

"I thought Stan would run a second camera," Rich said.

"No," Stuey laughed. "We've only got one."

"Then what in the hell is in the locked trailer?" Mrs. C stopped walking and confronted sweaty Stuey.

"What are you talking about?" Stuey was confused. Again.

"The goddamn trailer that I couldn't put my luggage in because it was full of lights and camera equipment," Mrs. C snapped.

"Oh that," Stuey backpedaled. "Well, um . . ." He stared uncomfortably at the ground. "I gotta come clean with you guys. You're such good people." I noticed his hands were shaking. Even though he was foul, I felt sorry for him. "The trailer is full of lights and cameras, but when they cancelled the show, they cancelled the insurance bond. There's about eight hundred thousand dollars' worth of equipment in there, but we're too nervous to use it," he ended quietly.

"Do you even know how to use it?" Mariah asked.

"Well, um . . . no," Stuey whispered, shaking like a leaf. "The crew, they knew how to use it, but . . ."

"It's okay, sweetie pie." Kim grabbed Stuey and pulled him to her ample bosom. "Everything will be fine. It will be a great show, I just know it." She patted his sweaty little back while he sobbed into her camoed chest. "Shh, shh, don't cry," she cooed.

"Enough with the waterworks, shiny boy." Edith yanked him off Kim. I think she believed he was enjoying Kim's bosom a little too much. She was probably correct. "I get the money and equipment thing, but do you know how to work the goddamn camera you're holding?"

"Oh yes," he blubbered, wiping his eyes with his loud Hawaiian shirt. "I'm really good on this camera."

"Fine," Rich said in a clipped British tone, giving Stuey a pointed look. "Let's get to it then."

It was the first time I'd heard Rich angry. It was kind of intimidating unless you were looking at him. It was hard to remove the horrible teeth and pear butt from the voice.

"According to my stopwatch, we need to walk north for eight more minutes and then we can go to work," Mariah said.

So we did.

The next three hours consisted of most of us examining tree trunks for pubic hair. I couldn't bring myself to do that, so I searched the ground for footprints that I knew I would never find. Four times Hugh had been sure he'd found some of Bigfoot's crotch tresses, only to have Mrs. C shoot him down and confirm it to be squirrel hair. Apparently, she and Edith had done a tremendous amount of varmint hunting in their youth. I was tempted to ask if they had ever eaten a groundhog, but I was trying to train myself not to ask questions I didn't want the answers to.

Stuey filmed with a vengeance. He talked the entire time he shot. I thought that was odd, but I supposed his voice could be removed in editing . . . just like my inappropriate use of the word *shit* in the intro. After hours of finding nothing but squirrel hair, deer prints, and what Mrs. C declared to be opossum poop, everyone was exhausted.

"This is ridiculous," Edith huffed. "It doesn't feel right and I'm hungry."

"I have to agree," Boo added pensively. "I don't get a vibe in this area. He hasn't been here."

"What in the hell are you talking about?" Stuey asked. "I have intel from our scientists that this is a prime area."

"Your scientists are brainless eunuchs, bless their hearts," Mrs. C snapped. "Bigfoot would not like this particular area."

"Why?" Stuey asked.

"Because there's no water near here or plant food source," Boo told him. "The trees are too tall, no good hiding places. The Yeti tends to like berries, roots, and human food, like pizza and chicken wings."

"For real?" Stuey asked doubtfully.

"Absolutely." Boo nodded.

"Let's go back and eat lunch," Rich suggested.

Rich looked bad. This kind of physical exertion had to be hard on someone of his girth. Kim was a little worse for the wear too. I was going to have a talk with both of them about healthier choices and exercise.

The cabin was clean and consisted of several rooms besides the bathroom. Stan had our lunch laid out on a long oak table for us when we arrived. His spirits were slightly better than they had been in the morning, but he was still mute. He and Stuey grabbed sandwiches and went into one of the bedrooms to look at footage. We all wanted to see it, but Stuey insisted we wait until it was edited. He gave us no choice. He locked the door behind him.

"I thought you were hungry," I said to Edith, who wasn't eating. I pushed a turkey bacon sub her way.

"I can't eat this roadkill," she muttered, getting up from the table. "I'll be outside." She got up from the table and left. Mrs. C followed, grumbling about dumb-ass shiny bastards getting food from god-forsaken shitholes like Rose and Popo's.

"So last night really affected the old gals," I said, tearing open a bag of chips.

"Nah, they're just pissed we didn't get to finish off the owner and bouncer, plus they've been eating all day," Mariah said.

"What do you mean?"

"They had beef jerky in their pockets. They've been snacking since we started. Although I think they left some of it buried in shallow holes to attract Bigfoot."

"Oh my God." I wrinkled my nose and giggled. "I thought they hadn't showered."

"Finish your lunch," Stan said, rejoining us. "We'll be leaving shortly."

"Are we going to another location?" Kim asked hopefully.

"Nope, we're done for today."

We all looked at each other. Was this how it was done? At least they weren't filming us 24/7. I had a sneaking suspicion that if we didn't find Bigfoot, which we wouldn't, they would secretly manufacture some kind of sighting and edit it in. If they could edit my foul language out, I'm sure they could edit a big fake Yeti in . . .

Filing out of the cabin and back out into the sticky July heat, I noticed the old ladies . . . disheveled and dripping with sweat. They held their suitcase between them like a baby. There was no way they could have held that monster piece of luggage that way unless it was empty. This morning it had weighed a ton. I knew because I'd helped them pull it out of the van. What in the hell was in there and what in God's name had they done with it? Images of a dead body buried in a shallow grave surrounded by beef jerky flooded my brain. Surely it couldn't have been a corpse . . . it would have smelled like hell—unless they had shrink-wrapped it.

Oh my God, my imagination had become warped. As awful as the old broads could be, they were not murderers. Both Kim and Rich eyed them for a long moment, but no one called them on anything. Did they have the same disturbing hunches I did?

"Allrightyroo, team, load your asses into the van and we'll meet you back at the lodge," Stuey yelled out the window of the sedan as they left us in the dust. Again.

"Something's going on with those shiny little fuckers," Edith said, not blessing their hearts.

"I agree," Mariah said. "I think they know exactly where Bigfoot is and aren't telling us."

"That's what I thought," Boo gasped. "For some reason they don't want us to find him."

"Oh, I don't know about that," Kim said carefully. "Maybe Stan, but not Stuey."

Hugh, back in full form, began grunting out the *Mission: Impossible* theme. I didn't know much, but I agreed that something weird was going on with the shiny guys and I saw with my own eyes that something was up with Mrs. C and Edith. A large part of me was curious, but a larger part whispered "beware of what you wish for." I decided to listen to the whisper. Sometimes the less you knew, the better off you were.

Chapter 20

The ride back was fast. Way too fast, but thankfully uneventful. If we'd been pulled over, it would've been awfully hard to explain why we were carrying eight hundred thousand dollars' worth of camera equipment that didn't belong to us in a trailer we couldn't open. Whatever. I just wanted to be alone. As much as everyone was growing on me, kind of like a nonpoisonous, friendly fungus, I wanted some time away. Hugh had gotten his voice back enough to do a Bee Gees concert that would stay trapped in my eardrums for years.

Edith and Mrs. C had fallen asleep in the back row and snored like truckers. They had clearly worn themselves out doing whatever the hell they were doing in the woods. I lacked the courage to ask what was in the suitcase and what they'd done with it, but I really did want to know. I considered bringing it up to the rest of the team, but the Bee Gees concert combined with the snoring made speaking impossible.

The dust cloud we knocked up in the parking lot was impressive. Kim could stop on a dime. She either had her foot slammed down on the gas pedal or slammed down on the brake. We all flew forward and the old ladies hit the floor with a thud.

"Goddamn it," Edith shouted. "Are we dead?"

"Nope," Kim yelled back, over our moaning. "We're home."

I wanted to slip into my room before anyone asked me to do anything, but the showdown in the parking lot was too good to miss. Heidi Kugelschmooson was throwing a fit on Stuey that was riveting.

"You told me I could come," she was whining to a freaked-out

Stuey and a very bored Stan. Her blond helmet head was rock solid and her outfit defied explanation. Suffice it to say she looked like a weather girl who hooked on the side.

"I'm sorry, baby," Stuey stammered.

"I went out with you and you said I could come along," she hissed, closing in on him. Was she going to punch the little guy? This was good. "Are you seeing someone else?" she shrieked. "Are you cheating on me?"

"I just met you yesterday, baby," Stuey stammered in bewilderment. "I haven't had any time to cheat."

"You told me to be here at four o'clock."

"I didn't say nothing about four o'clock," he said, backing away from her wrath. "Did we have plans to do anything at four o'clock, guys?" he asked us, trying to get her attention off himself. We shook our heads no as she whipped around and took in our motley crew.

Her gaze narrowed and lasered in on me, shooting me a look of death . . . or was her lethal stare aimed at Rich? He was standing so close, I couldn't be sure who she was trying to kill with her eyes. It had to be me. Did she think I was getting it on with Stuey and that's why he'd given her the wrong time?

"Maybe I'm mistaken," she said sweetly, turning on a dime. Can you say *schizophrenic*? "I'm sorry, Stuey baby. Heidi's so sorry. I'll make it up to you, snookums."

So much wrong here . . . her being attracted to Stuey, talking about herself in the third person, using the word *snookums*. In slow motion we all tried to back away and sneak into our rooms before Heidi started making it up to Snookums in the parking lot. I had my hand on my doorknob when she let out a shriek so loud I was sure I'd have hearing damage.

"Don't move. I have some questions for you." She stalked over to us as we huddled together like cows before a rainstorm. Wait a minute, this was ridiculous. Who the hell did this skank think she was?

"What do you want?" I stepped forward, blocking her from going at the rest of my group. "We are tired and have a very low threshold for anyone's temper tantrums at the moment. Especially yours."

For a brief second I could have sworn I saw admiration in her eyes, but as fast as it appeared . . . it was gone. I had to have imagined it.

"Did you find Bigfoot?" she asked me.

"No."

"We thought we found some pubes, but they turned out to be squirrel," Hugh volunteered.

"What?" Heidi asked, revolted.

"Nothing," I said, giving Hugh the "shut up" look. "What else do you want to know?"

"Did Stuey hit on anyone?"

"Everyone," I confirmed.

"Hey now," Stuey shouted and moved around to the back of the sedan to avoid punishment.

"That's what I thought." She nodded in disgust. "What time do you go out tomorrow morning?"

"We left at seven this morning," I told her. "I would assume we'll leave at seven tomorrow morning."

She turned to Stuey for confirmation and he nodded weakly. "I know we met yesterday, but I'm Heidi," she said, extending her hand to me.

"Kristy." I returned the handshake. She had a solid grip, not at all what I was expecting. Up close, I realized she was pretty underneath all the makeup and fake hair.

"I'll be here tomorrow with my crew," she said. "Sorry you had to see that little argument in the parking lot." God, if that was a little argument, I would hate to see what she considered to be a big one. She turned on her high heels and marched back over to where Stuey was now hiding under the car.

I shook my head and laughed. "Good luck with that," I muttered under my breath, turning to go back to my room.

"She's got a set of knockers on her," Edith said. "God bless her, she must have spent a year's salary to afford those."

Edith was half right. Heidi had a great pair, but I'd bet a lot of money they were real. Come to think of it, Heidi had a killer bod. It was just the hair, makeup, and clothes that made her look like a cartoon. I'd love to get ahold of her and fix her. Motherhumpin' ass-clowns, I needed to stop trying to solve the world's problems. Good old Heidi was probably quite happy with the way she looked. God knows it would take at least an hour or two every morning to accomplish a look like that. Plus, if I suggested she change anything, she'd more than likely deck my ass rather than thank me.

"When should we meet up for dinner?" Boo asked.

"How about forty-five minutes?" Kim suggested.

"You know, I think I'm going to stay in tonight," I said casually. I didn't want them to think I didn't want to be seen in public with them.

"Kristy, you have to eat," Rich said, taking my hand in his huge one. "It won't be as much fun without you."

A chorus of agreement came from my team, even the old bags. "Okay," I caved. Rich was right. I had to eat and God knows, Paul Bunyan Lodge and Getaway Resort did not have room service. "Fine, I'll meet you guys back here in forty-five." Mariah gave me a high five and we all went our separate ways.

Getting kicked out of restaurants two nights in a row was an accomplishment I never thought I'd achieve, but I never thought I'd go searching for Sasquatch either. Since Rose and Popo's wasn't an option, we tried Tooties Homestyle Hotdish Eatery. Turned out they had karaoke too. And imagine our surprise when they got offended at Hugh's rendition of a hard-core Snoop Dogg medley. At this rate we'd be eating peanut butter and jelly in our rooms soon.

The two good things were: we'd already finished our dinner and no fistfights ensued. We escaped with only verbal abuse and death threats. Thankfully we were gone before the cops showed up.

"Hugh," I said gently, not wanting to hurt his feelings. "You might want to rethink your artistic choices when you sing in public places where children are present."

"Ya think?" Mariah snorted. I gave her a stern look that wiped the smile right off her face.

"I think you're right, Kristy," Hugh said morosely. "I'm trying to be edgy and current, but I think I'm more of a disco–Top Forty kind of guy."

"I love your Top Forty selections," Boo said.

"I'm sort of fond of the movie and TV sound tracks," Mariah conceded.

"And I love when you butcher my favorite disco tunes, bless your heart," Edith informed Hugh from the back of the van.

"Thank you," Hugh said gratefully. "That means a lot. Kim says I should try for a recording contract, but . . ."

"But you're too much of a pussy, bless your heart, to try?" Mrs. C attempted to finish his sentence.

"Hugh is not a pussy," Rich said sharply, putting Mrs. C in her place.

"Sorry," she muttered.

The silence was long and awkward and Hugh looked like he might cry. I couldn't stand it. "Hugh, I have an idea." I mentally squashed down the part of my brain that was telling me that I would live to regret what I was about to say, and soldiered on. "Why don't you do the sound track for *Searching for Sasquatch*?"

"Do you think they'd let me?" He bounced like a child in the front seat.

"We won't even ask," I said with absolute and unhinged confidence. "You just do it. They don't have any money to pay someone, so you'd be doing them a favor."

"Oh my God," Hugh gasped, his eyes blazing with excitement. "What would I do?"

"Well . . ." I spoke slowly because I had no idea what was going to come out of my mouth next. "You, um, just stand next to Stuey the entire time and go for it. We have enough of us looking for, um . . ."

"Pubic hair." Kim helped me out.

"Yes." I cringed, but agreed. "I was going to say *proof*, but that's definitely more specific. You just stand with Stuey so you're close to the mic, and sing your ass off."

"That's a great idea!" Boo squealed. "Hugh, you might get a recording contract without even trying."

Hugh was now openly sobbing. I was both proud of and mortified by what I'd just done. I had a "fixer" problem. I wanted to make everyone around me okay . . . and I was pretty good at it. I wish I was as successful with myself as I was with others.

Rich squeezed my hand and I caught Kim's eye in the rearview mirror. She winked and blew me a kiss. At the end of a very long and bizarre day, I felt happier than I had in a long time.

"You're joking," I laughed into my phone. If I curled up into a tight ball on my lumpy hotel bed and shut my eyes, I could pretend Rena was in the same room with me instead of hours away in our cozy apartment.

"No," she giggled. "Aunt Moon-Unit has her house under lockdown. She says she's close to eradicating some kind of fucking chi. No one's allowed in and she hasn't come out."

"Does she have food?"

"Yeah, I left a couple of bags of groceries on her front porch this morning and her neighbor ripped me a new one."

God, I missed my best friend. "Why'd the neighbor go after you?"

"Because for some unknown reason, Aunt Moon-Unit spread salt-peter all over her yard."

"Oh hell, that was Edith and Mrs. C's idea, so the chi would stop having sex and multiplying."

"Oookay, that somehow doesn't surprise me," she chuckled. "I have no idea if the chi have stopped playing hide the salami. I was unaware that chi could even get it on, but apparently the neighbor's registered stud bulldog can't get his pink lipstick up."

"That's both disgusting and hilarious," I said, pointing my toes up at the mustard ceiling.

"The unhilarious part is that the beeotch neighbor, Mrs. Bloom-house, is going to sue Moon-Unit for causing canine erectile dys-function."

"Get out of town." I sat up, realizing the old lesbos could wreak havoc even from hundreds of miles away. "Is Moon-Unit upset?"

"Hell no," Rena said. "She thinks it's payback."

"Payback?"

"Yep," she snorted, trying not to laugh. "As the story goes, the late and great Uncle Fucker boinked Mrs. Bloomhouse on a semiregular basis, so Moon-Unit feels vindicated. Plus, that dog shits all over Moon-Unit's hostas."

"That's wrong on all levels." I readjusted myself on the bed so I couldn't see myself in the cracked mirror over the vanity as I posed my next question. I knew my face was red. I felt the heat crawling up my neck. "Um, Rena, I was wondering if you had, um . . ."

"No," she said matter-of-factly. "He left the same day you did."

My stomach dropped and my throat went dry. I squeezed my eyes shut tight and tried to keep the tears from rolling down my cheeks. I couldn't believe he was gone. "He left?" I whispered. "For good?"

"I don't know," she said softly. If she were here I knew she'd hold me in a bear hug and play with my hair. "I told Jack I would withhold sex if he mentioned Mitch's name, but I can find out if he knows anything—if you want me to."

"Um, no . . . it's better this way. I think."

"Okay, but if you change your mind . . ." she said.

"I did," I told her.

"You did what?" she asked, confused.

"I changed my mind. Ask Jack what he knows."

"Do you want to see him again?"

"I have no idea," I said honestly. "I just want to know if he's coming back."

"I'll ask," she said. "Jack might not know anything, but whatever I find out, I'll tell you."

"I love you, Rena."

"I love you too, Kristy."

I hung up and curled into a ball on the bed. I didn't care that I was still fully dressed. I tried to sleep, but it eluded me . . . Images of Mitch's beautiful face were burned into my mind . . . his laugh, how sweet and smart he was, his butt . . . Shitclowns, I needed to push him into a closet in my mind and lock it. He was gone and probably never coming back. No matter how much I wanted him to. I closed my eyes again and focused on my team, the sweet and semisweet bunch of misfits that we were. I wondered what tomorrow would bring. It simply couldn't be any more weird and unsettling than today . . . I hoped.

Chapter 21

"*He found that wearing clothes made him slightly less frightening to humans, if he kept his distance. The main problem with this strategy was that the sheer amount of hair all over his body made the clothing very itchy. Not to mention, it was damn near impossible to find a pair of pants large enough to house his massive pork sword.*

"*His fearless leader had given him a pair of crotchless pants to alleviate the pain of having to encase his jewels in suffocating denim, but it kind of defeated the purpose of disguising himself enough to fit into polite society. His isolation was tearing him apart. His true dream was to be a rock star, but even though he could sing like an angel, his exterior was too horrific.*

"*He cried out to the heavens. 'Why? Why am I such a hairy bastard with such a commodious skin flute?' He received no answer. Why had Zeus forsaken him? Or was it Buddha? Or maybe Bryant Gumbel . . .*

"*He had never seen another of his kind; maybe he was the only one. What kind of cosmic clusterfuck was that? His anger caused him to hatch a plan . . . If the humans didn't want to date him, he would screw with them . . .*"

"Oh my God," Heidi Kugelschmooson gasped, interrupting Boo's recitation. "What kind of revolting bestiality porno is that?"

Heidi had voiced the question that had been in my mind for days, but all it did was piss me off. I could say or think anything about my team I wanted . . . because I cared about them and they were mine. Heidi, on the other hand . . .

"It's the bible. The Bigfoot bible," I snapped. I paused for a second and had a weird déjà vu moment. WTF? Whatever. Seven in the morning was too early to get into a fight with Plastic Barbie, but she left me no choice. "It's written in code," I explained as if she were two years old. "You have to interpret the, um, foul and pornographic text in order to get to the true roots of the Bigfoot myth."

"Really," she said skeptically.

"Really," I shot back, hoping the conversation was over. Kim had picked up coffee and doughnuts before we congregated in the parking lot, so I quickly shoved a glazed one into my mouth to signify the end of the conversation.

"So, what in the hell did that repulsive passage mean?" Heidi asked, not one to give up easily. Assclowns, I could just imagine the article she would write later.

"It means that Bigfoot is a tragic and lonely beast. There is solid proof in that particular passage that there may be just one Bigfoot in existence. His intelligence level is on a par with or higher than humans' and clearly he's been gifted in the genital area," Boo told Heidi without flinching.

"He also enjoys humping trees and large furniture," Hugh added.

"Which is why we will be searching trees for pubic hair today," Mariah told Heidi. "We understand that you will be taking pictures and gathering information for your article, but if you want to come you will have to comb the woods for pubes also."

Heidi Kugelschmooson was shocked or possibly revolted into silence. I'm sure that was a first for her. We all enjoyed her traumatized expression, especially Rich. I guess he'd noticed how disgusted she was by his unusual appearance. Payback is a bitch.

"Where's Stuey?" she choked out, clearly wanting to escape our company.

"He and Stan will be out right before we leave, dear," Kim said, trying to be kind and make Heidi feel welcome. "Here, have a doughnut. Will you and your bald friends be riding in the van with us? I'm sure we could make room."

"No," she answered, declining the ride, but taking the doughnut. "We'll take our own car and follow. I'm not sure we can stay the entire time."

"Well, that's too bad." Kim smiled sweetly. "We really have a wonderful time together and you look like you could use some fresh air and good company."

"Or a breast reduction, bless your heart," Edith muttered.

Heidi whipped around on the old lesbo so quickly, I was surprised her wig didn't fly off. She took three steps toward Edith, completely invading her space. "What did you say?" Her eyes narrowed and Edith shrank back.

"We're on a quest of, um . . . deduction, bless your, um, heart," Edith said, her eyes wide with fear.

"Hmmm." Heidi tapped the toe of her high heel in the dusty gravel of the parking lot. She was dressed totally inappropriately for a hike through the woods, but I'm sure tight dresses and stilettos were the only items of clothing she owned. She eyed the trembling old woman for a moment. "It sounded like you made a comment about my chest," she said way too quietly.

"Oh, ah . . . nope," Edith said, laughing nervously at the obvious misunderstanding. "I never even noticed your huge hooters," she said, backing away.

"Good," Heidi snapped. "Let's keep it that way."

"Of course," Edith agreed meekly.

How in the hell did she do that? They'd been up my backside for a week about my boobs and no matter what I said, they kept it up. I suppose I didn't have that natural command Heidi did. People seemed to do what she wanted them to. She kind of reminded me of . . .

"Are you ready?" Stuey shouted, running around the corner of the building and scaring the hell out of all of us. "Hop into the van and let's get a move on!"

As we piled in, I noticed Heidi having a private chat with Stuey. She grabbed him by the collar of his starched polo and laid a big wet one on his gross little mouth. Stuey walked a very happy and unsteady line back to his sedan.

"I got a call from Moon-Unit last night," Kim said once we were safely in the van and out of earshot of Stan, Stuey, and Heidi.

"What did the crazy old coot have to say?" Mrs. C asked.

"Pot. Kettle. Black," Mariah mumbled.

"She said that Bigfoot is in the area, but they've been sending us in the wrong direction. She believes it's on purpose."

"I knew it," Boo said. "They don't want us to find him."

"I've thought long and hard about this," Kim said. "I think they may know they're sending us on a wild-goose chase, but it may be for the good of the show. If we found Yeti on the first day, the show would be over."

"That's a good point," Rich said. "What do you want to do about it?"

"I think we should follow their directions, knowing that the direction they don't want us to go in is most likely the area where we will find him."

"Do you think we should sneak back out here at night and do an independent search?" Mariah asked, clearly excited about the idea.

"No, absolutely not," Rich said sharply, making Mariah jump. "It's, um, not safe . . . or ethical."

"He's right," Boo agreed. "What if we locate Sasquatch on our own and scare him away? That would ruin the show."

"True," Hugh said slowly, "but if they find him, do you think they would harm him?"

The entire van went silent at that question. Would Stan and Stuey or possibly Heidi and the bald guys try to kill Bigfoot? Or trap him and put him in a zoo . . . or God forbid, experiment on him? WTF? Am I starting to believe Bigfoot actually exists? That there's some depressed wild creature with a gargantuan pecker running around the woods looking for love? Help me, Jesus.

"I don't think their intention is to hurt him," I said, "but maybe we could lead them on a wild-goose chase of our own."

"What do you mean?" Rich asked.

"I'm not really sure, but the more I think about it, the more I wonder if it's really okay to reveal Sasquatch on national TV."

"Praise Jesus," Kim bellowed. "She's a believer!"

"No, I'm not," I insisted. "I'm worried, just in case."

"Riiiight." Mariah grinned.

"Oh my God!" I shouted. "I don't believe in Bigfoot!" Everyone in the van shot me their best skeptical look. "All right, fine," I muttered. "I don't necessarily not believe anymore."

"What do you mean by wild-goose chase?" Hugh asked, grinning at my embarrassing turnaround.

"Honestly, I have no idea." I blew out a long breath and dropped my head back on the seat.

"I know," Boo said. "What if we plant and find clues in an area we know Sasquatch isn't in?"

"We could insist on staying in the same area," Kim said excitedly. "They would look like asses if they forced us to leave a potential sighting."

"I could cry really hard on camera if they tried to make us leave," Boo offered.

"I could damage their nuts," Mariah volunteered. "Off-camera, of course," she added as an afterthought.

"We could threaten them," Edith chimed in.

I wasn't so sure this would work. Not to mention, what kind of proof could we plant? How would we do it without getting caught? Was there actually a reason to go to all this trouble?

"We don't have any proof," Rich noted, reading my mind.

"Oh yes, we do, Mr. Man-boobs," Mrs. C said. She bent over and pulled a bizarre triangular beard-looking thing out of her ever-present sewing bag. It was attached to a hideous lime green knitted belt. The hair was dark and curly and it smelled vaguely of wet dog. I briefly wondered if it was alive.

"What in the hell is that thing?" I gasped, holding my nose.

"It's a merkin, shit for brains," Mrs. C informed me. "A genuine vagina wig made from poodle hair!" She beamed proudly and I threw up a little in my mouth.

The car went silent. I wasn't sure if it was in revulsion or admiration . . . Now I knew why no one had wanted to tell me what a merkin was. Why in the hell would anyone need, want, make, or have a merkin? Was it some weird lesbian sex toy?

"Um, it's all well and good that you carry merkins around with you," Mariah said, trying not to laugh, "but how is a vajayjay wig made out of poodle hair supposed to help us?"

Mrs. C rolled her eyes. "I will cut the cooter wig into eight pieces. I will then hand each of you an eighth of the hair pie. You will put it in your pocket. When that shiny bastard is filming someone else, you will run your section of poodle beaver over as many tree trunks as you can without being caught. The individual hairs of the love taco will get caught in the trees and we can play it off as Sasquatch pubes."

My brain had frozen on the term *love taco*. I didn't think I could get past it. Even if I went to therapy every day for the rest of my life, I would never get that explicitly visual paragraph out of my head. I was now stuck with poodle beaver, hair pie, cooter wig, and the worst of the worst . . . love taco.

"I think that might work," Kim said, impressed. "Good plan, Mrs. C."

Was no one going to comment on her butchering the word *vagina*?

"Maybe you should cut the poodle beaver into seven sections," Hugh offered. "I'll be singing next to Stuey all day and I don't think it would be wise for me to try to distribute any of the hair pie."

"Good point," Edith said, handing Mrs. C a pair of scissors. "You're not as stupid as I thought you were."

Hugh smiled at the backhanded, passive-aggressive compliment. I shook my head and glanced over at Rich, who looked at me with amusement.

"What?" I asked him, trying to bite back my laughter.

"Nothing." He smiled. "It's just fun to watch you."

"Why?" I said, exasperated. "Because I'm going to self-combust?"

"That among other things," he said softly. He gave me a look that made me strangely uncomfortable. I felt a zing of weird. WTF? I am not attracted to a guy with man-boobs, British teeth, and crotch hair on his head. Crapitty, crapitty, crap. What did he really mean by that? Please, God and Jesus and Brett Favre, don't let Rich be getting a crush on me. I want him as a friend. Only. Assclowns, if he thinks he likes me, it will screw everything up . . . I'll just stay away from him today and tomorrow and the next day . . . shit.

Chapter 22

"Oh for God's sake, is he going to sing all day?" Heidi groused as she unwillingly searched the trees for pubic hair.

I grabbed her and yanked her aside before Hugh could hear her griping. She'd been bitching for the last hour straight and I'd had enough. "Listen to me," I hissed quietly. "Hugh has some, um . . . self-esteem issues. Singing is good for him even if it's painful for everyone within hearing distance. So, yes, he is going to sing all day and you're going to enjoy it . . . or at least pretend to."

"You go, girl," she said, grinning and surprising me.

Why in the world did she cover herself up with the makeup and fake hair? She was gorgeous and somehow familiar . . . "Do I know you?" I stared at her and tried unsuccessfully to place her.

"Nope," she said, moving away. "You don't."

I watched her as she sidled up to Stuey and grabbed his tiny butt. Something wasn't right, but I couldn't put my finger on it . . .

"Thank you," Kim whispered, startling me. To keep from falling, I grabbed the tree that I was covertly pubing.

"Holy hell, Kim. You scared me," I said, wiping the poodle hair I'd wasted off my shirt.

"Sorry," she chuckled, helping me remove the damning strands from my clothes. "I wanted to thank you for sticking up for my Hubie. I know he's a bit unusual, but he's a beautiful person and I love him."

"You're welcome," I said with a big ball of emotion clogging my throat. "You guys are lucky to have each other."

"I know, dear." She smiled and tilted her big head to the side. "What about you, Kristy? Do you have a love in your life?"

"Um, well . . . I thought so, but . . ."

Kim stood quietly and watched my struggle. Did I?

"It's okay, sweetie. You don't have to tell me."

"No, no, it's not that. I just think I might have found it and screwed it up," I told her.

"If it was the real thing and meant to be, it will always be there," she said with confidence. "I chased Hubie for three years. He had no idea I even wanted him till the night I jumped him at a Sasquatch Singles gathering."

"Wow," I said, hoping there would be no graphic details.

"Yep," she reminisced fondly. "We got married two days later and have been madly in love ever since." She took my hand in hers. "Kristy, you are a beautiful girl on the outside, but more important, you are just as beautiful on the inside. You will find your love when you are ready to accept him."

"Do you think?" I choked out, feeling the tears well up in my eyes.

"I know." She gave me a hug. "You should let Boo touch you. She has the gift and might be able to tell you what your future holds."

After so many beautiful words, the last couple of sentences made me remember how crazy Kim really was. I nodded, afraid if I spoke, I would say something insulting about insane people.

"Well, dear, it was lovely chatting, but I need to keep distributing my pubic hair." After another quick hug she was off.

The morning in the woods was eventful. The bald photographers, whom we'd never been introduced to, were thrilled and shocked to be the lucky ones to first spot Bigfoot's private hair. There was hair everywhere. That merkin sure packed a punch. Heidi examined the hair and took copious notes.

Mariah and the old ladies stood in the shadows behind the largest trees they could find and tried desperately not to laugh. I was having a difficult time myself. Boo, Kim, and Rich were the only ones who were able to play it off as if they were surprised and delighted by the amazing discovery. Hugh was too deeply ensconced in his music to realize anything was amiss. Edith kept mouthing the word *merkin* to me when no one else was looking. I literally mutilated the inside of my mouth trying to hold it together.

Stuey had the strangest reaction of all. He was baffled by our findings. As the morning progressed and more hair was discovered, he behaved like a child on Christmas morning who'd never experienced Santa's bounty before. Stuey was so excited it was almost alarming. He even did a rendition of "Sweet Home Alabama" with Hugh. That one would take shock treatments to remove from my brain. By the time lunch rolled around, I was exhausted from holding back laughter. Heidi, with her notebook in hand, was interviewing everyone. Especially Rich and Stuey.

"I think we've found enough pubes to agree that Sasquatch has been here," Kim said, grinning from ear to ear. "I vote we come back to this exact spot tomorrow."

Everyone cheered and agreed . . . except Stuey. "I'll have to check with Stan on that," he mumbled, not making eye contact with anyone.

"Why?" Heidi demanded. "Is Stan the boss of you?"

"No, baby," he stammered. "I just have to . . ."

"Tell that shiny mute bastard Stan, bless his heart, that we're coming back here tomorrow or we all quit," Edith said. "We know Bigfoot is here and if that slimy little asshole has a problem with it, his testicles can have a conversation with Mariah's knee."

Boo chose that exact moment to start sobbing and Mariah began stretching her limbs to kick some ass. The old lesbos had done their threatening job well. Stuey paled, and his only friend, his singing partner, Hugh, deserted him to stand with his beloved wife, Kim.

"Um, okay," he whispered, knowing he was outnumbered. "We'll come back here tomorrow."

We walked our twenty minutes back to the cabin, happy that the real Sasquatch, if he truly existed, was safe for another day. Stan couldn't have been less impressed about the pubic hair if he tried. What in the hell was his deal? Did he suspect we were pulling something over on them? Did he know where Bigfoot really was? He was so cold I wouldn't have put it past him to kill our hairy hero . . . and why in the hell did they need us if they were just going to harm Sasquatch? Maybe they were setting us up. Maybe they were going to place the blame of Bigfoot's death on us. Wait a minute . . . Had I totally lost my mind and entered the land of Psychoville?

Yes. The answer was yes.

Heidi was furious that Stuey and Stan locked themselves in a room while we ate lunch. She tried wheedling and begging and then swearing, but to no avail. I thought it was pretty funny, but Rich seemed oddly disturbed.

"Are you okay?" I asked, handing him a Rose and Popo's sub.

"Um, yeah. Why?" he asked, unwrapping the sandwich and taking a bite.

"Well, Heidi seems to be really bothering you."

"Oh." He shook his head, swallowed, and ran his hand carefully through his gnarly hair. "I'm just a bit concerned for the safety of Sasquatch with the paper covering us so closely."

"What do you mean?"

"I just hope that woman doesn't reveal our location. All sorts of local yahoos will start coming out here to hunt down Yeti."

"Assclowns," I muttered. "I hadn't thought of that. Should we talk to her?"

"I'll take care of it," he said.

I was relieved that I didn't have to go toe to toe with Heidi again. I glanced around the room and realized Edith and Mrs. C were missing. Damn it, they were outside emptying the mysterious contents of yet another suitcase. Tomorrow I would slip out and follow them. If they were doing something illegal, I would stop them. As much as they still drove me to want to drink heavily, I did not want them getting in trouble with the law. I wasn't exactly sure what I would do if they were burying dead bodies, but the more I got to know them, the more certain I felt that their covert activity was something far more creatively disturbing than burying the dead.

"Time to go," Stan said as he rejoined us.

"So we'll be searching the same area again tomorrow?" Boo said, not trusting that Stuey had informed Stan.

"Yeah, yeah, sure," he said. "Just find Bigfoot."

"We'll find him," Hugh said, slowly sliding into the splits. "Don't you worry about that, my man."

Stan gave him an odd look, pulled out his cell phone, and left the cabin.

"Nice talking to you too," Mariah laughed and flipped Stan's back the bird.

"Sorry about Stan." Stuey stared at the floor and his shoulders drooped. "He's a little shy. He's really excited about all this, he just doesn't know how to show it."

We all stood silently and stared at Stuey.

"So, um," he continued after the awkward silence refused to end. "We sent some footage to TIT and they loved it!"

"That's wonderful, Stuey," Kim gushed. "They must be so proud of you."

She embraced him and Hugh gave him a high five.

"It's not me," he said modestly. "This whole trip is working out the way it's supposed to because of you guys."

"Stuey, you're no slouch," Boo said, squeezing his hand. "You're a wonderful singer. You and Hugh make a great team."

"Really?" He blushed furiously.

"Absolutely," she said, smiling.

"Okay." Stuey was a little puffed up now that he had fans. "Let's get you kids back to the lodge. Heidi?"

Heidi's head jerked back to the action in the middle of the room. She had been in deep and animated conversation with Rich. "What?"

"Are we still on for a hot date tonight?"

She giggled and tried to fluff her helmet. "Of course we are, Stuey baby."

Eww and gross. I wondered if Rich had had any success convincing her to keep our location out of the paper. Old Heidi seemed to have a few screws loose. I still couldn't place her; maybe she was right . . . maybe I didn't know her.

Thankfully on the ride home we went through a fast food drive-through. The thought of getting thrown out of another restaurant was too much for any of us to bear. I was happy with my chicken sandwich, fries, and vanilla milkshake. I was looking forward to a quiet evening in my mustard-colored hotel room.

"Hey, Rich," I said, stealing one of his fries. "Did the aggressive helmet-wig reporter agree to not give up our location?"

"She agreed." He nodded. "Why do you think she's wearing a wig?"

"Because I saw her brown hair sticking out of it the other day."

"Hmm." He dug into his fries and drifted off into his own world. Thankfully the weird feeling I'd gotten from him yesterday was gone.

I glanced up at the front seat and noticed Hugh feeding Kim as she drove like a bat out of hell. She giggled as he dangled onion rings in front of her lips. Realization hit me like a ton of bricks. Mitch was the one who'd got away . . . or rather the one I'd sent away. He could never be with me like Hugh was with Kim . . . And since that was what had happened, I needed to let it go. It had happened for a reason and there was someone out there who would feed me onion rings too. Well, maybe not onion rings, because I hated them . . . but french fries. I loved french fries. Strangely enough, I felt a weight lift from my shoulders. I could do this. I could forget about Mitch and keep living my life. Of course it helped that I would never see him again.

If I had to see him on any kind of regular basis, I'd be screwed. I pulled on my curls and smiled. I was going to be okay.

"What's going on inside that brain of yours?" Rich asked quietly.

"Dangerous things." I grinned. "No, actually, I just realized I will be okay."

"Did I miss something?" He grinned back. Thankfully the car was dark enough that his horrible teeth only looked crooked.

"Nope, I've just come to terms with a few issues that were floating around in my head."

"The guy?" he asked, raising his eyebrow over his green eye.

"Yep."

"And?"

"He's the one who got away. There's nothing I can do about it now, so I'm going to let it go. As long as I don't see him, and trust me, that won't be an issue, I'll be able to forget him. He hightailed it out of Minnesota the morning after we, um . . . whatever. Suffice it to say he's gone . . . and I will be okay."

Rich was quiet. I knew he was thinking about the horrid girl who had broken his heart. Soon I would have a sit-down with my sweet buddy. I would gently talk to him about a makeover of sorts. I would be very careful. I didn't want to hurt him, but I was hell-bound and determined to help him.

Chapter 23

A forty-five minute steamy hot shower, where I shaved, conditioned, moisturized, scrubbed, and pampered myself, made me feel like a new woman. My hair was wild and smelled like peaches. My skin felt soft and there was no trace of bug spray or merkin anywhere on my body. I pulled on my favorite pajama bottoms and a threadbare wifebeater. I loved the shirt. I hadn't been able to wear it much, because Jack was always in our apartment and the shirt was obscene. Rena called it my hoochie mama shirt. I reheated my unhealthy dinner in the antiquated microwave and I curled up on my lumpy bed for some trashy TV.

For a couple of hours I could pretend I wasn't in Duluth, Minnesota, hunting for a mythical creature that I wasn't even sure was mythical anymore. I found an alarming documentary about Amish teenagers getting wild and I knew all was right with my world . . . except someone was knocking on my door.

Shitmonkeys, I didn't have the energy to deal with anyone at the moment. Particularly someone I'd been living with 24/7.

"Who is it?"

"It's me, Boo," came a sweet little voice from the other side of the door.

"Hey, Boo." I smiled as I opened the door and welcomed her in. "What can I do for you?"

"Can I talk to you for a minute?"

"Sure." I wished the TV had a pause button. Those hungover Amish teenagers were just about to walk into a grocery store for the first time in their lives. Crap. I turned off the disaster about to happen on the TV and waited for the real thing. If Boo had come to talk, something was up.

"I'm worried," she said, sitting down on my bed.

"Uh-huh." I sat down next to her. "You want a fry?"

"Yeah." She took a bite. "These are gross."

"I know," I said, shoving a few in my mouth. "So what are you worried about?"

"About the show and Stan and Stuey. Something isn't right." She took a few more of the gross fries and ate them.

"If you dip them in catsup, they're not as bad," I said, offering her a packet.

"Thanks."

"So what makes you uncomfortable?"

"I touched Stuey's hand today . . . I don't think he's who he says he is."

"Who the hell is he?" I asked. Now I felt all weird and off. The gross fries and chicken sandwich sat in my stomach like lead.

"It doesn't work that way," Boo said pensively. "I don't see exacts. I get feelings and vibes from people. Sometimes I hear a message, but that doesn't happen often."

"So you think his name isn't Stuey?"

"Not necessarily and that's not even the point. I felt an angry fear and excitement in him. He's waiting for something . . . to happen."

"Well, hell . . . do you think he wants to kill Bigfoot?" I asked, doing an internal eye roll at myself. I could forget about trying not to believe anymore.

"That's what I thought at first, but now I'm not so sure," she murmured.

"Maybe you should tell this stuff to Kim and Hugh or Rich." I grabbed a bottle of water and tried to wash the nervous dryness down my throat. I didn't even believe in Boo's magic hoodoo, but something about what she was saying felt right.

"I went by Hugh and Kim's room and they, um . . . seemed kind of busy, so I didn't even knock." She blushed to the roots of her auburn hair and I prayed that my dinner would stay in my stomach.

"What about Rich?" I choked out. Bad evil images of Kim and Hugh getting it on made speaking and focusing difficult.

"I tried his door, but he wasn't home."

"That's weird," I said, doing some yoga breathing. I hoped that by centering myself I could bypass the inappropriate and unsavory porno going on in my brain.

"I thought so too. Maybe he's asleep," she said, lying back on my bed and getting comfortable. I realized I was going to miss the whole Amish debacle . . .

"I'll call Aunt Moon-Unit and have her do a search on Stan and Stuey," I said, tossing the rest of the fries in the trash.

"That's a great idea," she yawned.

"Boo, how old are you and Mariah?"

"I'm twenty-one and Mariah is twenty-three," she said. "Mariah kind of raised me after our mom checked out."

"Is your mom still around?"

"Don't know and don't care."

It was the harshest thing I'd ever heard pass Boo's lips. I knew there was a bad story there. I'd place a bet it was as ugly or uglier than mine . . .

"Sorry about that."

"I'm not. Do you want to know why my sister sounds like a man?" She sat up and stared me down.

"Do you want to tell me?" I asked. My gut clenched; I was feeling a little sick about what she might say.

"My mom was a crackhead. A violent crackhead." Boo's voice was even, betraying no emotion. "She liked to beat on Mariah . . . on her face. She broke her nose so many times that her septum is so deviated and screwed up, she sounds like a man."

I had nothing to say. My own understanding of being beaten by someone who's supposed to love you came crashing down around me. My body began to shake violently and I hopped up off the bed. "I'm so sorry," I whispered, trying to bury my own memories.

"I told you because I knew you would understand."

"What do you mean?" I asked more sharply than I'd intended.

"I've touched you, Kristy. I can tell things."

I nodded and sat back down on the bed. I felt naked and exposed . . . and strangely free. I didn't mind that she knew about my past; I was still a little unnerved about how she'd learned it, but I was starting to believe in things that I'd always scoffed at. "Why doesn't Mariah get her nose fixed?" A plan was forming in my head.

"I've offered to pay for it. I almost have enough money, but she won't let me."

"She needs to do it herself," I told Boo. "Let me think about this . . . I'll come up with a way that won't seem like charity to her."

"You would do that?" she asked, her eyes shining.

"Well, duh," I laughed. "Of course I would. It's what I do. It's what I'm good at."

Boo hopped off my bed and threw herself at me. She hugged me so hard I saw stars. Damn, these sisters were strong. She froze and slowly raised her small hands to my face. She placed her palms on either side of my head and closed her eyes. She was totally freaking me out.

"Oh, Kristy." She grinned. Her voice was breathy. "So many good and happy things for you . . . so many."

"Would you like to be more specific?" I asked nervously. It was hard to deny her gift. She had read my past abuse like a book.

"Nope," she giggled. "When I feel things like this, I never tell. It would be like spoiling Christmas."

"You suck," I laughed.

"Yep," she agreed. "I'm going to take your trash out or else your room will reek of french fries."

"Oh, okay."

"It smells so good in here it would be awful to ruin the mood with rotting french fries."

"Right," I muttered, reminded she was still a little coo-coo.

"Thank you for listening," she said. "I think you're wonderful."

"I think you are too." I hugged her tight and locked the door behind her. The french fry removal was weird, but I was grateful. It would have been rude to wake up to that nasty smell in the morning.

After a quick call to Aunt Moon-Unit's answering machine, I snuggled back into bed. I'd left her a detailed message about the discussion I'd had with Boo and asked her to run a background check on Stuey, Stan, and Heidi. I knew Boo only suspected the guys, but something wasn't quite right with Heidi either.

I found a new *Housewives* that I'd never seen before and I was finally alone. I could wallow in the ludicrous problems of women with too much Botox in their faces and too much time on their hands . . . except someone was at my door. Again.

I was tempted to shout "Go away," but I didn't have it in me. As long as it wasn't the old lesbos, I could handle it. They'd have a heyday with this shirt. The boob jokes would be endless. Although, if it were Kim and Hugh, I might have a difficult time keeping a straight face . . . or my dinner in my stomach.

"Coming," I muttered, wondering if Paul Bunyan Lodge and Getaway Resort had soda machines anywhere. I needed caffeine if I was going to be hosting visitors all night.

Yanking the door open, I tripped over my stupid hiking boot and fell into two very muscular and familiar arms that smelled heavenly. "Shit," I gasped and jumped back into my doorway like I had touched a raging inferno with my bare hands. I quickly slammed the door shut in the face belonging to the arms and dropped to the ground. My knees refused to hold me and my mind was racing like the final lap of the Indy 500.

What in the hell was he doing here and how did he know where to find me? Rena would never have given me up . . . Jack. That asshat Jack told him. I knew I never should have left my information on his machine. If only Rena wasn't so technically challenged and knew how to erase messages on her phone, I wouldn't have had to leave my location with Jack the fucktard.

What was I going to do? I knew it wasn't exactly mature to slam the door in his face, but my other instinct had been horrifying . . . I wanted to jump him. I wanted to tackle him and play tonsil hockey. Shitshitshit, would he go away if I just sat there with my eyes closed and not making a sound?

A light knock at the door was my answer.

"Who is it?" I asked, hoping I was mistaken about his identity.

"Kristy, it's Mitch," he chuckled. The sound of his voice did very warm and inappropriate things to my insides.

"Um, Mitch, it's really late and I have to go to bed, so if you could come back in about, um . . . two weeks or so, that would be better." It was silent on the other side of the door. My heart sank at the thought he would leave so easily. What an asshole. I was right not to love him anymore if he would leave with a half-assed pathetic excuse like that.

"Are you still there?" I called through the door.

No answer.

Oh my God. I did it again. How could I be so stupid? I'd been wallowing in my own self-pity for days because I'd made him leave . . . and now I'd done it again. My body felt like it was on fire and not in a good way. My heart was beating like it was going to fly out of my chest and my eyes welled with tears. Shithats, was this what love felt like? Or was I having a stroke?

I stood up slowly with the help of the doorknob. If he was still on the other side of the door, I would know we were meant to be, but if he was gone . . . Son of a bitch, why didn't the Paul Bunyan Crap Hole Lodge have peepholes? That had to be against some kind of safety code. It would be so much easier to just peep out and know what fate had in store for me. But noooo, I had to open the door and be devastated if he was gone. Of course, the longer I took to open the door, the more likely he would have left.

"Mitch, are you still there?"

"I am, Kristy."

"Why are you here?" I asked. I pressed my forehead to the door, took a deep breath, and tried to slow my pounding heart.

"Because I miss you. I can't stop thinking about you and I don't believe you really want me to go away."

"That's kind of presumptuous of you," I huffed, narrowing my eyes at the door.

There was a long silence. I wondered again if he'd left, but deep down I knew he was still there.

"Am I right?" he asked.

It was my turn to create a long silence. *It's better to tell the truth than lie . . . Lying takes too much brain power. The simple truth is always easier to remember . . .* "Yes, you're right."

"Will you open the door?"

"Will you be offended if I tackle you?" I needed him to know the dangers.

"I'd be honored," he laughed, sending little shock waves through me. I was in so much trouble.

I warily opened the door. How in the motherhumpin' hell did I not remember how gorgeous he was? He literally took my breath away. Well-worn jeans with a fitted light blue T-shirt to match his eyes, and work boots—he made my mouth water. And the memory of what was underneath . . . help me, Jesus.

I was floating above myself . . . felt hot, felt cold, felt the warm salty tears fall from my eyes and roll down my cheeks. What was happening to me?

"Don't cry, Goldilocks," he said, gently wiping my tears away.

"I'm sorry. I just . . ."

"You just what?" he said, piercing me with those damn eyes. Wait a minute . . . one was blue and one was green. How in the hell did I not notice that before?

"What's wrong with your eyes?"

"What do you mean?" he asked, rubbing his eyes as if I meant he had something stuck on them.

"Look at me," I said, moving close. They were both blue. I was losing it. Duluth was sucking my brain out. I could have sworn he had two different-colored eyes, but it must have been the light.

"So, are you going to invite me in?" He gave me a lopsided grin and I grabbed the door so I wouldn't fall.

"Are you going to behave?" I asked, watching him closely.

"Only if you want me to . . . The choice is yours."

I stepped back slowly, never taking my eyes from his face. "I'd like you to come in, Mitch."

His grin stopped my heart. "I'd love to."

And he did.

Chapter 24

The room grew very small all of a sudden and my choice of outfit seemed very bare. Mitch was having a difficult time keeping his eyes off my assets. Not that I took offense, but my assets, having a mind of their own, were letting him know how much they liked his admiration.

"So, Duluth is a neat little town," I babbled, moving around the tiny space. My hands were fisted into balls at my sides. I didn't trust them. "I haven't gotten out much, but there seems to be plenty of karaoke and all-you-can-eat restaurants. The people here are friendly unless you serenade them with X-rated music . . . Well, actually only when their children are with them. Although, they might get pissed even without their kids . . . I don't know. I haven't tested that theory yet and . . ."

"Kristy," Mitch laughed. "Relax."

I backed myself up against the wall on the other side of the room, as far away as I could get in the tiny mustard yellow dump. "I can't."

"Can I speak?" he asked, sitting down on my bed and giving me my space.

I nodded. I was terrified that if I opened my mouth I would tell him to strip.

"I want you to know that I'm sorry. I screwed up by not telling you the entire story." He paused and ran his hands through his hair.

My stomach plummeted to my toes. This was not going the way I wanted it to. He was supposed to express his undying love for me and tell me everything would be all right. Shitmonkeys.

"It's okay." I stared at the floor. "It was kind of you to come all the way to apologize, but I have a big day tomorrow and I have to get some sleep. So, um . . ."

"Shit, I'm screwing up again," he moaned.

I glanced up and noticed his hair was standing up all over the place. Clearly he took out his anxiety on his head. He looked so lost, and even though my heart was breaking again, I giggled.

"My angst is funny?" He smiled and raised his eyebrows.

"Nope. Your hair."

He stood up and checked himself out in the mirror. "You're right," he laughed. "Scary."

This was getting harder with every passing moment. I needed him to leave. We were on two very different pages . . . "Mitch, it's late and I . . ."

"Kristy, stop. Please let me finish."

"Okay." I slid down the wall and sat on the floor. I knew at the end of his "I'm sorry" speech I would dissolve into a puddle anyway. Breaking up twice just seemed so unfair, but I loved him enough to let him continue . . . even though it was killing me.

"I'm just gonna do this," he muttered. He took a deep breath and let it rip. "I am crazy about you. You're all I think about all day long. I can't concentrate. I can't sleep. I have never felt like this. Ever. I know I omitted some important things, but I was afraid you wouldn't take me seriously . . . and I screwed up. God." He sat back down on the bed and put his head in his hands. "I'm in love with you, Kristy," he said through his fingers. "And I don't know what to do about it."

Oookay, this was much better. I kept my eyes trained on the nasty, yellowish carpet. I wanted him to suffer for at least thirty-two more seconds . . .

"Can you say something? Please?" he asked. I could feel his eyes on me. My inner-hooker, a term Rena had coined, wanted to yell "Let's fuck," but I was not controlled by my inner-hooker . . . at least not right at that moment. But in two minutes—it'd be anybody's call.

I glanced up and got sucked into everything that was Mitch. His beauty, his kindness, his rockin'-hot bod, his bitable lips . . . and his love. How both of us could have fallen so quickly was a mystery to me, but in this magical moment I wasn't questioning anything.

"Do you still have the same job?" I asked.

"I do," he said so quietly I almost missed it.

"I don't care."

"You don't?" he asked, covering the small amount of space between us.

"Nope." I smiled, looking up at him. God, he was huge. "I've been miserable. I don't care anymore. I don't want to make any promises to each other that we can't keep. I know this may not last and I'll be heartbroken, but I just want to be happy . . . right now. Hell, I could get eaten by Bigfoot tomorrow or attacked by people who are pissed off about my friend Hugh's profane concerts or . . . Oh my God, I'm babbling."

"You are," he laughed and pulled me to my feet, "but I have a remedy for that."

"You do?" I whispered. His lips were so close to mine, I could taste him.

"I do."

His lips touched mine and I felt like I was flying. Which was a good thing because I knew my legs were not going to hold me up. I heard bed springs creak and for the life of me, I couldn't have told you where I was . . . because I didn't care. The only thing I knew for sure was that I was alone with Mitch and he was mine.

His tongue teased the seam of my lips. I giggled and kept them closed tight so he'd have to work for it, but when his hand closed over my breast and pinched my nipple, I squealed and gave him exactly what he wanted.

"I can't wait," I gasped, clawing at his clothes.

"Me neither." He yanked my shirt over my head and froze. "God-damn, you're gorgeous."

"And they're real," I laughed. He ran his hands over my breasts reverently, making little shocks jerk through my body and travel straight to my panties when he pinched my nipples.

"Very real," he whispered before his wet mouth closed over one of my painfully hard nipples. He drew hard, almost to the point of pain, and it was making me see Jesus. My back arched and I'm fairly sure I screamed. Everything with Mitch was just a little too much, a little too far, a little too hot, a little too rough . . . and I loved it. With every electrified fiber in my body, I luurve it.

"You don't wear a bra?" he asked as he expertly slid my pajama bottoms down before I noticed what he was doing.

"Not to bed, dorko." I pushed him down, unbuttoned and pulled his jeans and gray boxer briefs off, and came face-to-face with the largest erect penis I'd ever seen in my life. I mean, I knew it was very nice from my over-the-shoulder glance when I was cuffed to the silverware drawer, but up close and personal, it was a monster. I didn't realize I was motionless until I heard him laugh.

"Everything all right?" he asked. His eyes were hooded with desire, but they sparkled with amusement.

"Um, no . . . I just, um . . . you know. You're freakin' huge. I'm not sure that's going to fit inside me." I slapped my hand over my mouth and wanted to die. Talk about what not to say during foreplay . . .

"We'll just have to make sure you're very, very ready," he chuckled, pulling my mostly naked body flush against his. Lifting me up with seemingly no effort, he laid me down on my back. The lumpy bed felt like a million-dollar mattress to me now. "God, I want you bad."

"Me too," I said in a voice I didn't recognize. My inner-hooker had apparently gotten lodged in my throat.

Mitch hopped off the bed and dug through the pockets of his jeans, which I'd thrown across the room while in shock over his um, girth. "Oh shit," he muttered. In all his glorious nakedness he dropped to the floor on all fours and started searching the carpet as if his life depended on it. As fine as the view of his spectacular man-butt was, his behavior was a tad alarming.

"Um, Mitch?"

"Yep?" he said, combing the floor.

"Do we have a problem?"

"Do you have any condoms?" he asked.

"Nope."

"Then we have a problem."

I jumped off the bed in nothing but my purple thong and helped with the prophylactic search and rescue mission.

"Are you sure you had them?" I asked, looking under the bed.

"Positive," he muttered, ransacking his jeans again. "Son of a bitch," he moaned.

I glanced over and giggled. Even under duress, he was still sporting a massive hard-on. "Mitch?"

"Yes?" he answered, looking up at the ceiling for either divine intervention or condoms.

"I'm on the pill and I have a clean bill of health."

His pulled his gaze slowly from the ceiling and zeroed in on me with white hot intensity. "I have a clean bill too." He grinned like a wolf about to eat his prey. "In fact, I've never in my life had sex without a condom."

"Um, neither have I," I whispered, as my excitement took the express train to the stop between my legs.

I'm fairly sure he flew across the room. He scooped me up and tossed me back onto the bed. He stood there completely naked, looking every inch the Greek god that he was. He was the most exquisite man I'd ever seen; just looking at him made my body surge with heat.

"I cannot tell you what the thought of being inside of you with nothing to separate us is doing to my head right now." His voice was rough with desire and need. I couldn't say anything. I was too overwhelmed. "Take off your panties and open your legs. Now, Kristy."

My bossy alpha man was back and I almost came at the sound of command in his voice. Damn if he didn't know my buttons. I slowly slid my thong down my legs. His blue eyes held mine and I could barely breathe.

"Open for me, baby."

I hesitated. All of a sudden I was shy.

"Do it, Kristy," he whispered.

I did.

He ran his big hands down my inner thighs and stared at my most intimate places. "You are so beautiful." He bent down and kissed me where I'd rarely been kissed.

"Oh, Mitch," I gasped. "I don't think . . ."

"You don't think what?"

"I mean you don't have to, um . . . well. I just don't want you to think that . . ." I faded out and covered my heated face with my hands.

"Kristy, look at me," he demanded. I peeked through my splayed fingers. "I love what I'm doing right now. I. Love. It."

And I did too. I loved it into one of the most mind-shattering orgasms I'd ever had. For a brief moment I was worried I'd snapped his neck with my thighs . . .

While my body floated like water he slowly made his way back up. Kissing and tasting every inch of my skin. "I am so turned on right now I don't know what to do," he moaned into my ear and my body shuddered. I didn't think I had anything left but his voice was as hot as his tongue. He bit into my earlobe and my body convulsed around him. His lips closed over mine—I could taste myself and it was wildly erotic. "I can't wait anymore. I need to be in you . . . now."

Answering with coherent English was an impossibility so I wrapped my legs around his waist. He took my hand and put it on his engorged cock. "Guide me into you, baby." He was having a difficult time with speech. I couldn't speak at all.

He was like thick steel covered in silk. So hard and so smooth at the same time. I was so in love with this man. As nervous as I was about his size, I was also turned on beyond reason. I led him to my opening and helped him enter me. He pushed the head of his shaft into me and I gasped. I'd never felt anything so amazing in my life.

"God, you're so wet and tight," he hissed, one hand grasping my ass and the other tangled in my wild hair. He forced me to look at him as he slid into me inch by inch.

"Ohhh," I gasped. "Please . . . slow . . . Oh God," I whispered. It felt so good, my body was on fire, but I was still unsure if I could handle all of him. My body had softened to accommodate him, but . . .

"You are so hot," Mitch ground out through clenched teeth. "Nothing in my life has ever felt as good as you do."

He was filling me beyond capacity. He rubbed my clit with his thumb as he slowly pushed deeper into me. I was at that insane place between pleasure and pain that turned me on like nothing else could. I was losing control and my body was sending him messages before it was quite ready to handle the consequences. My hips started to buck and my body was writhing beneath his. He took my movement as a sign that I was ready for him. I felt his body tense and I tried to speak. I really did . . . to tell him to wait, but my traitorous inner-hooker kept twisting and turning and my arms pulled him closer. Sounds were coming from somewhere deep inside me. I couldn't stop him or myself. I didn't want to. With one deep and forceful thrust, he buried himself to the hilt.

I screamed.

I was spinning off an abyss and loud explosions were going off inside of me. My body jerked in protest. I could literally feel him pressed against my womb. I was sure he had torn me apart. Just when I was going to beg him to stop . . . something happened. The pain evaporated, my body adjusted, and an orgasmic fire began to glow in my belly. I gripped him inside of me and little fissions of heat consumed me. He groaned and pushed even deeper.

"You're mine, Kristy," he whispered. He was triumphant. His eyes blazed a beautiful icy blue.

My body started to tingle and there was a roaring in my ears. What had begun as pain had turned into the most intense pleasure I'd ever experienced. He was moving in and out of me . . . I was physically stretched to my limit. I wanted . . . Oh God, I wanted more. I arched and slammed my pelvis into his, meeting each thrust with a force I didn't know I was capable of. I was scared and excited and wildly out of control. I'd known it would be good, but this was . . . Oh. My. God. I was spiraling toward an orgasm that was going to kill me dead.

Just as I almost passed out with pleasure, I felt him stiffen on top of me. I felt his release and met it with my own. He had made me his and I had made him mine in the most intimate way possible.

"I love you," I whispered, running my hands through his hair and kissing his swollen lips with my own. "I think I might be dead," I giggled as I tried to push his dead weight off me.

He rolled off. Still breathing hard, he played with my hair. "Did you go to heaven or hell?"

"Heaven." I snuggled close. "How long can you stay?" I asked, dreading the answer.

"For a couple of hours, but I'll be back in two days." He pulled me even closer and I breathed him in. "I want you to fall asleep in my arms," he said quietly. "I'll leave after you're asleep."

"Do you promise you'll come back?" I stared at his chest and bit the inside of my cheek. I would not cry.

He gently lifted my face to his. "I promise."

"Okay then." I smiled and closed my eyes. I was playing a game with no rules. The winner would live happily ever after and the loser would get their heart ripped out . . . A sane person should run for the hills, but living in Duluth, searching for Bigfoot, qualified me as certifiable . . . and right in that moment, that was A-OK with me.

Chapter 25

"So, as I was saying, we've chosen to stay in this area because of the wealth of, um . . ." I fumbled, pulling my jacket tighter around me. It was a chilly July morning deep in the woods of Duluth.

"Pubes," Edith shouted.

"Shut the hell up," I hissed. "Oh shit, I mean shoot. Can you edit that out?" I asked Stuey.

"Yeah, yeah."

"Okay great." I took a cleansing breath and continued. "The sheer amount of what we believe to be Sasquatch hair in this particular area is astounding."

"Show some hair," Stuey said.

I grabbed the sandwich bag of shredded merkin with two fingers and held it up in front of the camera. "This is proof of Bigfoot's rather, um, unusual hobbies." *Help me Jesus.* "We found the hair on the trees and, you know, we, um collected it."

Mrs. C took the opportunity to shove me out of the way and finish the introduction.

"The pubes were found at crotch level embedded in the bark, proving that Sasquatch is a hairy son of a bitch that likes to hump trees. The scientists traveling with us, who shall remain nameless, have determined the hair to be pubic and of a species unfamiliar to the area." Mrs. C finished and was shoved out of the way by Edith.

"According to the Bigfoot bible, Sasquatch is masterfully built and hung like an ox. He may be the only one of his kind in existence. Therefore, his huge man-tool makes his life lonely and miserable. There are very few female humans or animals that could hop on that love stick and live to tell."

"Oh Jesus," a purple-faced Kim screeched and tackled Edith to the ground before she could continue. As the wrestling match on the ground escalated into what could qualify as a bitch-slap-fest, Boo shoved me back in front of the camera and gave me the silent signal to keep talking. I got momentarily sucked into her hideous lime green and Day-Glo orange sweater before I remembered the camera was still rolling. Shitmonkeys, what could I say after that?

"Some of our group, um . . . missed their, you know . . ."

"Medication," Mariah volunteered.

"Medication this morning and, ahhh . . . might be slightly confused. Soooo, I think I'll close here and invite you to watch us search for Sasquatch!" I smiled for the camera and hoped my face wasn't shiny. It might be chilly, but I'd worked up a whopper of a mortification sweat.

"And cut," Stuey said, lowering the camera and grinning like a fool. Why wouldn't he be grinning? We were providing some hugely embarrassing and disgusting reality TV. We were sure to be a hit . . .

"Let's find Bigfoot!" Hugh squealed and then broke into a Guns N' Roses medley. I was truly in hell, but it didn't matter because I was in love and I'd had the best sex of my entire life about eight hours ago. I could deal with anything today.

I glanced over and realized both Mariah and Boo were sporting the hideous shelter sweaters. As blindingly green, orange, and ugly as they were, I wished I had brought mine along. My thin jacket wasn't keeping me exactly warm.

"You ready to hunt?" Rich asked.

Sweet baby Jesus, what in the heck was he wearing? Drawstring, plaid Jeannie pants had replaced the sweats, and his muumuu was trimmed in silver thread. Maybe he was gay . . . It didn't matter, but I hoped he would trust me enough to be himself with me. I supposed today was as good a day as any to carefully broach the dental subject . . .

"I'm ready." I smiled. "Are we supposed to plant any more clues today?" I whispered as quietly as I could. I didn't want Stuey, Heidi, or the Baldies to hear me.

"No, I'm sure there are some poodle pubes left in the trees from yesterday," he chuckled.

"No doubt," I agreed.

As we made our way deeper into the woods, I noticed that Hugh had switched from Guns N' Roses to Enya. His playlist was alarmingly vast and unfortunate.

"You seem happy today," Rich commented as he searched the ground for footprints.

"I am. I'm happier than I've ever been in my life," I said, squatting down next to him and playing with some leaves.

"And why would that be?" he asked.

"Because I didn't screw it up."

"You lost me," he said.

"I didn't lose the guy."

"Did he call?"

"Nope," I grinned. "He showed up."

"At *Paul Bunyan*?" He stopped searching and gave me his full attention.

Damn, I could have sworn his right eye was brown and his left eye was green before, but today it was just the opposite. My observation skills clearly sucked. Whatever. "Yep, he showed up last night and we, um . . . talked for a really long time."

"And?"

"I love him and he loves me."

"That's wonderful, Kristy." He smiled and squeezed my hand. "I'm happy for you."

"Me too." Now that I was happy, it was time to help my big buddy. I wanted him to be happy and in love too. "Um, Rich, I was wondering if you'd ever been to the orthodontist before."

"Why would I do that?" he asked, baffled.

Fucktard, this was going to be more difficult than I had anticipated. "Well . . ." I racked my brain for a delicate approach. "I noticed that your teeth are just a tiny bit crooked and that can lead to your bite being off and then you'll have problems when you get older . . . you know?"

"Do you know a good orthodontist?" he asked, keeping his mouth as closed as he could while still trying to get words out.

I felt sick at his embarrassment, but there was no turning back now. "Yes, as a matter of fact I do. It's my roommate, Rena's, dad, and he does majorly discounted work."

"I could certainly pay for a small adjustment," he said. "I make a good wage as a magician."

"I'm sure you do," I sputtered, worried that I'd offended him even more, "but I didn't know if you had a magician's dental plan and um, I just thought that . . ."

"I think you are a lovely and caring girl," he said, saving me from myself. He gave me a closed-mouth smile and I felt bad for bringing his shortcomings up. I would definitely hold off on the exercise and eating plan till another day. "I might check this gentleman out when we get back."

"I'd be happy to go with you," I offered, relieved that he didn't seem too angry or hurt.

"I would like that very much."

We continued our footprint search in a comfortable silence. I pondered if I'd ever get to mention his hair to him. Maybe I'd just bring him by the Steves' salon and let them broach that subject. The Steves had a wonderful way of making people think whatever they wanted to do to them was the person's own idea. It was a talent I didn't have. That's exactly what I would do. I didn't want Rich to think I was judging everything about him . . . I just wanted to help make the outside as attractive as the inside.

"Can I join you two lovebirds?" Heidi Kugelschmooson asked.

WTF? Was she serious? I glanced up at her and gave her a hard stare. She looked ridiculous. Her stilettos and skin-tight minidress looked silly out in the middle of the forest and her nipples announced that she was freezing. I wondered how she hadn't snapped an ankle yet.

"Ahhh, Miss Kugelschmooson," Rich said in his crisp kind-of-British accent. "I'm afraid you are mistaken. Kristy and I are just friends. She has a lovely and devoted boyfriend who adores her and I myself prefer the bachelor status at the moment. As to your joining us, the answer is no."

Heidi narrowed her eyes at Rich and stomped off to bother someone else.

"You certainly laid that on a little thick," I giggled. "Why didn't you want her to search with us, I mean, besides the fact she's annoying as all get-out?"

"Isn't that reason enough?" he asked.

"I suppose it is."

Aside from the WWE match between Edith and Kim, the rest of the morning was fairly uneventful. We did find more pubes, well, Mrs. C did. It made me wonder if she had distributed another merkin. I was tempted to ask her how many she had, but stopped myself in time. My self-training to refrain from asking questions that I knew would haunt me was going well. Heidi was playing Stuey for all he was worth. Why in the hell was she doing that? She couldn't possibly be attracted to him. Did she already know him? The puzzle was getting more complicated and I had never been good at puzzles. I hoped Aunt Moon-Unit would have some information soon on our trio of Bigfoot-killer suspects.

"I'm so hungry, I could eat a goddamn poodle," Edith yelled, giving us all the spastic eyebrow when Stuey wasn't looking.

I snorted and turned away. I was unsure if that meant she actually wanted to eat a poodle or if it was some gross sexual reference to eating the merkin or if she had finally lost her mind. It was probably a combination of all three.

"She's going to get us busted," Mariah huffed.

"Personally, I think Stuey is too stupid to catch on to anything," Boo said as we walked back to the cabin for lunch. "But I'm not so sure about Heidi Kugelschmooson and her bald buddies. They give me the creeps." She shuddered.

"Have you touched them?" I asked. I'd finally drunk the Kool-Aid. I was a firm believer in Boo's gift. My still-present afterglow from last night's sex-a-thon made me a believer.

"It's odd," she mused. "I've tried, but every time I get close enough, they move. It's like they know I have this ability."

"That's impossible," Mariah said, putting her arm around her younger sister. "There's no way they could know, unless someone told them and I can guarantee no one from our group would do that."

I agreed with Mariah. No one would have even thought to talk about Boo's gift. I'm not even sure the old lesbos knew about it. Hugh was too busy rocking out and Kim would protect all of us with her own life. Rich . . . Rich was the most trustworthy person I'd ever come across. No . . . no leaks from our side.

"What in the fuck is that?" Mariah stopped dead in her tracks and gaped at the cabin.

I stopped beside her and stared. What in the *fuck* had happened while we were out rooting around for bogus Bigfoot evidence? All the windows of the cabin had been covered with thick plywood and nailed shut. It looked like an abandoned building or one that had gotten all the windows shot out of it.

"Stan reinforced the cabin while we were out," Stuey said proudly. "We're going to store the expensive camera equipment in here instead of letting it sit in the trailer unattended all the time."

It was the first semi-intelligent thing I'd heard him say, although I wasn't sure how comfortable I'd be with leaving eight hundred thousand dollars' worth of cameras and lights in the woods in the middle of nowhere. Thankfully . . . not my problem.

"Well, it looks like hell, but I'm hungry," Edith said, stomping into the cave that used to be a light-filled cabin.

We obediently filed in after her to be met by Stan and a big take-out bag full of subs from Rose and Popo's. I zeroed in on the old ladies. I knew they'd leave at some point. I'd seen them shové another huge suitcase into the van's cargo hold that morning. Today, I was going to follow them . . .

"God bless you and your shiny little asscracks," Mrs. C bitched to Stan and Stuey, "but can't you homo, um . . . sapiens find some goddamn food that isn't from an establishment that caters to fucktards?"

I couldn't believe she'd used my favorite word. Did it mean we had a kinship? I prayed not.

"It's the only place open at six in the morning," Stan said, ignoring her upset and throwing the sandwiches on the table. "Eat, or not. I don't care."

"Not," Edith said, giving her sister a covert look. Mrs. C nodded back and they headed outside. I knew it would take them a few minutes to pull out the suitcase, so I leisurely grabbed a sub and went out after them. Thankfully everyone had been too busy getting their lunch to notice my escape. Plus, the simple fact that there was only one lamp in the now very dark cabin made slipping away quite easy.

I stayed hidden behind Stuey's sedan and watched them drag the suitcase from the van. After a quick scan of the area, they nodded at each other and hightailed it into the woods. Holy Lutheran God, I'd never seen them move so fast in the entire time I'd known them. They were headed to the exact area where we suspected Bigfoot was really hiding. Were they searching for him on their own? Maybe they were trying to scare him off so he couldn't be captured. I wondered if Kim knew what they were up to.

In a move of what I suspected would be gargantuan stupidity, I followed them. It turned out to be less stupid and more mind-boggling than anything I could have imagined.

About fifteen minutes in, they stopped and pulled what appeared to be lime green and Day-Glo orange knitted hammocks from the suitcase, along with heavy bark-colored rope and metal clamps. WTF?

"How many did we set yesterday?" Edith asked from halfway up a huge tree.

How in the hell did she get up there and how did I miss that? Wait a minute . . . those lime green and orange hammocks looked alarmingly familiar. No. Freakin'. Way. Mrs. C and Edith were the anonymous sweater donors? I'd been wearing a sweater made by crotchety old lesbians who were obsessed with my boobs?

Ooo, I had their number now. Their nasty, God bless them, skanky personalities were a cover for two old ladies who truly cared. Well, they were still nasty and skanky . . . but they cared. Maybe Grandma was right. There was more to Edith and Mrs. C than met the eye, but that still didn't explain what they were doing.

I watched in utter shock as Mrs. C shimmied up a tree about ten feet from the one Edith was hanging out of.

"We set seven yesterday. We need to set at least six today. Catch," she yelled as she tossed a long cord of bark-colored rope her sister's way. It was difficult to see because the rope blended perfectly with the trees. And what in the hell were they setting six of today?

"You throw like a sissy," Edith cackled as she hung upside down from a limb and attached her rope to the tree with clamps.

"Takes one to know one," Mrs. C panted as she shimmied back down the tree. "Get your ass down here and help me finish."

"Are we going to test this one?" Edith asked, sliding down the tree like a fireman on a pole. *Shit, that had to hurt.* Yet she seemed fine and hustled over to secure the hammock to the ropes.

"I think we should. These are different pulleys than the ones we used yesterday. They have more spring action," she added gleefully.

They secured the eye-scorching hammock to the ropes hanging from the trees, pulled it down to the forest floor, and covered it with leaves. They were so skilled that I couldn't make out the knitted atrocity on the ground. I held my breath and waited for what came next.

"Get a log, you old dyke," Mrs. C told Edith.

"You get it," she shot back. "I got the log yesterday."

"Fine, you lazy heifer," Mrs. C groused.

She grabbed a log off the ground that had to weigh at least fifty pounds. She lifted it with ease and tossed it onto the leaf-covered hammock. The weight of the log caused the hammock to violently snap up and choke the log, leaving it dangling about ten feet in the air. I bit back a gasp and inched farther away from the certifiable nutbags. What in God's name were they doing?

"Fantastic!" Edith squealed and gave her sister a high five. "Spray it."

Mrs. C pulled out a spray bottle and squirted the entire hammock. "That should do it."

Edith quickly made her way back up her tree, released a latch on the clamp, and the log fell back to earth with a thud. They quickly buried the hammock under leaves again and were back on the move.

"That Moon-Unit is a crazy old coot, bless her heart, but thank the Good Lord Lutheran Jesus that she had a recipe to make Sasquatch repellent. I'd have a coronary if we harmed Bigfoot," Edith grunted as she pulled the suitcase along.

"We just need to make goddamn sure none of our group goes down this path."

"This is the only path they won't send us down, you know that. You're the one that overheard the conversation." Edith swatted her sister in the back of the head.

"What was it that slimy little shiny prick said?" Mrs. C stopped and tried to remember.

"If you're getting senile, you old queer, I'll put you in a home so fast," Edith warned, laughing. "What he said was, they can take any path except the southwest one. The million-dollar payday is at the end of that path and if anyone fucks it up he'll kill them."

"That's right." Mrs. C grinned. "Won't they be surprised when they go to find their million-dollar prize and end up strung up like floating sacks of shit?"

The women paused in their tracks and laughed so hard I almost giggled. Their glee at stringing up Stan, Stuey, and possibly Heidi and the Baldies was contagious. I bit down hard on my lip to keep from joining them. I didn't want them to know they were being watched. I wouldn't put it past them to string me up for spying on them. The one thing I didn't get was the secrecy . . . Was it because they'd be busted as the phantom sweater makers? Or because they didn't want anyone else to get in trouble? If I had to bet, I'd say sweaters.

I sucked in a big breath of fresh air and blew it out slowly. The gals had disappeared into the trees. It was safe for me to go back. I didn't think I would share what I'd seen with anyone just yet, not even Rich. I was unsure why, but it felt right.

As I wandered back, a huge weight lifted from my shoulders. My relief that Sasquatch would be safe was palpable. Wait a minute . . . Did I actually believe that crap? I stopped and reassessed . . . I was pretty sure I did. I glanced up at the sky to make sure it wasn't falling . . . It wasn't. Hi, my name is Kristy . . . and I believe in Bigfoot. Shit.

Chapter 26

We stopped for Mexican take-out on the way home. I couldn't order a taco or even say the word. The old ladies had forever ruined my favorite Mexican treat with their litany of vaginal terms, including my favorite, the dreaded love taco . . . hair pie wasn't far behind. I ordered a burrito and some chips and salsa. I wondered if Mitch liked Mexican. I realized there were so many things I had yet to discover . . . and I couldn't wait.

Everyone else in the van ordered tacos. The irony was almost too much to bear. Rich ordered ten. I blanched inwardly and realized the talk about nutrition was going to have to come sooner rather than later.

"I think the cabin feels spooky with the windows all boarded up," Boo said. "I don't like it."

"Do you get a bad vibe?" Kim asked, concerned.

"It doesn't work that way. I feel nothing from objects, only people."

"What are you dumb-ass idiots, bless your hearts, blabbering about?" Edith asked, shoving a taco into her mouth. I supposed she was hungry. She'd missed lunch due to her covert tree swinging and trap setting.

"Boo has a gift," Kim told her. "Through touch, she can read things about people."

"I call bullshit," Mrs. C shouted.

I whipped around and confronted her before Mariah could jump over the seat and kick her ass. "You believe in Bigfoot, but you can't fathom someone having psychic abilities?"

"That's right, Little Miss Hooters," Edith said with a mouthful of taco. I averted my eyes so I wouldn't heave.

"Well, you're wrong," I said, keeping my eyes glued to her forehead. "Boo has a gift and that's all there is to it."

"Prove it," Mrs. C challenged.

"Give me your hand," Boo said, leaning back over her seat toward the ladies.

"Groundhog!" Kim shrieked, swerving to avoid squashing the rodent. I guess killing all of us was okay. Thankfully we were all wearing seat belts . . . except for Boo. Boo went flying and was saved from bashing headfirst into the window by Rich's big flabby arms. She gasped and stared at Rich with such an intensity, I felt uncomfortable. He stared back equally hard. Boo, with a smirk on her face, gave him a curt nod and reached out for the old ladies. WTF? Had she discovered something about Rich?

"Give me your hand," she told Edith.

"All right," Edith snorted. "Tell me my future, O Great Madam Boo."

"Listen here, you old lesbo," Mariah grunted, taking off her seat belt and beginning her climb back to rip Edith a new one.

"Shhh, it's okay, Mariah," Boo said in a soothing tone. "Sit back down." Mariah did.

Taking Edith's hand, Boo closed her eyes and started to giggle. I wondered if she saw the old bags shimmying trees and making sweaters.

"Give me my hand back," Edith hissed, getting nervous.

Boo's grip tightened. I could tell by Edith's grimace. Boo held on tight and continued to giggle.

"What?" I asked. I couldn't take it. Edith had worked up a sweat and I was sure she didn't doubt Boo's gift anymore. That, or Boo was breaking her fingers.

Boo let go and grinned from ear to ear. "You are a good woman, Edith. You are loving and you care about others . . . deeply."

"Horsecrap," she muttered, massaging her hand.

"You can't fool me," Boo laughed. "In fact, I think I adore you and want you for a grandma."

"Holy hell," Mariah groaned. "They're actually good?"

"Really, really good." Boo nodded. "Both of them."

"You're full of shit, little girl," Mrs. C threatened. "We are not good. Never have been and never will be, so just get that out of your fool head this minute."

Boo laughed with delight. The sound rang through the van and made everyone smile . . . except the old gals.

"We are not good!" Edith shouted. "All of you, wipe those smiles off your pieholes or I'll do it for you . . . with my boot."

"Don't you love my sweater?" Boo asked me as she crawled back to her seat.

"I do," I said, fingering the soft knitted material. "The colors obviously tell us the knitters have no taste whatsoever, but they're beautifully made and soooo cozy. I have one at home that I wear all the time."

"I just think the fact that someone makes them anonymously and gives them to the shelter is wonderful," she said with great satisfaction in her voice.

I glanced into the rearview mirror and covertly examined the old girls. They looked like deer caught in the headlights, terrified that Boo was going to out them. Good Lord, they were more disturbed to be known for being kind than for being nasty old gay women.

I figured this was the only chance I would get, so I went for it. "Someday I'd like to be able to thank whoever makes these. It's the little things that make a world of difference. And whoever they are, they've made a difference."

A quick peek back at the rearview mirror confirmed all my suspicions. Edith and Mrs. C smirked proudly at each other. I'd never out them for their kindness, but I sure as hell was glad I was able to thank them . . . in a roundabout way.

My room seemed empty and cold without Mitch in it. I was literally counting the hours until I would see him again. He hadn't given me a time, but that was okay. He'd said two days . . . which meant tomorrow.

Settling down with my burrito, I checked my e-mail. Damn, nothing from Moon-Unit yet. I thought about calling her, but certain days of the week she went to bed at six, and I couldn't remember which days. She claimed she had dream communication with extraterrestrials on specific days of the week. While I used to roll my eyes at that kind of talk . . . now, I wasn't so sure. Rena would crap her pants if she knew what I was thinking.

I replied to a few questions from Louise at the shelter. Everything was going great and she had it all under control. I couldn't wait to tell her the sweaters were from Edith and Mrs. C. There was no way in hell I was going to e-mail her that juicy little nugget. I wanted to see her face.

As I was putting my laptop away, the mail beeped and I saw an e-mail from Mitch. I clicked immediately and blushed from my head to my toes as I read in explicit detail his plans for my body. My inner-hooker was not at all embarrassed. She was loving it. How could his words alone whip my insides into a frenzy? My nipples tightened and everything south of my belly button clenched in anticipation. He was very clear that using Vinnie the Vibrator was a no-no. I had to wait and save everything for him. Oh. My. God. He said he would know if I cheated and I would be punished . . . I thought about defying him just so I could get punished. I would looooove to be punished by Mitch. The thought made me have to change my panties. Damn, tomorrow couldn't come soon enough.

After a quick and very cold shower, I settled in with some bizarre documentary about underground Mormons, their multiple wives, and their hordes of children. If that wasn't enough to get my mind off sex, I didn't know what would be. I watched in shock and horror as the dad of thirty-two was unable to remember the names of his kids. It was a train wreck. I was actually relieved by the knock at my door.

Mariah and Boo stood outside with cookies and chocolate milk in hand.

"Can I help you guys?" I grinned.

"We were watching some God-awful fucked-up show about Mormons and decided bothering you would be a lot more fun," Mariah said, barging into my room before I invited her. "Holy shit! You're watching it too."

"He can't remember the names of his kids," I said, ripping open the cookies and settling back down on the bed. "It's disgusting."

"You know not all Mormons are like that." Boo poured three plastic glasses of chocolate milk and handed them around.

"Yes," Mariah agreed grudgingly, "but who's going to watch a show about normal Mormons?"

"Point," I said, accepting my chocolate milk and my fate for the evening. I was glad they were here. It would keep me away from Vinnie and from breaking Mitch's very direct and sexy demand. "Boo, did you feel something odd when Rich grabbed you?"

She was quiet while she considered her answer. Crap, was he going to have a heart attack or something? No . . . she'd smiled at him. She wouldn't smile if he was going to die.

"I did," she slowly acknowledged.

My heart was in my mouth. "Is he okay?" I whispered. "Is he sick?"

"No, no, nothing like that," she assured me. "He's okay. He's very, very, very okay."

"I suppose you're not going to expand on that?" I raised my eyebrow and waited.

"Nope." She grinned. "I promised him I wouldn't tell."

"When?" Mariah asked. "I've been with you all evening."

"When we were in the van. He communicated with me."

"That makes sense. He is a magician after all." Mariah downed her milk and poured another glass.

"What in the hell does that mean?" I laughed. "He does tricks . . . illusions. He doesn't read minds."

"He's not psychic," Boo said, "but he is very strong, mentally. I've never had anyone talk back to me before. It was fun."

"So he's not going to drop dead of a heart attack?" I asked.

"No. The only thing I can say is that appearances can be, um . . . well, somewhat deceiving."

"Like that's not cryptic," Mariah groaned.

It was cryptic, but it did make sense. It was easy to dismiss Rich. His looks were unsettling at the very least, but his insides were beautiful. It was a good lesson about not judging people. I couldn't help but think there was more to the story . . . I guess I'd have to settle for knowing he wasn't going to drop dead from being obese. And if I had anything to do with it, he wouldn't be huge for long.

"Do you guys want to go play ring and run on the lesbos?" Mariah suggested.

I considered it for a moment, before I remembered I was twenty-eight. "Mariah, that is not nice."

"I know"—she grinned unapologetically—"but doesn't it sound fun?"

We laughed hard at the thought of doing such a stupid thing. So hard, I didn't hear the knock at my door until it turned into banging.

"What the . . . ?" I jumped up off the bed and went to see who it was. When did I become party central?

"Hi, can I . . . ?" My greeting died in my throat when I came face-to-face with Edith, Mrs. C, a huge bottle of vodka, and a pack of cards. WTF?

"We heard you idiots all the way down in our room. If there's a party, we're crashing," Edith informed me and shoved me out of the way.

"Do you little backward-ass jack-offs know how to play poker?" Mrs. C inquired in a pleasant voice that was in total opposition to her language. Maybe they didn't even realize how offensive they were . . . Nah.

"I will happily kick your ass and take your money." Mariah narrowed her eyes at the old girls.

"We'll see about that, you little green-haired douche bag," Edith cackled. She pulled the desk over to the bed and put the remaining chairs in the room around it. There still weren't enough places to sit. "Hang on," she muttered. She opened my door and grabbed two folding chairs that were leaning against the wall. Good God, they had no intention of leaving . . . they'd brought their own chairs. Crapballs. This was going to be a long night.

"Where's Kim?" Mrs. C asked.

As if on cue, someone banged on the door, but it didn't sound good. Whoever was on the other side of the door was sobbing uncontrollably.

I flew across the tiny space and yanked open the door. Kim stood on the other side. She was a hot mess. Her camouflage makeup was running down her face, her eyes were bloodshot red, and her clothes were a rumpled disaster.

"Oh my God," I gasped, pulling her into the room. "What happened?"

"I didn't . . . didn't realize . . . that you . . . that you had um, company," she blubbered, moving to leave. "I'll come back . . . la . . . later."

"Sit your fat, overcamouflaged ass down on that bed and start talking," Edith demanded. "Did Hugh do something to you?"

Kim started sobbing anew.

"Goddamn it," Edith shouted. "Mariah, get your knees ready. We're going to go destroy some 'nads."

Mariah bent over to stretch out before she went out and ripped Hugh's testicles off. This was quickly turning into the night from hell. Even the Mormons sounded appealing at this point.

"No!" Kim shouted through her tears. "Hugh didn't do anything. It's me . . . it's all me."

"What happened?" Boo asked gently.

"Well, I told Hubie that I needed to go for a walk and he said okay and then he told me that he was going to practice for the show tomorrow and I said okay and then I asked him if he wanted me to get him a soda from the machine and he said no and then he asked me if I liked Kenny Rogers or Donny Osmond better and I said I liked John Tesh because he used to be on that entertainment show and then . . ."

"Jesus Christ on a cross," Mrs. C shrieked. "Get to the goddamn point. You're killing me."

I did agree with her, but I never would have put it so harshly.

"Sorrrry," Kim said and burst into a fresh set of tears.

"Shhhh." Boo wrapped her arms around her. "Everything will be okay."

"It will?" Kim sniffed, giving Boo her hand.

Boo paused for a moment and looked directly into Kim's eyes. "I promise, but we have a little work to do tonight."

"What in the name of hell is going on here?" Mrs. C groused. "I'm ready to destroy some man-jewels and you're telling her everything is okay? The only reason a woman blubbers like that is because of a man."

"Or a woman," Edith added.

"Right," Mrs. C agreed. "So spit it out or I'm gonna go down there and slice it off with a dull butter knife."

"A plastic dull butter knife," Mariah said through gritted teeth. Both the lesbians looked at Mariah with newfound admiration. They approached her slowly and offered their hands. Mariah shook them and they all turned to look at Kim expectantly.

"Okay," Kim said, gathering herself. She wiped her tears, further smearing the leftover camouflage face paint she insisted on wearing every day. "I'm just going to say it . . ."

"Today?" Edith inquired rudely. Boo shot her a look that shut her up and made her cheeks heat. "Sorry," she muttered, possibly even meaning it for the first time.

"Hubie is going to be a rock star soon and all kinds of beautiful women will be throwing themselves at him. I mean, Hubie is hot now, but when he's famous, the women will go wild. I'm just . . . I'm just . . ." She took a deep breath. "I'm worried I won't be enough woman for him when he's rich and famouuuuuus," she squeaked and began sobbing again.

It was everything I could do not to lose it right then and there. Hubie was the farthest from hot I'd ever seen in my life and the chances of him becoming a rock star were about zero . . . but Kim was serious . . . and seriously hurting. Biting my tongue in half would be a terrible idea, so I sucked in on my lower lip so hard I tasted blood. The excruciating pain was enough to keep me from falling to the floor in hysterics.

"If that bastard throws you over for a nubile twenty-year-old with fun-puppy implants, I will feed him his nuts while I stick his tally-whacker up his bunghole," Edith bellowed.

The entire room went into silent shock. The visual alone was enough to make us all candidates for massive psychiatric intervention. It was laugh or vomit . . . thankfully we started to laugh. Hard. Even Kim. The laughter would die down and then one person would get it going again and we would all lose it. In the end, I believe it lasted about twenty minutes. My stomach muscles were killing me and my mouth hurt from smiling. Damn, it felt great. I hadn't laughed that hard in a long time.

"Kim, Hugh adores you and nothing will ever change that. You're the one with the problem," Boo said. "You need to have more self-confidence."

"Look at me," she moaned. "I used to be hot." She dug through her pocket and pulled out a crinkled and well-loved wedding photo. It was amazing. Her dress was camo along with Hugh's tux, but the most notable part of the picture was that they both had on full camouflage face paint.

"I think you look exactly the same," Edith commented.

"Really?" Kim asked, perking up.

Mariah examined the picture closely. "Your hair might have been a little more strawberry blond then," she said thoughtfully.

"And your boobies might have been a little higher," Mrs. C added.

"Her num-num's are perfectly fine, you old dyke," Edith hissed, punching her sister in the shoulder.

Mrs. C examined the picture and then gave Kim a good once-over. "You're right. Her funbags still look perky."

"Hey," Mariah accused, "I thought you didn't like that term."

"What? Funbags?" Mrs. C asked.

"No." Mariah rolled her eyes. "Dykes."

"Oh," Edith said. "We forgot that one. I'm quite fond of *dyke*. You can use that whenever you want to."

"Good to know." Mariah nodded.

"Enough of that," Boo chastised the women. "We are here for Kim and I think she could use a little of our expertise."

"Did you like your hair color in the picture?" Mariah asked Kim. I felt a bit nauseous. I knew where this was headed.

Kim examined the photo. "Yes, I loved it."

"No prob. Where in the fuck is a drugstore?" Mariah asked.

"There's one down the street from Rose and Popo's," Boo remembered. "Do you have money?"

Mariah pulled a man's wallet out of her back pocket and checked it. "Yep, there's a ton in here."

Boo gave her an odd look, but quickly nodded her head. "Fine, get some tinfoil, makeup, and nail polish too."

"I'm on it." She turned to leave and froze. "Do you dykes want to come? I was thinking we could make a quick stop at Rose and Popo's for some man-jewel smashing."

The old ladies jumped up so fast my head spun. Right as they were almost out the door, Kim, Boo, and I yelled "NO!"

"Why not?" Edith pouted. "I was so primed to stomp some testies."

"That's exactly why," Boo snapped. "We do not have the time to bail your sorry butts out of jail tonight. And Mariah Carey, if I find out you kicked even one ball sac up into someone's chest cavity, I will be really mad."

"Fine," she huffed. "I'll be back in a half hour."

The old ladies sulked while Boo and I made Kim wash all the green and black paint off her face. Boo washed Kim's hair in the sink and then we waited . . . I was really scared. I mean, Mariah's hair was green, for God's sake. What in the hell was she going to do with Kim's? The word *strawberry* in Mariah's description had me thinking the next time Hugh saw his wife, she'd be sporting pink hair. I took a deep breath and decided to take the wait-and-see approach. We could always redye Kim's hair if we needed to . . . *Help me, Jesus.*

Chapter 27

T he bathroom door was open, but they wouldn't let us see what they were doing. My nerves were doing a tango in my stomach. What was Kim going to look like when she came out? I'm sure Boo wouldn't let Mariah do anything heinous to her, but Boo might think Mariah's green locks were awesome. Shitclowns.

"You want a shot?" Edith offered, holding up the big ole bottle of vodka. I was more of a beer girl, but having something to take the edge off sounded like a fine idea.

"Yes, did you bring . . . ?" Before I could finish my question, she pulled six shot glasses out of her sewing bag. I wondered if they had been living with the merkin . . . "All righty then."

She handed me the shot and straddled one of the folding chairs she'd been so kind to provide. I looked around my room. I didn't have any folding chairs . . . Oh, good God, did they pack folding chairs? They certainly had big enough suitcases to have done it. I wondered what the hell else they had brought.

"You want to play?" Mrs. C asked, shuffling the deck with the skill of a Vegas cardshark.

"Do you cheat?" I winced as I downed my shot. Assmonkeys, that burned. I was rudely reminded why I preferred beer.

"Yep, do you?"

I threw back another shot and felt much warmer and happier all of a sudden. "Tonight I do. Deal 'em up, lesbo."

"You got it, hooters," Edith laughed.

I got my ass kicked. I realized that I sucked at cheating and they didn't. I watched Edith pull two aces from under the desk and was amazed I'd never seen her put them under there to start with. They'd probably be good magician assistants for Rich . . . I giggled at the thought of them in skimpy little magician sidekick outfits.

"I don't know what you're laughing at, Buppies. You owe me fifty dollars," Mrs. C said.

"Oh, horseshit," I laughed and downed another shot. "You cheated so bad. I tell you what, when we get back to Minneapolis, I'll pay you with Monopoly money."

"Or you could let us actually run and manage the shop," Edith mumbled.

I paused for a long time and let what she had just said sink into my brain. If they were almost anyone else in the whole world, it would be a much simpler decision. I blew out a long breath. "Oh, Edith, Edith, Edith. How in God's name do you think that would work out? . . . For real." I stared at her. She couldn't hold my gaze and looked down in shame.

Fucktard. My brain was telling me one thing and my instincts were telling me something else altogether. Clearly the three shots had muddled my thinking.

"Oooookay," I said slowly, giving myself ample time to back out of what I was about to do. "One round of twenty-one. No cheating. If you win, you can run the shop for one month . . . on your own. If you terrorize the customers or run my grandma's business into the ground, you're gone . . . Deal?"

"And if you win?" Edith asked.

"Hmmm." I pulled on my curls. "I forgot to think this whole thing out," I admitted. "If I win . . . you two give up the rights of your five-year contract and work for real. I won't fire you unless you give me no choice."

"God damn, Hooters runs a tough bargain," Mrs. C said, giving her sister a nervous glance.

"I'll take it," Edith said, slamming her hand down on the table. "You deal." She handed the cards to her sister and started praying.

Mrs. C shuffled the deck, but she didn't look happy. I watched her closely. They were so good at cheating, it was fascinating. It all looked fair so far. She dealt the cards, one up and one down to each of us. We both had a jack facing up. I peeked at my facedown card and inhaled a quick breath. An ace. I had won unless Edith had the same hand. Asswhackers, why did that make me feel so sick?

"Hit me," Edith snapped at her sister.

She didn't have the same hand I had. She wouldn't have asked for another card if she did. I closed my eyes and had a silent talk with the only woman who might approve of what I was about to do . . . *Grandma, if you can hear me, I might be about to do something really stupid. I know you wanted job security for the old dykes—don't worry, they like that word—but they're hideous employees. We've lost customers and they made big strong construction workers weep and almost quit. I'm beginning to see why you liked them, but I'm not sure that's enough. It takes a while to peel through the layers. They're kind of like onions . . . stinky but good for you . . . and they're good at spicing things up in a profane and offensive way. But I'm not so sure that's good for business. Fuckmonkeys. Oops, sorry. Please don't be angry with me . . .*

"Hit me," I said, sending out a silent prayer to Jesus and Brett Favre. Mrs. C dealt me an eight. "Wow, look at that! I went over. You win, Edith." I tried to shove my cards into the middle of the deck and be done with it, but they were having none of it.

"Gimme those." Mrs. C yanked the cards out of my hand and paled. She handed the cards to Edith, who gave me a questioning stare.

"Did your knockers absorb your brain?" Edith asked.

"No, I must have, um . . . misjudged my, you know . . ." I was cornered. I didn't like being cornered, especially when I had done something nice. Stupid, but nice. "All right, listen up, you old queers. I did it on purpose. I may live to regret this moment the rest of my natural life, but right now it feels like the right thing to do. Buuut, since I did throw the game, I get to add one more nonnegotiable item to the contract."

"Is that fair?" Edith asked her sister.

"I'm gonna go with a yes on that one," Mrs. C said. "What do you want?"

"Every Saturday and Sunday you two will teach underprivileged teens and low-income women to knit. You will be kind to them and you will teach them to make things they need for themselves and their children . . . scarves, mittens, hats, stuff like that."

"No swearing at all?"

"None, and no statements that require a 'bless your heart,'" I told Edith.

They did a little twin telepathy and gave each other a curt nod. "We'll take it."

"Oh shit, you will?" I gasped.

"Yep." Mrs. C grinned. "Regretting it already?"

"Kind of," I admitted, grinning back.

"Here," Edith said, shoving another vodka shot into my hands. "This will make everything better."

"Will you two really be able to curb your insults?" I asked.

"That will be a challenge, Watermelons." Edith shook her head regretfully and tossed back her shot.

I tossed back my own and was hit with inspiration, possibly drunken inspiration, but whatever. "I'll tell you what, you can keep insulting me as much as you want as long as you don't go after the customers and the shelter women. Free reign. Once a week I'll let you take your best shots."

"Will you attack back?" Edith asked.

"Absolutely. And occasionally I'll bring guest attackers."

"Like that little asshat Mariah Carey?" Mrs. C questioned.

"Yep and my roommate Rena would be fantastic."

A slow smile split both of the old lesbos' faces. "You've got yourself a deal!" Edith shouted and did a jig that culminated in a dizzy spell and her ass landing on the floor. She was looking a little green.

"If you puke in my room, I will make you eat it. Do you understand me?"

"Yes," she muttered as she crawled back to her chair.

"Did somebody say my name?" Mariah asked, coming out of the bathroom.

"Yeah, we're going to have a once-a-week, no-holds-barred, name-calling fest with the lesbos when we get back to Minneapolis. Do you want in?" I asked, handing her a shot.

"Of course." She grinned and downed her shot. "Are you guys ready to see the new and improved Kim?"

"We've been waiting two goddamned hours, you little swamp-ass," Mrs. C snapped. "This better be good."

"Oh, it will be, you crotchety old dyke," Mariah laughed. "Come on out, Kim."

"Can I look in the mirror yet?" she called from the bathroom.

"No," I heard Boo say. "Not until everyone sees you."

Boo came out first, followed by a lovely woman with a very flattering layered bob. Wispy bangs complemented her heart-shaped face. Her hair was a gorgeous dark honey blond with strawberry blond highlights. She was wearing subtle makeup that made her sparkling gray eyes pop. Her nails were a soft blush pink and her full lips matched her nails. WTF?

"Kim?" I choked out.

The room was silent. Even the old queers couldn't think of one horrid thing to say. She was simply beautiful. Had Mariah and Boo actually done this? And how had they done it with a box of drugstore hair dye?

"Is it bad?" Kim whispered. Our reaction terrified her.

"God, no," I sputtered. "Just the opposite. You're beautiful."

"I am?" Kim's eyes started to well with tears.

"For shit's sake," Edith snapped, "don't cry. You'll run your mascara."

"It's okay," Boo said, taking Kim's hand and leading her to the mirror above where my desk used to be before we played the life-changing poker game on it. "I used waterproof."

Kim walked in front of the mirror and froze. For a brief moment I thought she didn't like what she saw. She leaned into the mirror and carefully traced her reflection. "I'm pretty," she whispered.

"No need to be all vain about it," Mrs. C said. "You're very pretty, you've got a nice large rack, and a big booty. Men like juicy bums. So enough about you. Who wants a shot?"

"For God's sake, don't be such an asswad," Edith snapped at her sister. "Kim, you look lovely, but clearly Boo and Mariah had something good to work with."

I was speechless for so many reasons. Kim was beautiful and Edith was being kind. Was the world ending?

"I don't know what to do with myself." Kim was positively giddy. "Part of me wants to stand here and stare at myself for a couple of hours, but that's just ugly behavior."

She paced the room like a caged tiger. She was making me dizzy . . . no wait, that was all the vodka I'd consumed.

"Boo and Mariah, I don't know what to say. You have changed my life. I feel like I can take on any nubile fake-breasted groupie that goes after my Hubie when he gets famous."

"Plus, if you sit on them you could kill them," Mrs. C added.

Everyone gave her the evil eye. "What?" she shouted. "I'm just sayin' . . ."

"I think you should go see your hubby." I smiled at Kim. "You're gonna knock his socks off!"

"That's exactly what I'm going to do," she said, running around the room and hugging everyone . . . twice. "I love all of you and I will have your backs till the day I die!"

"Get the hell out of here," Mrs. C groaned. "I can't take much more of this mushy crap."

Without further ado, Kim raced out of my room and back to her rock star hubby.

"Well, at least somebody's going to be getting it tonight," Mrs. C muttered, reshuffling the cards. I wondered if she planned to cheat Mariah and Boo out of some money . . .

"I'd have to put that into the category of TMI," Mariah stated, pouring herself another shot. "Anyone else?" she asked, holding the bottle up.

"Pour a round for everyone," Edith said, settling herself back down at the card table. "Wait a minute. Boo, are you old enough to drink?"

"Yep, but I don't."

"Why's that?" she asked.

"Alcoholic crackheads run in my family," Boo told her, pulling out her bible.

"Good enough," Edith said. "What in the hell is your excuse?" she asked Mariah.

"It's my dream to become one."

"Good enough," Edith replied. Boo giggled and threw a pillow at her sister.

"Who's in?" Mrs. C bellowed. "I'm ready to play cards."

I decided to just lie on my bed and watch. I'd done enough damage playing with the lesbians for the evening. Plus, I was feeling slightly woozy from the shots. Boo chose to recite passages from the bible. Mariah was the only one brave enough . . . or stupid enough . . . to play with the old gals.

"Mariah, how in the hell did you make Kim's hair look like that?" I sat up on the bed and crawled over next to her.

"It was easy. I cut off all the dead shit and layered it. Then I did a new base color in a darker blond and painted in the highlights," she said and downed her shot.

I was speechless . . . almost. "How in the hell did you learn how to do that?"

She shrugged her shoulders and poured another shot.

"The Internet," Boo said. "And it's not easy. She's amazing."

I had a vague recollection of Mariah doing her anger management classes on the Internet too. "Did you do the makeup?" I asked the green-haired wonder.

"Nope, that was Boo."

I turned my focus to Boo and waited.

"Internet," she giggled. "We don't have any money for things like classes. We have to eat and stuff like that." She was so matter-of-fact about something I totally understood. Being hungry sucked. Living in a car sucked worse. I shook my head and remembered I'd overcome all of that. I am the person I am today because of it.

"Why haven't either of you pursued a career in beauty?"

"No license," Mariah told me.

"You can't get certified on the Internet?"

"She could have if she was taking the class legally," Boo admitted. "But it cost too much, so we hacked our way in."

"I could forge you a license, and not a soul in the world would question it," Edith said as if it were the most natural thing in the world to create fake IDs.

"She's good," Mrs. C chimed in. What in the hell had they done in their youth?

"Nah, don't want to do it. People suck. I'd end up sending more to the hospital than any respectable place would allow."

Silently I agreed with her . . . but I did have an idea.

"Why are you looking at me like that?" Mariah narrowed her eyes at me.

"Like what?"

"Like you do at the shelter when you're going to send me into some bogus form of hell."

"I have no idea what you're talking about," I huffed and looked away before she realized how hard I was plotting. It would have to wait until we got home anyway . . . but it would happen.

"Can I read to you guys?" Boo asked.

"Sure," I said, getting comfortable. I was afraid I'd fall asleep. No more shots for me . . . Okay, one more.

"Hairy Sam was furious with the butt-ass stupid fucked-up ways

he was depicted by Americans living in the Pacific Northwest. He cut some slack to those living in the rural South because most of them were into inbreeding. He had no issues with alternate lifestyles, but that one was gross even by his low standards.

"He and his captain decided to play a game called Fuck with the Future. Aside from the fact that they enjoyed time traveling together, his captain was in a constant search for a woman with two vaginas.

"Hairy Sam would show up and make sure idiots all over the world caught glimpses of him. He left footprints and pubic hair everywhere."

I sat up with a jerk and almost passed out. The room was tilting a little to the left. Was the bible starting to sound familiar because I was drunk? Or because I'd actually heard this before? I racked my liquored-up brain for the answer, but nothing came. WTF? Maybe if I could stay awake for a little more of it, I'd be able to remember. I cuddled back into my lumpy bed and listened . . .

I woke up curled into a little ball. I was being spooned by Edith, who was being spooned by Mariah, who was being spooned by Mrs. C, who was being spooned by Boo. What the fu . . . ?

"Um, guys? As much as I love all of you, this just seems wrong. Like, against-my-religion wrong."

"Oh my God," Boo screamed, snapping out of her slumber. "Kristy, you're alive."

"Of course I'm alive. Why wouldn't I be alive?" I said, pushing a still-passed-out Edith off me. Ewww, the back of my shirt was wet . . . from her drool. I gingerly pulled my shirt over my head and quickly changed before everyone else woke up.

I glanced at the bedside clock. It was three in the freakin' morning. The party was so over.

Mrs. C sleepily rolled herself off my bed. How in the hell had we all fit on the bed? "Sorry for saying your hooters were fake."

"What are you talking about?" An icy tendril of fear started twisting through my insides. I vaguely recalled . . .

"Well," she yawned, "when you showed them to everybody, they jiggled so much, I knew they were real."

"Jesus Christ in high heels," I yelled. "I thought that was a dream. Wait . . . then you owe me five hundred dollars."

"Aww shit," she muttered. "I was hoping you were too drunk to remember that part."

"Turn down the TV," Edith hissed. "I'm trying to sleep."

"Then you need to try sleeping in your own room," I said, shoving her and her drooly mouth off my bed.

"Kristy!" Mariah shouted as she woke up. She tackled me in a hug, possibly breaking a rib and making me realize I was still a little drunk. "It was frightening. We were so worried with all the singing and dancing and then exposing yourself and then . . ."

"Enough," I snapped, cutting her off. "Enough with the scary Kristy imagery. I get it."

"Can I take a turn?" Boo politely asked.

"Will it be long?" I asked.

"No."

"Okay," I relented against my better judgment.

"It was horrific, like the *Exorcist* head-spin-off horrific, or *Alien* baby-ripping-out-of-stomach horrific."

"Thank you," I said.

"No prob."

"Oookay, party's over. Time for everyone to go home. Now." I opened my door and ushered them out. I had a bad feeling I would be living down this particular evening for years. Fucktard. I was never putting my lips to vodka again.

I heaved a huge sigh of relief when I was finally alone. I knew I needed to do two things before I went back to bed. Ibuprofen and water. If I didn't I would be useless in . . . four hours, when I had to be out in the parking lot. Assmonkeys, how could I have been so stupid?

I unzipped the side pocket of my suitcase and searched for my ibuprofen. Got it, thank you, Jesus. I felt something rectangular and bumpy. What the hell? Oh my God . . . the bible. A wave of apprehension swept through me. I yanked it out of the suitcase and ripped the wrapping paper off it and almost vomited. The near-puke wasn't caused by the alcohol still churning through my veins . . . it was caused by *Pirate Dave and His Randy Adventures*, written by Evangeline O'Hara, the novel-stealing skank that Rena and the porno grannies had brought to ruin. This book was the work of the profane and repulsive imagination of my best friend and roommate, Rena. Motherhumpin' cowballs, my entire belief in Bigfoot was rooted in one of the biggest jokes of the century. God, I was so stupid . . . and stupid.

I felt panicky and nauseous. Why in the hell hadn't I opened that damn present the first day? What was I supposed to do with this information? Did I tell everyone the bible was a stream of consciousness, filthy rant from Rena's head? I could just imagine the look on Boo's face . . . Hell, Mariah would probably break my nose or knee my ovaries up into my mouth.

Along with the sickness I was experiencing over discovering the true origins of the bible, I could feel my hangover coming on with a vengeance. I threw back six ibuprofen and chugged three glasses of water. I would tell them . . . No, I wouldn't. Yes, I had to. Shitshitshit, was I supposed to? Had I found the bible tonight for a reason? This was too much to deal with at three thirty in the morning.

I would talk to Rich privately first thing. He was levelheaded and kind. He'd tell me what to do. He would never lead me astray. My panic slowly receded and my breathing went back to normal. I had no idea what I was going to do about this, but knowing I could go to Rich was as comforting as knowing that Mitch was coming back tomorrow night. Why? I had no clue . . . but it was.

Chapter 28

Morning had broken . . . unfortunately my hangover had not. At least I wasn't the only one who looked like hell warmed over. Mariah had a baseball cap pulled low over her eyes and was wearing the same clothes she'd had on last night. The old ladies were sporting Jackie O sunglasses and their hair looked like rats had slept in it.

I'd at least had the wherewithal to have showered. I tried to tame my hair, but touching my head was a no-no. I was hoping after a few doughnuts and several cups of strong coffee, all would be right with my world.

The rest of the crew looked chipper, especially Kim and Hugh. He was following her around like a lovesick puppy and she was loving every minute. She looked as pretty as she had last night and I noticed she had forgone her usual full-camo face paint. Hugh's customary heavy metal morning serenade had turned into a medley of sappy love songs. They held hands and I'm pretty sure I spotted a hickey on her neck.

"Good morning, sunshine," Rich whispered.

"Thank you."

"For what?" he asked.

"For not talking loud." I grimaced.

He handed me two glazed doughnuts and a cup of coffee. I was in love. "Rich," I said with a mouthful of doughnut, "could I talk to you about something?"

"Certainly." He led me over to a bench by Paul Bunyan's right leg. Thankfully we were shaded. The bright sunlight was not my friend this morning.

I was hesitant. Part of me was afraid of how he would answer. "Do you, um . . . really, you know, believe?"

"In Bigfoot?"

"Um, yeah."

"Do you?" he asked, turning the tables. My brain wasn't functioning at full capability and his question threw me. I was on my way to telling him Boo's bible was full of lies, so I figured I would be honest about everything. Besides, I was an even worse liar than I was a cheater.

"I didn't, but then I was starting to and then I found out something really, really bad and now I don't think I do anymore."

He took a sip of coffee and watched me closely. His green and brown eyes stared intently into mine.

"Why are you looking at me like that? Do you think I'm a bad person?" Crapballs, I never should have asked him anything. I'd just thought . . .

"I think you're a wonderful person," he said. "I'm simply processing what you just said."

"Did it make any sense?" I wondered aloud, shoving the rest of the doughnut into my mouth.

"Not much," he admitted.

I swallowed my doughnut and blew out a frustrated breath. I'd already started . . . I might as well finish. If he felt betrayed or angry, I'd have to deal with it. "Okay, I'll explain, but you have to answer two questions first."

He looked at me expectantly and waited.

"Do you believe in Bigfoot and where in the hell are you from?" His accent was killing me. It sounded fake, because there were so many variations.

"As to the question of the existence of Sasquatch, I believe in the possibility," he said slowly. "And my homeland is Australia, but I've spent time in England, Scotland, South Africa, and Kentucky."

"But you're a magician," I sputtered, trying to make sense of his vast amount of travel.

"I worked cruise ships for a while and was fortunate enough to get to visit places all over the world."

Wow, maybe the accent made sense. Maybe he was one of those people who picked up the local dialect without even realizing it. I felt bad for doubting him. "Okay," I mumbled. I felt my cheeks heat, so I bent down to retie my tennis shoes.

"So what do you want to talk about?"

Unfortunately I had only two laces and there were only so many ways to tie them. I sat back up and stared at my hands.

"Kristy, are you okay?" He lifted my chin so I had no choice but to look at him.

"The bible is a lie," I whispered.

"Which part?" he asked.

"All of it."

"Oookay," he said, giving me an odd look. "I get that Noah's ark is difficult to swallow, but you think the entire thing is fiction?"

"Oh my God," I giggled. "Not that one."

"Is it the loaves and fishes? I find that story a bit suspect, or maybe the parting of the Red Sea . . ."

"No, Rich, you're referring to the wrong bible. I'm talking about the Bigfoot bible."

He glanced up at the morning sky and tried to suppress a grin. He gingerly ran his hands through his nappy hair and composed himself. "So you think the Bigfoot bible is fiction?"

"I don't think. I know. And why are you trying not to laugh?" I asked, annoyed that he wasn't taking me seriously.

"I'm trying not to laugh because I've always thought the Bigfoot bible was fiction . . . very alarming fiction," he said, smoothing his muumuu.

"You did?" I gasped. "Why didn't you say anything?"

"Because everyone needs something to believe in."

That certainly shut me up. It was a profound and completely unselfish sentiment. Who in the hell did I think I was? My headache mocked my self-righteousness by pounding like a rock band in my brain. Rich was correct. How much good would it do to tell them? None. It would do no one any good. It would be embarrassing and mean.

"How do you know it's fake?" Rich asked, watching my inner turmoil with concern.

"Because my roommate wrote it to destroy an over-Botoxed, novel-stealing bitch," I sighed.

"How did you put it all together?"

"I didn't until last night. It had sounded bizarrely familiar at certain points, but I couldn't place it. I'd never actually read the book. Rena would just tell me bits of the story."

"Is this the Evangeline O'Hara disaster?"

"Yeah," I laughed without much humor. "How did you know?"

"I love the Anderson Cooper show and the night she went down on national television was one of the most entertaining evenings I've had in front of the tube."

"That was a good one," I giggled, remembering how Evangeline had gotten her just deserts, and all the women she'd been blackmailing and stealing from had gotten their due. "Thank you," I said, giving him a quick hug. God, he smelled good . . . at least he had that going for him.

"For what?" He gently wiped the doughnut glaze from my mouth.

"For setting me straight. You really are a beautiful human being, Rich."

He blushed and it was actually kind of cute in a disturbing way. When we got back to Minneapolis, he wasn't going to know what hit him. I was soooo going to fix him. All he needed was . . . well, he needed a lot, but I was the gal to make it happen.

"Come on people, chop-chop," Stuey yelled, coming from around the back of the building. Why in the hell did he always come from the back of the building? All the doors to the rooms were in the front . . . Maybe he took a final pee in the woods every morning.

"For God's sake," Edith hissed. "Keep your voice down or I'll rip your larynx out."

"She can do it. I've seen it," Mrs. C warned Stuey. "Twice."

That statement made everyone pause. I was fairly certain she was telling the truth. What in the hell was their former occupation? Their skills, when added up, made no sense whatsoever. I should have pried when we were all drunk. Assmonkeys, I was usually good at taking advantage of opportunities. Knitting, tree-shimmying, trap-laying, larynx-ripping, cheating twin lesbians . . . equals? No clue.

"Okay," Stuey whispered, as Heidi and the Baldies pulled up. "Let's get loaded and get out of here."

"Hey, swamp-ass," Edith called out to Stuey. "Why in the hell is the trailer still locked if all the equipment is out of it? I want to put my goddamn suitcase back here."

She stood at the trailer and rattled the door. Mariah walked over and examined it closely.

"I can pick it, if you want," she told Edith.

"Noooo, no, no, no," Stuey said, running over and dragging the huge suitcase to the cargo hold under the van. "I lost the key. It must be out at the cabin. Hell," he muttered, "I've been losing everything. Has anyone seen my wallet?"

A chorus of no's answered him, and he appeared agitated and pissed. Unfortunately, I had a very good idea where his wallet might have ended up. The smirk on Mariah's face was the nail in her coffin.

"When we get out to the cabin, you will drop the wallet on the ground where he'll be sure to find it. Do you understand me?" I whispered in Mariah's ear.

"Fine." She rolled her eyes and grinned.

"How much money did you take out of it?"

"Not enough that he'll miss it. He's got thousands of dollars in there," she said.

"For real?" I asked. Why would Stuey be running around with that much cash? Maybe the TIT network had finally cancelled the credit card . . . Whatever. The money did not belong to Mariah and she was not keeping it. Period.

Heidi Kugelschmooson, in an obscene outfit, moseyed over, gaped at Kim's new look, and exchanged a few flirty sentences with Stuey until Stan yanked his partner aside.

"You lost your fucking wallet?" he hissed.

Stuey paled and pulled Stan away from the group. I watched them argue out of earshot and it didn't look friendly at all. Shit, was Mariah in possession of the rest of the budget for the show? This day was starting off bad. I prayed to Brett Favre it wouldn't get worse.

"Jesus Christ in a miniskirt, that wig is hideous," Mariah mumbled as she watched Heidi wobble off to her SUV.

"Do you think she's bald or something?" I asked, agreeing with her assessment.

"Nope. I think she has thin hair or she's under the impression that blondes have more fun. She wears contacts too."

"Lots of people wear contacts," I said, hoping there were more doughnuts in the van. They were my perfect hangover food.

"She wears colored contacts," Mariah told me. She hopped up into the van and strapped in.

"How do you know?" I was fascinated with Heidi and her bizarre disguise. I'd seen the brown hair sticking out of the wig and it didn't look thin at all. It looked healthy and shiny. Was the getup for the weather girl gig? My gut said she'd be a lot prettier without all the crap.

"She got a merkin pube stuck in her eye yesterday and I saw her take out her brown contact." Mariah passed an almost-full box of doughnuts back to me in my seat. I wondered if anyone would notice if I polished off a dozen or so. My ass would probably notice, but my hangover didn't care very much about my ass.

I shoved a doughnut in my mouth and remembered I was still in the middle of a conversation with Mariah. "What color were her real eyes?" I asked through my wad of hangover food.

"A striking icy blue. I don't know why in the hell she would cover up that color . . . unless she had something to hide."

I mulled over what Mariah had said as I ate my fourth doughnut of the morning. Was she in on something with Stuey and Stan? Was she trying to kill Bigfoot too? Wait a minute . . . there's no such thing as Bigfoot. I knew that, but did they?

"I've got Moon-Unit on the line," Kim shouted excitedly, driving as erratically as ever. I wanted to slap her in the back of the head for talking so loud, but hearing what Moon-Unit had to say was far more important than the fact that my brain had just partially exploded in my skull. "I'll put her on speaker!"

"Hello? Can you hear me?" Moon-Unit sounded a bit tinny and far away, but it was comforting to hear her voice.

"Yes, we can, dear," Kim said. "Did you find anything?"

"Yes and no," she said.

Fucktard, I hoped this wasn't going to be an unbalanced cryptic conversation.

"What did you find out about Stuey and Stan and Heidi?" I asked. I noticed Rich tense next to me. He knew something was off too.

"First things first," Moon-Unit yelled into the phone. "I am approximately twenty-four hours away from killing the evil chi. There's been some divine intervention from a traveling band of hobgoblins. I was concerned the hobgoblins had come to start a war with my trolls, but thankfully I was mistaken. As a matter of fact, several of the trolls and hobgoblins have mated."

"What in the fuck would their offspring be called?" Edith yelled from the back of the van.

Oh. My. God. Was I the only one with a hangover in this vehicle?

And why in the hell were we discussing the mating particulars of things that didn't exist, except in the minds of insane people?

"They have informed me that they will be called trobgobrolls. It's a wonderful step to bringing peace to the land of Spoctersprocket."

I'd had enough. "Moon-Unit, what about Stuey, Stan, and Heidi?"

"Oh yes, yes," she bellowed. "Your Heidi Kugelschmooson doesn't exist at all. She shows up in no database whatsoever."

"Did you use the links we sent you?" Mrs. C asked.

"Yes, I did," Moon-Unit answered. "I am impressed with you two. I had no idea."

"Yeah, whatever." Edith cut her off before she could say anything else. "What about the shiny little bastards?"

I noticed that Hugh had been humming a soft version of the theme from *Law & Order* throughout the entire conversation, Boo was taking notes, and Rich looked nauseous. I was a bit queasy to hear that Heidi didn't exist. What did that mean?

"As for Stan Angelusi and Stu Greenberg, there are a ton of them, but none that match up with our guys."

"What do you mean?" Boo stopped taking notes and spoke up.

"There's no record of them working for TIT anywhere, and I can't place those two at any production company in Los Angeles."

"Impossible," Kim gasped and almost swerved off the road.

"Goddamn it, Kim, if you kill us I will hunt you down and drag you to my condo in hell," Edith hissed.

"Sorry," Kim sputtered, sitting up straighter and closer to the steering wheel.

"Are they in the data bank we sent you the link to?" Mrs. C asked in a clipped and professional voice I didn't recognize. I felt Rich turn around and look at her.

"No," Moon-Unit replied.

"Then they're not using their real names," Edith said without a shred of doubt in her voice.

Holy hell, what had we gotten ourselves involved in? Stan and Stuey weren't Stan and Stuey? Heidi Kugelschmooson didn't exist? WTF? Wait. A. Minute.

"Mariah, give me the wallet," I insisted, reaching over the seat.

"Aww, come on, I said I would return it," she moaned.

"You said no such thing," I reminded her. "I told you that you were going to return it. Hand it over. Now."

She reluctantly gave me the wallet. My hands shook, but I was sure I was onto something. I opened it. Motherhumpin' assclowns, there was a shitwad of hundred-dollar bills inside, but that wasn't what I was after. I frantically rifled through the cards. Got it! I pulled Stuey's license out and an icy chill blasted through my body, which did absolutely nothing to improve my hangover.

"Try looking up Herman Stooshman," I said, examining the license. "He's from New York and the birthdate is 6/26/70."

"Herman what?" Moon-Unit asked.

"Stooshman," I repeated. "S-T-O-O-S-H-M-A-N."

"Is that the only one you've got?" she asked.

"Yep."

"Good enough. I'll get right on it."

"Moon-Unit, you old lunatic, I'm sending you another link from my phone. I'll send the security clearance separately," Edith yelled. "Do you understand what I'm saying?"

"That you'll kill me if I say where any of the information came from," she stated in a logical fashion.

"You got it," Edith said, satisfied with Moon-Unit's answer. I had a sick feeling she wasn't kidding. Rich was positively sweating next to me.

"Do I get to keep the wallet?" Mariah asked excitedly.

I looked down at the wallet in my hands. This news definitely changed the plan. I had no idea what the right thing to do was, but for now . . .

"Yes, you get to keep it until I tell you otherwise." I handed it back to her, grabbed another doughnut, and mentally cussed out David Hasselhoff. This whole fucking thing was his fault.

Chapter 29

The rest of the morning was uncomfortably bizarre. Rich had advised that we act as if nothing was amiss. I was such a sucky liar, I stayed as far away from Stuey and Stan as I could. Unfortunately, Heidi Kugelschmooson was another story. She was on me like white on rice.

"So, Kristy, what exactly do you do in Minneapolis?" she asked. She was wearing a dress that defied gravity. I was sure she had used titty tape, or at least I hoped she had. I could almost see her nipples. Eww.

"I run a women's shelter," I said and focused on patting down trees for pubes in the area we were searching. I snuck glances at her when I was sure she wasn't looking. No sign of her dark brown hair and icy blue eyes, only her cleavage. Why didn't she exist and what was she hiding? It certainly wasn't her boobs.

"That's wonderful. Are you involved with anyone?" she asked, pretending to examine the bark for Bigfoot's private hair.

"Thank you and yes," I replied. What was this? Twenty Questions?

"Is it serious?"

"Um, sure." Good God, was she going to ask how big his thingie was?

"Have you ever been married before?"

"Why would you ask me something like that?" I stopped and confronted her. Her prying was strange, it was like she was . . . oh my God, *boobs*. All I could see were *boobs*. It was everything I could do to keep my eyes on her face. Did she still think I had something going on with her Stuey? I mean Herman.

"Just curious." She smiled, shrugging her shoulders nonchalantly.

"Well, Miss Curious, your questions are a little too personal and I don't think they have anything to add to any article you may or may not be writing. How would you like it if I asked you all sorts of unnecessary questions?" Crap. I probably shouldn't have said any of that. Damn it, I needed a handler. I couldn't be trusted not to spill the beans. I frantically glanced around for a good liar to save me from myself. The only person nearby was Rich. I couldn't imagine he was very good at lying.

"Have at it, Little Miss Sunshine," she challenged, narrowing her eyes.

WTF? Was she daring me? I knew I should walk away. That was exactly what I should do. Yep, I would walk away and I wouldn't talk to her for the rest of the day. I still wasn't firing with all cylinders due to the evil vodka juice I'd thrown back last night . . . Walk away.

"Why are you disguising yourself? And if you were going to choose a wig, why would you choose one that looks like a blond helmet? It's highly unattractive and so 1990. And just so you know"— I leaned into her—"the brown contacts aren't fooling anybody."

Fucktard, that was definitely not walking away.

I expected her to deck me or at the very least, insult the hell out of me. I couldn't have been more wrong . . . She laughed. Not derisively. She laughed with delight.

"You've got spunk, little girl." She clapped me on the back. "I think I like you."

That was not a normal reaction to being insulted . . . not by a long shot. Although, for some unknown reason her approval thrilled me. WTF? She could be a busty axe murderer and I was happy she liked me? I needed to get out of this place. The only thing keeping me from running back to Minneapolis from Duluth on foot was the fact that I would see Mitch tonight. Two nights ago seemed like a hundred years.

After our unusual and unsettling bonding, Heidi seemed content to let me be. She stayed close to Stuey-Herman and laughed at all the jokes he told to her boobs. The rest of the morning went by uneventfully and at lunchtime we wandered back to the cabin in silence. Hugh, deep in thought, wasn't even providing his usual midday Beyoncé concert. I suppose one could be grateful for small favors.

"Hey, kids," Stuey-Herman shouted. "Why the long faces? We'll find that hairy bastard! I can feel it in my bones!"

"Did you find your wallet?" Mariah asked him. My breath choked in my throat for a moment, causing a coughing fit. What in the hell was she up to?

"No." His mood changed from jovial to something slightly frightening at warp speed. "If any of you find it, I need it back. Do you understand?"

We all nodded and murmured yes. Shiny little Stuey-Herman wasn't as sweet and mild mannered as I had thought. Although losing thousands of dollars could make anyone grumpy. Since we had the information we needed, maybe Mariah should drop the wallet as planned . . .

"No," Rich said quietly, his voice so soft I was unsure if I had heard him correctly.

"What?"

"No, Mariah should not give the wallet back," he said, taking my arm and putting a little distance between us and the rest of the group.

"How did you know what I was thinking?"

"Your pretty face is like an open book," he said, smiling. "You'd be terrible at poker."

"Trust me," I giggled, remembering my disastrous game from the drunken evening before, "I suck at poker . . . and lying and cheating."

"Just have Mariah hang on to it until we know more," Rich suggested.

I nodded, took his hand, and we caught back up with the group.

Lunch was from Rose and Popo's again. As expected, the old gals slipped out to do their thing. Everyone ate quietly and Stan's mood was blacker than black. He and Stuey spent the entire lunch break arguing behind locked doors. Heidi ate her sandwich very close to the shouting match and kept fiddling with her hearing aid. Wait . . . She wore a hearing aid? How in the sacred and frightening name of David Hasselhoff's Speedo had I missed the fact that she was hearing impaired? Had I been so focused on her cleavage and her helmet head that I'd missed the fact that she had hearing issues?

Dang it, now I felt bad for being so mean earlier. Not that she hadn't deserved it, but . . . I suppose I could try to be a little kinder to everybody. My sub felt like a lead ball in my stomach. I wasn't sure if it was because the doughnuts didn't like the sandwich or because my snarky behavior was getting a payback.

I closed my eyes and focused on Mitch. The man-butt of my dreams. Falling for a guy I'd known only a few days sounded more like a cheesy movie than my life, but it had happened. Thinking about him did crazy things to my insides and even more shocking things to my heart. I knew it could all blow up in my face, but I also knew I could die tomorrow . . . Whatever time I could have with Mitch would have to be enough. I would be devastated if he asked me to give up the shelter and turn my back on everything I'd worked so hard for. I loved him enough that I knew I would never demand he give up his dream for me. He was different from the other dorks I'd dated. Besides being able to make me melt into a pile of goo at his feet, he was kind and smart and funny and had a package that . . . shit, that wasn't the important thing. Well, it wasn't *un*important, but the size of his thingie and his abs and his butt and his thick shiny dark hair and his icy blue eyes and his oral talent and the way he smelled . . . those were just extras. Really, really niiice extras . . .

Stuey-Herman's reentrance jerked me out of my fantasy world. I wasn't sure if he'd been crying or if he was so angry his face had mottled. He buried his head in Heidi's cleavage for a moment and pulled himself back together.

"We're going to spend the next two hours or so searching for my wallet," he informed us. Stan stood in the doorway behind him with no expression on his face whatsoever.

"What about the keys to the trailer?" Boo asked, reminding him that he had lost those too. He shot her a look that made the hair on my arms stand up. Mariah instinctively moved in front of her sister.

Stuey-Herman caught himself and laughed like Boo had made a good one. "Oh, don't worry, little Boo. They were on the floor of the sedan. Thank you for asking."

"You're welcome," she said from behind her protective sister.

"Allrightyroo, if you're finished eating, let's go find my fucking wallet." He sounded like a cheerleader at a pep rally where it was okay to swear. We mutely followed him back out of the cabin and into the warm midday sun. I just had a feeling that the pesky lost wallet wasn't going to show up. Call me crazy . . .

To everyone's great surprise and intense, *maybe a bit overintense*, disappointment, after two hours of concentrated searching, we were unable to locate Stuey-Herman's wallet.

"Goddamn it," he shouted. "Where in the fuck is it?"

"Maybe you left it at Rose and Popo's," Mariah suggested innocently.

Did she have a death wish? Stuey-Herman froze and I watched his tiny pea brain try to retrace all his steps up to losing his wallet. He blew out a frustrated breath and gave Mariah a smile that didn't come close to reaching his eyes.

"Nope, Stan got the sandwiches. He paid."

"Are you sure Stan didn't take it? Like as a joke or something?" Mariah's serious face belied the evil twinkle in her eyes.

"That cocksucker," Stuey-Herman hissed between clenched teeth. "I'll be right back."

He ran into the cabin and slammed the door behind him. The sounds from inside were horrifying. Muffled grunts and thuds . . . screaming and moaning. We all stood rooted to the ground. It sounded like someone was getting killed in there.

"Shit," an ashen-faced Mariah mumbled. "I was just fucking with him."

"What do we do?" Kim asked, visibly trembling.

"We do nothing," Rich told us in a voice that brooked no bullshit. "If it gets worse, you will get into the van and leave."

"How could it get worse?" Boo asked, moving close to her sister.

"Well, if you hear a gun go off, I'd suggest you move your lily white asses out of here," Edith grunted, hopping back and forth from foot to foot like a prizefighter waiting to go into the ring.

The violence seemed to escalate and I wanted to cry. "Maybe we should drop the wallet. This is not worth it."

"You have his wallet?" Heidi asked with an excited gleam in her eyes.

Oh, shitfucktardmotherhumpinswampassbutts, what had I just done? I might as well go knock on the door and hand it to him . . . I'd just told his freakin' gal pal. If Stuey-Herman was willing to kill Stan over the wallet . . . what would he do to us?

"Come with me," Rich said tersely to Heidi and the Baldies. "Mariah, give me the wallet." He held out his hand and Mariah complied. "The rest of you get back in the van."

"I'm not going anywhere!" an adrenaline-filled Mrs. C spat. "You go talk to Blondie and the Baldies and I'll take care of everything here."

"Roger that," Edith said, doing push-ups on the ground at her twin sister's feet. Rich gave her a long and hard stare that Mrs. C returned with no problem.

"Suit yourself, but if it turns bad, you get them into the van and out of here," he said in a clipped tone. Heidi and her sidekicks followed Rich and the wallet to the back of the cabin.

"What's he going to do?" Kim asked.

"Pay her off, I imagine," Hugh guessed. "Why else would he want the wallet?"

"Do you think he'll give it to her?"

"Doesn't matter," Mariah informed us proudly.

My stomach plunged to my feet. "Oh God, Mariah, what did you do?" I demanded, wanting to take her over my knee and spank her.

"I kept his license and some of the money," she snickered.

"How much of the . . . No, don't tell me, I don't want to know." I paced back and forth. I wanted to jump out of my skin. How had we gotten into this mess and what in the hell was really going on? Wait . . . "Did you leave enough money in there for Rich to pay them off if he has to?"

"Yep, there's a little over a thousand in there," she said, refusing to meet my eyes.

That meant she had five to ten thousand somewhere on her body. I would not ask where. I'm sure it would gross me out and truthfully I wanted to forget about all of this.

"Should we call the police?" Boo asked.

"Quiet." Edith put her hand up to hush us. "They've stopped. Act normal," she hissed and resumed her exercise routine.

Was that normal? I was so confused and scared, I started doing deep knee bends and yoga breathing. Were we all going to die? Was I actually doing calisthenics with Edith so I could *appear normal*? I was going to have to go to a hypnotist to make me forget this past week when we got back . . . if we got back.

Stuey-Herman and Stan came out of the front of the cabin at the same time Rich, Heidi, and the Baldies came from around the back of the cabin. Heidi was focused and moving at a quick, almost masculine pace, but the minute she saw her shiny little paramour, the swing went back into her hips and the pout returned to her lips.

Rich looked pissed and the bald guys looked . . . bald. They rarely had much of an expression and they seemed to fade into the woodwork of wherever they were. Oftentimes I forgot they were even around and I still didn't know their names. Weird.

Stan and Stuey-Herman were bloody. They both looked like they had lost the fight. Stuey had an ugly shiner developing and crimson blood spilled from Stan's split lip and was dripping down his chin. Neither man was walking steadily and Stan's arm appeared to be hanging at a strange angle. Moon-Unit needed to call back quickly. My gut said to go home, but I had a feeling no one else would agree. If all of this violence and bad behavior had to do with Bigfoot, I was going to have to come clean about the bible being fake. If I could convince my group that he didn't exist, they might be willing to leave. I knew they were staying now to protect something that wasn't really out there.

"Allrightyroo," Stuey choked out. "Let's head on back to the hotel. We have a huge day tomorrow."

"Are you okay?" Boo asked, stepping forward and taking his hand.

Ohh, crapitty, crap, crap. I knew exactly what she was doing. Stuey looked down at her small hand clasped in his and actually seemed moved by her concern. He grimaced as he leaned into her and gave her an awkward hug. Boo reached up and gently touched his almost-closed eye.

"You need some ice," she said, "and Stan needs some stitches and possibly a cast. Would you like us to drive you to the hospital?"

"No, no, no, we're fine," Stuey laughed. "Just a little friendly tussle. Right, Stan?"

"Right. Fine," he answered.

"You guys head on back. We'll meet up with you soon."

"Are we going out tonight, snookie-pants?" Heidi cooed, pulling Stuey away from Boo and shoving her hooters in his face.

"Not tonight, baby. I got some stuff to do."

"Like editing the footage?" Mariah asked. Fucktard, she was making me a nervous wreck. Her insistence on baiting Stuey was bad on so many levels.

"Yeah, yeah, that's exactly what I gotta do. Those fuckers at TIT aren't gonna know what hit them. All those pubes were impressive. The show will be a hit."

"Time to go," Stan said abruptly. "Get in the van and leave."

I was worried about leaving them alone together. It seemed like such a bad idea, but Rich and the lesbos were ushering us like a herd of cows to the van.

"I'm not sure we should . . ." I said as Edith pushed me into the van.

"Yes, we should," she whispered. "We need to reconnoiter and find out more information. This does not feel good to me."

"Do you think they're going after Bigfoot this afternoon?" Hugh asked. His eyes were full of fear and he was on the verge of crying.

"Possibly," Edith muttered, "but if they do they're in for an ugly surprise."

I had visions of Stan and Stuey hanging from the trees, wrapped in lime green and Day-Glo orange nets. I laughed despite the strange situation we were in. Once we were locked and loaded into the van, I considered telling them what I knew about the bible. But I held off on revealing the true origin because even though I knew the bible was a crock, for some reason there was a small part of me that still believed Sasquatch might be out there.

"Would you guys like to go to a restaurant this evening?" Kim asked, starting the van and tearing out of the dirt driveway.

"I'm kind of tired and want to go to the lodge," I said. Why hadn't I told them about Mitch coming? I knew everyone would be thrilled . . . except maybe Rich. I was sure he had a little crush on me and if I was being honest, I had a little crush on him too . . . Not in a physical way, God forbid. The thought of that was . . . it was, um, wrong on every level and to be blunt, gross. But I liked him and admired him and loved spending time with him. He would be my friend for a long time . . . I could feel it.

"I'd like to get back too," Rich agreed. "It's been a long day."

"Do we need to dissect the data?" Mrs. C asked. "The situation is unstable and I don't like not knowing what the fuck is going on."

"It's like going into the jungle blind," Edith added. "You can get ambushed and strung up in a tree. Then some little swamp-ass bastard will come up and carve out your innards and feed you your entrails while he sings nursery rhymes."

Where in the fucking hell did that come from?

"We have to wait for the information from Aunt Moon-Unit," Boo said, cringing at the imagery that Edith had provided.

We rode in silence for a while. Kim's driving was less erratic, thank you, Jesus. Hugh, never one to miss an opportunity, filled the silence with a classical piece of unknown origin. Due to the many key changes, I was guessing it was an original. As awful as it was, it was beautiful. Hugh was solid and kind, a genuinely happy person. I envied him and Kim. As kooky as they were, they had gotten it right.

"What did you learn when you touched Stuey?" Kim asked Boo. I'd almost forgotten about that . . .

"Nothing specific," she said, frustration clear in her voice, "but he is very excited and angry. He's anticipating something, but his thoughts are so tangled, it's difficult to guess. Lots of visions of Heidi's boobs though."

"That girl has no shame, walking around looking like a cheap hooker," Edith said. "I can't figure her out. I thought for a while she was already acquainted with the shiny fucks, but now I don't believe that."

"You think she has her own agenda for Sasquatch?" Hugh asked, pausing the concert.

"I definitely think she and her overexposed watermelons have an agenda, but I'm not sure if it has anything to do with Yeti." Mrs. C shook her head with disgust.

"Mexican?" Kim called out to the van.

She was greeted by moaning and a chorus of yeses. I even considered ordering tacos after swearing I would never eat them again because of the vagina diatribe. As if sensing my hesitation, Edith decided to help me out.

"Do you want me to wipe the love taco from your mind?" she inquired.

How in the hell did everybody know what I was thinking? Was I that readable? "Will it destroy any other cuisine for me?" I shuddered at the thought of her ruining Italian or Japanese food too.

"Nah," she laughed. "Sometimes by layering in visuals on top of visuals, you can train the brain to accept only the ones you can tolerate."

WTF? That sounded like some intense therapyspeak or some self-preservation tactics for times of war . . . She constantly surprised me.

"Do you want help or not?"

"Sure, I guess," I said, already regretting my answer.

"Close your eyes and listen carefully," she whispered.

I nodded my head and shifted slightly so I was out of her line of spit.

"Front butt . . . pee pot . . . num-num . . . sugar bowl."

Well, that did it. I was able to order tacos and I would never put sugar in my coffee again. Thank you, Edith.

Chapter 30

After a much-needed shower and about twenty minutes of primping, I sat down on my lumpy bed and waited . . . and waited. Me and waiting were not good buddies. My mind tended to go places that were as ridiculous as they were unimaginable.

Thanking my lucky stars that my hangover had finally disappeared, I refolded all the clothes in my drawers. Crap, I was going to have to do laundry soon. I was getting down to the last of my panties and I was not one of those earthy gals who could turn them inside out and wear them a second time. I vaguely recalled Hugh saying there were washers, dryers, and a detergent vending machine around the side of the building. Maybe I would throw a load in now and get it out later . . . Yep, that's what I would do. If I sat there and did nothing I would imagine Mitch laid up in a hospital somewhere at the least, and dead at the worst.

I quickly scooped up all my panties, jeans, and T-shirts and threw them into a bag. If I were at home I wouldn't have even considered mixing colors in the wash, but I wasn't at home and I was running out of clothes. I didn't think searching for Sasquatch in my pj's was a good idea.

I stepped out of my little room and into the twilight zone.

"If I do a back handspring, you'll owe me three hundred dollars, you old dyke," Edith yelled at Mrs. C.

"I said standing backflip, heifer," Mrs. C. countered while walking on her hands across the parking lot. WTF?

"Um . . . What are you guys doing?" I asked. I was not taking either of them to the emergency room later. I had a rendezvous.

"Getting in shape to kick some ass." Edith grinned.

"Were you guys in the circus?" That had to be it. It didn't explain all of their strange behavior, but . . .

They cackled like I was a brilliant stand-up comedian. I rocked back and forth on my feet, watching them and hoped they didn't have strokes from their uproarious laugh attack. "Yeah," Edith gurgled, trying to get a grip. "You could call it a circus."

Clearly they hadn't been in the circus, but I knew they weren't going to come clean on their past.

"Where are you going?" Mrs. C asked. She now had her leg wrapped up around her neck. She looked like a human pretzel.

It took a moment before I could form words. "Laundry," I sputtered.

"Want to do ours too?" she asked.

"Nope," I said, looking away. I was having a painful visceral reaction to her inhuman position.

"What if I do a toe touch?" Edith offered.

"Like jump in the air and touch your toes?" I asked, mortified.

"Yep." She nodded proudly and started stretching out.

I considered it for a brief moment and then realized the image of Edith splayed spread eagle in the air would live with me forever.

"I'll pass," I said as politely as I could.

"Your loss," she grunted as she continued her workout.

I had nothing to say that wouldn't sound snarky, so I nodded and headed for the machines. Maybe Kim knew their backgrounds. I'd have to ask.

The washing machine was right where Hugh had said it would be and I was surprised at how clean it was. The Paul Bunyan Lodge and Getaway Resort might be ugly, but at least it was sanitary. I did find it rather odd that we were the only guests, but with the economy what it was, I guessed that folks weren't vacationing as much this summer.

I wandered around the back of the building. I peeked around for anything interesting that might have captured Stuey's attention. He always came from back there every morning. Holy hell, I was getting paranoid. I was on a reality show shoot not a stakeout.

I took a deep breath of fresh air, pushed my overactive imagination into the far corner of my brain, and admired the majestic forest that surrounded the lodge. I'd forgotten to notice the natural beauty around me with all the craziness going on. Minnesota wilderness was like no other. It had a quiet, stoic beauty . . . kind of like the people here. I glanced around one last time, making sure I hadn't missed anything, and then hurried back to my room.

I rounded the corner of the building and my heart lodged in my throat. Thankfully the old lesbos were gone because Mitch was standing outside my room. He was leaning against the building in his jeans, T-shirt, and rockin'-hot motorcycle boots. He hadn't noticed me, so I was able to admire from a distance. God, no man had the right to be as beautiful as he was.

I felt shaky and short of breath. What in the hell was wrong with me? I should be happy he was here, but all I felt was relief he wasn't dead. Was this how it was going to be? What happened to the "I'll take him when I can have him" scenario? Would I spend the rest of my life worried that he'd never come back and I'd never know why? I almost turned and ran like a coward, but he seemed to feel me and turned to stare.

A slow sexy smile spread across his handsome face and I grabbed the side of the building so I didn't fall to the ground. Every doubt I had evaporated. What kind of magic sauce was that boy working? And why did he have such an effect on me?

He crooked his finger, silently instructing me to come to him. No problem there. I'd have to be chained to a wall to be able to resist him. Although I was slightly off about there being no problem. My knees were a quivering mess and I needed the walls and doorknobs of the rooms I passed to hold me upright. I had a fleeting thought I might appear drunk, but there was nothing to do about it. It was wobble or fall. I chose wobble.

"Hi, Kristy." He grinned, pulling on my still-damp curls. "I've come to pick you up for a date."

"A date?" I looked around the parking lot for his car but only saw the vehicles from our group. "Where's your car?" I asked in a voice that sounded a little phone-sex-operator-ish even to my own ears.

"Don't have one." Those crazy-hot blue eyes roved all over my body. Somehow they had the same effect as his hands would have. Heat suffused me and I found myself involuntarily leaning into him. "God, Kristy, if you don't stop looking at me like that, I'm going to break down your door and cuff you to your bed."

"Promise?" I grinned and ran my fingers lightly over his lips.

He groaned and shoved me up against my door. He crushed my

mouth with his and my insides exploded into a happy dance. I wrapped my arms around his neck and laced my hands into his thick hair. Damn, he could kiss and he tasted like heaven.

"Okay," he whispered against my lips. "I'm going to do this right. I don't want you to think I'm just showing up for a booty call."

"You mean I'm not gonna get any booty?" I pouted and ran my tongue over his bottom lip. I slid my hands from his hair and trailed them down his broad shoulders to his chest.

He looked up to the sky and groaned. "If you don't remove your hands right now, there is a fine chance we'll be arrested for lewd public behavior."

I giggled and gave his perfect man-butt a squeeze before I stepped away. It did tingly things to my girlie parts to know I made him feel the same way he made me feel.

Holding me at arm's length, he gave me a devastating lopsided grin. "I am taking you out for a drink and then I am taking you back here to explore the various and sundry uses for handcuffs."

"That got us into a little trouble before," I said, backing away from him. A wave of excitement coursed through me and my breathing felt funny.

He narrowed his eyes and watched my retreat with interest. "You do realize you are challenging me right now."

"Yep," I said softly, backing away some more. His predator's instinct was so fine tuned, I could feel it, and it made the party in my panties ratchet up a few notches.

"You sure you want to do that?" he asked silkily, adjusting his stance.

"Yep," I said flippantly. My heart was pounding so hard in my chest, I was sure he could hear it. I very slowly backed up a few more steps, my eyes never leaving his. He might know how to push my buttons, but I was having a hell of a good time learning how to push his.

I glanced quickly to my right, wondering if I could make it to Paul Bunyan before he could catch me. If I could get that far, there was a good chance I could fend him off. Of course, fending him off wasn't really my goal . . . but the game was hot. The morning glory growth around Paul's ginormous legs made it impossible for Mitch to take a shortcut through the middle to corner me.

I stared at the ground for a moment and waited for his body to relax. I needed him to think I'd given up. I saw a slight shift in his body from the corner of my eye . . . and I ran. I ran like the devil was after me. And he was. The hot sexy one with killer eyes and an ass to match.

I shrieked as I felt him on my heels. His laugh made me giggle. I reached Paul, grabbed onto his huge red leg, and held on for all I was worth. So much for thinking I could outrun Mitch . . .

He buried his face in my hair and wrapped his arms around my waist. I could feel his uneven breathing against my cheek and his very happy camper grinding into my bottom. He tried to wriggle me off Paul's leg, but I held fast.

"Do you want to be spanked or tickled?" he whispered into my ear, clasping my body tightly to his.

"Neither," I gasped. "At least not out here."

"Well, then, how about this?" His hands slid from my waist to my breasts. He cupped them in his big hands and gently squeezed, sending chills through me. I felt drugged, my body was tingly and sluggish. I knew I would let him do anything he wanted to, happily, but . . .

"Mitch, we should stop," I told him, pressing my breasts more fully into his hands.

"Because um . . . wait, I can't remember why we have to stop."

"Possibly because we're outside in front of your hotel and anyone could see us?"

"That works," I laughed. I let go of Paul and relaxed into Mitch's embrace. My head fit perfectly in the hollow between his shoulder and his neck.

"Come on, pretty girl, let me take you out."

"There's nothing really within walking distance," I told him, wondering how he'd gotten here without a car. He took my hand in his and gently pulled me over to the check-in area of the hotel. I'd been here a week and hadn't even set foot on this side of the lodge.

"Are we calling a cab?" I asked, loving the feel of his warm calloused hand.

"Nope." He gave me a quick kiss. My heart fluttered and I almost tripped over the huge motorcycle that popped up from out of nowhere.

"Shit," I muttered, trying to regain my balance. Mitch steadied me and copped a major feel of my ass at the same time.

"Hop on, Goldilocks. I'm going to take you for a ride you won't forget."

If that wasn't the understatement of the century, I didn't know what was . . .

Rose and Popo's was rockin' when we walked in. I couldn't believe this was where he'd taken me. I said a silent prayer that I wouldn't be recognized . . . we had been banned from the place. Well, the rest of my group had. I'd actually been outside with Rich when all the ugly went down.

"What would you like?" Mitch asked, guiding me to the bar.

You. Naked. Every part of my body was hyperaware of him. I could feel the heat of his hand on my back through the thin material of my shirt and it made me want to jump him. Bad. "Um, a beer, please."

"Coming right up," he said and covertly grabbed my ass.

I watched with amusement at first and then jealousy after a few minutes. Waitresses and random women were literally falling over themselves to get close to him. All boobs and big white smiles. He was pretty, but this was ridiculous. *He belonged to me.* To be fair, he didn't encourage any of it, but it still made me want to bitch slap about thirteen overzealous women. He was mine and I was going to prove it.

Shoving one particularly busty blonde aggressor out of the way, I grabbed Mitch by the collar of his T-shirt, pulled him down to me, and laid on one of the hottest, most obnoxious kisses I'd ever given anyone. It backfired just a little when I had to grab a rotund bald man for balance because I practically blacked out.

"Sit," Mitch said, extracting me from my new bald paramour and leading me to a table. "What was that?"

I wanted to slap the smug grin off his face. I was embarrassed and felt out of control. I realized how little I knew of the man sitting in front of me. He was a rock star in the sack and he was funny and kind and I'd already imagined my life with him, but how would I be able to trust that, when he was away from me, he would still be mine?

"I don't know you," I muttered. "And now I feel embarrassed and stupid because I wanted to deck the boobie blonde and so I . . ." I trailed off and just wanted to leave.

"And so you?" He reached across the table and took my hand.

Dang it, I couldn't think when he touched me. "Mitch, I keep thinking I can do this and then I don't know if I can," I sighed. "I don't normally want to attack random women." I winced and tried to pull my hand back, but he held it fast.

"I liked it."

"You liked it?" I used my free hand to rearrange everything and anything I could find on the table.

"Look at me," he said quietly.

I raised my eyes to his and got sucked back into the place I wanted to be.

"I like that you want to claim me, because God knows I want to rip the heads off half the men in this bar."

I wrinkled my nose and giggled. "You do?"

"Yep," he said, taking my other hand. I wasn't sure if he needed to touch me or needed me to stop alphabetizing the sugar packets. "I don't like other men ogling what's mine."

"God, we're a pair," I laughed.

"Kristy, you do know me and I know you."

"Mitch," I said, shaking my head. "I don't know if we have a foundation strong enough to rock as hard as we're going to."

"I believe we do." He let go of the alphabetizing hand and sank his free hand into my hair.

"Can I tell you some things?" I asked, leaning my head into his hand.

"Please do."

"I have some trust issues." I closed my eyes, enjoying the feel of his hand in my hair and continued. "My dad disappeared when I was young and I haven't gotten a male-female relationship right since. I thought I wanted what I never had . . . you know, a husband who came home every night and a white picket fence and two point five children, but . . ."

"But?"

I opened my eyes and stared into his. "But I want you . . . and it scares me to death."

His quick intake of breath and the tightening of his hand in my hair thrilled me to my toes. "Do you believe in things you can't see all the time?" He watched me with an intensity that unnerved me.

"Like Bigfoot?" I giggled, needing to lighten the electric current running between us.

"Ookay," he grinned. "That would work."

"I believe in the possibility," I said, quoting my beautiful friend Rich.

"Then I need you to believe in the possibility of us. I may not be with you all the time, but I will love you no matter where I am."

Something snapped and my eyes filled with tears. A wall inside me semishattered with his words.

"Will you let me come home with you?" he asked.

I held my breath and closed my eyes. I knew what the next words out of my mouth were going to be and I knew once I uttered them, there was no going back. I took a deep breath and slowly opened my eyes. The big beautiful man in front of me looked like a vulnerable little boy.

"I will always let you come home with me, Mitch. Always."

Chapter 31

Riding fast on a motorcycle wrapped around my own Prince Charming was a damn good way to spend the evening. We rode around the outskirts of Duluth for about an hour at speeds that made me shriek with joy. I was flying and it was magical. Absolutely perfect.

Back at the lodge, Mitch parked his motorcycle and I dragged him down to the washing machine. Thankfully, I remembered I needed to switch my clothes from the washer to the dryer. I would hate to wear wet panties in the morning. Going commando, while kind of sexy, was not really my idea of a good time. That took thirty-seven minutes. Two of those minutes consisted of the clothing transfer and the other thirty-five involved making out like horny teenagers.

"We're going to get busted out here," Mitch mumbled with his lips planted firmly against my neck and his hands making their way inside the back of my jeans.

"Let's go to my room," I gasped as his teeth nipped lightly at my neck.

He took an unsteady step back and narrowed his eyes. "I'll race you."

"No way," I giggled. "You'll kick my ass."

"I'm at a slight disadvantage here," he said, referring to the impressive bulge in his jeans.

I considered my options while staring at the front of his pants.

"You're making it harder by looking," he chuckled.

"Really?" I was loving the power I had.

"Yep. Really."

"Can I have a head start?" I asked, hopping off the washer.

He leaned forward, trapping me against the machines. "If I win, I make the rules tonight," he said softly, making me shudder in anticipation.

"And if I win?" I challenged.

"You won't."

"We'll just have to see about that," I whispered, running my hand over what had to be a painful erection at this point.

He closed his eyes and groaned. I was nobody's dummy. I slipped away and got my head start . . . and I still lost. Of course, the situation was a win-win as far as I was concerned, so I didn't give a monkey's butt about losing.

I almost broke the key off in the door. We couldn't get in there fast enough, but when we did it got weird.

"So, um . . . can I get you something to drink?" I asked, all of a sudden feeling shy. Why in the hell was I shy? He was just touching my naked butt and I'd latched onto his package like I owned it.

"No, I'm good," he said, sitting on the desk that was still by the foot of my bed from the poker game last night. The thing weighed a ton and I couldn't move it back.

"That's good," I giggled, "because I don't actually have anything to offer you."

He grinned and ran his hands through his hair. He seemed as uncomfortable as I did. "I like the way you've rearranged the room," he said, watching me flit around the small space.

"Oh, the girls were over last night and we played a little poker," I told him, explaining the odd setup. "I couldn't get it back over to the wall." I shrugged and sat on one of the folding chairs that Edith had forgotten to retrieve.

"Allow me." Mitch pushed the desk back to the wall as if it weighed nothing. I'd bet five bucks he could bench press me. "How'd it go?"

"What?"

"The game. Did you win?"

"Nope," I laughed. "They cheated and I sucked."

"Did you lose a lot?" He sat down on the edge of my bed and pulled my chair close. As awkward as this was, I couldn't help but notice he was still sporting something very hard in his pants.

"No, I didn't lose money. What I lost could possibly make me lose my mind, but I'll just have to wait and see."

He waited for more, but it was too complicated to share right then. He slowly leaned in and pressed his forehead to mine. I closed my eyes and breathed him in.

"Why is this weird?" I whispered into his mouth.

He was very still for a moment and then sat back and stared straight into my soul with those damn blue eyes. "Maybe because neither one of us has made love with someone that we were truly in love with," he said in a low gruff voice that sent all sorts of unfamiliar feelings ricocheting through my body.

"Maybe we shouldn't have sex tonight." I kicked off my tennis shoes and removed my socks.

"You're probably right." He stood up and quickly removed his own boots and began unbuttoning his jeans.

"We should take it slow." I grinned and pulled my T-shirt over my head. I got discombobulated as I watched him ease his shirt off. His rock-hard abs were movie star worthy and the crisp sprinkling of dark chest hair that tapered down to a sexy V right below the waistband of his jeans made me dizzy.

"It's an interesting concept." His eyes were hooded as he slid his jeans off. His white boxer briefs hid nothing and my wisp of silk panties were now soaked. This was the most intense nontouching foreplay I'd ever had.

"We're being very adult about this," I told him, easing off my chair as I yanked off my jeans, leaving my barely there light pink thong and matching lacy bra on. "Would you like to play poker?" I giggled.

"Strip?"

"Well, considering the amount of clothing, or rather, lack thereof . . . it would be a fairly short game."

"True," he said, approaching me like a starving animal stalking its prey.

Wanting to add flames to the building inferno, I backed away. His eyes flashed and his grin knocked the air right out of my chest.

"What are you doing, Kristy?" His voice held a hint of danger in it that weakened my knees and set off fireworks in my panties.

"I don't know," I whispered, drawing my bottom lip into my mouth.

"Oh, I think you do."

The room was so charged with sexual energy, I thought I was going to have an orgasm merely from the way he was looking at me. God, was it going to get better and better each time with him? I wasn't sure I could live through much better. Although, I suppose dying from a massive orgasm would be a good way to go.

Speak . . . I needed to speak. I was close to passing out or even worse, having an embarrassing screaming orgasm all by myself right in front of him. Words . . . use words. Fucktard, I could barely remember how to talk . . .

"You're supposed to make the rules," I stammered, backing into the wall. "You won the race."

"Yep." He stilled, enjoying the fact I had nowhere to run. I was firmly trapped between the wall and the bed. I'd maneuvered that one nicely . . .

"So what are they?" My heart was hammering in my ears. I wondered if he really had handcuffs.

"There are no rules," he said, moving into my space. "Because this isn't a game. This is real."

Oh. My. God. Of all the things he could have said, I was not prepared for that. My knees buckled and I fell to the bed. He was on me so fast I didn't even see him move.

"Take off your bra," he demanded in a tone that made me shiver. I quickly flicked the front clasp and released my aching breasts. He gently took one of my painfully erect nipples into his mouth and lightly nipped. My hissed intake of breath made him chuckle. "You like that?"

"Yes," I ground out through clenched teeth, arching my back and offering more of myself to him.

"God, you are so fucking beautiful." His mouth found my other breast and his hands worshipped my body until I thought I would burst.

"Mitch, I need . . ." I gasped. "Oh God."

"What do you need, baby?"

"I need you," I whimpered.

"What do you need me to do?" His hot breath in my ear flew to all the nerve endings south of my belly button.

"I need you to fuck me," I gasped, writhing underneath him.

"Jesus Christ," he muttered, his eyes wild. He ripped my thong from my body and kicked out of his boxer briefs. "I can't wait," he said, roughly parting my legs and pushing his body into mine.

"Neither can I," I moaned, wrapping my legs around his back and lifting my hips to take more of him inside me.

"I don't want to hurt you," he groaned, trying to hold back.

"I like a little pain," I whispered with my lips against his neck.

"Oh, fuck," he groaned and buried himself to the hilt.

I think I screamed, but I was too far gone to know what came out of my mouth. For all I knew I was speaking in tongues or possibly Russian. My body was on fire and I met every mind-blowing thrust with a force and passion that only Mitch could draw out of me. His kisses were hard and searching. I laced my fingers through his hair and pulled. His lips seared a path down my neck to the spot on my shoulder that made me see God.

He raised his head and sank his fingers into my hair. Resting his weight on his elbows, he slowed his pace from frantic to slow burn, burying himself in and out of my body at a lazy speed that made waves of electricity throb through me.

"Look at me," he said in a gruff voice. "Watch me while I fuck you. Watch what you do to me."

I melted into him. This was so much more than sex. It fundamentally changed me . . . rearranged my atoms or something crazy like that. I gasped for air as his fingers burned into my hips, holding me the way he wanted me. The sounds coming from me were unfamiliar and my nails raked his back. I couldn't get close enough. And his eyes . . . he sucked me into a place that I never wanted to leave.

I was racing toward something I was sure I wouldn't live through, but I was hell-bent on getting there. "Mitch," I cried out. "Faster . . . please, God, faster."

His laugh of pure masculine satisfaction made everything inside me tighten. I gripped the thick length of him with my body; he swore and raised his eyes to the ceiling. All bets were off and all control was gone. I was on the scariest, most exhilarating ride of my life and there was no going back. He pounded into me with a speed and force that made me see stars. I bit down on his neck to muffle my screams . . . and then I exploded. Shattered into a million pieces. I vaguely heard him shout his release as I slowly floated back to earth.

"Oh my God," he muttered, refusing to let me put even an inch between us. "I think I just became one with Jesus."

"I know I did," I giggled and ran my tongue over his collarbone. "I guess really digging somebody does make it better."

He slid out of my body and took my face in his hands. "Really digging? Is that all?"

"Um . . . no. That's not all," I said quietly.

"Say it."

"I love you," I whispered. His crooked grin made my heart flutter and I tried to bury my face in his chest.

"No hiding," he said. "I love you too."

I nestled into his arms and realized I fit perfectly. He stroked my hair and slowly rattled off what he liked best about my body parts . . . all of them.

"You have to shut up." I was mortified and tried to roll away. It was embarrassing to listen to him talk about my tight wet lady parts when we weren't in the middle of a fuck-a-thon.

He tightened his grip and laughed. "You make me so happy, and I'm not just talking the sex."

"I wish this moment didn't have to end," I sighed, "but it does."

We were silent for a while, each lost in our own thoughts. I ran my hands over his chest and shoulders, trying to memorize the way he felt beneath my fingertips.

"It won't always be like this," he muttered into my hair.

"What do you mean?"

"I want to give you everything you want . . . I want you to have your white picket fence and your twelve point five kids and your . . ."

"Twelve point five?" I gasped. "I never said twelve point five. I said two point five."

"Oh, you're kidding. I was sure you said twelve point five," he teased. "I guess it was just wishful thinking. I always wanted my own football team."

"Two." I punched him in the shoulder. "I said two point five."

"Anyhoo," he said grinning, "I want to give you . . ."

"Shhh." I put my finger over his lips. "I don't want you to give up anything for me. I love you like this. I could never give up my shelter for someone . . . it makes me who I am."

"But . . ."

"No buts." I rolled on top of him and looked him in the eye. "Part of who you are is what you do and I want you . . . all of you." I leaned in and pressed my open lips to his and told him with my body all the things I'd just said with my voice.

"You're mine, Kristy," he whispered against my lips. "And I'll be back soon."

"When?"

"Soon." He shook his head in frustration. "Goddamn it, I want to tell you about what I do . . . but I can't." He blew out an angry breath and held on to me like I was going to disappear.

"It's okay. You don't have any idea of half of the stuff I'm doing," I said, thinking about my bizarre group of friends and the unsettling way the reality show was turning out.

"I know you're searching for Bigfoot with the lesbians, the gal who rearranges noses, and a big fat guy with bad teeth."

I sat up and stared at him. "How do you know all that? I didn't tell you that." Did I? God, if I did, I didn't remember.

"Rena," he said quickly. "You must have told Rena, and Jack told me."

"Oh." I nodded. I didn't recall talking about Rich's teeth to Rena, but clearly I had. "They're actually all good people. Strange, but good."

"They're lucky to have you," he said, pulling me back down and nibbling on my ear.

"Is your case in this area?" I asked. "Wait, you don't have to tell me."

"I don't want you to be afraid to ask me anything. I will always tell you what I can and yes, my case is in this area."

"Is it dangerous?"

"I hope not," he said. "I truly hope not."

I curled up next to him as close as I could get. The thought of something happening to him was unacceptable. He was mine and I was keeping him. "You have to promise me you'll be careful. I want my three point five kids."

"I thought it was two," he chuckled.

"I changed my mind," I giggled and decided I would hold on tight until he had to go.

Chapter 32

I got to hold on to Mitch for another half an hour before he had to go. It involved some cuddling and some toe-curling making out. I would never get enough of his lips. Ever. After one last soul-scorching kiss he promised he would be back soon and would call me daily unless he was out of range.

I had never felt this strongly about anyone in my life. I had wondered when it would be my turn. I had wanted what Kim and Hugh and Rena and Jack had . . . and now I had it. My relationship was a little unconventional, but I didn't care. I was head over heels in love with Mitch and we would make it work. Maybe I would become a secret agent too, and we could go off on missions together. I rolled my eyes at myself and my ridiculous daydreams and snuggled deeper into my covers. I could still smell Mitch on my pillow and I buried my face in it.

"Assmonkeys," I moaned to no one in particular from underneath my comfy pile of blankets. "My laundry . . ."

I rolled out of my cozy, lumpy bed and yanked on the first things my fingers touched. I looked sort of homeless in my ratty sweats, inside-out T-shirt, and mismatched tennis shoes, but who in the hell was I going to run into at this time of night? I'd simply zip down to the dryer, grab my clothes, and run back. Plus, if I ran into anyone from my crew, they wouldn't think twice about my outfit. The acrobatic lesbians would probably like it.

It was chillier than I'd expected. It always amazes me how cool it gets in the summer in Minnesota, especially up north. It was a little spooky being outside this late. The Paul Bunyan Lodge was deserted. I felt like I was in one of those horror movies where the audience is yelling at the screen for the stupid girl to go back into her room and bolt her door shut because she's about to get killed.

On the outside chance that might be the case, I hauled ass toward the machines. A heated conversation between a man and a woman stopped me dead in my tracks. I quickly wedged myself behind a pole so I wouldn't be bludgeoned to death. The voices sounded familiar . . . Mitch and Heidi? But that wasn't possible. I peeked around the pole and listened.

He had left a half hour ago. Why was he still here and what was he doing with her? Was she hitting on him the way she did with every man she came across? I glanced down at my horrifically unsexy outfit and cringed. She was still in her eye-dropping hooker dress. Shit . . . I could step out and save him, but I didn't want his last memory of our evening to be of me in this ridiculous getup. Whatever, he loved me . . . I'd save him. I stepped out to reclaim what was mine and froze. Something felt very wrong. My stomach clenched in dread and a flicker of apprehension coursed through me. I quickly slipped back behind my pole.

"You are not the boss of me," she hissed. "You were in charge for many years, but that's not the case anymore, so back off."

"Listen to me," he shot back angrily. "We may not be living under the same roof anymore, but you are and always will be my responsibility . . . whether you like it or not."

Oh my God, I felt sick. What the fuck was going on? Why were Heidi Kugelschmooson and Mitch arguing in the parking lot? And how did they know each other? And why did it sound like they knew each other really, really well?

I stayed hidden and listened. This was turning out way worse than getting chopped into bits by a masked axe murderer.

"You look like a slut and you're putting yourself and others in danger." He grabbed her by the shoulders and kept her from walking away.

"I'm not putting anyone in danger," she snapped. "I'm good and I know what . . ."

"I know." Mitch cut her off. "I know you're good. It's just . . . I can't lose you. I love you. You mean everything to me. I already lost . . ."

"Mitch, I love you. I have always loved you and I always will, but you have to let me go. I'm not her." She held her arms out and he slowly walked into them.

Ice ran through my veins and I thought I was going to throw up. This could not be happening. How could I be so fucking stupid and how could he be so mean? Why had he said all those things to me if he was in love with someone else? Was he sadistic, or did he have a gal in every state he happened to fly through? The thought tore at my insides. Maybe he had families tucked away everywhere, with two point five kids and a dog and a yard. Maybe he was just a fucktard like all men . . . but I loved him.

I slowly stepped out from behind my pole and took two steps toward Mitch and his lover, Heidi. My shattered heart was pounding wildly in my ears and breathing was difficult. I hadn't realized the tears were streaming down my face until I tasted the salty water on my lips.

"Oh shit," Heidi muttered, pushing Mitch away.

"What? You won't even let me hug you anymore?" he said.

"No." Heidi's voice was agitated and full of something I couldn't put my finger on. Did she know about me? "Look," she said hoarsely, pushing Mitch in my direction.

"Oh my God, Kristy." Mitch paled and stepped toward me.

I backed away, but this was no game. I choked back a sob and put my hand up. "Don't come near me."

He blanched and ran his hands through his hair. The same hands that had touched me . . . and then touched her.

"How much did you hear?" he asked.

"Enough," I said, trying to swallow back the bile in my throat.

"Fuck," Heidi groaned, stepping up next to Mitch. He shot her a look of death and she backed away.

"This is not what you think," he said.

"Stop," I said, wiping the tears away with the back of my hand. "I am so fucking stupid, so stupid. I thought you were different . . . I thought you . . ." I was crying now. For real. I wanted to run away from him. I wanted to scream. I wanted to crawl out of my skin and I wanted to hurt him the way I was hurting. I thought my dad leaving was bad . . . that was nothing compared to how shredded I felt at that moment.

"Kristy, I know this looks bad."

"Do you?" I laughed hysterically, on the verge of breaking.

"What's the bad part? The part where I caught you, or the part where I tell you I never want to see your face ever again in my life?"

"Oh shit," Heidi groaned and looked up to the heavens. She seemed upset and on the verge of tears herself.

"Shut up," I hissed. "I don't want to hear your voice or lay my eyes on you ever again. You'll have your two- or three- or four-timing lover back in about a minute, but right now it's my turn, you bitch."

"Kristy," Mitch said forcefully. "She is not a bitch and you've got this all wrong."

It would've hurt less if he had physically hit me. I was used to that kind of pain. I'd grown up with that and I knew how to compartmentalize that kind of hurt, but I had no idea what to do with this . . . How could he defend her? How much more humiliation was I going to stand there and take?

"You have to trust me when I tell you you've misunderstood what you saw." He sounded desperate.

My mind was a crazy mixture of hope and fear. Was I a typical abuse victim? Always ready for more. Fuck, I'd been through enough therapy to stand up for myself, even though there would be nothing left of me after this.

"Kristy, he's telling the truth." Heidi's voice was quiet, but intense. "There is nothing going on here. Not like you think."

"Please, Kristy," Mitch pleaded. He took another step closer and I took another step back.

I took a deep breath and used the pole to steady myself as I felt my world crumble around me. The tears wouldn't stop and I didn't try to hold them back. I couldn't. "I'd like to know how watching you profess your love to someone else and hearing her return it right after you left my bed is a misunderstanding." My voice was emotionless and cold. I had very little left, and unless he pulled a miracle excuse out of his ass . . . I was gone.

"You have to trust me. This looks like something that it's not."

I knew he wanted to come to me, but it was the last thing in the world I wanted. I feared my reaction to him. I was mortified to realize I wanted him to choose me over her. If he grabbed me right now and told me he'd never see her again, I'd believe him . . . which was why I wasn't letting him get close enough to touch me.

"Why should I trust you?"

"Because I love you." His voice broke with huskiness.

I closed my eyes and let the picture of him holding Heidi run through my mind. He was such a mean man. Why did I still want to believe him? Was great sex muddling my brain, or was it because I loved him too?

"If you want me to trust you, then tell me what's going on." To my own ears, my voice sounded like the same child who'd asked her horrid father why he had to leave . . . "Tell me what I saw."

Mitch's fists clenched at his sides and Heidi turned and walked away. His jaw was working and his eyes were hooded with sorrow and rage. "I can't," he said.

"I'm sorry, what?" I was sure I'd heard him wrong. Was this a joke or my life?

"I said I can't explain this right now. I need you to trust me." His gaze was like a laser, trying to burn a hole into me.

I looked at him for a long moment. I wanted to memorize his face because I knew with certainty that I would never see it again.

"I can't," I whispered, silently handing him what was left of my heart. "I can't trust you if you don't trust me. I can't see you anymore. Please leave me alone."

I turned and walked back to my room, but not before I noticed the tears in his eyes. It didn't matter. I supposed he wasn't used to getting caught . . . I was proud of myself that I didn't run. I held my head high and I walked away from the man I'd thought I would spend the rest of my life with. I knew this one would take a long time to get over, but as raw and as dead as I felt right now . . . I knew I would. I'd gotten over horrible things in my life. This might be the hardest, but I was a strong girl . . .

He knocked quietly and steadily on my door for about two hours, making sleep impossible. I buried my head in my pillow and sobbed until the knocking stopped. I continued to sob until my alarm went off the next morning. I might have gotten a little sleep in, but I wasn't sure and didn't care.

"Oh God," I groaned, realizing that when my life had blown up in my face last night, I'd forgotten my laundry. Thankfully I'd set my alarm really early. In all my wisdom, I'd decided a long run would be a good idea in the morning. Of course, the thought of sobbing out in the open air for five miles or so didn't appeal after a night with no sleep, but hopefully no one would be up when I cried myself down to the dryer to get my clothes.

No such luck. I slipped out of my room, praying that Mitch was gone. He was definitely gone. A small part of me was disappointed, but the logical part of my brain knew it was for the best. No Mitch, but Rich was leaning against the van and he looked like hell . . . maybe even worse than I did.

"Hey." I spared him a quick wave and tried to move quickly by. I didn't have it in me to talk to anyone right now. Even Rich.

"Kristy." The unhappiness in his voice stopped me. What in the hell had happened to him? Surely it couldn't be as bad as what had happened to me, but then again . . . everything was relative.

"Are you okay?" he asked.

"Of course." *Not.* I gave him a bright smile that didn't reach my eyes. "Are you?" He really did look bad. Like he hadn't slept at all. Welcome to my club.

"I'm a bit under the weather," he mumbled.

I noticed his cheeks looked puffier than normal. How did someone get that weird cheek fat? It seemed like he had wads of cotton stuffed up there. What in the hell was my problem? I needed to get over judging this man on his looks. He was one of the loveliest people I'd met in a long time. Hell, I'd be better off with someone like Rich. Eww . . . Even though I was trying not to be shallow, he just did not get my mojo going . . .

"Can I get you anything?" I asked, remembering I had some cold medicine and allergy pills in my room.

"No." He smiled, sadly. "It's nothing a hug wouldn't solve."

I stared at my big bizarre-looking friend for a moment and realized I could use a hug too. A hug from a trustworthy friend who wasn't going to fuck me over. I moved into his big fleshy arms and rested my head on his man-boobs. He smelled wonderful and it made my heart ache. He clearly used the same laundry detergent or soap as Mitch. If I closed my eyes, I could almost pretend it was Mitch holding me . . . well, a soft, squishy, unattractive version of Mitch.

"Why are you up so early?" he asked.

When I tried to pull away to answer, he refused to let go. Hmm, a little odd, but the hug was nice so I gave in. "I forgot to get my laundry out of the dryer last night."

"Oh," he said, resting his chin on the top of my head.

"Listen to me, you fucking asshole," Stuey hissed, coming around from the back of the building. "Today is the day. They pushed it up and that's that."

"I'm sick of your bullshit," Stan muttered. "You better be right about this or we're both going down."

Rich, with quick hands and sure moves, relocated us so we were between the van and the trailer . . . out of Stan and Stuey's sight line. He put his finger to his lips and I nodded. What were they talking about?

"What about the idiots?" Stan asked.

"They take the rap. The big guys told us to plant it on someone else and we have," he laughed. "What's your fucking problem?"

"This is the stupidest idea you've ever had, and why I'm going with it is beyond me," Stan replied tersely. "Getting involved with the blond bitch has fried your little brain."

"I never even got into her pants, just a few cops of her tits," he groaned. "I got some major blue balls here."

"Yeah, well let your goddamn wife take care of that when you get home."

Okay, gross, gross, and double gross. I guess Heidi was being true to Mitch by not screwing Stuey-Herman, but the thought that he'd touched her in any way was repulsive. Mitch and Heidi deserved each other. I buried my head in Rich's chest so he wouldn't see my tears. I was still too raw to explain anything to anyone.

"So we're really gonna take the big hairy bastards down today?" Stan laughed without much humor.

"Yep," Stuey said. "And we'll leave the trash with the idiots and get the fuck out of town."

"Perfect," Stan snorted, "but if anything goes south . . . you're dead."

"Not if I kill you first," Stuey-Herman growled and then laughed like a hyena.

I stiffened in Rich's arms. What in the hell did that mean? Had they really found Bigfoot? It sounded like they planned to kill him and blame it on us . . . or kill each other in the process. WTF? How would they benefit from that? Was it to screw over the TIT network? Although, according to Moon-Unit, they had no ties to TIT. I was so tired and confused, I couldn't make any sense of what I'd just heard. In fact, I wasn't even sure I'd heard them correctly.

I stifled a gasp when the van started and began to move. Rich, with amazing dexterity for a man so huge, quickly moved us so the trailer didn't run us over. Why were Stuey and Stan leaving Paul Bunyan with both the sedan and the van? How were we supposed to save Sasquatch with no ride out to the cabin?

"Rich, what's happening?"

He was quiet as we watched the van leave the parking lot. "I'm assuming they're going to fill the van with gas. They do that every morning, but as far as the rest of that conversation . . . I'm not sure."

"They're going to kill Bigfoot and set us up." For the second time in less than twenty-four hours, I felt the bile rise up in my throat.

"I won't let that happen," Rich assured me, and for some bizarre reason, I believed him. "Go get your laundry and get ready. I'll meet you back out here with the rest of the crew in an hour and a half," he told me.

"Okay." I didn't want to leave him, but I did as I was told. This moment felt like the quiet eye of the storm . . . I worried what the actual storm was going to bring. "Should I call the police?"

"I'll take care of that. Now go." He gave me a strained smile and a quick hug. I watched him as he strode back to his room and I ran down to the dryer. *Please, God, let today be over soon.*

Chapter 33

After getting my laundry, I went back to my room, took a shower, and lay down for a few minutes. Apparently a few minutes turned into an hour or so because a banging on my door knocked me out of a deep slumber.

"Crapmonkeys," I shrieked as I looked at my alarm clock. "I'm coming," I shouted as I yanked on clean jeans, a T-shirt, and matching tennis shoes. God, how could I have fallen back asleep with Armageddon coming? It took me six minutes of frantic movement coupled with a bunch of creative swearing before I was ready. I almost choked myself to death with my toothbrush, I was moving so fast.

"I'm here," I gasped, tearing out of my room into the parking lot.

Mariah, Boo, Mrs. C, and Edith were standing out in the middle of the gravel drive, looking around. Kim, Hugh, and Rich were nowhere to be found. I wondered if Rich had fallen back asleep too.

"Where did those little shiny dumb-asses put the van?" Edith asked with her hands on her hips.

"I saw them drive it off about an hour and a half ago," I said, still trying to catch my breath. "I think they went to get gas."

"Where? In Canada?" Mrs. C snapped. "I'm ready to go, and those slimy little bastards are out joyriding in a van with an empty trailer attached to it."

I realized the old gals weren't saying "bless your heart" anymore. "Where is everyone else?"

"Don't know." Mariah shrugged. Holy cow, her hair was purple. "You look exhausted," she commented.

"Yep," I agreed, not offering anything more.

"Bad night?" Boo asked kindly.

I sucked my bottom lip into my mouth and nodded. I was afraid to speak. I refused to cry any more over Mitch. At least not in public . . . I glanced up as an SUV turned into the parking lot. Oh hell, this was awesome, just fucking awesome. I tensed and felt ill as I watched Heidi Kugelschmooson and the Baldies pull up. What in the hell was she doing here? Had she come to rub it in? I turned my back on her arrival and gave myself a pep talk. *I can do this; I will stay away from her and I will not slap, pinch, bite, or dismember her in any way.*

"I need to talk to you," Heidi insisted loudly as she hopped out of the truck and strode toward me. The Minnesota accent was gone as were the slutty clothes. She wore jeans, boots, a T-shirt, and a baggy jacket. Aside from the horrible wig, she looked amazing. I hated her.

"I have nothing to say to you," I said through clenched teeth. "You will stay away from me and I will do the same." Everyone watched in fascination as Heidi and I exchanged terse words.

"You will listen to me and we will do it in private," she demanded. God, she sounded just like Mitch. I supposed that came from living with someone for as long as they apparently had.

"Back off," I snapped. "You won. I lost. Don't you dare try to rub it in my face or assume that I'm stupid enough to believe your pathetic lies."

"Holy shit," Mariah muttered. "This is good."

"Hit her," Edith whispered under her breath. "Punch her in the knockers. I'll bet they pop."

Heidi narrowed her eyes at Edith, and Edith shrank back behind me.

"You hurt him, and I won't let that happen," she said, advancing on me.

"You have got to be kidding me," I shouted. "You and your blond helmet have some huge testicles to throw that in my face." My breathing was erratic. I was flabbergasted at her words. "What? Am I supposed to share? You are fucking crazy," I hissed.

"Can I take her out?" Mariah begged, bouncing up and down beside me.

"Let her do it," Mrs. C grunted in my ear. "She's good."

I turned and looked at Mariah, so willing to fight for my honor, her purple hair shining in the morning sun. Her eyes were wild and she was ready to bust down . . . and I wanted her to. I knew I should tell her no, that there was a chance Heidi could kick her ass, but . . .

"Yes," I said, "but—" I grabbed her before she threw herself at my nemesis. "We're going in together."

"Awesome." She grinned and grabbed my hand.

"*No!*" Boo screamed, stepping between Heidi and Mariah and me. "There will be no fighting. Bad things are coming, I can feel it. We have no time for this."

I stopped and dropped my head in embarrassment. What the hell had I been thinking? Just because Heidi had the man I loved, that was no excuse to fight. Actually, nothing was an excuse to fight.

"Sorry," I muttered.

"Me too," Heidi said.

"You two will shake on it and we will get back to the business at hand," Boo stated firmly. "I have no idea what went on between the two of you, but you will work it out later." She reached for my hand and Heidi's at the same time. She grabbed Heidi's first and froze. My hand was forgotten as she glared at Heidi. Heidi became uncomfortable and tried to withdraw her hand, but she was no match for Boo's strength. Boo might be tiny, but when her psychic thing got going, she was superwoman. "Oh my God," Boo mumbled. "No way."

"Stop it," Heidi insisted. "Right now."

"Tell her," Boo said coldly. "You will tell her right now . . . or I will. Not only that, I'll let my sister and the lesbos have at you and I'll help."

The Baldies, who had always faded into the woodwork, stepped up beside Heidi. They looked menacing and all of a sudden the situation had taken an ugly turn. What had Boo sensed? I wasn't sure how much more I could handle. Was Heidi Mitch's wife?

Heidi gazed at Boo with wonder and had the audacity to grin. "Fine," she relented without much of a fight. "This should have been dealt with last night."

I was shaking and I needed to sit. Edith came up behind me and supported me with her skinny old frame. Mrs. C moved in and put her arm around my shoulder.

Heidi bent forward and removed her contacts, revealing a pair of icy blue eyes so similar to Mitch's I gasped. She then reached up and pulled off her helmet, keeping her eyes glued to mine. Her chin-length hair was a dark chocolate brown and she was striking.

Odd and impossible thoughts ran through my brain. I recalled her telling Mitch that she wasn't some other woman. Did that mean his . . . ?

"I'm not his girlfriend," she said softly. "I'm his sister."

A thrill shot through me. He had told me to trust him last night and I had told him to go, but why hadn't he just told me the truth? "Who's the other woman that you claimed not to be?" I asked, amazed at the similarities between brother and sister.

"Our sister who died. I got into this for the same reason Mitch did."

"Why wouldn't he tell me?" The tears started again and Edith shoved a delicate embroidered hanky into my face. While I mopped my eyes, I idly wondered if she had made it.

"Because I'm undercover and it could endanger my life," she said, trying to make me understand. "So instead he destroyed his own happiness," she admitted grimly.

I leaned back into the comfort of Edith and Mrs. C. I felt faint and strange. Trying to place all the puzzle pieces was making me dizzy. Are we the undercover operation? Is *Searching for Sasquatch* just a cover for something else far bigger? Did Mitch really come to see me, or was I convenient because I was already here? Why did they need us? How in the hell did we tie into the big picture? As I was about to start my inquisition, Kim and Hugh ran out of their room, shouting.

"Sweet baby Moses in a blanket," she shrieked. "Moon-Unit got the info and it's bad."

She stopped and attempted to catch her breath. While she recuperated, Hugh gave us a spastic and freaked-out rendition of the theme from *Jaws*. Boo rubbed her back and tried to calm her down.

"Kim, what did Moon-Unit say?"

"Stuey," she panted. "I mean Herman . . . rap sheet . . . long. Prison and drugs and illegal buying and selling of endangered species . . . bad, bad," she gasped.

The old ladies ran back to their room, muttering something about a showdown, and Heidi and the Baldies began quickly walking back to their SUV.

"Wait," I yelled. "I saw them this morning. Rich and I did. They were saying something about today being the day, killing the hairy bastards and setting up the idiots."

"Did they see you and Rich?" Heidi asked in a clipped voice, going into agent mode.

"No, Rich hid us and we listened."

"Is there more than one Bigfoot?" Hugh asked, referring to their mention of hairy bastards. "Are they going to sell him . . . or them . . . into the black market?"

We stood and silently contemplated the many crazy and horrific possible scenarios.

"Where's Rich?" Mariah asked, looking around.

"Oh my God." Heidi paled. "Is he gone?"

"No, I'll bet he fell asleep like I did. He looked like hell this morning," I said, walking over to his door to knock. Heidi gave me a strange stare. I ignored her and banged on Rich's door. No answer. I tried again . . . harder. The same.

"Shit," Heidi mumbled and began pacing. My gut clenched. Rich hadn't felt well this morning. Maybe he was having a heart attack and I was too wrapped up in myself to insist he go to the hospital. Fucktard. I banged harder. I knew CPR and I needed to get into his room. Now.

"Pick it." I pulled Mariah out of the crowd around me. "Pick the lock."

She pulled a pocketknife out of her back pocket and had the door opened in seconds. I had no time to even think about the fact she was so good at getting into locked places. I shoved past her and ran into the room. It was empty. Where was he?

Clothes, books, stacks of gauze, and bottles of cream or maybe glue littered his desk. Boo checked the bathroom and Mariah searched under the bed. I almost laughed in the midst of my oncoming hysteria. Like Rich would even fit under the bed.

"Bathroom's clear," Boo said.

"Bed's clear," Mariah added. "Except for this." She held up an odd purple police manual. Where had I seen that before? No time to think . . . We needed to find him. I had a bad feeling and I didn't even have Boo's abilities.

"That son of a bitch." Heidi's angry tone hit my stomach in a painful place. "Dave, Dan, check the side of the building for his motorcycle." They took off at a run. "I will kill him, if someone else doesn't get to him first," she muttered, making my blood run cold.

Who was she talking about? Mitch or Rich? And what in the hell was her real name?

Reading my mind, Boo asked. "What's your name?"

"Couldn't you tell from your voodoo?" Heidi snapped, clearly wound up about Rich's disappearance.

"I wouldn't ask if I knew," Boo replied calmly.

"Sorry. It's Candace. Candace Sanderson."

"Is Mitch's name really Mitch?" I asked, wondering if he'd lied about that too.

She considered me for a long moment. "Yes, my brother's name is Mitch and he loves you."

"I love him too," I said quietly.

"Well, I sure as hell hope you get to tell him that." She left the room and went in search of the Baldies, who actually had names.

"It's gone," the Baldie named Dave said.

"Damn it, we've gotta go . . . What in the hell is that?" Candace gasped.

We raced out of the room to see what had happened now. Oh. My. God. I blinked to make sure my eyes weren't playing tricks. Nope, they weren't.

Walking down the sidewalk toward us, Mrs. C and Edith were locked and loaded . . . literally. They were armed to the teeth. They carried pearl-handled pistols in side holsters and nunchucks over their shoulders. They had shed their sweats for combat fatigues, boots, and army green T-shirts. I barely registered the fact that they were braless. The rest was too scary.

Edith had a knife tucked into her boot and it looked like Mrs. C had some kind of samurai sword strapped across her back. WTF?

"No fucking way," Mariah blurted, beyond impressed.

"What, may I ask, do you think you're doing?" a shocked Candace demanded as she circled the paramilitarized twins.

"Gonna take care of the problem," Edith grunted, cracking her knuckles.

"Don't you think Herman and whatever Stan's name is will be slightly alarmed and clued in if you show up like that?" Kim inquired, reasonably.

They threw on big jackets, effectively covering their arsenal.

"Knife." Mariah pointed to Edith's exposed weapon.

"Thanks," she said and shoved it down into her boot.

"We have to go," Candace told the Baldies. "They've either got him or he's got them."

"Do we call in backup?" the one named Dan asked.

"Yep," she said, running toward the SUV. "They're about two hours out. No one was expecting anything this soon."

"What about us?" Boo called out as we all ran after her.

"You stay here," she instructed.

"Absolutely not," Mrs. C said, blocking Candace from getting to the truck.

"Out of my way," she barked. "I know what I'm doing and you don't."

"Would you like to put money on that?" Edith said, coming up behind Candace.

Candace was effectively trapped between two armed and insane lesbians. I watched her consider her options carefully. Smiling, she shook her head ruefully. "Suit yourselves."

"Pile in, troops," Edith shouted. Candace winced and grabbed her hearing aid.

"Jesus Christ," she groaned. "Can you not see that I'm wearing a listening device, you old bat?"

"I can see it plain as day." Edith grinned and slapped a high five with her sister. "Plain as day."

How much of a gullible idiot had I been? Candace wasn't hard of hearing, she'd been listening to Stuey and Stan's conversations . . . and how did I not know that the old gals were into guerrilla warfare? Although, I was sure there was more to that story . . .

We quickly piled in. All of us. All ten of us. Thank you, Jesus, it was an extended vehicle, but it was still a tight fit . . . like can-of-sardines tight.

"I'm going to call and see if Moon-Unit has any more info," Kim said from underneath Hugh and Mariah. I was wedged between the Baldies, who were told by Candace if they so much as touched me that Mitch would kill them. They tried desperately to keep their distance, but space was limited.

"Got her," Kim shouted, causing Candace to yank her listening device out of her ear.

"Can you hear me?" Moon-Unit called out.

"We can hear you, dear," Kim answered.

"I believe you're all in danger. The aliens have come and told me that the show has nothing to do with Bigfoot."

"You mean they're not trying to kill Sasquatch?" Hugh asked, clearly relieved.

"Oh, they would if they could," Moon-Unit said, "but he was warned off by the tree sprites. From what I understand, he is safe."

I wasn't sure whether to laugh or cry. The simple fact that the majority of the people in the truck believed what she was saying was mind-blowing. The problem was, some of what she was saying did pertain to possibly keeping us from getting caught in the crossfire of something we didn't understand. I caught Candace's questioning look in the rearview mirror and I shrugged. How to begin to explain . . .

"What I still don't understand is why the hell we're here and involved." Mrs. C stated what we'd all been wondering.

"I think you're a cover for something else they have going on up there," Moon-Unit surmised.

"Candace, can you enlighten us on that one?" I asked sarcastically.

"Nope."

"If you could, would you?" I wondered how far I could push.

"Nope, but I will tell you I have no idea why you're here. It's what I was sent in to find out."

"Can you still hear me?" Moon-Unit's tinny voice yelled.

"Yes, dear," Kim said.

"They are probably armed and dangerous. Edith and Mrs. C, are you prepared?"

"Roger," the old gals grunted in unison.

"Good. Find the source and destroy it. Ohhh," she squealed, "Kristy, this is very important for you to know. It will change your life. I found the evil chi and I destroyed it with my bare hands, a machete, and my dentures. I can't believe I didn't realize it all along, but the trolls said I wasn't to blame. Chi can be quite insidious . . . but that's for another conversation with a lot of alcohol involved."

"How does this affect me?" I was a nervous wreck. Was I going to inherit a colony of trolls or worse? I needed her to get to the end of the story so I could relax. She was killing me.

"Oh, it's all good, sweetie. Are you all ready?"

"Yes," everyone in the entire car shouted, even the Baldies and Candace.

"The evil chi is . . ."

The phone went dead. *Are you kidding me?*

"Call her back," Edith snapped. "I need to know what the fuck the old whack job found."

Pot. Kettle. Black. Again.

"I can't get her," Kim said frantically. "It won't go through."

Par for the course of my life. I always seemed to have about half of the information . . . Shitclowns.

Chapter 34

The van and trailer were parked outside the cabin. The sedan was parked right alongside. Mitch's motorcycle was beside the front door, but no one was in sight. Holy hell, did they have both Rich and Mitch?

"Listen to me," Candace hissed. "This is a clusterfuck waiting to happen. We never should have brought all of you out here, but you may be safer with us than being sitting ducks at the hotel."

Great. This had gone from an easy, but embarrassing, gig to earn fifty thousand dollars for the shelter, to a life-and-death situation. I would bet my left boob—*it's the bigger one*—that the fifty thousand was as fictitious as the show. I might die today for nothing.

"Edith and Mrs. C, protect the group. Dan, Dave, and I are going into the cabin. Roger?" Candace snapped.

"Roger that," Edith replied in the same cadence. "Everyone, out of the car and stay low to the ground. Stay together and be prepared to run."

I lay on the ground next to Boo and prayed to every religious deity I could think of. After about five of the longest minutes of my life, Candace stepped back out of the cabin.

"Mrs. C," Candace yelled from the door. "Do you have smelling salts?"

Why in the hell would she think Mrs. C had smelling salts?

"I'm on it," she said, pulling a small bottle out of her pocket. Of course she had smelling salts . . .

"Bring everyone in here," Candace shouted. "It's not pretty, but I think we'll be safer in here."

Staying low, we duckwalked over to the cabin and waddled into a hell like I'd never known. Three dead bodies of men I'd never seen before were lying on top of each other by the entrance. They'd been shot at point-blank range. I'd seen enough *Law & Order* to recognize that. I clutched Mariah and tried hard not to throw up or scream. I didn't think either one of those activities would be particularly helpful right now. I'd never seen a murdered body before and I hoped I never would again. I turned away from the atrocity and looked around. The room had been trashed; stuffing was everywhere. I didn't recall a couch, but I'd never been in the locked rooms before. My eyes tried to adjust to the darkened cabin. I was now sure the windows hadn't been covered to protect any camera equipment. I doubted there ever had been any camera equipment. I stepped on something hard and it cracked beneath my feet. Glancing down I realized it was teeth.

Oh my God. I ran to the bathroom and threw up. Had they ripped out the men's teeth before they'd killed them? Were Stan and Stuey really capable of this? I rinsed my mouth out and splashed cold water on my face. I stared hard at myself in the mirror and started making deals with God. First and foremost, if I got out of here alive, I'd stop busting on David Hasselhoff. That would be nearly impossible, so I thought it was a good first offer. Secondly, I'd forgive and lay off Tandy McOath, the Junior Miss shoe stealer . . . actually that thought made me feel good. I shoved a piece of gum in my mouth and went out to see how I could help. I was shaking like a leaf, but I was trying.

The Baldies, Candace, and the old ladies were squatting down by someone on the floor. Was it Rich . . . or Mitch? Was he alive? Candace was as tense as I'd ever seen a person, and my heart was in my mouth. Mariah, Boo, Kim, and Hugh were lined up against the wall, watching in horror.

I knew CPR, I reminded myself. I forced my feet, which wanted to stay glued to the floor, to move. Moving like I was underwater, I made my way across the room toward whoever was lying there. If I could be valuable, I was going to be . . . no matter how difficult.

It was Rich. He'd been beaten badly. His arms were tied behind his back and his feet were bound. One of his eyes was swollen shut, his stuffing had been ripped out, and his wig had partially come off, revealing his thick brown hair and his teeth . . . Wait. What? I stood there, blank, amazed, and very shaken. My mind swirled with confusion and betrayal. This. Was. Not. Happening.

Baldie Dan reached into Rich's mouth and removed huge wads of gauze and his cheeks went down. Screams of frustration lodged at the back of my throat. I was the stupidest, most gullible idiot that had ever been born. I turned to find the teeth I had stepped on . . . they were dentures. Dentures for someone who wanted to appear to have hideous teeth. I hated him. He had played me harder than I'd ever been played in my life. The nausea rose back up and I was tempted to race back to the bathroom . . . but first I needed to know if he was alive.

"Can you remove the contact from the swollen eye?" Candace asked Baldie Dave. He nodded curtly and pried the bloody socket open and removed the green contact, revealing a bloodshot icy blue eye. "The other one," Candace directed in a pained whisper. Dave removed the other contact and pulled the rest of the wig from Rich's head.

"Take him out of the suit," Dan ordered Dave. "We need to make sure he hasn't been shot."

Candace swore and ran her hands through her hair in a move so reminiscent of her brother I wanted to cry. As soon as I knew he was okay, I could hate him as much as I wanted to, but right now I just needed to know he wasn't going to die.

"Once he's free, give me the salts," Candace told Mrs. C. Edith pulled the knife from her boot and meticulously cut the ropes that bound Mitch's hands and feet.

"How did he let this happen?" Candace muttered. "I didn't think those little bastards could have taken him down like this."

"Can I touch him?" Boo asked, moving forward.

"Be my guest," Candace said, making room.

The Baldies had finished removing the suit and there was no denying that Rich was Mitch. I was more numb than I had been last night because I had no idea how I felt . . . Everyone moved to get a better view, except me. I was too afraid I would try to kill him once I knew he was okay, so I kept my distance. Boo knelt down and took one of his limp hands in her own. She closed her eyes and rocked back and forth.

"He was tranquilized," she said in a hollow monotone. "They shot him with a tranquilizer gun, tied him up, and then they beat him as he was passing out."

"What about the dead bodies?" Candace demanded.

"They were already here," an ashen-faced Boo whispered.

"Those fuckers," Candace hissed. "Can you tell how long ago he was tranqued?" she asked Boo.

Boo took his hand again and concentrated. "It was still a little dark out," she said in the same monotone. "I would guess two to three hours ago."

Dave picked up a bottle off the floor and examined it. "It should be wearing off about now," he said, "if this is the amount they used."

"Give me that." Edith reached for the bottle. "Salt him," she told her sister. "This dose and this amount should have worn off already." She sniffed the bottle.

"What are you doing?" Kim asked, near tears.

"Making sure it's not laced with anything else."

"You can do that?" Mariah asked, awestruck.

"You bet your ass I can," Edith said smugly, licking the open rim of the bottle.

"Jesus Christ, don't drink it," Candace gasped. "We don't need another tranqued-out casualty."

Edith cackled and flipped Candace the bird. "Please, I've have so much of this shit in my system over the years, I'm immune."

"Ain't that the truth," Mrs. C laughed and licked the bottle too.

They eyed each other for a long moment while we all watched in shock, waiting for them to keel over. WTF? What had they been? It had to be military, but it was mind-boggling to think of them anywhere other than the knitting shop insulting the bejesus out of everyone.

"It's clean," Edith said. "Not laced. This boy should be awake. Gimme the salts, sister."

"Can I ask you a question, just in case we die today?" Mariah squatted down next to Mrs. C . . . her new hero.

"Sure, Purple. Have at it."

"What does the C stand for and why are you a Mrs.? I thought you were a dyke."

Baldie Dave sucked in a huge amount of air, fully expecting Mariah to get her ass kicked for calling an old woman a dyke.

"It's okay," Boo assured him. "They like that term. That, lesbo, and queer."

He nodded his head, color suffusing his face all the way to his bald head.

"I'm a dyke through and through," Mrs. C said. "The Mrs. is for respect and the C stands for Coco." She gave a hard stare around the room, daring anyone to laugh. No one did.

"Can I call you Coco?" Mariah whispered, fearing for her life, but unable to stop herself . . . as usual.

Mrs. C sat silently for a long moment while Edith passed the salts under Mitch's nose. "Yes, you can. I'm tired of the fucking Mrs. C thing anyway. Henceforth all of you will address me as Coco."

Everyone nodded and no one laughed except Edith . . . who was the only one who could have gotten away with it.

"Would anyone like some background music?" Hugh asked, desperate to do his part.

"That would be lovely, darling." Kim smiled and took his hand.

"How about some Elton John," Baldie Dan suggested. "I really enjoyed your medley last Tuesday."

Hugh blew up like a puffer fish and started with "Someone Saved My Life Tonight" . . . very appropriate.

Right at "sugar bear," Mitch woke up. He was groggy, but his eyes searched the room, landed on me . . . and didn't waver.

"Can you get up?" Candace asked, stepping into his line of vision.

"Move," he croaked. "I need to see her."

Candace backed away and I could feel his eyes on me as if they were his hands. I couldn't look at him. I was so relieved he was okay, but at the same time I wanted to destroy him.

"Come here," he said gruffly.

I didn't move.

"Please, Kristy, come to me." His voice was low and filled with pain. I wanted to imagine part of it was emotional, but I knew better. He'd lived a lie and played with me like I was a toy.

"Oh, for the love of Jesus in a bikini, get your ass over there," Coco ordered. "We all know he's an untrustworthy lying sack of shit, but he clearly loves you and you feel the same way or you wouldn't have wanted to whack his sister earlier when you thought he was hosing her . . . so go on with your bad self."

I was pretty sure "Jesus in a bikini" was the least offensive part of that sentence. I refused to make eye contact, but I made my way over. I knew if I didn't, Coco would pick me up and plop me down next to him. Although, if I was honest with myself, I wanted to be near him more than I wanted to breathe . . . but that didn't make him any less of a shithat assmonkey.

He got himself to a sitting position and pulled me close to his body. I went limp and let him do what he wanted. I didn't have the strength to do anything else.

"I may be a sack of shit, but I'm not untrustworthy," he said urgently, lifting my chin so I had to look at him. I closed my eyes and refused to cooperate. "I've been on this case for months. They're drug dealers . . . big ones. I followed them to Minneapolis. We were trying to pinpoint the ringleaders. Unfortunately three of them are lying dead in the corner. When I realized all of you were in danger, I changed how I was going in and became one of the group instead of outside surveillance. I wanted to protect you and I wanted to be near you," he finished softly.

I opened my eyes and stared at his battered, beautiful face. "I don't even know you. Everything about you has been a lie or a secret."

"I'm Rich too," he said, trying to keep me from pulling away. He had me physically because he was stronger, but the emotional part was going to be a much more difficult battle. "I'm your friend who adores you . . . who knows all sorts of important and special things about you. I'm that guy too."

Normally I'd be mortified to have all of my dirty laundry paraded around, but since I wasn't sure we were going to make it out of here, I let it all hang out. Besides, he'd tricked everyone here . . . well, almost. Not Heidi and the Baldies and not Boo. She knew and she was happy for me, told me all sorts of good things were going to happen in my life. Maybe she was still right . . . I was hoping I had all the facts now, so my decisions would be based on reality. But did anybody ever have all the facts?

"Are you really a magician?" I asked, trying not to smile.

He lit up like a child when he realized he might still have a chance. "Actually, I am." He grinned. "I had to learn for a case, years ago. I thought it was fun and I kept it up."

"You're an asshole," I said lightly.

"Agreed." He nodded, grinning.

"And a shithat and an assmonkey and a jerky son of a bitch." I bit down on my lower lip to keep from giggling.

"Agreed, agreed, and agreed . . . Anything else?"

"Can I add something?" Candace begged, wanting a piece of the action.

"Nope," Mitch said, finally able to stand. He pulled me up and pressed me against his body. "Kristy, I love you and all I wanted to do was protect you. I would die for you."

I leaned in and carefully wrapped my arms around his body and heard him breathe a huge sigh of relief. I did love him. I loved him and Rich and his secrets and I might even grow to love his sister . . . As I started to tell him I was cut off by a scream.

"Well, isn't this touching," Stuey-Herman spat, holding a very sharp knife to Boo's throat, "but fun time is over, kids. Well, at least yours is . . ."

Chapter 35

A thin trickle of blood rolled down Boo's neck where Stuey's knife had pricked her. Her eyes were huge and she was shaking like a leaf. Mariah's eyes were wild and I knew she wanted to kill Stuey with her bare hands. Edith held her in a firm grip.

"Let the innocent ones go," Mitch said, moving me behind him. "You don't want to kill Boo. You'll be hunted like a dog if you do."

Stuey laughed and it made the hair stand up on my neck. How in the hell did I ever think he was a semidecent guy? He was a douche and one hell of a good actor. "You've made it so easy for me." He leered at Candace. "Now I don't have to make a trip back to the hotel because you brought them to me."

Candace said nothing and glared at Stuey with repulsion. "You know," he said to Candace while running the knife carefully up and down Boo's fragile neck, "I think I liked you better as a blonde."

"We made a deal," Mitch ground out, pulling the focus back to him. "I gave you my name and you said you'd leave them alone."

Candace's head whipped around to Mitch in utter shock. I didn't understand the significance, but it was huge if Candace's reaction was anything to go by.

"You are worth quite a lot, Mitch Sanderson. I know plenty of guys who'd like to see you dead, but do you really think I'd pay up on a deal with a fed?" He shook his greasy little head in disgust. "Stan," he shouted, "get your sorry ass in here."

"My name is Fred," Stan said, his usual chipper self. I realized that Stuey was definitely the brains in this operation. All along I'd thought it was Stan . . . Why that surprised me, I didn't know. I'd missed every clue around me the entire time . . . I'd make one hell of a detective. *Not.*

"I believe some of our friends are armed. I'll ask once nicely and then I'll carve the little girl's neck up. Throw your weapons over here."

Mitch gave a curt nod to our group and Candace, the Baldies, Edith, and Coco began to disarm. Guns, nunchucks, and knives slid toward the insane little drug dealers. I snuck a quick glance at Coco when I realized she hadn't given up her samurai sword. Her jacket concealed it and since so many weapons hit the deck, it must have been unimaginable to Stuey that there might be more. Mariah's pocketknife was missing from the pile as well as the knife that Edith had used to cut Mitch free. I hoped to God they knew what they were doing. This was not a game.

"Stan, remove the arsenal and I'll clue our good buddies in on the plan."

"Fred," he corrected in a pissy tone as he gathered the weapons and took them out of the cabin.

"Well, Mitch Sanderson," he sneered. "I am the kingpin you've been looking for. I'm the one in charge and I'm running the show."

"Hmmm," Mitch said, shaking his head in confusion. "Your name has never really come up. Now, those guys"—he pointed to the pile of dead bodies in the corner—"I definitely recognize them."

"Goddamn it, I'm the kingpin," Stuey screamed in such a rage, he threw Boo to the floor and she scrambled away. Realizing his mistake, he quickly pulled a gun from his pocket. "It's automatic," he ground out, "so even if you rush me, I'll take out at least four of your innocents before you take me down."

"We're not going to do anything stupid," Mitch calmly assured him. "There's no reason to kill all these people. You've got me. That should be sufficient."

"And me," Candace added.

"And me," the Baldies and old lesbos said in unison.

"I'll do it too," Mariah added. The rest of us nodded in favor of going with the group.

Mitch rolled his eyes and groaned.

"It's lovely to see you all so ready to die for each other. It will be much more fun for you, I'm sure. I'm curious . . ." He aimed his gun at Candace. "What's your real name, sweet thing?"

She glanced at Mitch and a silent sibling telepathy passed between them. "What do I get if I tell you?" she countered.

He grinned and licked his wet thin little lips. "A quick death, my love. A very quick death."

"As opposed to?"

"A very slow and painful one." He smiled.

"I'm going to reach into my pocket for my ID. You good with that?"

"Oh yeah, baby, just go real slow."

Candace reached into her pocket and pulled out a man's wallet. With the quickest sleight of hand I'd ever seen, she lifted an ID out and replaced it with another. There was no way Stuey could have noticed. They only reason I saw it was because I was behind her and I heard Mitch's quick intake of breath. She slid the wallet over and backed away.

Stuey yanked the ID out of the wallet and laughed. "You used your real name, you stupid fed," he barked. "Heidi Kugel. Nice, very nice."

No one breathed and no one moved. I was terrified my slightest movement would clue him in to the fact that Candace had pulled a fast one.

"Sooo, here's the deal, friends . . . Stan, bring in the surprise," he yelled.

Stan walked in and put a box on the table and walked right back out without saying a word.

"Inside that box is a bomb. A bomb that will tear you to shreds and destroy this lovely little cabin and our sedan, but enough clues will remain to implicate the dead assholes in the corner, the sweet little drug-smuggling Bigfoot group, and a couple of dirty feds."

"Why us?" Hugh asked. I could tell he felt betrayed by Stuey. They had done several concerts together. To Hugh, that was sacred.

"Why you? Why you?" Stuey laughed. It was such an ugly sound, I felt sick to my stomach. I moved closer to Mitch and breathed him in. "I chose the stupidest group of losers I could find. A group so fucking stupid that they would drive around in a van and trailer loaded down with eight million dollars in drugs without asking questions. Leased under their name and driven only by them," he sneered. I thought Hugh was going to cry or kick him in the face. "A group so fucking clueless that if they had gotten pulled over by the cops, I would have walked away and they would have spent a nice long time in jail for drug possession . . . massive drug possession. A group so motherfucking stupid they would run around looking for a creature that doesn't exist while I conducted million-dollar drug deals right under their noses. That's why I chose you. The show was a cover so the idiotic people of Duluth didn't get suspicious."

"Did you ever film us at all?" Hugh asked quietly.

"No, Hugh. There was never any film in the camera at all. And yet again, you people were too stupid to notice. So you see, Mitch Sanderson and Heidi Kugel, I am the kingpin and now I'm a very rich kingpin. I killed my competition and . . ."

"*I* killed them," Stan shouted, coming back into the room. "You stood there like a pussy and screamed."

"Shut up," Stuey hissed. "You may have pulled the trigger, but it was my plan . . . all mine."

Hugh nodded his head, turned to Kim, and buried his head in her chest. He also did something strange with his hand. Oh. My. God . . . Hugh had just taped Stuey's entire villainous monologue on his phone. God, if we didn't get blown to bits, Stuey and Stan were so going down . . .

"You pathetic losers have ten minutes left of your lives and then . . ."

"Thirty," Stan interrupted him.

"What?"

"They have thirty minutes. You said to set the bomb on a thirty-minute timer and I did."

"No," he said through tight lips. "I said set the thirty-minute timer to go off in ten minutes, you ass."

"My bad." Stan shrugged his shoulders and walked out of the cabin.

"Okay, fine," Stuey huffed. "You have about twenty-three or twenty-four minutes left while we make our getaway. I'll be sure to let the authorities know where to find you after you burn to a crisp."

"Did you ever find your wallet?" Mariah asked.

I stopped breathing and dug my nails into Mitch's back.

"No, I did not."

"The only trail we didn't look on is the southwest one. Maybe it's out that way," Edith suggested, mildly.

"Well, it just so happens that's the way we're leaving, so I may get lucky yet. Oh"—he grinned—"I'll be needing your phones. My battery died."

I peeked out from behind Mitch's back and caught the evil grin that passed between the lesbians. We might not get out of here alive, but I had a feeling the Slime Guys might find themselves a little hung up.

After collecting our phones, Stuey calmly walked out of the cabin. The sound of multiple locks being set made my heart drop. I didn't think even Mariah was good enough to pick us out of that. Besides, they were on the outside of the door. Fucktard.

"Are they gone?" Kim asked.

No car started, but Candace pulled her listening device out and pressed her ear to the door. "They're on foot. They're talking about walking to a meeting point . . . and getting picked up."

Edith and Coco slapped each other high fives and went to examine the bomb.

"Don't touch that," Mitch said tersely. "Dave and Dan, how much bomb training have you had?"

"Hopefully enough." Dan was sweating and Dave looked like he was going to hurl. With Mitch, they carefully approached the box and slowly opened the lid. No one in the room was breathing. I glanced at my watch. That had taken a full five minutes.

"This is complicated," Dan muttered, sweating profusely now. Mitch leaned in and studied the bomb.

"Oh, for the love of Jesus Christ in a thong, get the fuck out of my way," Coco hissed, shoving the Baldies to the side.

"Stop," Mitch snapped harshly. "What makes you qualified to go near that bomb? This is not a game."

"I'm old and mean. I've been around more blocks than you'll ever see in your lifetime. Trust me when I say I know what I'm doing," she told him in a tone that made me scared out of my mind and hopeful at the same time.

"Explain," he said in a clipped tone. He approached her warily and placed himself between her and the bomb.

Edith walked up behind her twin and stood at attention. They looked fierce and determined and sad. "Vietnam. Special Forces . . . four tours. Now move," Edith demanded in a tone that would brook no bullshit.

Mitch backed away with a look of awe and shock on his face.

"But you're women," Mariah gasped.

"Not just women . . . we're dykes," Coco said in a serious voice that sent me over the edge.

I lost it. I knew the inappropriate laughing monster had possessed me, but this day had been too much and it didn't seem like it was going to get better anytime soon. It was either laugh or cry and my brain clearly chose laughter . . . so did everyone else's.

"All right, enough," Edith shouted, laughing too. "I can't concentrate with you swamp-asses making all that noise. Mariah, see if you can pick the locks. Kristy, help her. You bald motherfuckers see if you can remove the boards from the windows. Boo, Candace, and Kim, look for another exit. Hugh, I'd like to hear some Barry Manilow while I deactivate this son of a bitch. Mitch, you versed in bombs?"

"Specialized," he replied.

Everyone stood frozen with fright and then Hugh started singing . . . and it was beautiful.

"You heard the woman. Move. We have less than fifteen minutes," Mitch said. "Go, go, go."

It was a controlled chaos. Mitch, with calm authority, directed everyone to their post and then he and the dykes went to work.

"Damn," Mariah muttered. "I got the main lock, but I think it's padlocked from the outside . . . Problem here," she called out.

"Name it," Mitch said while still focusing on the bomb.

Mariah explained and was met with silence.

"Kristy," Coco directed, "I can't move at the moment unless we'd all like to be blown to smithereens. You're going to carefully remove my sword and puncture a hole in the door big enough for Mariah to get her arm through."

"Oookay," I said. "Are you sure you don't want Mariah to do it? She's stronger."

"Can't risk her lock-picking hands. You don't need yours," she said absently, absorbed in her task.

"You can do it, baby," Mitch told me, not looking up.

"Right." I took a deep breath and removed the sword like I was performing brain surgery. The clock was ticking and the atmosphere in the cabin was stifling. I could hear the Baldies banging on the boards and the murmurs of frantic searching from the rest of the crew. My job was simple and straightforward. Take the ginormous, heavy sword and punch a hole in the door. Don't worry about breaking my hands because as long as the hole gets punched, my hands are unimportant collateral damage. Got it.

It sounded much easier in my head than physically doing it. The sword had to weigh fifteen pounds, but with the adrenaline I had pumping, I could probably lift a car. Sweating like a whore in confession, I backed up and ran at the door with the sword in my hand. The jolt of contact was jarring and painful. The crack I heard in my wrist made the collateral damage issue very real . . . and I didn't make a hole.

"Get on that door, Kristy," Mitch ordered. "The bomb is more sophisticated than I thought."

"Who knew those shiny bastards were so smart," Edith spat angrily. "I don't feel good about this."

The Baldies' pounding increased tenfold and the whimpers from Kim brought home the gravity of the situation.

"There's a crawl space entrance," Candace called out. "I'll try to pry the door off."

"Dave, Dan," Mitch said sternly. "Go to Candace."

"Roger that," Dave shouted from the back room. "The windows won't budge without a crowbar."

"Dave," Mitch ordered, still totally immersed in the bomb. "Redirect. Find something strong. Try to fashion a crowbar . . . look for a bed frame."

"On it."

My punching a hole in the door, even if I permanently destroyed my hands, was no longer an option. It was a necessity. Fucktard. I stepped back and prayed to my favorite quarterback, Brett Favre . . . Minutes left in the game and a Hail Mary from Jesus was all I needed. It was now or never. With strength I didn't know I possessed, I slammed the sword through the door, breaking most of my fingers, the sword, and thankfully the door. There was a hole just large enough for Mariah's arm. She'd be working blind, but it was as good as it was going to get.

"Crawl space open," Candace yelled. "It's tight."

"I'll go," Boo said.

"Seven minutes," Hugh said, taking a quick break from his crooning.

"Fuck," Mitch muttered. "Mariah, status on the door."

"Got two," she grunted. "Feels like three more."

"Candace," he shouted. "Crawl space?"

"Boo's in. Unsure of status."

I felt helpless standing there and watching my hands swell. There was no way in hell I was going to complain, but I wanted to sob. I looked at Mitch and knew that I loved that man more than I loved my own life. I just hoped I would still have a life to love him with . . .

"No go," Coco said in a furious tone. "If we cut, we're dead."

"Agreed," Mitch ground out. "Abandon. Help the others. Mariah?"

"One more," she gasped.

"Five minutes," Hugh called out. The singing had stopped.

"Got it," Mariah shouted.

"Out," Mitch ordered. "Everybody out. Now."

Panic ensued as everyone made a run for the door. Mitch grabbed me and hauled me out.

"Gather at the van," Candace yelled. "Head count. Now."

She rattled off names as we came into view. "Mitch, Kristy, Dan, Dave, Kim, Hugh, Mariah, Coco, Edith . . . We good?"

"Oh my God," Mariah shrieked. "Where's Boo?"

"Fuck." Mitch took off at a run, followed by Candace, Edith, and Coco.

Kim held Mariah back. "Too many will make it dangerous."

"Back up and get down," Dan said, moving us farther out.

All eyes were glued to the front door of the cabin.

"Two minutes," Hugh whispered.

"She can't die." Mariah grabbed my shoulders. "She's all I've got."

"Mitch will save her," I promised. If I said it, it would be true. It had to be true. There were no other options.

"One minute."

I began to count backwards from sixty, willing them with every fiber of my being to come out . . . but they never did.

The cabin blew with a thunderous noise and a blinding explosion. The sedan went up with the cabin and I realized that was the way they'd wanted it . . . no trace. It was a sight that would be burned into my mind for the rest of my days. The Baldies covered us with their bodies so we weren't hit with debris, but the heat of the roaring blaze and the smell of burning wood, charred metal, and gasoline were inescapable.

Mariah's scream of anguish sounded inhuman. It ripped me

straight to my soul. It was only matched by the equally horrific sounds coming from my own mouth. Forgetting my balloon-size hands, I took Mariah into my arms and rocked her back and forth. It was not supposed to end this way. I was supposed to get the guy and have my foul-mouthed surrogate dyke grandmas at my wedding. Boo, Mariah, Kim, Candace, and Rena were going to be my bridesmaids and Hugh was supposed to provide the music.

Amongst the debris on the ground, I spotted Boo's worn and coverless Bigfoot bible. The thought of never seeing her sweet little face again brought on a fresh wave of sobbing.

"What in the fuck is going on here?"

Holy shit, did people come back as ghosts that quick? "You're dead," I stammered.

"Interesting," the ghost of Coco said, stretching her bony arms over her head and bringing them down only to swat me in the back of the head.

"Ouch."

"Did that bitch slap feel like a dead person to you?" She grinned.

"Not really," I said, hoping I hadn't finally jumped off the crazy cliff and landed in Hallucinationville.

"We're not dead, you asshat."

"But . . ." I was still in shock.

"We got out through the crawl space," she informed us.

"But it was small," Mariah whispered, clearly having the same doubts as to the corporality of Coco that I was having.

"Oh, please," she cackled. "I crawled through shitholes full of rats and body parts. That was nothing."

I stood up on shaky legs and was whipped off my feet by a dirty and very alive Mitch. I wrapped my arms around him and held on tighter than I'd ever held anything. "I love you," I gasped, laughing and crying at the same time. "I love you so much."

"I love you too, baby. Always."

A filthy and disheveled Candace gently handed a trembling Boo to her sister. Mariah took her in her arms and held her while they both cried.

"We have to go," Candace said.

Mitch groaned and ran his hands through his hair. He grabbed me by the shoulders and stared right through me and straight to my heart.

"I will come back to you. I will always come back to you. Promise me you'll wait . . . promise me."

"I promise." Tears were streaming down my face. The last thing in the world I wanted was for him to leave, but it's what he did and he was good, so very good. I was a big girl and loved him in a way I couldn't fully comprehend yet. He was so strong for me . . . I could be the same for him.

"Mitch," I said, "go get those slimy assmonkeys."

His grin almost set me on my ass and I knew I had done the right thing.

"Go, go, go," Candace yelled to Mitch and the Baldies. "Backup is on the way. Edith, Coco, get everyone to the hospital, and Hugh . . . give the feds your phone. It will save a lot of time." She winked at him and took off after her partners and her brother, but not before she gave Coco and Edith a military salute.

"You didn't give Stuey your phone?" Mariah asked, fully impressed.

"I have three." Hugh grinned. "He only asked for one."

"Dear God," Kim worried. "Do you think they'll find them?"

"Oh, there's no doubt about that," Edith smirked.

"I have a feeling they'll find them hanging out just about two hundred feet or so into the woods," Coco added knowingly.

And that's exactly what happened.

Epilogue

The library smelled the same and looked the same. It hadn't changed at all . . . but I had. It seemed a million years had passed since the last time I'd been here.

Being back in Minneapolis was wonderful, but I missed my crew . . . even the old dykes. Who, much to everyone's surprise except mine, were doing an amazing job running the knitting shop. The classes I insisted on their teaching at the shelter were a huge hit too. They hadn't insulted one person, although it was rumored they were giving free lessons in profanity along with sweater making.

Not one to welsh on a deal with God, I called Tandy McOath and apologized, which led to her apology, which led to a really awkward lunch at Chinese Farts. Mrs. Wang surprised us with a creamy cheesy fried rice topped with Tater Tots and sweet-and-sour sauce. Since hurling on the table was out of the realm of possibility, we both had to taste it and swallow it. Once Mrs. Wang's back was turned, we hightailed it to the bathroom and vomited in adjacent stalls. It was a bonding experience that led me to ask her to give free sewing lessons down at the shelter. Unfortunately I gave her my cell number too and she called me at least seven times a day. Thank the sweet baby Jesus for caller ID.

I glanced up at the clock on the wall. Crap, I was early. I wandered around the library and considered skimming a few books, but with a cast on one arm and splints on most of my fingers, I decided against it. Three broken fingers on my left hand and four fingers on my right plus a broken left wrist made doing everyday things a bit difficult.

"You're early," came a loud and discombobulated voice through the stacks.

"Shit." I grabbed the side of a shelf and slapped my hand over my mouth so I wouldn't scream. Pain burst through both of my hands and I wanted to deck Mariah. "Don't do that," I hissed.

"Dude," she laughed, coming around the corner, "you need to relax. I didn't know if you would come."

"Of course I came. Why wouldn't I come?"

"So you're a believer?" She raised her eyebrow and smirked.

"I wouldn't go that far . . . but let's just say I'm open to possibilities." I grinned and ran my splints through her hot pink hair. "Pretty."

"Yep. I know you had something to do with it."

"With what?" I looked up at the ceiling. I was the suckiest liar ever and I knew where this was going.

"My job at the salon. My becoming Steve and Steve's new project. The fact that I have insurance now . . ."

"I have no idea what you're talking about." I felt the stupid telltale heat creep up my neck. I wondered if there were online classes on lying . . .

"You just can't stop yourself." She narrowed her eyes and crossed her arms over her chest.

I wanted to deny it. I even started to . . . but I couldn't. She was right: for better or worse, I needed to fix people's lives. It made me happy.

"You changed my life," she said quietly. "I'm better because of you."

"Nope," I disagreed. "You're a better you because of you. I just helped a little."

She considered me for a few moments. "You're such a dork," she giggled.

"Yep, and you're an assmonkey," I countered. "You ready to go in?"

"I am if you are."

Not only had the Steves been blown away by Mariah's natural talent, they adored her and treated her and Boo like the daughters they'd always wanted. Boo was going to cosmetology school on the Steves' dime and Mariah was getting her formal training from the dynamic gay duo themselves. Mariah had used the money from Stuey's wallet to get her and her sister an apartment in a safer area. She'd come to me for approval and I'd given it on the condition that this would be the end to her life of crime. She told me she'd try . . .

Boo had confided in me that Mariah had gone for a consultation about her deviated septum, now that she had insurance, and I cried. Hard.

I glanced up and saw my best friend and the love of her life heading my way. "Why are you here?" I laughed as Rena dragged Jack through the library toward the back meeting room.

"I hear I'm famous for writing that big fat fucking pile of shit, *Pirate Dave and His Randy Adventures*. I've come to sign autographs," she informed me with a twinkle in her eye.

"Oh my God, Rena. They think it's true. Well, at least that it has a subtext that's true. Don't be mean," I begged.

"Kristy." She rolled her eyes. "First of all, I'm not mean and secondly maybe it is all true . . ." She waggled her eyebrows, grabbed a pained-looking Jack, and flounced into the room.

Rena and Jack were doing great . . . better than great. Turned out he used the bonus money from the mayor for decking my old beau, Ethan/Nathan, to buy Rena an engagement ring. They were getting married next spring and I was going to be her maid of honor. Aunt Moon-Unit had gotten her minister's license over the Internet and was going to officiate. Rena's mom had blown a gasket and threatened Moon-Unit with sure death if she brought up trolls or aliens during the ceremony.

Speaking of . . . Moon-Unit had gone to Wisconsin to meditate before we got back from Duluth. Apparently there was a large gathering of shape-shifting tree sprites meeting there.

"Swamp-ass," Edith greeted me as I made my way toward the front of the room.

"Dyke." I nodded and flipped her off. We'd had our first insult session two days earlier. Her and Coco versus Rena, Mariah, and me. I'd learned more swearwords in two hours than I ever would need to know in one lifetime. We had to call it a draw. Between Rena's mouth and Mariah's, we held our own against the foul-mouthed decorated war veterans.

I glanced around and saw Kim and Hugh flirting up a storm with each other. They were going to open up their own karaoke restaurant and bar and call it Sing for Your Supper. Hugh would be the MC and main singer seven nights a week.

Everybody was getting their happy endings except for me . . . but that wasn't exactly true. I didn't have the fifty thousand for the shelter, but I was working hard on raising enough to keep us afloat into the next year. And even though I hadn't seen or heard from Mitch, I knew he loved me and would be back when he could. I just missed him so much I ached.

"Ladies and gentlemen and lesbos," Kim said, clearing her throat. "I have some exciting news. Our group, along with several under-cover federal agents, has been publicly recognized for bringing down one of the largest drug rings in the country!"

The crowd went nuts and Hugh broke into one of the most alarm-ing Miley Cyrus concerts I'd ever heard.

"Everybody, quiet down," she bellowed, grinning from ear to ear. "There will be a formal presentation at the end of the meeting! Also, our very own Moon-Unit is back and she has some incredible news!"

Moon-Unit made a spectacular entrance from the back of the room. Her hair was lime green and she wore a silver jumpsuit. I choked on my own spit trying to hold back a scream. I glanced over at Mariah, who gave me the thumbs-up sign. I sternly reminded myself never to let Mariah touch my hair. Ever.

"As many of you know, I have succeeded in killing the chi and I have communed with the aliens. They come in peace and want to mate with us, but that's not what I'm here to discuss."

I snuck a quick peek at Rena and Jack. They were pale and looked nauseous. Possibly a bit of regret at having asked Moon-Unit to offi-ciate at their wedding?

"Kristy, where are you?" Moon-Unit shouted.

"Here." I stood up in fear and waited for the rest of the story. I'd missed the fact that she was carrying a large pillowcase with her. I suppose her outfit had blinded me to everything else.

"In this bag is the evil chi," she explained. "I was going to burn it, but the aliens said if you put evil to good use, the great ball of gaseous life force will be one with you and rain down karmic favors."

I looked around the room to see if anyone was following her, be-cause I sure as hell wasn't.

"I was once married to a man my niece calls Uncle Fucker. He couldn't keep his joystick in his pants and fornicated with at least eight to ten of my neighbors. If he was still alive, I'd remove his john-son with a pair of pliers and some rubbing alcohol." All the men in the room winced. "But he's dead, so I won't have that pleasure. Anyhoo, when that cheating bastard died, I received a large life insurance settlement which I cashed in by mistake. I refused to use that tallywhacker's money, so I shoved it in a pillowcase and threw it into the guest room closet. That dirty money from that whoring man-tool's policy was causing the bad chi! It's been in there for ten years and it's going today!"

I was so confused I was dizzy. Was she going to set a bag of money on fire in the library? They were so not going to let us come back here.

"Kristy, I know those shiny little drug-dealing peckers falsely promised the shelter fifty thousand dollars, but I can do better. I would like to donate the proceeds from the life of a man-whore to the shelter. Burning five hundred thousand dollars seemed like such a waste, so come and get it!"

I was in shock. Was this real? I wanted Mitch to be here so badly right now, but that was okay. I'd e-mail him later. Everyone in the room started screaming with joy . . . including me. Five hundred thousand dollars for the shelter was my every wildest dream come true . . . and then some. "Are you sure?" I sputtered. "It's so much money."

"Never been more sure about anything in my life. Jack is armed and he'll drive you to the bank after this," she said. Clearly she didn't know anything about banks . . . it was nine thirty at night. I ran up to her and gave her a big hug. I handed the money to Jack because I was too afraid to hold it.

"Allrightyroo," Kim yelled. "We have one more piece of business and then we'll call it a night. Jack, I believe you're going to handle this."

"Yep," he said, walking to the front of the room. "I have the pleasure of announcing the guest who is here to officially present you with your award. The government of Minnesota, the government of the United States, and people all over the country are grateful to you for your part in ending one of the most heinous and violent drug rings in the U.S. Three of the top ringleaders are dead and two vicious henchmen are going to jail for a very long time thanks to your good work and an outstanding taped confession." He gave Hugh a thumbs-up and continued. "To present you with the award is a former federal agent. He worked for the DEA for a long time and then he fell in love with some nutty chick and decided he couldn't be away from this woman for even a day for the rest of his life. I told him he was insane and that this woman was crazy, but he wouldn't believe me. Somehow he finagled his way onto the Minneapolis police force and is now just a regular old cop like me."

I couldn't move. My heart was beating like a jackhammer and I knew I was seconds from passing out. Today had to be a dream. Things did not happen this way for me. My broken hands were shaking and everyone was looking at me. I put my head down into my hands to try to hide my tears.

"Hi, baby," the most beautiful man in the world whispered. He gently lifted my chin, gave me a lopsided smile, and stole my heart again. "I want a white picket fence and a beautiful wife and seven point five kids."

"Two. Two point five," I corrected him, giggling through my tears. I reached out and touched his face and prayed I wasn't dreaming. "Wait," I gasped. "Did you just ask . . ." I stopped. My face felt warm and I was sure I resembled a tomato. God, what if I'd misunderstood him?

"I guess I didn't do that quite right."

"No shit, Sherlock," Rena yelled from across the room.

"Hurry up and get to it," Edith griped. "I'm missing my programs."

"Oh, shut up, you old bull dyke," Coco huffed. "I'm enjoying this."

"Fine," Mitch laughed, rolling his eyes at our vocal audience. He got down on one knee and I stopped breathing. "I love you more than I've ever loved anyone. It was my choice to go civilian. I made it when I gave Stuey my real name, and I've never felt so happy or free . . . I want to spend the rest of my life with you. I promise I will do everything in my power to make you happy and I will never leave. Ever. Kristy, will you marry me?"

I think I said yes before I attached myself to his mouth. I must have, because the room broke out into the loudest cheering of the evening. Hugh serenaded us with a pop version of the "Wedding March" and all the people I loved ran over to congratulate us. Mitch picked me up and put me on his lap, holding on so tight I could barely move.

I buried my face in his neck and breathed him in. I was sitting in my own happy ending's lap and my life couldn't have been more perfect . . . and to think I had David Hasselhoff to thank for all this. Of course, David Hasselhoff would never realize what an important role he'd played in my happiness, but if I ever have a son . . . I think I'll name him David.

AND THE TITLE IS . . .

Oftentimes the title of a book changes. The original title the author intended wasn't quite right. Of course, I work with the bestest publishers evah, so they always let me come up with alternatives. Mind you, I have a couple of really good insane-brained friends who help me. I thought you might enjoy seeing the potential titles we came up with for this book. Some were just to make my editor, Alicia Condon, laugh, and the others were titles I loved. Soooo, thank you to James Kall, Kris Calvert, and JM Madden. I believe we came up with some doozies this time!

1. The Big Hairy Deal *(you know what they say about big feet . . .)*

2. The Bigger They Are . . .

3. She Likes Them Big and Hairy

4. Stop, Squatch, and Roll

5. Is That a Squatch in Your Pocket
or Are You Just Happy to See Me?

6. Why Didn't You Tell Me It Got Harder?

7. How Hard Can It Be?
Part Two . . . Bigfoot. Really?

8. Size Matters:
A Girl, a Guy, and Bigfoot

9. Things Just Got Hairier

10. A Hard Man Is Good to Find

11. Looking for the Big One

12. And Yeti Said He Loved Me . . .

13. Lust and Found

14. Big Man Hunt

15. The Harder the Man, the Bigger He Falls

Don't miss Robyn Peterman's next wild adventure in romance, *Cop a Feel*, coming next June.

Prologue

"Is your name even David?" I asked as I yanked my panties back on.

"Is yours Melanie?" he inquired, buttoning his jeans.

"I asked first," I countered wondering for the umpteenth time why being an idiot came so easily to me.

"Not David."

"Not Melanie."

We dressed in silence. I glanced around the hotel room and felt the need to do damage. Unsure whether I wanted to damage him or myself, I decided to get the hell out before I did something else I would regret.

"You know, I can't believe I've been sleeping with you on and off for a year and I don't know your real name," I said as I slipped my gun into its holster on my hip, promising myself I would never lay eyes on his ridiculously gorgeous nude body again.

"Back at ya, Ice."

"Ice?"

"Like your eyes, pretty girl. Icy blue and cold. I figure since you're not going to tell me your real name, I'll just give you one that fits."

"How about I call you Ass?" I snapped. What in the hell was wrong with me? He hadn't forced me to do anything I wasn't more than willing to do. True, he hadn't given his real name, but neither had I.

"I've been called worse," he chuckled, revealing even white teeth and an orgasm-inducing smile. "When will I see you again?" He adjusted his bulletproof vest and slipped his knife back into his boot.

"Let me think," I purred, enjoying how my change of tone stopped him in his tracks and piqued his interest. "Never. You will never see me again. I'm not interested and I'm tired of screwing someone I can't trust to tell me his real name."

"Turn about is fair play." He grinned. He checked the safety on his gun and secured it at his hip. "And I think you were pretty interested twenty minutes ago when I made you see Jesus."

"Oh. My. God. You did not just liken sex with you to a biblical experience," I sputtered. His ego was bigger than his dick and his dick was nothing to scoff at.

"If the shoe fits . . ."

"Listen, David," I ground out between clenched teeth. "You're a decent lay and all, but you're not that good. I'm turning over a new leaf and I'm done having meaningless sex with asshats."

"Good luck with that, Ice," he replied enjoying himself too much for my liking. He beat me to the door and flipped the lock. "I'll see you around," he shot back over his shoulder as he walked away.

"Don't bet on it," I muttered and grabbed my purse.

"Oh, baby, I'm a gambling man," he laughed as he disappeared from my sight and hopefully my life.

I slumped down on the sex-destroyed bed and dropped my head into my hands. I had to get my damned life together. Was this all I had to look forward to? Mind blowing sex with assholes not named David? The sex had been biblical, but the after-shame was getting debilitating. I was far better than this. What would my mother think? Or my brother, for that matter? I shuddered at the thought. I was an accomplished woman at the top of my game and I deserved more than I allowed myself to have.

Done. I was done.

I grabbed my ID and my handcuffs, which had unfortunately been put to very obscene use about a half an hour ago, and left. I considered leaving my non-traceable Go-Phone in the room so there was no chance of another hook-up, but I needed it for work. With one last wistful glance at the sin-bed, I walked out of that room and into my new and improved life.

Chapter 1

Three months later

The office was small but tidy. My gut clenched in anticipation of the dressing down I was about to receive. I glanced at the organized stacks of paper waiting to be filed sitting neatly next to a pile of romance novels. I grinned and grabbed one; anything to take my mind off my latest major fuck up. I'd been out of the hospital for nearly a month and I was ready to work again. I just needed to take my stern talking to and get on with it. I paged through the book and snorted. Why my boss kept this crap here was a mystery to me. I wondered if he read these books.

Romance was for people who believed in fairy tales and I didn't. Life was real and most people were bad. I skimmed the book and rolled my eyes. Nobody looked that good first thing in the morning and making out without brushing your teeth at seven am was not my idea of a good time. Damn, the sex was pretty good.

Of course, that made me think about not David, the egotistical wonder dick. I hadn't Go-Phoned him and he hadn't Go-Phoned me and since we hadn't made any other strangers-with-benefits rendezvous, I hadn't seen him in months. That smarted a little bit, but it was for the best. Great sex was great sex. I could get that anywhere. Although, he'd kind of ruined me. I hadn't slept with anyone but him in over a year. Whatever. At least he didn't know that.

I nervously tucked the stiff blond hair behind my ear. Where in the hell was Steve? I knew I had it coming. I'd blown my cover twice in six months and that didn't bode well. I'd considered cutting my hair and coloring it before my meeting to show my boss, yet again, how easily I could disguise myself, but I figured a wig would do the trick.

Blonde wasn't really my color, but the last time I'd gotten an ass-chewing I'd worn a red wig. Men preferred blondes according to Marilyn Monroe and although Steve was gay, I figured being blonde couldn't hurt.

The ruckus in the hallway yanked me out of my pity party.

"This is ridiculous," a female voice shrieked. "You're not a fag. You fathered our two children and slept with me for . . ."

"Enough," my boss Steve ground out. "We're divorced and I am happily re-married. You're not allowed here and if I have to get a re-straining order I will."

"You can't marry a man. It's against God's will. You'll burn in hell and you'll deserve it," his not so lovely ex-wife hissed.

"Jesus Christ, Helen. You need to leave now before I do something I will regret. Although there's not much I would regret at the moment."

"I'll leave," she said airily. "But you'll come back to me. Take this and read it. See the light, Steve. When you do, I'll be waiting."

"Don't hold your breath," he muttered.

I heard her heels clack down the hall. And that right there was why I would never get married. I'd rather chew glass and swallow it than deal with that kind of bullshit. Not that I'd get a divorce because I'd realized I was gay, but there were myriads of reasons not to be involved with anyone. Ever.

"Sorry about that," Steve sighed as he entered the office and tossed the Bible she'd obviously given him into the trash. "That was stressful to say the least."

"Um, are you okay?"

"I'm just dandy." He grimaced and took a seat behind his desk.

My boss Steve was a great looking man in his late forties. Sandy blond hair and built like a brick shit-house. An ex-Navy Seal. From what I knew about him, he could kill a man with his bare hands and I was fairly sure he'd been tempted to do just that to his ex-wife. He had two kids that he was devoted to and a husband that he adored. Clearly that didn't sit well with his ex-wife.

"Sorry you had to hear that," he said. "That doesn't belong here."

"No problem," I said feeling awful that I was adding to the weight of the world that had very obviously landed on his shoulders. "So, um . . . you wanted to see me?"

Steve tented his fingers, rested his chin on them and stared at me. I fidgeted with my wig and put the novel back on the edge of his desk. Fuck, why wouldn't he say something? Never one to let a silence live out its life . . . I filled it.

"So I know you're a little unhappy with me at the moment, but I had no choice. Back up was stalled in traffic and the fucker was going to get away. I had to move. He sold to kids," I said at light speed in an effort to make him see there was no other way. "Three sixteen year olds had already OD'd and he was scheduled to get a shipment that would hook and kill God knows how many others and I . . ."

"Do you have a death wish?" Steve asked quietly.

Shitballs. Yelling I could take. Yelling I could understand and process. Quiet was bad, really bad.

"No, I . . ."

"It seems to me that you do," he said and tiredly ran his hands through his hair. "You broke procedure and could have been killed.

"But I wasn't and I . . ."

"This time," Steve interrupted me in a hard voice that shut me up quick. "This time you weren't killed, by sheer luck . . . not skill. You blew your cover with a cartel that wants your ass and will stop at nothing to get it."

"I stopped a thirty million dollar transaction and I won't apologize," I told him adjusting my wig that had slipped forward due to the fact I'd forgotten to pin the stupid ugly thing on.

"Show me your stomach."

Goddamnit, I didn't have time for this. "My stomach is fine," I replied, straightening the neat piles on his desk.

"Show me your stomach."

I heaved a put upon sigh and reluctantly lifted my shirt to reveal an angry jagged red scar. I'd taken a knife to the gut in my latest assignment gone awry. Of course the other guy fared much worse . . . like six feet under worse. Luckily his knife had missed all my major organs and arteries.

"Jesus Christ, Candace," he muttered. "That's it. I won't go to your funeral young lady."

"You're not my dad," I shot back, worried about where the conversation was headed. He never called me Candace . . . always Candy or kid or idiot. Not Candace.

"Nope, I'm much worse. I'm your boss."

"So what are you saying? I'm fired? I'm reassigned? I'm what?" I asked in a voice I didn't recognize.

"You need a break. You're too involved; lost your objectivity," Steve said watching me closely. "The drug dealers and the kids are hitting too close to home."

He was right and he was wrong; not that I'd admit the right part. I was an undercover DEA agent because my sister had died from a drug overdose when we were little more than kids. My brother Mitch had become an agent first. Needless to say no one was overjoyed when I chose the same profession. My mother's fear of losing another child had almost debilitated her, but doing nothing had almost destroyed me. It was my way of paying tribute and it fit me. I was good at it. I needed it. I'd had to fight my parents and my brother on my decision. To this day, I felt their disapproval and doubt. It mattered to none of them that I'd been at the top of my recruit class, spoke three languages fluently and had more weapons expertise than even my hotshot big brother.

My boss Steve had been the only one who had believed in me after I'd come out of training. He'd taught me the finer arts of jimmying car doors and disguise. He'd taught me the difference between revenge and justice. He'd been harder than hell on me and I loved and appreciated every moment of it. He'd believed in me and now he didn't . . .

"I know I screwed up and I promise you that I . . ."

"Save it," he said slapping a folder down on his desk in front of me. "This is your medical report. To say that you're lucky is an understatement. This . . ." He pushed the folder toward me angrily. "This is proof of what being emotionally involved can do. It makes you sloppy and useless to me."

I said nothing. He was right. I was a constant blur of motion. Trying to fill up holes I couldn't define.

"There is strength in stillness and order. Protocol exists for a reason. Staying centered and uninvolved means you live to see another day," Steve said pulling out another file.

"I know all that," I insisted. God, if I lost this job I had nothing. Less than nothing.

"Intellectually, maybe," he conceded. "But you're a liability to me at the moment and you're in no shape physically to go undercover."

"So you're firing me?"

"Hell no," Steve chuckled. "You're one of the best agents I have. Once you've healed and gotten your head back on straight, I'll kick your ass and send you back out."

I breathed a sigh of relief and my tense body went slack. Fuck, I thought my life was ending. In that moment I understood how much my work defined who I was. Whether that was good or bad I had no clue . . . it simply was. Certain that sharing my revelation with Steve would be a bad thing, I kept my mouth shut. Difficult, as there was a silence I was tempted to fill.

"So what am I supposed to do?" I asked myself as well as my boss.

"Do you want to go to your parents?"

"God no," I shouted and then slapped a hand over my mouth.

Steve's eyes narrowed and he waited. He knew my parents. He knew my brother. Hell, my brother Mitch had been one of his best agents until he fell in luuurrve and got out to become a plain old boring cop.

"If my mom knew about my stomach, she'd lock me in the house and go into a deep depression. I'm twenty-nine and I will not go back," I snapped.

"A family that loves you is not the worst thing in the world," Steve said in his fatherly tone. I hated the fatherly tone.

"Yeah, well, a family that disapproves of what I do isn't going to be too excited about a knife wound in my belly. Just sayin'." I grabbed the silly romance novel and changed the subject. "You read this crap?"

"No, Kevin does," he laughed.

Kevin, Steve's partner, was every bit as good looking as Steve. Many straight women had shed real tears upon learning the two men were gay and happily committed. Where Steve was intense and brooding, Kevin was light and joy. They were wonderful parents to Steve's kids; far better than his religious zealot ex-wife, Helen.

"Well, these books are ridiculous. Happily ever after's don't exist," I snorted.

Steve shook his head sadly. "Ah, you have much to learn, Candy."

"Give me a break," I snorted.

"Exactly my plan. You're going on light duty until the doctors and I deem you ready for the field again." He opened the folder in his hand and skimmed the contents.

"Light duty? You're kidding me. Do you want me to file and answer phones?" I asked sarcastically.

"Nope," he grinned. "I'd like to keep my business. Your social skills leave much to be desired."

"Social skills are for civilians and fucktards," I snapped, unfortunately proving his point.

Steve cocked his head to the side and waited for me to bury myself deeper. I was a loose cannon, but I wasn't stupid. I stayed quiet. Difficult, but possible.

"God help the man who tries to tame you," he laughed and removed several sheets from the folder.

"No man will ever tame me," I told him confidently. "Romance is for sissies."

"How exactly should I take that? As a slur to my manhood or my sexual preference?" he asked, eyebrows raised.

"No, I . . . shit. Um, I meant that it's, you know . . ." I mumbled and felt the heat crawl up my neck.

"Candy, you're missing out on a few things in life. Like a life mainly. I want you to take this light duty time to ease up and live a little. Have some fun for God's sake."

I had no freakin' clue what he was talking about. A life? I had a life. I saved lives. And I had fun. I, um enjoyed tons of things, like . . . Whatever. This was ridiculous.

"Just give me my pansy-ass light duty assignment and let me get back to work."

Steve observed me critically for a moment, then went from father mode back to boss mode. "Fine. A dear friend of mine has received some threats on her life. I'm fairly sure they're innocuous, but Kevin is freaked out and wants protection for her."

"You want me to find and eliminate the threats?" I asked, my expression hopeful. Maybe light duty wouldn't suck as much as I thought.

"Not exactly," he said, folding the papers in his hands and placing them inside the romance novel I'd just made fun of. "I want you on her and watching for trouble."

"You want me to be a bodyguard?" I gasped, unable to hide my

shock and dismay. I was an undercover agent for shit's sake. Not a
rent-a-cop babysitter.

"Yep," Steve said ignoring my stinky attitude. "Sue is a professor
and an author. She's scheduled to headline an author's convention in
a week and I want you on her. Innocuous or not, a threat is a threat."
He handed me the book with a smile.

"Wait, I have to guard a woman named Sue who writes trashy romance novels because someone may or may not want a piece of her?"

"That sounds about right," he said. "On, and she goes by Shoshanna.
Shoshanna Lehump."

I waited for the punch line, but it didn't come. Who in the hell
would go by the name Shoshanna LeHump? She sounded like a
stripper.

"You're serious," I said pinching my thighs to keep from laughing
just in case he was.

"As a heart attack. Shoshanna married Kevin after her husband
died so he could get his green card. They divorced when we met.
Shoshanna actually officiated our wedding ceremony. You remember,
the one you were invited to, but couldn't come because you were
recovering from being shot in the ass."

That was a low blow. I hadn't been shot in the ass by anyone. It
was actually quite big of Steve to state it that way. I had shot myself
in the ass. I'd been testing a new firearm. The gun had been faulty
and the safety was put on backward. Hence, when I put it in my back
pocket it went off and I shot myself in the ass.

"I'm a little confused," I said ignoring his comment about my ass
debacle.

"In a round about way, Kevin and I met because of Shoshanna. We
owe her."

"She introduced you guys while she was married to Kevin?"

"No, no," Steve laughed. "But that does sound like something
she would do. She's our angel because if she hadn't married Kevin,
he would have been deported and we never would have met. She's
the reason my life is full."

I was so tempted to roll my eyes, but I loved Kevin. And I loved
Steve. And they loved each other. Hell, Steve sounded just like my
pussy-whipped brother Mitch. He fell in love with Kristy when we
were all on a bizarro drug bust that involved Bigfoot. Kristy had
nothing to do with the crimes. She was with a crew of loonies

searching for Bigfoot and was unknowingly the cover for a nasty drug cartel. At first I didn't like her, but she proved herself in the end. Of course, it also helped that she didn't really believe in Bigfoot.

"So what's with the trashy novel?" I asked as he handed it over.

"Shoshanna wrote it. I would suggest you read it so you get a feel for her. Inside I've put a list of potential suspects. You can question them this week before you leave for Wisconsin."

I looked the list over. Several professors at the U where this Shoshanna gal worked seemed to have rather large issues with either her success as an author or her subject matter. Some old woman named Evangeline O'Hara, who had been blackmailing Shoshanna for stories for what looked like twenty years was also on the list.

"Holy shit," I muttered. "Here's your threat. The O'Hara woman has a motive like I've never seen."

"I'd tend to agree if she wasn't still in jail," Steve said. "Her calls and mail are monitored."

"I'll interview her."

"Absolutely and the professors at the U. Sue's one of the foremost profs of Women's Studies and these jackoffs are trying to get her tenure removed."

"Jealousy?"

"Possibly. More likely closed minded bigotry towards her subject matter."

"Women's Studies?" I asked, surprised. "What are they? Dinosaurs?"

"Not what she teaches, what she writes," he corrected my misassumption.

"What in the hell does she write? Porno?" I laughed.

"Some might refer to it as porno, but it's technically classified as erotic romance," Steve said logically.

Again I waited for the punch line. Again it didn't come.

"So, um . . . is there anything in the University's by-laws that make her, um . . . sex books negate her contract?" I asked. I almost said fuck books. Thank you God that that one hadn't slipped.

"It's somewhat vague, but Shoshanna's lawyers are convinced she'd win and most of the board is backing her," he said. "But it's unpleasant and drawing unwanted attention to the University. The longer it goes on the more precarious her position is."

"I don't get it. She would win in court. What's the biggie?"

"The biggie," Steve smiled at my choice of word, "is that Shoshanna loves the University and would leave before she caused too much trouble and bad press. It would be a sad day for her, the students and academia if that were to happen."

"Why would someone hurt her then? Wouldn't it be smarter to just draw it out till she leaves on her own recognizance?"

"Yes and no," Steve said. "She's up for several prestigious awards and two of the suspects in particular are up for the same award. I don't really get it, but apparently in the world of academia the more papers with stars on it you get the more important you seem to be in that strange sub-culture."

"You think someone would kill or hurt her for that?" I asked memorizing the names for later.

"Doubtful, but I've seen stranger." Steve handed me a card.

"Here's Shoshanna's address. You're expected at dinner tomorrow night. Kevin and I will be there as well as your brother, Kristy, Rena and Jack."

That sounded like hell to me. To be stuck in a room with a porno writer and three sickeningly in-love couples would be enough to make me tear my own head off. My brother and his fiancé, Kristy, were bad enough, but Rena and Jack, their best friends were down right nauseating.

"I don't think I can make that," I hedged, racking my brain for a good excuse.

"You have plans? Cancel them. This is work related and you need to have a good time occasionally."

"I have a date," I blurted out, my mouth way ahead of my brain.

"Bring him," Steve said, waiting for me to cop to lying.

"Well, um . . . David is a little weird and I'd, you know . . . rather not subject him to my brother before I know if he really, um . . . you know."

"What does this David do?" he asked.

"I think he's a . . . banker."

"I see," Steve said, seeing entirely too much.

"Fine," I huffed, pissed at myself for lying and pissed at Steve for making me. "I'll come. Is Kevin cooking?"

"You bet." He smiled his first real smile of the meeting. "Shoshanna can't boil water and Kevin still cooks for her a couple of nights a week."

"Oh shit," I muttered. "What about the cartel that wants my ass?"

"Taken care of. Sent two agents to Mexico and ended it."

Fuck. I hated that. I hated that two people had to risk their lives to cover my fuck up. Maybe Steve was right. I needed to get my head on straight.

"Are they okay?" I asked.

"Yep. Got back today. Hell of a ride. Been down there three months."

Three months? "Can I thank them?"

"Nope. These guys are deep cover. They don't exist in any database. Not going to screw with that. Just know it's taken care of."

"Right," I said, more furious than ever with myself. My vengeance against drug dealers had resulted in two of Steve's hard core guys having to go to Mexico and clean up my mess. Not gonna happen again. Ever.

"It's done Candy," Steve said recognizing my frustration. "They're back and fine, but it could have gone any way. I wasn't planning on this, but shit happens. Remember that next time you want to go Rambo on a job."

"You have my word," I promised.

"Good. Now get out of my office. I have work to do. Oh, and by the way," he smirked. "Blonde's not your color. Stick with your natural brunette. It's beautiful."

"Yes Sir." I gave him a mock salute and left. His chuckle followed me down the hall as I yanked the itchy blonde wig off my head and tossed it in the trash. I'd been living on luck and a prayer . . . and that stopped today.

Chapter 2

The private law enforcement gym was practically empty. It smelled a little musty and the equipment had seen better days, but I loved the place. I'd earned my black belt in karate in this very gym and felt a real sense of peace here that I sometimes had a hard time finding in my daily life. Steve's implication that I had no life rankled—possibly because it might be true. I just wasn't sure I was brave enough or cared enough to actually do anything about it.

Scanning the free weights, I settled on the lighter side. My healing knife wound kept me from a full workout, but I was getting stronger every day. My physical therapist was blown away by my progress. I was just pissed I wasn't back to full form yet. I dropped my gym bag on the floor and grabbed some five pounders.

"What are you? A pussy?" an unfortunately familiar voice demanded.

Jesus Christ, who in the hell did I fuck over in a former life to have to keep running into the evil lesbian sisters?

"Nope, I had a little mishap at work and have to take it easy. What's your excuse?" I asked eyeing her appalling choice of workout wear. Both Mrs. C and her sister, Edith, were somewhere in their sixties and tended to favor sequins. Even at the gym.

Edith clad in a shiny gold exercise top cackled and punched her sister in the arm. "Yeah, what's your excuse, you old dyke?"

Mrs. C grunted and walloped her sister back. I idly wondered if they'd get into an all out brawl. At least they weren't boring . . .

"Heard you got stabbed in the gut," Mrs. C said while she simultaneously smacked her sister in the back of the head. Edith came right back and knocked her sister's feet out from underneath her.

How in the fuck did they know that? "Well, that seems to be the rumor," I muttered wondering how long I could take dealing with them before I did damage. Although, that would be an unwise choice on my part considering they had been in Vietnam, Special Forces . . . four tours. I was fairly sure only a few high placed government officials knew of their existence.

"Yep," Edith crowed as she helped her sister back to her feet. "But rumor also has it that you put a dick-weed drug dealer six feet under."

"How in the hell do you guys hear all this stuff?" I asked. The info was classified and didn't hit the media in any way shape or form. "You two run a knitting store, for God's sake."

The just stood there and grinned. A smile pulled at my lips because they looked so ridiculous and they either had no clue or didn't care. I'd met them on the same drug bust where my brother Mitch had met his fiancé Kristy. They were part of the certifiably insane group of nut jobs searching for Bigfoot. Turns out they were far more than poorly dressed lesbian Sasquatch enthusiasts . . . they helped save the day by booby trapping the trees with knitted snap traps.

"How is it that you lovely ladies are allowed to work out here?" I asked as I switched to twenty pound weights. I was no pussy. I was a dumb ass.

"Give me those goddamned things," Edith snapped, yanking the weights from my hands. "You wanna reopen that wound?"

"No," I huffed, annoyed that my pride had gotten the better of me.

"Anyhoo, we work out here because we're doing some government contract work here and there and the fine city of Minneapolis has no choice but to let us hone our fine machines in their gym," Mrs. C said, sliding slowly into the splits. Edith, not one to be outdone . . . joined her.

Had I entered an alternate universe? I was going to be a bodyguard for a smut writer and these two sparkling limber dingbats were picking off bad guys for the government when they weren't manning a knitting store?

As I stared at them on the floor, I idly wondered if I could do the splits. Holy hell, I really did need a life.

"So," Edith grunted, "heard you got quite the cushy assignment."

"I would truly love to know where you get your info."

"Not gonna happen." She gave me a wink.

"Figures," I muttered. I walked over to the treadmill and prayed our conversation was over.

"You are one lucky chickee," Mrs. C said rolling out of the splits. "Edith here would give her left boob, it's the bigger one, to go to the SCREW-Con."

"I'm sorry, what the hell did you just say?" I asked, sure I'd heard her incorrectly.

"I said Edith's left boob is bigger than her . . ."

"Not that part," I snapped. "The other part."

"The SCREW-Con." She cackled at the look of horror on my face. "Society of Contemporary Romance Erotic Writers. Screw. You get it?"

"Yeah, I got it. Now quit fucking with me." I blew out an exasperated sigh and waited for the punch line . . . and it never came.

"Sweet baby Jesus in assless chaps, you really didn't know," Edith yelled, enjoying my discomfort. I certainly wasn't a prude, but I had no desire to go to a convention called SCREW.

"Clearly I didn't." I put my earbuds in, cranked up the volume on my iPod and turned on the treadmill. This conversation was done. If there was anything else to know, I didn't want to know it. Despite the fact that Steve was my boss, I was going to rip him a new one for this. Being taken unaware by two sequin wearing lesbians with uneven boobs was not on my schedule today . . . and apparently being ignored wasn't on theirs.

"You'll be body-guarding one of the hottest pieces of ass alive," Mrs. C informed me while removing my earbuds.

"Sweet baby Moses in leather and a ball gag, I pray daily for Shoshanna LeHump to switch teams and come over to the dyke side," Edith shouted in full agreement of the sexual magnetism of the infamous LeHump.

Stunned to silence and having no comeback for that one, I stared at them while debating my next move. Taking them down might set me back medically and running meant I really was a pussy. So I tried the next best thing.

"You guys wanna go shoot some stuff? I'm about to implode and I need to find something inanimate to kill."

"Now your talking, sister," Edith said yanking me off the treadmill and out of the gym.

The gun range was empty. After signing in, the old gals announced that the targets were insulting and had just what we needed to spice it up. They set up targets that made Mel, the owner cringe and threaten to ban us for life. Edith had a couple of words in private with Mel and to my great surprise, he turned a blind eye. Those crazy women set up an old computer, two toasters, a vacuum and a mini-fridge that they just so happened to have in the back of their car. They drew tiny bull's-eyes on the appliances and started making wagers. Color me impressed. Maybe these gals weren't so bad.

"Youth before beauty," Mrs. C grunted, getting into her zone.

Laughing, I put on my ear protectors and goggles. Holding my Glock in my hand made me go to my calm happy place. I aimed and I fired—over and over and over.

"What the fuck?" Mrs.C gasped. "Guns down."

We holstered. She walked over to the appliances and whistled.

"What?" Edith shouted, still wearing her hearing protection.

"Clean bull's-eye on every one."

"Clean a bull's what?" Edith yelled.

"Take your goddamned head gear off and get a look at this shit," Mrs. C said, squatting down to get a better view.

Both women eyed my handiwork silently, crossed back over to me and stared.

"Do it again," Mrs. C demanded. "Do it right now."

"No prob." I grinned and reloaded. And I did it again—and one more time for good measure.

"Jesus Christ in a corset, you should have sniped with us in Nam," Mrs. C whispered reverently.

"Wasn't born yet," I said enjoying myself for the first time in a while.

"I've never seen anything like it. I think I came in my shorts," Edith added, saluting me.

"Gross," I groaned backing away.

"Don't worry yourself," she cackled. "You're too young, too skinny and too straight. It's your shooing that gave me a woody."

"Guys, enough. I'm a good shot. I'm supposed to be. I'm an undercover DEA agent, for God's sake." I rolled my eyes and debated if they needed an anatomy lesson. Although who knew? Maybe they had dicks . . .

"She the best I've ever seen," Mrs. C muttered.

"Not better than Mag the Hag," Edith insisted.

Both women dropped to their knees, genuflected and quietly murmured Mag the Hag repeatedly.

Fuck, just when I was beginning to think they were kind of normal.

"Do you think it's possible?" Edith asked her sister, eyeing me suspiciously.

"Could be," Mrs. C said rising to her feet.

"Um, guys you're kind of freakin' me out here." Maybe it was time to go. Mrs. C's iron grip on my arm made escape impossible.

"She died in my arms. She was the best sharp shooter that ever lived." Edith's eyes welled with tears making me notice her glittery yellow eye shadow. How had I missed that?

"I'm sorry, I know how it is to lose someone you love."

"I didn't love her," Edith laughed. "I hated her fucking guts, but I admired the hell out of her and would have done her if she was a dyke."

"Okay, then—gotta go," I told them removing my goggles and peeling Mrs. C's claw off my arm.

"Mag the Hag, are you in there?" Mrs. C screeched in to my ear, definitely damaging my hearing.

"What the fuck is wrong with you? You're insane and a menace to society. Not to mention, your dress sense is vomitous," I shouted and put my hand to my ear to check for blood.

"It's her," Edith said dropping to her knees in front of me.

"Who's her?" I asked glancing around in alarm.

"You. You're Mag the Hag reincarnated," Mrs. C rejoiced trapping me in a bear hug. "God, I've missed you, you stinky bitch."

"I'm not Mag the Hag," I said, but being wedged in Mrs. C's armpit it came out a little muffled.

"Of course you are," Edith tsked and bent to kiss my feet.

"This is the most glorious and fucked up thing to happen in at least three weeks!" Mrs. C claimed, hugging me tighter.

"I really think you ladies need some help," I squeaked trying to get some air into my squashed lungs.

"I'm gonna call Homer in DC. This will blow his mind," Edith giggled after she'd finished adoring my feet. "He'll offer you a job so fast it will make your head spin."

"Thanks, but no thanks," I gasped, miraculously breaking away from Mrs. C. "I have a job already and I'm not Madge or who ever you whack-jobs think I am. I'm Candy and you're bat shit crazy."

"Exactly what Mag the Hag would have said," Edith shot back, secure in her debatable sanity that I was their reincarnated buddy.

"Okay then, I'll just be going." I grabbed my gun and quickly stowed it away. "I'll see you guys when hell freezes over and I hope you have an interesting rest of your lives." I made a run for the door.

"Hell froze over last Tuesday," Mrs. C shouted joyously as I hustled away. "We'll see you this weekend. We have a lot of catching up to do. You've been dead for years!"

"Not gonna happen," I muttered as I slammed the door behind me only to be followed by their laughter as I hightailed it out of the building.

ABOUT THE AUTHOR

Robyn Peterman writes because the people inside her head won't leave her alone until she gives them life on paper. Her addictions include laughing really hard with friends, shoes (the expensive kind), Target, Coke with extra ice in a Styrofoam cup, bejeweled reading glasses, her kids, her superhot hubby, and collecting stray animals.

A former professional actress with Broadway, film, and TV credits, she now lives in the South with her family and too many animals to count. Writing gives her peace and makes her whole—plus having a job you can do in your PJs works really well for her. You can follow Robyn at robynpeterman.com. She loves to hear from her fans.

www.ingramcontent.com/pod-product-compliance
Lightning Source LLC
Chambersburg PA
CBHW020438270626
47155CB00022B/624